A Pleasure to Burn

NOVELS

The Martian Chronicles

Fahrenheit 451

Dandelion Wine

Something Wicked This Way
Comes

Death Is a Lonely Business

A Graveyard for Lunatics

Green Shadows, White Whale

From the Dust Returned

Let's All Kill Constance

Farewell Summer

Ahmed and the Oblivion
Machines: A Fable

SHORT STORY COLLECTIONS

Dark Carnival

The Illustrated Man

The Golden Apples of the Sun

The October Country

A Medicine for Melancholy

R is for Rocket

The Machineries of Joy

The Autumn People

The Vintage Bradbury

S is for Space

Twice 22

I Sing the Body Electric

Long After Midnight

The Small Assassin

The Mummies of Guanajuato

Beyond 1984: Remembrance
of Things Future

This Attic Where the Meadow
Greens

The Ghosts of Forever

NONFICTION

A PLEASURE TO BURN

Fahrenheit 451 Stories

RAY BRADBURY

Donn Albright, *Volume Editor*
Jon Eller, *Textual Editor*

NEW YORK • LONDON • TORONTO • SYDNEY • NEW DELHI • AUCKLAND

HARPER ● PERENNIAL

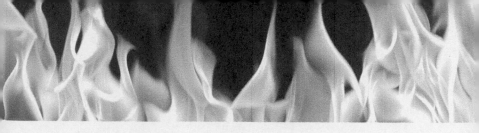

CONTENTS

Bonus Stories

THE REINCARNATE

AFTER A WHILE YOU WILL GET OVER THE INFERIORITY complex. Maybe. There's nothing you can do about it. Just be careful to walk around at night. The hot sun is certainly difficult on you. And summer nights aren't particularly helpful. So the best thing for you to do is wait for chilly weather. The first six months are your prime. The seventh month the water will seep through and the maggots will begin. By the end of the eighth month your usefulness will dwindle. By the tenth month you'll lie exhausted and weeping the sorrow without tears, and you will know then that you will never move again.

But before that happens there is so much to be thought about, and finished. Many thoughts to be renewed, many old likes and dislikes to be turned in your mind before the sides of your skull fall away.

It is new to you. You are born again. And your womb is silk-lined and fine-smelling of tuberoses and linens, and there is no sound before your birth except the beating of the Earth's billion insect hearts. Your womb is wood and metal and satin, offering no sustenance, but only an implacable slot of close air, a pocket within the mother soil. And there is only one way you can live, now. There must be an emotional hand to slap you on the back to make you move. A desire, a want, an emotion. Then the first thing you know you quiver and rise and strike your brow against silk-skinned wood. That emotion surges through you, calling you. If it is not strong enough, you will settle down wearily, and will not wake again. But if you grow with it, somehow, if you claw upward, if you work tediously, slowly, many days, you find ways of displacing earth an inch at a time, and one night you crumble the darkness, the exit is completed, and you wriggle forth to see the stars.

Now you stand, letting the emotion lead you as a slender antenna shivers, led by radio waves. You bring your shoulders to a line, you make a step, like a new born babe, stagger, clutch for support—and find a marble slab to lean against. Beneath your trembling fingers the carved brief story of your life is all too tersely told: Born—Died.

You are a stick of wood. Learning to unbend, to walk naturally again, is not easy. But you don't worry about it. The pull of this emotion is too strong in you, and you go on, outward from the land of monuments, into twilight streets, alone on the pale sidewalks, past brick walls, down stony paths.

You feel there is something left undone. Some flower yet unseen somewhere where you would like to see, some pool waiting for you to dive into, some fish uncaught, some lip unkissed, some star unnoticed. You are going back, somewhere, to finish whatever there is undone.

All the streets have grown strange. You walk in a town you have never seen, a sort of dream town on the rim of a lake. You become more certain of your walking now, and can go quite swiftly. Memory returns.

You know every cobble of this street, you know every place where asphalt bubbled from mouths of cement in the hot oven summer. You know where the horses were tethered sweating in the green spring at these iron posts so long ago it is a feeble maggot in your brain. This cross street, where a light hangs high like a bright spider spinning a light web across this one solitudinous spot. You soon escape its web, going on to sycamore gloom. A picket fence dances woodenly beneath probing fingers. Here, as a child, you rushed by with a stick in hand manufacturing a machine-gun racket, laughing.

These houses, with the people and memories of people in them. The lemon odor of old Mrs. Hanlon who lived there, remember? A withered lady with withered hands and gums withered when her teeth gleamed upon the cupboard shelf smiling all to their porcelain selves. She gave you a withered lecture every day about cutting across her petunias. Now she is completely withered like a page of ancient paper burned. Remember how a book looks burning? That's how she is in her grave now, curling, layer upon layer, twisting into black rotted and mute agony.

The street is quiet except for the walking of a man's feet on it. The man turns a corner and you unexpectedly collide with one another.

You both stand back. For a moment, examining one another, you understand something about one another.

The stranger's eyes are deep-seated fires in worn receptacles. He is a tall, slender man in a very neat dark suit, blond and with a fiery whiteness to his protruding cheekbones. After a moment, he bows slightly, smiling. "You're a new one," he says. "Never saw you before."

And you know then *what* he is. He is dead, too. He is walking, too. He is "different" just like yourself.

You sense his differentness.

"Where are you going in such a hurry?" he asks, politely.

"I have no time to talk," you say, your throat dry and shrunken. "I am going somewhere, that is all. Please, step aside."

He holds onto your elbow firmly. "Do you know what I am?" He bends closer. "Do you not realize we are of the same legion? The dead who walk. We are as brothers."

You fidget impatiently. "I—I have no time."

"No," he agrees, "and neither have I, to waste."

You brush past, but cannot lose him, for he walks with you. "I know where you're going."

"Do you?"

"Yes," he says, casually. "To some childhood haunt. To some river. To some house or some memory. To some woman, perhaps. To some old friend's cottage. Oh, I know, all right, I know everything about our kind. I know," he says, nodding in the passing light and dark.

"You know, do you?"

"That is always why the dead walk. I have discovered that. Strange, when you think of all the books ever written about the dead, about vampires and walking cadavers and such, and never once did the authors of those most worthy volumes hit upon the true secret of why the dead walk. Always it is for the same reason—a memory, a friend, a woman, a river, a piece of pie, a house, a drink of wine, everything and anything connected with life and—LIVING!" He made a fist to hold the words tight. "Living! REAL living!"

Wordless, you increase your stride, but his whisper paces you:

"You must join me later this evening, my friend. We will meet with the others, tonight, tomorrow night and all the nights until we have our victory."

Hastily. "Who are the others?"

"The other dead." He speaks grimly. "We are banding together against intolerance."

"Intolerance?"

"We are a minority. We newly dead and newly embalmed and newly interred, we are a minority in the world, a persecuted minority. We are legislated against. We have no rights!" he declares heatedly.

The concrete slows under your heels. "Minority?"

"Yes." He takes your arm confidentially, grasping it tighter with each new declaration. "Are we wanted? No! Are we liked? No! We are feared! We are driven like sheep into a marble quarry, screamed at, stoned and persecuted like the Jews of Germany! People hate us from their fear. It's wrong, I tell you, and it's unfair!" He groans. He lifts his hands in a fury and strikes down. You are standing still now, held by his suffering and he flings it at you, bodily, with impact. "Fair, fair, is it fair? No. I ask you. Fair that we, a minority, rot in our graves while the rest of the continent sings, laughs, dances, plays, rotates and whirls and gets drunk! Fair, is it fair, I ask you that they love while our lips shrivel cold, that they caress while our fingers manifest to stone, that they tickle one another while maggots entertain us!

"No! I shout it! It is ungodly unfair! I say down with them, down with them for torturing our minority! We deserve the same rights!" he cries. "Why should we be dead, why not the others?"

"Perhaps you are right."

"They throw us down and slam the earth in our white faces and load a carven stone over our bosom to weigh us with, and shove flowers into an old tin can and bury it in a small spaded hole once a year. Once a year? Sometimes not even that! Oh, how I hate them, oh how it rises in me, this full blossoming hatred for the living. The fools. The damn fools! Dancing all night and loving, while we lie recumbent and full of disintegrating and helpless passion! Is that right?"

"I hadn't thought about it," you say, vaguely.

"Well," he snorts, "well, we'll fix them."

"What will you do?"

"There are thousands of us gathering tonight in the Elysian Park and I am the leader! We will destroy humanity!" he shouts, throwing back his shoulders, lifting his head in rigid defiance. "They have neglected us too long, and we shall kill them. It's only right. If we can't live, then they have no rights to live, either! And you will come, won't you, my friend?" he says, hopefully. "I have coerced many, I have spoken with scores. You will come and help. You yourself are bitter with this embalming and this suppression, are you not, else you would not be out tonight. Join us. The graveyards of the continent will explode like overripened apples, and the dead will pour out to overflow the villages! You will come?"

"I don't know. Yes. Perhaps I will," you say. "But I must go now. I have some place ahead of me to find. I will come."

"Good," he says, as you walk off, leaving him in shadow. "Good, good, good."

Up the hill now, as quick as you can. Thank God there is a coolness upon the Earth tonight. If it was a hot night it would be terrible to be above the ground in your condition.

You gasp happily. There, in all its rococo magnificence, is the house where Grandma sheltered her boarders. Where you as a child sat on the porch Fourth of July, watching sky rockets climb in fiery froth, the pinwheels cursing, sputtering sparks, the fire-crackers beating at your ears from the metal cannon of Uncle Bion who loved noise and bought fifty dollars worth of crackers just to explode them with his hand-rolled cigarette.

Now, standing, trembling with this emotion of recapturence, you know why the dead walk. To see again things like this. Here, on nights when dew invaded the grass, you crushed the wet petals and grass-blades and leaves as your boy bodies wrestled, and you knew the sweetness of now, now, TONIGHT! who cares for tomorrow, tomorrow is nothing, yesterday is over and done, tonight live, tonight!

Inside that grand old tall house the incredible Saturday nights took place, the Boston-baked beans in hordes saturated with thick juices, panoplied with platforms of bacon. Oh, yes, all of that. And the huge black piano that cried out at you when you performed musical dentistry upon its teeth . . .

And here, here, man, remember? This is Kim's house. That yellow light, around the back, that's her room. Do you realize that she might be in it now, painting her pictures or reading her books? In one moment, glance over that house, the porch, the swing before the door where you sat on August evenings. Think of it. Kim, your wife. In a moment you will see her again!

You bang the gate wide and hurry up the walk. You think to call, but instead slip quietly around the side. Her mother and father would go crazy if they saw you. Bad enough, the shock to Kim.

Here is her room. Glowing and square and soft and empty. Feed upon it. Is it not good to see again?

Your breath forms upon the window a symbol of your anxiety; the cold glass films with fog and blurs the exact and wonderful details of her existence there.

As the fog vanishes the form of her room emerges. The pink spread upon the low soft bed, the cherry-wood flooring, brilliantly waxed; throw-rugs like bright heavily furred dogs slumbering acenter it. The mirror. The small cosmetic table, where her sorcery is enacted in an easy pantomime. You wait.

She comes into the room.

Her hair is a lamp burning, bound behind her ears by her moving, she looks tired, her eyes are half-lidded, but even in this uncertain light, blue. Her dress is short and firm to her figure.

Breathlessly, you listen against the cold shell of glass, and as from deep under a sea you hear a song. She sings so softly it is already an echo before it leaves her mouth. You wonder what she thinks as she sings and combs out her hair at the mirror.

The cold brine of you stirs and beats. Certainly she must hear your heart's cold thunder!

Thoughtless, you tap upon the window.

She goes on stroking her hair gently, thinking that you are only the autumn wind outside the glass.

You tap again, anxiously, a bit afraid.

This time she sets down the comb and brush and rises to investigate, calm and certain.

At first she sees nothing. You are shadowed. Her eyes, as

she walks toward the window, are focused on the gleaming squares of glass. Then, she looks *through*. She sees a dim figure beyond the light. She still does not recognize.

"Kim!" You cannot help yourself. "It is I! I am here!"

Your eager face pushes to the light, as a submerged body must surge upon some black tide, suddenly floating, triumphant, with shimmering dark eyes!

The color drops from her cheeks. Her hands open to release sanity which flies away on strange wings. Her hands clasp again, to recapture some last sane thought. She does not scream. Only her eyes are wide as windows seen on a white house amidst a terrific lightning-shaft in a sudden summer squall, shadeless, empty and silvered with that terrific bolt of power!

"Kim!" you cry. "It is I!"

She says your name. She forms it with a numb mouth. Neither of you can hear it. She wants to run, but instead, at your insistence, she pulls up the window and, sobbing, you climb upward into the light. You slam the window and stand swaying there, only to find her far across the room, crucified by fear against the wall.

You sob raggedly. Your hands rise clean toward her in a gesture of old hunger and want. "Oh, Kim, it's been so long—"

TIME IS NON-EXISTENT. For five full minutes you remember nothing. You come out of it. You find yourself upon the soft rim of bed, staring at the floor.

In your ears is her crying.

She sits before the mirror, her shoulders moving like wings trying to fly with some agony as she makes the sounds.

"I know I am dead. I know I am. But what can I try to do to this cold? I want to be near your warmness, like at a fire in a long cold forest, Kim . . ."

"Six months," she breathes, not believing it. "You've been gone that long. I saw the lid close over your face. I saw the earth fall on the lid like a kind of sounding of drums. I cried. I cried until only a vacuum remained. You can't be here now—"

"I *am* here!"

"What can we do?" she wonders, holding her body with her hands.

"I don't know. Now that I've seen you, I don't want to walk back and get into that box. It's a horrible wooden chrysalis, Kim, I don't want its kind of metamorphosis—"

"Why, why, why did you come?"

"I was lost in the dark, Kim, and I dreamed a deep earth dream of you. Like a seventeen-year locust I writhed in my dream. I had to find my way back, somehow."

"But you can't stay."

"Until daybreak."

"Paul, don't take of my blood. I want to live."

"You're wrong, Kim. I'm not that kind. I'm only myself."

"You're different."

"I'm the same. I still love you."

"You're jealous of me."

"No, I'm not, Kim. I'm not jealous."

"We're enemies now, Paul. We can't love any more. I'm the quick, you're the dead. We're opposed by our very natures. We're natural enemies. I'm the thing you most desire, you represent the thing I least desire, death. It's just the opposite of love."

"But I love YOU, Kim!"

"You love my life and what life means, don't you see?"

"I *don't* see! What are we like, the two of us sitting here, talking philosophically, scientifically, at a time when we both should be laughing and glad to see one another."

"Not with jealousy and fear between us like a net. I loved you, Paul. I loved the things we did together. The processes, the dynamics of our relationship. The things you said, the thoughts you thought. Those things, I still love. But, but—"

"I still think those thoughts and think them over and over, Kim!"

"But we are apart."

"Don't be merciless, Kim. Have pity!"

Her face softens. She builds a cage around her face with convulsive fingers. Words escape the cage:

"Is pity love? Is it, Paul?"

There is a bitter tiredness in her breathing.

You stand upright. "I'll go crazy if this goes on!"

Wearily, her voice replies, "Can dead people go insane?"

You go to her, quickly, take her hands, lift her face, laugh at her with all the false gaiety you can summon:

"Kim, listen to me! Listen! Darling, I could come every night! We could talk the old talk, do the old things! It would be like a year ago, playing, having fun! Long walks in the moonlight, the merry-go-round at White City, the hot dogs at Coral Beach, the boats on the river—anything and everything you say, darling, if only—"

She cuts across your rapid, pitiable gaiety:

"It's no use."

"Kim! One hour every evening. Just one. Or half an hour.

Any time you say. Fifteen minutes. Five minutes. One minute to see you, that's all. That's all."

You bury your head in her limp, dead hands, and you feel the involuntary quiver shoot through her at your rapid contact. After a moment, she dares to move, slightly. She leans back, her eyes tightly closed, and says, simply: "I am afraid."

"Why?"

"I have been taught to be afraid, that's all."

"Damn the people and their customs and their old-wives tales!"

"Talking won't stop the fear."

You want to grasp, hold, stop her, shake sense into her, to clasp her trembling and comfort it as you would a wild bird trying to escape your fingers. "Stop it, stop it, Kim!"

Her trembling gradually passes like movements on a disturbed water pool calming and relaxing. She sinks down upon the bed and her voice is old in a young throat. "All right, darling." A pause. "Anything you say." Swallowing. "Anything you wish. If—it makes you happy."

You try to be happy. You try to burst with joy. You try to smile. You look down upon her as she continues talking vaguely:

"Whatever you say. Anything, my darling."

You venture to say, "You won't be afraid."

"Oh, no." Her breath flutters in. "I won't be."

You excuse yourself. "I just had to see you, you understand? I just had to!"

Her eyes are bright and focused now on you. "I know, Paul, how it must feel. I'll meet you outside the house in a few minutes. I'll have to make an excuse to mother and dad to get out past them."

You raise the window and put one leg out and then turn to look back up at her before vanishing. "Kim, I love you."

She says nothing, but stares blankly, and shuts the window when you are outside, and she goes away, dimming lights. Held by the dark, you weep with something not quite sorrow, not quite joy. You walk to the corner to wait out the time.

Across the street, past a lilac shrub, a man walks stiffly. There is something familiar about him. You remember. He is the man who accosted you earlier. He is dead, too, and walking through a world that is alien only because it is alive. He goes on along the street, as if in search of something.

Kim is beside you now.

An ice cream sundae is a most wonderful thing. Resting cool, a small white mountain capped by a frock of chocolate and contained in glass, it is something you stare at with spoon poised.

You put some of the ice cream in your mouth, sucking the cold. You pause. The light in your eyes embers down. You sit back, removed.

"What's wrong?" The old man behind the ancient fountain looks at you, concerned.

"Nothing."

"Ice cream taste funny?"

"No. It's fine."

"Fly in it?" He bends forward.

"No."

"You ain't eating it?" he says.

"I don't want to." You push it away from you and your lump of heart lowers itself precariously between the lonely bleak walls of your lungs. "I am sick. I am not hungry. I can't eat."

Kim is at your left, eating slowly. At your sign, she lays aside her spoon, also, and cannot eat.

You sit very straight, staring ahead into nothing. How can you tell them that your throat muscles will no longer contract efficiently enough to allow food. How can you speak of the frustrated hunger flaming in you as you watch Kim's dainty jaw muscles close and open, finishing the white coolness of the ice within her mouth, tasting and liking it.

How can you explain of the crumpled shape of your stomach lying like a dried apricot against your peritoneum? How describe that desiccated rope of intestine that is yours now? That lies coiled neatly, as if you heaped it by hand at the bottom of a cold pit?

Rising, you have no coin in your hand, and Kim pays, and together you swing wide the door and walk out into the stars.

"Kim—"

"That's all right. I understand," she says. Taking your arm, she walks down toward the park. Wordless, you realize that her hand is very faintly against you. It is there, but your feeling of it is lost. Beneath your feet, the sidewalk loses its solid tread. It now moves without shock or bump below you, a dream.

Just to be talking, Kim says, "Isn't that a marvelous smell on the air tonight? Lilacs in bloom."

You test the air. You can smell nothing. Panic rises in you. You try again, but it is no use.

Two people pass you in the dark, and as they drift by, nodding to Kim and you, as they gain distance behind, one of them comments, fading, "—Don't you smell something— funny? I wonder if a dog was killed in the street today . . ."

"I don't see anything—"

"—well—"

"KIM! COME BACK!"

You grasp her fleeing hand. It seems that it is this moment she has waited for in a tensed, apprehensive, and semi-gracious silence. The passing of the people and their few words are a trigger to thrust her away, almost screaming from you.

You catch her arm. Wordless, you struggle against her. She beats at you. She twists, and strikes at your binding fingers. You cannot feel her. You cannot feel her doing this! "Kim! Don't, darling. Don't run away. Don't be afraid!"

Her brooch falls to the cement like a beetle. Her heels scuff the hard stony surface. Her breath pants from her. Her eyes are wide. One hand escapes and stretches out behind her as she leans back, using her weight to pull free. The shadows enclose your struggle. Only your breath sounds. Her face glows taut and not soft any more, breaking apart in the light. There are no words. You pull back, your way. She pulls in her direction. You try to speak softly, soothingly, "Don't let people frighten you about me. Calm down—"

Her words are bitten out in whispers:

"Let go of me. Let go. Let go."

"No, I can't do that."

Again the wordless, dark movement of bodies and arms. She weakens and hangs limply sobbing against you. At your touch she trembles very deeply. You hold her close, teeth chattering. "I want you, Kim. Don't leave me. I had such plans. To go to Chicago some night. It only takes an hour on the train. Listen to me. Think of it. To eat the most elegant food across fine linen and silver from one another! To let wine lift us by our bootstraps. To stuff ourselves full. And now—" you declare harshly, eyes gleaming in the leaf-dark, "Now—" You hold your thinned stomach, pressing in that traitor thing lying dry and twisted as a paint tube there. "And now I can't taste the cool of ice cream, or the ripeness of berries, or apple pie or—or—"

Kim speaks.

You tilt your head. "What did you say?"

She speaks again.

"Speak louder," you ask of her, holding her close. "I can't hear you." She speaks and you cry out, bending near. And you hear absolutely nothing at first, and then, behind a thick cotton wall, her voice says,

"Paul, it's no use. You see? You understand now?"

You release her. "I wanted to see the neon lights. I wanted to find the flowers as they were, to touch your hand, your lips. But, oh god, first my taste goes, then I cannot eat at all, and now my skin is like concrete. And now I cannot hear your voice, Kim. It's like an echo in a lost world."

A great wind shakes the universe, but you do not feel it.

"Paul, this is not the way. The things you desire can't be had this way. It takes more than desire to insure these things."

"I want to kiss you."

"Can your lips feel?"

"No."

"Love depends on more than thought, Paul, because thought itself is built upon the senses. If we cannot talk together, hear together, or feel, or smell the night, or taste the food, what is there left for us?"

You know it is no use, but with a broken voice you argue on: "I can still *see* you. And I remember what it WAS like!"

"Illusion. Memory is an illusion, nothing more. It is a fire that needs constant tending. And we have no way to tend it if you cannot use your senses."

"It's so unfair! I want life!"

"You will live, Paul, I promise that. But not THIS way, the impossible way. You've been dead over half a year, and I'll be going to the hospital in another month—"

You stop. You are very cold. Holding to her shoulders, you stare into her soft, moving face. "What?"

"Yes. The hospital. Our child. Our child. You see, you didn't have to come back. You are always with me, Paul. You are alive." She turns you around. "Now I'll ask you. Go back. Everything balances. Believe that. Leave me with a better memory than this of you, Paul. Everything will work for the best, eventually. Go back where you came from."

You cannot even cry. Your tear-ducts are shriveled. The thought of the baby comes upon you, and sounds almost correct. But the rebellion in you will not be so easily put down. You turn to shout again at Kim, and without a sign, she sinks slowly to the ground. Bending over her, you hear her few weak words:

"The shock. The hospital. Quick. The shock."

You walk down the street, she lies in your arms. A grey film forms over your left eye. "I can't see. The air does things to me! Soon, I'll be blind in both eyes, Kim, it's so unfair!"

"Faith," she whispers, close, you barely hear the word.

You begin to run, stumbling. A car passes. You shout at it. The car stops and a moment later you and Kim and the man in the car are roaring soundlessly toward the hospital.

In the middle of the tempest, her talking stands out. "Have

faith, Paul. I believe in the future. You believe it too. Nature is not that cruel or unfair. There is compensation for you somewhere."

Your left eye is now completely blind. Your right eye blurs ominously.

Kim is gone!

The hospital attendants run her away from you. You did not even say goodbye to her, nor she to you! You stand outside, helpless, and then turn and walk away from the building. The outlines of the world blur. From the hospital a pulsing issues forth and turns your thoughts a pale red. Like a big red drum it beats in your head, with loud, soft, hard, easy rhythms.

You walk stupidly across streets, cars just miss striking you down. You watch people eat in gleaming glass windows. Watch hot dogs sizzling juices in a Greek restaurant. Watch people lift forks, knives. Everything glides by on noiseless lubricant of silence. You float. Your ears are solidly blocked. Your nose is clogged. The red drum beats louder, with an even tempo. You long and strive and strain to smell lilacs, taste bacon, or remember what a mockingbird sounded like cutting pieces from the sky with the trilling scissors of his beak. All those wonderful memorious things you try to capture.

Sour-sick, an earthquake of thought and confusion shaking you, you find yourself swaying down a ravine path in Elysian Park. The dead, the dead are walking tonight. They gather tonight. Remember the man who talked to you? Remember what he said? Yes, yes, you still have some fragments of memory. The dead are banding tonight, forming a unit to swarm over the homes of the warm living people, to kill and decimate them!

That means Kim, too. Kim and the baby.

Kim will die and have to grope and stumble and gabble like this, stinking and falling away from the bone and have dull ears and blind eyes and dry, eroded nostrils. Just like *you*.

"No!"

The ravine rushes on both sides and under you. You fall, pick yourself up, fall again.

The Leader stands alone as you grope your way to him by the silent creek. Sucking hoarse breaths you stand before him, doubling your fists, wondering where the horde of the undead are, you do not see them. And now the Leader talks to you, explaining, shrugging angrily:

"They did not come. Not one of those cold dead people showed up. You are the only recruit." He leans wearily against the tree, as if drunk. "The cowards, the persecuted swine."

"Good." Your breath, or the illusion of breath, slows. His words are like cold rain on you, bringing confidence and quiet. "I'm glad they didn't listen to you. There must be some reason why they didn't obey you. Perhaps—" you grope for the logic of it . . . "perhaps something happened to them that we can't understand, yet."

The Leader makes a bitter move of his lips, shaking his head back. "I had wild plans. But I am alone. And I see the futility of it now. Even if all the dead should rise, they are not strong enough. One blow and they fall in upon their members like a fire-gutted log. We grow tired so soon. Above the earth our discrepancies are hastened. The lift of an eyebrow is slow, painful toil. I am tired—"

You leave him behind you. His muttering passes away. The red pounding beats in your head again like horses' hooves on soft turf. You walk from the ravine, down the street, and into the graveyard, with mute purpose.

Your name is on the grave-stone still. The cavity awaits you. You slide down the small tunnel into the waiting wooden cavity, no longer afraid, jealous or excited. The complete withdrawal of your various senses has left you little but memory, and that seems to dissolve as the boxed satin erodes and the hard square wood softens. The wood becomes malleable. You lie suspended in warm round darkness. You can actually shift your feet. You relax.

You are overwhelmed by a luxury of warm sustenance, of deep pink thoughts and easy idleness. You are like a great old yeast contracting, the outer perimeter of your old fetidness crumbling, being laved away by a whispering tide, a pulsation and a gentleness of moves.

The coffin is now a round dim shell, no longer square. You breathe sufficiently, not hungry, not worried, and are loved. You are deeply loved. You are secure. The place where you are dreaming shifts, contracts, moves.

Drowsy. Your huge body is washed down in movements until it is small, tiny, compact, certain. Drowsy, drowsy on a slumberous singing tide. Slow. Quiet. Quiet.

Who are you trying to remember? A name plays at the rim of a sea. You run to get it, the waves pluck it away. Somebody beautiful you try to think of. Someone. A time, a place. Oh, so sleepy. Close round darkness, warmth, tiredness. Soundless shell. Dim tide pulsing. Quiet contraction.

A river of dark bears your feeble body on a series of loops and curves, faster, faster and yet faster.

You break into an openness and are suspended upside down in brilliant yellow light!

The world is immense as a new white mountain. The sun blazes and a huge red hand binds your two feet close as another hand strikes your naked spine to force a cry out of you.

A woman lies below, tired; sweet perspiration beads her face, and there is a wide singing and refreshened and sharpened wonder to this room and this world. You cry out into it with a newly formed voice. One moment upside-down, you are swung right side up, cuddled and nursed against a spiced-sweet breast.

Amid your fine hunger, you forget how to talk, to worry, to think of all things. Her voice, above you, gently tired, whispers over and over:

"My little new born baby. I will name you Paul, for him. For him . . ."

These words you do not comprehend. Once you feared something terrifying and black, but what it was you do not know now. It is forgotten in this flesh warmth and cackling content. For but a moment a name forms in your thimble-mouth, you try to say it, not knowing what it means, unable to pronounce it, only able to choke it happily with a fresh glowing that arises from unknown sources. The word vanishes swiftly, leaving a quickly fading, joyous soon-erased after-image of triumph and high laughter in the tiny busy roundness of your head: "Kim! Kim! Oh, Kim!"

PILLAR OF FIRE

HE CAME OUT OF THE EARTH, HATING. HATE WAS HIS FA-
ther; hate was his mother. It was good to walk again. It was
good to leap up out of the earth, off of your back, and stretch
your cramped arms violently and try to take a deep breath!

He *tried*. He cried out.

He couldn't breathe. He flung his arms over his face and
tried to breathe. It was impossible. He walked on the earth, he
came out of the earth. But he was dead. He couldn't breathe.
He could take air into his mouth and force it half down his
throat, with withered moves of long-dormant muscles, wildly,
wildly! And with this little air he could shout and cry! He
wanted to have tears but he couldn't make them come either.
All he knew was that he was standing upright, he was dead, he
shouldn't be walking! He couldn't breathe and yet he stood.

The smells of the world were all about him. Frustratedly,
he tried to smell the smells of autumn. Autumn was burning
the land down into ruin. All across the country the ruins of
summer lay; vast forests bloomed with flame, tumbled down
timber on empty, unleafed timber. The smoke of the burning
was rich, blue, and invisible.

He stood in the graveyard, hating. He walked through the world and yet could not taste nor smell of it. He heard, yes. The wind roared on his newly opened ears. But he was dead. Even though he walked he knew he was dead and should expect not too much of himself or this hateful living world.

He touched the tombstone over his own empty grave. He knew his own name again. It was a good job of carving.

WILLIAM. LANTRY

That's what the grave stone said.

His fingers trembled on the cool stone surface.

BORN 1898—DIED 1933

Born *again* . . . ?

What year? He glared at the sky and the midnight autumnal stars moving in slow illuminations across the windy black. He read the tiltings of centuries in those stars. Orion thus and so, Auriga here! And where Taurus? There!

His eyes narrowed. His lips spelled out the year:

"2349."

An odd number. Like a school sum. They used to say a man couldn't encompass any number over a hundred. After that it was all so damned abstract there was no use counting. This was the year 2349! A numeral, a sum. And here he was, a man who had lain in his hateful dark coffin, hating to be buried, hating the living people above who lived and lived and lived, hating them for all the centuries, until today, now, born out of hatred, he stood by his own freshly excavated grave, the smell of raw earth in the air, perhaps, but he could not smell it!

"I," he said, addressing a poplar tree that was shaken by the wind, "am an anachronism." He smiled faintly.

HE LOOKED AT THE GRAVEYARD. It was cold and empty. All of the stones had been ripped up and piled like so many flat bricks, one atop another, in the far corner by the wrought iron fence. This had been going on for two endless weeks. In his deep secret coffin he had heard the heartless, wild stirring as the men jabbed the earth with cold spades and tore out the coffins and carried away the withered ancient bodies to be burned. Twisting with fear in his coffin, he had waited for them to come to him.

Today they had arrived at his coffin. But—late. They had dug down to within an inch of the lid. Five o'clock bell, time for quitting. Home to supper. The workers had gone off. Tomorrow they would finish the job, they said, shrugging into their coats.

Silence had come to the emptied tombyard.

Carefully, quietly, with a soft rattling of sod, the coffin lid had lifted.

William Lantry stood trembling now, in the last cemetery on Earth.

"Remember?" he asked himself, looking at the raw earth. "Remember those stories of the last man on Earth? Those stories of men wandering in ruins, alone? Well, you, William Lantry, are a switch on the old story. Do you *know* that? You are the last dead man in the whole damned world!"

There were no more dead people. Nowhere in any land was there a dead person. Impossible? Lantry did not smile at this. No, not impossible at all in this foolish, sterile, unimaginative, antiseptic age of cleansings and scientific methods! People died, oh my god, yes. But—*dead* people? Corpses? They didn't exist!

What *happened* to dead people?

The graveyard was on a hill. William Lantry walked through the dark burning night until he reached the edge of the graveyard and looked down upon the new town of Salem. It was all illumination, all color. Rocket ships cut fire above it, crossing the sky to all the far ports of Earth.

In his grave the new violence of this future world had driven down and seeped into William Lantry. He had been bathed in it for years. He knew all about it, with a hating dead man's knowledge of such things.

Most important of all, he knew what these fools did with dead men.

He lifted his eyes. In the center of the town a massive stone finger pointed at the stars. It was three hundred feet high and fifty feet across. There was a wide entrance and a drive in front of it.

In the town, theoretically, thought William Lantry, say you have a dying man. In a moment he will be dead. What happens? No sooner is his pulse cold when a certificate is flourished, made out, his relatives pack him into a car-beetle and drive him swiftly to—

The Incinerator!

That functional finger, that Pillar of Fire pointing at the stars. Incinerator. A functional, terrible name. But truth is truth in this future world.

Like a stick of kindling your Mr. Dead Man is shot into the furnace.

Flume!

William Lantry looked at the top of the gigantic pistol shoving at the stars. A small pennant of smoke issued from the top.

There's where your dead people go.

"Take care of yourself, William Lantry," he murmured. "You're the last one, the rare item, the last dead man. All the other graveyards of Earth have been blasted up. This is the last graveyard and you're the last dead man from the centuries. These people don't believe in having dead people about, much less walking dead people. Everything that can't be used goes up like a matchstick. Superstitions right along with it!"

He looked at the town. All right, he thought, quietly, I hate you. You hate me, or you *would* if you knew I existed. You don't believe in such things as vampires or ghosts. Labels without referents, you cry! You snort. All right, snort! Frankly, I don't believe in *you,* either! I don't *like* you! You and your Incinerators.

He trembled. How very close it had been. Day after day they had hauled out the other dead ones, burned them like so much kindling. An edict had been broadcast around the world. He had heard the digging men talk as they worked!

"I guess it's a good idea, this cleaning up the graveyards," said one of the men.

"Guess so," said another. "Grisly custom. Can you imagine?

"Being buried, I mean! Unhealthy! All them germs!"

"Sort of a shame. Romantic, kind of. I mean, leaving just this one graveyard untouched all these centuries. The other graveyards were cleaned out, what year was it, Jim?"

"About 2260, I think. Yeah, that was it, 2260, almost a

hundred years ago. But some Salem Committee they got on their high horse and they said, 'Look here, let's have just ONE graveyard left, to remind us of the customs of the barbarians.' And the gover'ment scratched its head, thunk it over, and said, 'Okay. Salem it is. But all other graveyards go, you understand, all!"

"And away they went," said Jim.

"Sure, they sucked out 'em with fire and steam shovels and rocket-cleaners. If they knew a man was buried in a cow-pasture, they fixed him! Evacuated them, they did. Sort of cruel, I say."

"I hate to sound old-fashioned, but still there were a lot of tourists came here every year, just to see what a real graveyard was like."

"Right. We had nearly a million people in the last three years visiting. A good revenue. But—a government order is an order. The government says no more morbidity, so flush her out we do! Here we go. Hand me that spade, Bill."

William Lantry stood in the autumn wind, on the hill. It was good to walk again, to feel the wind and to hear the leaves scuttling like mice on the road ahead of him. It was good to see the bitter cold stars almost blown away by the wind.

It was even good to know fear again.

For fear rose in him now, and he could not put it away. The very fact that he was walking made him an enemy. And there was not another friend, another dead man, in all of the world, to whom one could turn for help or consolation. It was the whole melodramatic living world against one William Lantry. It was the whole vampire-disbelieving, body-burning, graveyard-annihilating world against a man in a dark suit on a dark autumn hill. He put out his pale cold hands into the city illumination. You have pulled the tombstones, like teeth, from the yard, he thought. Now I will find some way to push your damnable Incinerators down into rubble. I will make dead people again, and I will make friends in so doing. I cannot be alone and lonely. I must start manufacturing friends very soon. Tonight.

"War is declared," he said, and laughed. It was pretty silly, one man declaring war on an entire world.

The world did not answer back. A rocket crossed the sky on a rush of flame, like an Incinerator taking wing.

Footsteps. Lantry hastened to the edge of the cemetery. The diggers, coming back to finish up their work? No. Just someone, a man, walking by.

As the man came abreast the cemetery gate, Lantry stepped swiftly out. "Good evening," said the man, smiling.

Lantry struck the man in the face. The man fell. Lantry bent quietly down and hit the man a killing blow across the neck with the side of his hand.

Dragging the body back into shadow, he stripped it, changed clothes with it. It wouldn't do for a fellow to go wandering about this future world with ancient clothing on. He found a small pocket knife in the man's coat; not much of a knife, but enough if you knew how to handle it properly. He knew how.

He rolled the body down into one of the already opened and exhumed graves. In a minute he had shoveled dirt down upon it, just enough to hide it. There was little chance of it being found. They wouldn't dig the same grave twice.

He adjusted himself in his new loose-fitting metallic suit. Fine, fine.

Hating, William Lantry walked down into town, to do battle with the Earth.

THE INCINERATOR WAS OPEN. IT NEVER CLOSED. THERE was a wide entrance, all lighted up with hidden illumination, there was a helicopter landing table and a beetle drive. The town itself was dying down after another day of the dynamo. The lights were going dim, and the only quiet, lighted spot in the town now was the Incinerator. God, what a practical name, what an unromantic name.

William Lantry entered the wide, well-lighted door. It was an entrance, really; there were no doors to open or shut. People could go in and out, summer or winter, the inside was always warm. Warm from the fire that rushed whispering up the high round flue to where the whirlers, the propellers, the air-jets pushed the leafy grey ashes on away for a ten mile ride down the sky.

There was the warmth of the bakery here. The halls were floored with rubber parquet. You couldn't make a noise if you wanted to. Music played in hidden throats somewhere. Not music of death at all, but music of life and the way the sun lived inside the Incinerator; or the sun's brother, anyway. You could hear the flame floating inside the heavy brick wall.

William Lantry descended a ramp. Behind him he heard a whisper and turned in time to see a beetle stop before the entrance way. A bell rang. The music, as if at a signal, rose to ecstatic heights. There was joy in it.

From the beetle, which opened from the rear, some attendants stepped carrying a golden box. It was six feet long and there were sun symbols on it. From another beetle the relatives of the man in the box stepped and followed as the attendants took the golden box down a ramp to a kind of altar. On the side of the altar were the words, "WE WHO WERE BORN OF THE SUN RETURN TO THE SUN." The golden box was deposited upon the altar, the music leaped upward, the Guardian of this place spoke only a few words, then the attendants picked up the golden box, walked to a transparent wall, a safety lock, also transparent, and opened it. The box was shoved into the glass slot. A moment later an inner lock opened, the box was injected into the interior of the flue and vanished instantly in quick flame.

The attendants walked away. The relatives without a word turned and walked out. The music played.

William Lantry approached the glass fire lock. He peered through the wall at the vast, glowing, never-ceasing heart of the Incinerator. It burned steadily, without a flicker, singing to itself peacefully. It was so solid it was like a golden river flowing up out of the earth toward the sky. Anything you put into the river was borne upward, vanished.

Lantry felt again his unreasoning hatred of this thing, this monster, cleansing fire.

A man stood at his elbow. "May I help you, sir?"

"What?" Lantry turned abruptly. "What did you say?"

"May I be of service?"

"I—that is—" Lantry looked quickly at the ramp and the door. His hands trembled at his sides. "I've never been in here before."

"Never?" The Attendant was surprised.

That had been the wrong thing to say, Lantry realized. But it was said, nevertheless. "I mean," he said. "Not really. I mean, when you're a child, somehow, you don't pay attention. I suddenly realized tonight that I didn't really *know* the Incinerator."

The Attendant smiled. "We never know anything, do we, really? I'll be glad to show you around."

"Oh, no. Never mind. It—it's a wonderful place."

"Yes, it is." The Attendant took pride in it. "One of the finest in the world, I think."

"I—" Lantry felt he must explain further. "I haven't had many relatives die on me since I was a child. In fact, none. So, you see I haven't been here for many years."

"I see." The Attendant's face seemed to darken somewhat.

What've I said now, thought Lantry. What in God's name is wrong? What've I done? If I'm not careful I'll get myself shoved right into that damnable firetrap. What's wrong with this fellow's face? He seems to be giving me more than the usual going over.

"You wouldn't be one of the men who've just returned from Mars, would you?" asked the Attendant.

"No. Why do you ask?"

"No matter." The Attendant began to walk off. "If you want to know anything, just ask me."

"Just one thing," said Lantry

"What's that?"

"This."

Lantry dealt him a stunning blow across the neck.

He had watched the fire-trap operator with expert eyes. Now, with the sagging body in his arms, he touched the button that opened the warm outer lock, placed the body in, heard the music rise, and saw the inner lock open. The body shot out into the river of fire. The music softened.

"Well done, Lantry, well done."

BARELY AN INSTANT LATER another Attendant entered the room. Lantry was caught with an expression of pleased excitement on his face. The Attendant looked around as if expecting to find someone, then he walked toward Lantry. "May I help you?"

"Just looking," said Lantry.

"Rather late at night," said the Attendant.

"I couldn't sleep."

That was the wrong answer, too. Everybody slept in this world. Nobody had insomnia. If you did you simply turned on a hypno-ray, and, sixty seconds later, you were snoring. Oh, he was just *full* of wrong answers. First he had made the fatal error of saying he had never been in the Incinerator before, when he knew damned well that all children were brought here on tours, every year, from the time they were four, to instill the idea of the clean fire death and the Incinerator in their minds. Death was a bright fire, death was warmth and the sun. It was not a dark, shadowed thing. That was important in their education. And he, pale thoughtless fool, had immediately gabbled out his ignorance.

And another thing, this paleness of his. He looked at his hands and realized with growing terror that a pale man also was non-existent in this world. They would suspect his paleness. That was why the first attendant had asked, "Are you one of those men newly returned from Mars?" Here, now, this new Attendant was clean and bright as a copper penny, his cheeks red with health and energy. Lantry hid his pale hands in his pockets. But he was fully aware of the searching the Attendant did on his face.

"I mean to say," said Lantry. "I didn't *want* to sleep. I wanted to think."

"Was there a service held here a moment ago?" asked the Attendant, looking about.

"I don't know, I just came in."

"I thought I heard the fire lock open and shut."

"I don't know," said Lantry.

The man pressed a wall button. "Anderson?"

A voice replied. "Yes."

"Locate Saul for me, will you?"

"I'll ring the corridors." A pause. "Can't find him."

"Thanks." The Attendant was puzzled. He was beginning to make little sniffing motions with his nose. "Do you—*smell* anything?"

Lantry sniffed. "No. Why?"

"I *smell* something."

Lantry took hold of the knife in his pocket. He waited.

"I remember once when I was a kid," said the man. "And we found a cow lying dead in the field. It had been there two days in the hot sun. That's what this smell is. I wonder what it's from?"

"Oh, I know what it is," said Lantry quietly. He held out his hand. "Here."

"What?"

"Me, of course."

"You?"

"Dead several hundred years."

"You're an odd joker." The Attendant was puzzled.

"Very." Lantry took out the knife. "Do you know what this is?"

"A knife."

"Do you ever use knives on people anymore?"

"How do you mean?"

"I mean—killing them, with knives or guns or poison?"

"You *are* an odd joker!" The man giggled awkwardly.

"I'm going to kill you," said Lantry.

"Nobody kills anybody," said the man.

"Not any more they don't. But they used to, in the old days."

"I know they did."

"This will be the first murder in three hundred years. I just killed your friend. I just shoved him into the fire lock."

That remark had the desired effect. It numbed the man so completely, locked him so thoroughly with its illogical aspects that Lantry had time to walk forward. He put the knife against the man's chest. "I'm going to kill you."

"That's silly," said the man, numbly. "People don't do that."

"Like this," said Lantry. "You see?"

The knife slid into the chest. The man stared at it for a moment. Lantry caught the falling body.

THE SALEM FLUE EXPLODED AT SIX THAT MORNING. THE great fire chimney shattered into ten thousand parts and flung itself into the earth and into the sky and into the houses of the sleeping people. There was fire and sound, more fire than autumn made burning in the hills.

William Lantry was five miles away at the time of the explosion. He saw the town ignited by the great spreading cremation of it. And he shook his head and laughed a little bit and clapped his hands smartly together.

Relatively simple. You walked around killing people who didn't believe in murder, had only heard of it indirectly as some dim gone custom of the old barbarian races. You walked into the control room of the Incinerator and said, "How do you work this Incinerator?" and the control man told you, because everybody told the truth in this world of the future, nobody lied, there was no reason to lie, there was no danger to lie *against*. There was only one criminal in the world, and nobody knew HE existed yet.

Oh, it was an incredibly beautiful setup. The Control Man had told him just how the Incinerator worked, what pressure gauges controlled the flood of fire gasses going up the flue, what levers were adjusted or readjusted. He and Lantry had had quite a talk. It was an easy free world. People trusted people. A moment later Lantry had shoved a knife in the Control Man also and set the pressure gauges for an overload to occur half an hour later, and walked out of the Incinerator halls, whistling.

Now even the sky was palled with the vast black cloud of the explosion.

"This is only the first," said Lantry, looking at the sky. "I'll tear all the others down before they even suspect there's an unethical man loose in their society. They can't account for a variable like me. I'm beyond their understanding. I'm incomprehensible, impossible, therefore I do not exist. My God, I can kill hundreds of thousands of them before they even realize murder is out in the world again. I can make it look like an accident each time. Why, the idea is so huge, it's unbelievable!"

The fire burned the town. He sat under a tree for a long time, until morning. Then, he found a cave in the hills, and went in, to sleep.

He awoke at sunset with a sudden dream of fire. He saw himself pushed into the flue, cut into sections by flame, burned away to nothing. He sat up on the cave floor, laughing at himself. He had an idea.

He walked down into the town and stepped into an audio booth. He dialed OPERATOR. "Give me the Police Department," he said.

"I beg your pardon?" said the operator.

He tried again. "The Law Force," he said.

"I will connect you with the Peace Control," she said, at last.

A little fear began ticking inside him like a tiny watch. Suppose the operator recognized the term Police Department as an anachronism, took his audio number, and sent someone out to investigate? No, she wouldn't do that. Why should she suspect? Paranoids were nonexistent in this civilization.

"Yes, the Peace Control," he said.

A buzz. A man's voice answered, "Peace Control. Stephens speaking."

"Give me the Homicide Detail," said Lantry, smiling.

"The *what?*"

"Who investigates murders?"

"I beg your pardon, what are you talking about?"

"Wrong number." Lantry hung up, chuckling. Ye gods, there was no such a thing as a Homicide Detail. There were no murders, therefore they needed no detectives. Perfect, perfect!

The audio rang back. Lantry hesitated, then answered.

"Say," said the voice on the phone. "Who *are* you?"

"The man just left who called," said Lantry, and hung up again.

He ran. They would recognize his voice and perhaps send someone out to check. People didn't lie. *He* had just lied. They knew his voice. He had lied. Anybody who lied needed a psychiatrist. They would come to pick him up to see why he was lying. For no *other* reason. They suspected him of nothing else. Therefore—he must run.

Oh, how very carefully he must act from now on. He knew nothing of this world, this odd straight truthful ethical world. Simply by looking pale you were suspect. Simply by not sleeping nights you were suspect. Simply by not bathing, by smelling like a—dead cow?—you were suspect. Anything.

He must go to a library. But that was dangerous, too. What were libraries like today? Did they have books or did they have film spools which projected books on a screen? Or did people have libraries at home, thus eliminating the necessity of keeping large main libraries?

He decided to chance it. His use of archaic terms might well make him suspect again, but now it was very important he learn all that could be learned of this foul world into which he had come again. He stopped a man on the street. "Which way to the library?"

The man was not surprised. "Two blocks east, one block north."

"Thank you."

Simple as that.

He walked into the library a few minutes later.

"May I help you?"

He looked at the librarian. May I help you, may I help you. What a world of helpful people! "I'd like to 'have' Edgar Allan Poe." His verb was carefully chosen. He didn't say 'read'. He was too afraid that books were passé, that printing itself was a lost art. Maybe all "books" today were in the form of fully delineated three-dimensional motion pictures. How in hell could you make a motion picture out of Socrates, Schopenhauer, Nietzsche, and Freud?

"What was that name again?"

"Edgar Allan Poe."

"There is no such author listed in our files."

"Will you please check?"

She checked. "Oh, yes. There's a red mark on the file card. He was one of the authors in the Great Burning of 2265."

"How ignorant of me."

"That's all right," she said. "Have you heard much of him?"

"He had some interesting barbarian ideas on death," said Lantry.

"Horrible ones," she said, wrinkling her nose. "Ghastly."

"Yes. Ghastly. Abominable, in fact. Good thing he was burned. Unclean. By the way, do you have any of Lovecraft?"

"Is that a sex book?"

Lantry exploded with laughter. "No, no. It's a man."

She riffled the file. "He was burned, too. Along with Poe."

"I suppose that applies to Machen and a man named Derleth and one named Ambrose Bierce, also?"

"Yes." She shut the file cabinet. "All burned. And good riddance." She gave him an odd warm look of interest. "I bet you've just come back from Mars."

"Why do you say that?"

"There was another explorer in here yesterday. He'd just made the Mars hop and return. He was interested in supernatural literature, also. It seems there are actually 'tombs' on Mars."

"What are 'tombs'?" Lantry was learning to keep his mouth closed.

"You know, those things they once buried people in."

"Barbarian custom. Ghastly!"

"*Isn't* it? Well, seeing the Martian tombs made this young explorer curious. He came and asked if we had any of those authors you mentioned. Of course we haven't even a smitch of their stuff." She looked at his pale face. "You *are* one of the Martian rocket men, aren't you?"

"Yes," he said. "Got back on the ship the other day."

"The other young man's name was Burke."

"Of course. Burke! Good friend of mine!"

"Sorry I can't help you. You'd best get yourself some vitamin shots and some sun-lamp. You look terrible, Mr.—?"

"Lantry. I'll be good. Thanks ever so much. See you next Hallows' Eve!"

"Aren't you the clever one." She laughed. "If there *were* a Hallows' Eve, I'd make it a date."

"But they burned *that*, too," he said.

"Oh, they burned everything," she said. "Good night."

"Good night." And he went on out.

OH, HOW CAREFULLY HE WAS BALANCED in this world! Like some kind of dark gyroscope, whirling with never a murmur, a very silent man. As he walked along the eight o'clock evening street he noticed with particular interest that there was not an unusual amount of lights about. There were the usual street lights at each corner, but the blocks themselves were only faintly illuminated. Could it be that these remarkable people were not *afraid of the dark?* Incredible nonsense! *Everyone* was afraid of the dark. *Even he* himself had been afraid, as a child. It was as natural as eating.

A little boy ran by on pelting feet, followed by six others. They yelled and shouted and rolled on the dark cool October lawn, in the leaves. Lantry looked on for several minutes before addressing himself to one of the small boys who was for a moment taking a respite, gathering his breath into his small lungs, as a boy might blow to refill a punctured paper bag.

"Here, now," said Lantry. "You'll wear yourself out."

"Sure," said the boy.

"Could you tell me," said the man, "why there are no street lights in the middle of the blocks?"

"Why?" asked the boy.

"I'm a teacher, I thought I'd test your knowledge," said Lantry.

"Well," said the boy, "you don't need lights in the middle of the block, that's why."

"But it gets rather dark," said Lantry.

"So?" said the boy.

"Aren't you afraid?" asked Lantry.

"Of what?" asked the boy.

"The dark," said Lantry.

"Ho ho," said the boy. "Why should I be?"

"Well," said Lantry. "It's black, it's dark. And after all, street lights were invented to take away the dark and take away fear."

"That's silly. Street lights were made so you could see where you were walking. Outside of that there's nothing."

"You miss the whole point—" said Lantry. "Do you mean to say you would sit in the middle of an empty lot all night and not be afraid?"

"Of what?"

"Of what, of what, of what, you little ninny! Of the dark!"

"Ho ho."

"Would you go out in the hills and stay all night in the dark?"

"Sure."

"Would you stay in a deserted house alone?"

"Sure."

"And not be afraid?"

"Sure."

"You're a liar!"

"Don't you call me nasty names!" shouted the boy. Liar was the improper noun, indeed. It seemed to be the worst thing you could call a person.

Lantry was completely furious with the little monster. "Look," he insisted. "Look into my eyes . . ."

The boy looked.

Lantry bared his teeth slightly. He put out his hands, making a claw-like gesture. He leered and gesticulated and wrinkled his face into a terrible mask of horror.

"Ho ho," said the boy. "You're funny."

"*What* did you say?"

"You're funny. Do it again. Hey, gang, c'mere! This man does funny things!"

"Never mind."

"Do it again, sir."

"Never mind, never mind. Good night!" Lantry ran off.

"Good night, sir. And mind the dark, sir!" called the little boy.

Of all the stupidity, of all the rank, gross, crawling, jelly-mouthed stupidity! He had never seen the like of it in his life! Bringing the children up without so much as an ounce of imagination! Where was the fun in being children if you didn't imagine things?

He stopped running. He slowed and for the first time began to appraise himself. He ran his hand over his face and bit his finger and found that he himself was standing midway in the block and he felt uncomfortable. He moved up to the street corner where there was a glowing lantern. "That's better," he said, holding his hands out like a man to an open warm fire.

He listened. There was not a sound except the night breathing of the crickets. Faintly there was a fire-hush as a rocket swept the sky. It was the sound a torch might make brandished gently on the dark air.

He listened to himself and for the first time he realized what there was so peculiar to himself. There was not a sound in him. The little nostril and lung noises were absent. His lungs did not take nor give oxygen or carbon-dioxide; they did not move. The hairs in his nostrils did not quiver with warm combing air. That faint purling whisper of breathing did not sound in his nose. Strange. Funny. A noise you never heard when you were alive, the breath that fed your body, and yet, once dead, oh how you missed it!

The only other time you ever heard it was on deep dream-less awake nights when you wakened and listened and heard first your nose taking and gently poking out the air, and then the dull deep dim red thunder of the blood in your temples, in your eardrums, in your throat, in your aching wrists, in your warm loins, in your chest. All of those little rhythms, gone. The wrist beat gone, the throat pulse gone, the chest vibration gone. The sound of the blood coming up down around and through, up down around and through. Now it was like listening to a statue.

And yet he *lived*. Or, rather, moved about. And how was this done, over and above scientific explanations, theories, doubts?

By one thing, and one thing alone.

Hatred.

Hatred was a blood in him, it went up down around and through, up down around and through. It was a heart in him, not beating, true, but warm. He was—what? Resentment. Envy. They said he could not lie any longer in his coffin in the cemetery. He had *wanted* to. He had never had any particular desire to get up and walk around. It had been enough, all these centuries, to lie in the deep box and feel but *not feel* the ticking of the million insect watches in the earth around, the moves of worms like so many deep thoughts in the soil.

But then they had come and said, "Out you go and into the furnace!" And that is the worst thing you can say to any man. You cannot tell him what to do. If you say you are dead, he will want not to be dead. If you say there are no such things as vampires, by God, that man will try to be one just for spite. If you say a dead man cannot walk he will test his limbs. If you say murder is no longer occurring, he will make it occur. He was, *in toto*, all the impossible things. They had given birth to him with their damnable practices and ignorances. Oh, how wrong they were. They needed to be shown. He would *show* them! Sun is *good,* so is *night,* there is nothing wrong with dark, *they* said.

Dark is horror, he shouted, silently, facing the little houses. It is *meant* for contrast. You must fear, you hear! That has always been the way of this world. You destroyers of Edgar Allan Poe and fine big-worded Lovecraft, you burner of Halloween masks and destroyer of pumpkin jack-o-lanterns! I will make night what it once was, the thing against which man built all his lanterned cities and his many children!

As if in answer to this, a rocket, flying low, trailing a long rakish feather of flame. It made Lantry flinch and draw back.

IT WAS BUT TEN MILES TO THE LITTLE TOWN OF SCIENCE Port. He made it by dawn, walking. But even this was not good. At four in the morning a silver beetle pulled up on the road beside him.

"Hello," called the man inside.

"Hello," said Lantry, wearily.

"Why are you walking?" asked the man.

"I'm going to Science Port."

"Why don't you ride?"

"I *like* to walk."

"*Nobody* likes to walk. Are you sick? May I give you a ride?"

"Thanks, but I like to walk."

The man hesitated, then closed the beetle door. "Good night."

When the beetle was gone over the hill, Lantry retreated into a nearby forest. A world full of bungling helping people.

By God, you couldn't even *walk* without being accused of sickness. That meant only one thing. He must not walk any longer, he had to ride. He should have accepted that fellow's offer.

The rest of the night he walked far enough off the highway so that if a beetle rushed by he had time to vanish in the underbrush. At dawn he crept into an empty dry water-drain and closed his eyes.

The dream was as perfect as a rimed snowflake.

He saw the graveyard where he had lain deep and ripe over the centuries. He heard the early morning footsteps of the laborers returning to finish their work.

"Would you mind passing me the shovel, Jim?"

"Here you go."

"Wait a minute, wait a minute!"

"What's up?"

"Look here. We didn't finish last night, did we?"

"No."

"There was one more coffin, wasn't there?"

"Yes."

"Well, here it is, and open!"

"You've got the wrong hole."

"What's the name say on the gravestone?"

"Lantry. William Lantry."

"That's him, that's the one! Gone!"

"What could have happened to it?"

"How do I know? The body was here last night."

"We can't be sure, we didn't look."

"God, man, people don't bury empty coffins. He was in his box. Now he isn't."

"Maybe this box was empty."

"Nonsense. Smell that smell? He was here all right."

A pause.

"Nobody would have taken the body, would they?"

"What for?"

"A curiosity, perhaps."

"Don't be ridiculous. People just don't steal. Nobody steals."

"Well, then, there's only one solution."

"And?"

"He got up and walked away."

A pause. In the dark dream, Lantry expected to hear laughter. There was none. Instead, the voice of the gravedigger, after a thoughtful pause, said, "Yes. That's it, indeed. He got up and walked away."

"That's interesting to think about," said the other.

"Isn't it, though?"

Silence.

LANTRY AWOKE. It had all been a dream, but God, how realistic. How strangely the two men had carried on. But not unnaturally, oh, no. That was exactly how you expected men of the future to talk. Men of the future. Lantry grinned wryly. That was an anachronism for you. This was the future. This was happening *now*. It wasn't 300 years from now, it was now, not then, or any other time. This wasn't the Twentieth Century. Oh, how calmly those two men in the dream had said, "He got up and walked away." "—interesting to think about."

"Isn't it, though?" With never a quaver in their voices. With not so much as a glance over their shoulders or a tremble of spade in hand. But, of course, with their perfectly honest, logical minds, there was but one explanation; certainly nobody

had *stolen* the corpse. "*Nobody* steals." The corpse had simply got up and walked off. The corpse was the only one who could have *possibly* moved the corpse. By the few casual slow words of the gravediggers Lantry knew what they were thinking. Here was a man that had lain in suspended animation, not really dead, for hundreds of years. The jarring about, the activity, had brought him back.

Everyone had heard of those little green toads that are sealed for centuries inside mud rocks or in ice patties, alive, alive oh! And how when scientists chipped them out and warmed them like marbles in their hands the little toads leapt about and frisked and blinked. Then it was only logical that the gravediggers think of William Lantry in like fashion.

But what if the various parts were fitted together in the next day or so? If the vanished body and the shattered, exploded incinerator were connected? What if this fellow named Burke, who had returned pale from Mars, went to the library again and said to the young woman he wanted some books and she said, "Oh, your friend Lantry was in the other day." And he'd say, "Lantry who? Don't know anyone by that name." And she'd say, "Oh, he *lied*." And people in this time didn't lie. So it would all form and coalesce, item by item, bit by bit. A pale man who was pale and shouldn't be pale had lied and people don't lie, and a walking man on a lonely country road had walked and people don't walk anymore, and a body was missing from a cemetery, and the Incinerator had blown up and and and—

They would come after him. They would find him. He would be easy to find. He walked. He lied. He was pale. They would find him and take him and stick him through the open fire-lock of the nearest Burner and that would be your Mr. William Lantry, like a Fourth of July set-piece!

There was only one thing to be done efficiently and completely. He rose in violent moves. His lips were wide and his dark eyes were flared and there was a trembling and burning all through him. He must kill and kill and kill and kill and kill. He must make his enemies into friends, into people like himself who walked but shouldn't walk, who were pale in a land of pinks. He must kill and then kill and then kill again. He must make bodies and dead people and corpses. He must destroy Incinerator after Flue after Burner after Incinerator. Explosion on explosion. Death on death. Then, when the Incinerators were all thrown in ruin, and the hastily established morgues were jammed with the bodies of people shattered by the explosion, then he would begin his making of friends, his enrollment of the dead in his own cause.

Before they traced and found and killed him, they must be killed themselves. So far he was safe. He could kill and they would not kill back. People simply do not go around killing. That was his safety margin. He climbed out of the abandoned drain, stood in the road.

He took the knife from his pocket and hailed the next beetle.

IT WAS LIKE THE FOURTH OF JULY! The biggest damned firecracker of them all. The Science Port Incinerator split down the middle and flew apart. It made a thousand small explosions that ended with a greater one. It fell upon the town and crushed houses and burned trees. It woke people from sleep and then put them to sleep again, forever, an instant later.

William Lantry, sitting in a beetle that was not his own, tuned idly to a station on the audio dial. The collapse of the Incinerator had killed some four hundred people. Many had been caught in flattened houses, others struck by flying metal. A temporary morgue was being set up at—

An address was given.

Lantry noted it with a pad and pencil.

He could go on this way, he thought, from town to town, from country to country, destroying the Burners, the Pillars of Fire, until the whole clean magnificent framework of flame and cauterization was tumbled. He made a fair estimate—each explosion averaged five hundred dead. You could work that up to a hundred thousand in no time.

He pressed the floor stud of the beetle. Smiling, he drove off through the dark streets of the city.

THE CITY CORONER HAD REQUISITIONED an old warehouse. From midnight until four in the morning the grey beetles hissed down the rain-shiny streets, turned in, and the bodies were laid out on the cold concrete floors, with white sheets over them. It was a continuous flow until about four-thirty, then it stopped. There were about two hundred bodies there, white and cold.

The bodies were left alone; nobody stayed behind to tend them. There was no use tending the dead; it was a useless procedure; the dead could take care of themselves.

About five o'clock, with a touch of dawn in the east, the first trickle of relatives arrived to identify their sons or their fathers or their mothers or their uncles. The people moved quickly into the warehouse, made the identification, moved quickly out again. By six o'clock, with the sky still lighter in the east, this trickle had passed on, also.

William Lantry walked across the wide wet street and entered the warehouse.

He held a piece of blue chalk in one hand.

He walked by the coroner who stood in the entranceway talking to two others. ". . . drive the bodies to the Incinerator in Mellin Town, tomorrow . . ." The voices faded.

Lantry moved, his feet echoing faintly on the cool concrete. A wave of sourceless relief came to him as he walked among the shrouded figures. He was among his own. And—better than that, by God! he had *created* these! He had made them dead! He had procured for himself a vast number of recumbent friends!

Was the coroner watching? Lantry turned his head. No. The warehouse was calm and quiet and shadowed in the dark morning. The coroner was walking away now, across the street, with his two attendants; a beetle had drawn up on the other side of the street, and the coroner was going over to talk with whoever was in the beetle.

William Lantry stood and made a blue chalk pentagram on the floor by each of the bodies. He moved swiftly, swiftly, without a sound, without blinking. In a few minutes, glancing up now and then to see if the coroner was still busy, he chalked the floor by a hundred bodies. He straightened up and put the chalk in his pocket.

Now is the time for all good men to come to the aid of their party, now is the time for all good men to come to the aid of their party, now is the time for all good men to come to the aid of their party, now is the time. . .

Lying in the earth, over the centuries, the processes and thoughts of passing peoples and passing times had seeped down to him, slowly, as into a deep-buried sponge. From some death-memory in him now, ironically, repeatedly, a black type-writer clacked out black even lines of pertinent words:

Now is the time for all good men, for all good men, to come to the aid of—

William Lantry.

Other words—

Arise my love, and come away—

The quick brown fox jumped over . . . Paraphrase it. The quick risen body jumped over the tumbled Incinerator . . .

Lazarus, come forth from the tomb . . .

He knew the right words. He need only speak them as they had been spoken over the centuries. He need only gesture with his hands and speak the words, the dark words that would cause these bodies to quiver, rise and walk!

And when they had risen he would take them through the town, they would kill others and the others would rise and walk. By the end of the day there would be thousands of good friends walking with him. And what of the naïve, living people of this year, this day, this hour? They would be completely unprepared for it. They would go down to defeat because they would not be expecting war of any sort. They wouldn't believe it possible, it would all be over before they could convince themselves that such an illogical thing could happen.

He lifted his hands. His lips moved. He said the words. He began in a chanting whisper and then raised his voice, louder. He said the words again and again. His eyes were closed tightly.

His body swayed. He spoke faster and faster. He began to move forward among the bodies. The dark words flowed from his mouth. He was enchanted with his own formulae. He stooped and made further blue symbols on the concrete, in the fashion of long-dead sorcerers, smiling, confident. Any moment now the first tremor of the still bodies, any moment now the rising, the leaping up of the cold ones!

His hands lifted in the air. His head nodded. He spoke, he spoke, he spoke. He gestured. He talked loudly over the bodies, his eyes flaring, his body tensed. "Now!" he cried, violently. "Rise, *all* of you."

Nothing happened.

"Rise!" he screamed, with a terrible torment in his voice.

The sheets lay in white blue-shadow folds over the silent bodies.

"Hear me, and act!" he shouted.

Far away, on the street, a beetle hissed along.

Again, again, again he shouted, pleaded. He got down by each body and asked of it his particular violent favor. No reply. He strode wildly between the even white rows, flinging his arms up, stooping again and again to make blue symbols!

Lantry was very pale. He licked his lips. "Come on, get up," he said. "They have, they always have, for a thousand years. When you make a mark—so! and speak a word—so! they always rise! Why not you now, why not you! Come on, come *on,* before *they* come back!"

The warehouse went up into shadow. There were steel beams across and down. In it, under the roof, there was not a sound, except the raving of a lonely man.

Lantry stopped.

Through the wide doors of the warehouse he caught a glimpse of the last cold stars of morning.

This was the year 2349.

His eyes grew cold and his hands fell to his sides. He did not move.

ONCE UPON A TIME PEOPLE SHUDDERED when they heard the wind about the house, once people raised crucifixes and wolfbane, and believed in walking dead and bats and loping white wolves. And as long as they believed, then so long did the dead, the bats, the loping wolves exist. The mind gave birth and reality to them.

But. . .

He looked at the white sheeted bodies.

These people did not believe.

They had never believed. They would never believe. They had never imagined that the dead might walk. The dead went up flues in flame. They had never heard superstition, never trembled or shuddered or doubted in the dark. Walking dead people could not exist, they were illogical. This was the year 2349, man, after all!

Therefore, these people could not rise, could not walk again. They were dead and flat and cold. Nothing, chalk, imprecation, superstition, could wind them up and set them walking. They were dead and *knew* they were dead!

He was alone.

There were live people in the world who moved and drove beetles and drank quiet drinks in little dimly illumined bars by country roads, and kissed women and talked much good talk all day and every day.

But he was not alive.

Friction gave him what little warmth he possessed.

There were two hundred dead people here in this warehouse now, cold upon the floor. The first dead people in a hundred years who were allowed to be corpses for an extra hour or more. The first not to be immediately trundled to the Incinerator and lit like so much phosphorus.

He should be happy with them, among them.

He was not.

They were completely dead. They did not know nor believe in walking once the heart had paused and stilled itself. They were deader than dead ever was.

He was indeed alone, more alone than any man had ever been. He felt the chill of his aloneness moving up into his chest, strangling him quietly.

William Lantry turned suddenly and gasped

While he had stood there, someone had entered the warehouse. A tall man with white hair, wearing a light-weight tan overcoat and no hat. How long the man had been nearby there was no telling.

There was no reason to stay here. Lantry turned and started to walk slowly out. He looked hastily at the man as he passed and the man with the white hair looked back at him, curiously. Had he heard? The imprecations, the pleadings, the shoutings? Did he suspect? Lantry slowed his walk. Had this man seen him make the blue chalk marks? But then, would he interpret them as symbols of an ancient superstition? Probably not.

Reaching the door, Lantry paused. For a moment he did not want to do anything but lie down and be coldly, really dead again and be carried silently down the street to some distant burning flue and there dispatched in ash and whispering fire. If he was indeed alone and there was no chance to collect an army to his cause, what, then, existed as a reason for going on? Killing? Yes, he'd kill a few thousand more. But that wasn't enough. You can only do so much of that before they drag you down.

He looked at the cold sky.

A rocket went across the black heaven, trailing fire.

Mars burned red among a million stars.

Mars. The library. The librarian. Talk. Returning rocket men. Tombs.

Lantry almost gave a shout. He restrained his hand, which wanted so much to reach up into the sky and touch Mars. Lovely red star on the sky. Good star that gave him sudden new hope. If he had a living heart now it would be thrashing wildly, and sweat would be breaking out of him and his pulses would be stammering, and tears would be in his eyes!

He would go down to wherever the rockets sprang up into space. He would go to Mars, one way or another. He would go to the Martian tombs. There, there, by God, were bodies, he would bet his last hatred on it, that would rise and walk and work with him! Theirs was an ancient culture, much different from that of Earth, patterned on the Egyptian, if what the librarian had said was true. And the Egyptian—what a crucible of dark superstition and midnight terror that culture had been! Mars it *was,* then. Beautiful Mars!

But he must not attract attention to himself. He must move carefully. He wanted to run, yes, to get away, but that would be the worst possible move he could make. The man with the white hair was glancing at Lantry from time to time, in the entranceway. There were too many people about. If anything happened he would be outnumbered. So far he had taken on only *one* man at a time.

Lantry forced himself to stop and stand on the steps before the warehouse. The man with the white hair came on onto the steps also and stood, looking at the sky. He looked as if he was going to speak at any moment. He fumbled in his pockets, took out a packet of cigarettes.

THEY STOOD OUTSIDE THE MORGUE TOGETHER, THE TALL pink, white-haired man, and Lantry, hands in their pockets. It was a cool night with a white shell of a moon that washed a house here, a road there, and further on, parts of a river.

"Cigarette?" The man offered Lantry one.

"Thanks."

They lit up together. The man glanced at Lantry's mouth. "Cool night."

"Cool."

They shifted their feet. "Terrible accident."

"Terrible."

"So many dead."

"So many."

Lantry felt himself some sort of delicate weight upon a scale. The other man did not seem to be looking at him, but rather listening and feeling toward him. There was a feathery balance here that made for vast discomfort. He wanted to move away and get out from under this balancing, weighing. The tall white-haired man said, "My name's McClure."

"Did you have any friends inside?" asked Lantry.

"No. A casual acquaintance. Awful accident."

"Awful."

They balanced each other. A beetle hissed by on the road with its seventeen tires whirling quietly. The moon showed a little town further over in the black hills.

"I say," said the man McClure.

"Yes."

"Could you answer me a question?"

"Be glad to." He loosened the knife in his coat pocket, ready.

"Is your name Lantry?" asked the man at last.

"Yes."

"*William* Lantry?"

"Yes."

"Then you're the man who came out of the Salem grave-yard day before yesterday, aren't you?"

"Yes."

"Good Lord, I'm glad to meet you, Lantry! We've been trying to find you for the past twenty-four hours!"

The man seized his hand, pumped it, slapped him on the back.

"What, what?" said Lantry.

"Good Lord, man, why did you run off? Do you realize what an instance this is? We want to talk to you!"

McClure was smiling, glowing. Another handshake, another slap. "I *thought* it was you!"

The man is mad, thought Lantry. Absolutely mad. Here I've toppled his Incinerators, killed people, and he's shaking my hand. Mad, mad!

"Will you come along to the Hall?" said the man, taking his elbow.

"Wh-what hall?" Lantry stepped back.

"The Science Hall, of course. It isn't every year we get a real case of suspended animation. In small animals, yes, but in a man, hardly! Will you come?"

"What's the act?" demanded Lantry, glaring. "What's all this talk?"

"My dear fellow, what do you mean?" The man was stunned.

"Never mind. Is that the only reason you want to see me?"

"What other reason would there be, Mr. Lantry? You don't know how glad I am to see you!" He almost did a little dance. "I suspected. When we were in there together. You being so pale and all. And then the way you smoked your cigarette, something about it, and a lot of other things, all subliminal. But it is you, isn't it, it *is* you!"

"It is I. William Lantry." Dryly.

"Good fellow! Come along!"

THE BEETLE MOVED SWIFTLY through the dawn streets. McClure talked rapidly.

Lantry sat, listening, astounded. Here was this fool, McClure, playing his cards for him! Here was this stupid scientist, or whatever, accepting him not as a suspicious baggage, a murderous item. Oh no! Quite the contrary! Only as a suspended animation case was he considered! Not as a dangerous man at all. Far from it!

"Of course," cried McClure, grinning. "You didn't know where to go, whom to turn to. It was all quite incredible to you."

"Yes."

"I had a feeling you'd be there at the morgue tonight," said McClure, happily.

"Oh?" Lantry stiffened.

"Yes. Can't explain it. But you, how shall I put it? Ancient Americans? You had funny ideas on death. And you were among the dead so long, I felt you'd be drawn back by the accident, by the morgue and all. It's not very logical. Silly, in fact. It's just a feeling. I hate feelings but there it was. I came on a, I guess you'd call it a hunch, wouldn't you?"

"You might call it that."

"And there you were!"

"There I was," said Lantry.

"Are you hungry?"

"I've eaten."

"How did you get around?"

"I hitch-hiked."

"You *what?*"

"People gave me rides on the road."

"Remarkable."

"I imagine it sounds that way." He looked at the passing houses. "So this is the era of space travel, is it?"

"Oh, we've been traveling to Mars for some forty years now."

"Amazing. And those big funnels, those towers in the middle of every town?"

"Those. Haven't you heard? The Incinerators. Oh, of course, they hadn't anything of that sort in your time. Had some bad luck with them. An explosion in Salem and one here, all in a forty-eight-hour period. You looked as if you were going to speak; what is it?"

"I was thinking," said Lantry. "How fortunate I got out of my coffin when I did. I might well have been thrown into one of your Incinerators and burned up."

"That would have been terrible, wouldn't it have?"

"Quite."

Lantry toyed with the dials on the beetle dash. He wouldn't go to Mars. His plans were changed. If this fool simply refused to recognize an act of violence when he stumbled upon it, then let him be a fool. If they didn't connect the two explosions with a man from the tomb, all well and good. Let them go on deluding themselves. If they couldn't imagine someone being mean and nasty and murderous, heaven help them. He rubbed his hands with satisfaction. No, no Martian trip for you, as yet, Lantry lad. First we'll see what can be done boring from the inside. Plenty of time. The Incinerators can wait an extra week or so. One has to be subtle, you know. Any more immediate explosions might cause quite a ripple of thought.

McClure was gabbling wildly on.

"Of course, you don't have to be examined immediately. You'll want a rest. I'll put you up at my place."

"Thanks. I don't feel up to being probed and pulled. Plenty of time in a week or so."

They drew up before a house and climbed out.

"You'll want to sleep naturally."

"I've been asleep for centuries. Be glad to stay awake. I'm not a bit tired."

"Good." McClure let them into the house. He headed for the drink bar. "A drink will fix us up."

"You have one," said Lantry. "Later for me. I just want to sit down."

"By all means sit." McClure mixed himself a drink. He looked around the room, looked at Lantry, paused for a moment with the drink in his hand, tilted his head to one side, and put his tongue in his cheek. Then he shrugged and stirred his drink. He walked slowly to a chair and sat, sipping the drink quietly. He seemed to be listening for something. "There are cigarettes on the table," he said.

"Thanks." Lantry took one and lit it and smoked it. He did not speak for some time.

Lantry thought, I'm taking this all too easily. Maybe I should kill and run. He's the only one that has found me, yet. Perhaps this is all a trap. Perhaps we're simply sitting here waiting for the police. Or whatever in hell they use for police these days. He looked at McClure. No. They weren't waiting for police. They were waiting for something else.

McClure didn't speak. He looked at Lantry's face and he looked at Lantry's hands. He looked at Lantry's chest a long time, with easy quietness. He sipped his drink. He looked at Lantry's feet.

Finally he said, "Where'd you get the clothing?"

"I asked someone for clothes and they gave these things to me. Darned nice of them."

"You'll find that's how we are in this world. All you have to do is ask."

McClure shut up again. His eyes moved. Only his eyes and nothing else. Once or twice he lifted his drink.

A little clock ticked somewhere in the distance.

"Tell me about yourself, Mr. Lantry."

"Nothing much to tell."

"You're modest."

"Hardly. You know about the past. I know nothing of the future, or I should say 'today' and day before yesterday. You don't learn much in a coffin."

McClure did not speak. He suddenly sat forward in his chair and then leaned back and shook his head.

They'll never suspect me, thought Lantry. They aren't superstitious, they simply *can't* believe in a dead man walking. Therefore, I'll be safe. I'll keep putting off the physical checkup. They're polite. They won't force me. Then, I'll work it so I can get to Mars. After that, the tombs, in my own good time, and the plan. God, how simple. How naïve these people are.

McCLURE SAT ACROSS THE ROOM for five minutes. A coldness had come over him. The color was very slowly going from his face, as one sees the color of medicine vanishing as one presses the bulb at the top of a dropper. He leaned forward, saying nothing, and offered another cigarette to Lantry.

"Thanks." Lantry took it. McClure sat deeply back into his easy chair, his knees folded one over the other. He did not look at Lantry, and yet somehow did. The feeling of weighing and balancing returned. McClure was like a tall thin master of hounds listening for something that nobody else could hear. There are little silver whistles you can blow that only dogs can hear. McClure seemed to be listening acutely, sensitively for such an invisible whistle, listening with his eyes and with his half-opened, dry mouth, and with his aching, breathing nostrils.

Lantry sucked the cigarette, sucked the cigarette, sucked the cigarette, and as many times, blew out, blew out, blew out. McClure was like some lean red-shagged hound listening and listening with a slick slide of eyes to one side, with an apprehension in that hand that was so precisely microscopic that one only sensed it, as one sensed the invisible whistle, with some part of the brain deeper than eyes or nostril or ear. McClure was all chemist's scale, all antennae.

The room was so quiet the cigarette smoke made some kind of invisible noise rising to the ceiling. McClure was a thermometer, a chemist's scales, a listening hound, a litmus paper, an antennae; all these. Lantry did not move. Perhaps the feeling would pass. It had passed before. McClure did not move for a long while and then, without a word, he nodded at the sherry decanter, and Lantry refused as silently. They sat looking but not looking at each other, again and away, again and away.

McClure stiffened slowly. Lantry saw the color getting paler in those lean cheeks, and the hand tightening on the sherry glass, and a knowledge come at last to stay, never to go away, into the eyes.

Lantry did not move. He could not. All of this was of such a fascination that he wanted only to see, to hear what would happen next. It was McClure's show from here on in.

McClure said, "At first I thought it was the finest psychosis I have ever seen. You, I mean. I thought, he's convinced himself, Lantry's convinced himself, he's quite insane, he's told himself to do all these little things." McClure talked as if in a dream, and continued talking and didn't stop.

"I said to myself, he purposely doesn't breathe through his nose. I watched your nostrils, Lantry. The little nostril hairs never once quivered in the last hour. That wasn't enough. It was a fact I filed. It wasn't enough. He breathes through his mouth, I said, on purpose. And then I gave you a cigarette and you sucked and blew, sucked and blew. None of it ever came out your nose. I told myself, well, that's all right. He doesn't inhale. Is that terrible, is that suspect? All in the mouth, all in the mouth. And then, I looked at your chest. I watched. It never moved up or down, it did nothing. He's convinced himself, I said to myself. He's convinced himself about all this. He doesn't move his chest, except slowly, when he thinks you're not looking. That's what I told myself."

The words went on in the silent room, not pausing, still in a dream. "And then I offered you a drink but you don't drink and I thought, he doesn't drink, I thought. Is that terrible? And I watched and watched you all this time. Lantry holds his breath, he's fooling himself. But now, yes, now, I understand it quite well. Now I know everything the way it is. Do you know how I know? I do not hear breathing in the room. I wait and I hear nothing. There is no beat of heart or intake of lung. The room is so silent. Nonsense, one might say, but I know. At the Incinerator I know. There is a difference. You enter a room where a man is on a bed and you know immediately whether he will look up and speak to you or whether he will not speak to you ever again. Laugh if you will, but one can tell. It is a subliminal thing. It is the whistle the dog hears when no human hears. It is the tick of a clock that has ticked so long one no longer notices. Something is in a room when a man lives in it. Something is not in the room when a man is dead in it."

McCLURE SHUT HIS EYES A MOMENT. He put down his sherry glass. He waited a moment. He took up his cigarette and puffed it and then put it down in a black tray.

"I am alone in this room," he said.

Lantry did not move.

"You are dead," said McClure. "My mind does not know this. It is not a thinking thing. It is a thing of the senses and the subconscious. At first I thought, this man thinks he is dead, risen from the dead, a vampire. Is that not logical? Would not any man, buried as many centuries, raised in a superstitious, ignorant culture, think likewise of himself once risen from the tomb? Yes, that is logical. This man has hypnotized himself and fitted his bodily functions so that they would in no way interfere with his self-delusion, his great paranoia. He governs his breathing. He tells himself, I cannot hear my breathing, therefore I am dead. His inner mind censors the sound of breathing. He does not allow himself to eat or drink. These things he probably does in his sleep, with part of his mind, hiding the evidences of this humanity from his deluded mind at other times."

McClure finished it. "I was wrong. You are not insane. You are not deluding yourself. Nor me. This is all very illogical and—I must admit—almost frightening. Does that make you feel good, to think you frighten me? I have no label for you. You're a very odd man, Lantry. I'm glad to have met you. This will make an interesting report indeed."

"Is there anything wrong with me being dead?" said Lantry. "Is it a crime?"

"You must admit it's highly unusual."

"But, still now, is it a crime?" asked Lantry.

"We have no crime, no criminal court. We want to examine you, naturally, to find out how you have happened. It is like that chemical which, one minute is inert, the next is living cell. Who can say where what happened to what. You are that impossibility. It is enough to drive a man quite insane."

"Will I be released when you are done fingering me?"

"You will not be held. If you don't wish to be examined, you will not be. But I am hoping you will help by offering us your services."

"I might," said Lantry.

"But, tell me," said McClure. "What were you doing at the morgue?

"Nothing."

"I heard you talking when I came in."

"I was merely curious."

"You're lying. That is very bad, Mr. Lantry. The truth is far better. The truth is, is it not, that you are dead and, being the only one of your sort, were lonely. Therefore you killed people to have company."

"How does that follow?"

McClure laughed. "Logic, my dear fellow. Once I *knew* you were really dead, a moment ago, really a—what do you call it—a vampire (silly word!) I tied you immediately to the Incinerator blasts. Before that there was no reason to connect you. But once the one piece fell into place, the fact that you were dead, then it was simple to guess your loneliness, your hate, your envy, all of the tawdry motivations of a walking corpse. It took only an instant then to see the Incinerators blown to blazes, and then to think of you, among the bodies at the morgue, seeking help, seeking friends and people like yourself to work with—"

"You're too damned smart!" Lantry was out of the chair. He was halfway to the other man when McClure rolled over and scuttled away, flinging the sherry decanter. With a great despair Lantry realized that, like a damned idiot, he had thrown away his one chance to kill McClure. He should have done it earlier. It had been Lantry's one weapon, his safety margin. If people in a society never killed each other, they never *suspected* one another. You could walk up to any one of them and kill him.

"Come back here!" Lantry threw the knife.

McClure got behind a chair. The idea of flight, of protection, of fighting, was still new to him. He had part of the idea, but there was still a bit of luck on Lantry's side if Lantry wanted to use it.

"Oh, no," said McClure, holding the chair between himself and the advancing man. "You want to kill me. It's odd, but true. I can't understand it. You want to cut me with that knife or something like that, and it's up to me to prevent you from doing such an odd thing."

"I *will* kill you!" Lantry let it slip out. He cursed himself. That was the worst possible thing to say.

Lantry lunged across the chair, clutching at McClure.

McClure was very logical. "It won't do you any good to kill me. You *know* that." They wrestled and held each other in a wild, toppling shuffle. Tables fell over, scattering articles. "You remember what happened in the morgue?"

"I don't care!" screamed Lantry.

"You didn't raise *those* dead, did you?"

"I don't care!" cried Lantry.

"Look here," said McClure, reasonably. "There will never be any more like you, ever, there's no use."

"Then I'll destroy all of you, all of you!" screamed Lantry.

"And then what? You'll still be alone, with no more like you about."

"I'll go to Mars. They have tombs there. I'll find more like myself!"

"No," said McClure. "The executive order went through yesterday. All of the tombs are being deprived of their bodies. They'll be burned in the next week."

They fell together to the floor. Lantry got his hands on McClure's throat.

"Please," said McClure. "Do you see, you'll *die*."

"What do you mean?" cried Lantry.

"Once you kill all of us, and you're alone, you'll die! The hate will die. That hate is what moves you, nothing else! That envy moves you. Nothing else! You'll die, inevitably. You're not immortal. You're not even alive, you're nothing but a moving hate."

"I don't care!" screamed Lantry, and began choking the man, beating his head with his fists, crouched on the defenseless body. McClure looked up at him with dying eyes.

The front door opened. Two men came in.

"I say," said one of them. "What's going on? A new game?"

Lantry jumped back and began to run.

"Yes, a new game!" said McClure, struggling up. "Catch him and you win!"

The two men caught Lantry. "We win," they said.

"Let me go!" Lantry thrashed, hitting them across their faces, bringing blood.

"Hold him tight!" cried McClure.

They held him.

"A rough game, what?" one of them said. "What do we do *now*?"

THE BEETLE HISSED ALONG the shining road. Rain fell out of the sky and a wind ripped at the dark green wet trees. In the beetle, his hands on the half-wheel, McClure was talking. His voice was a susurrant, a whispering, a hypnotic thing. The two other men sat in the backseat. Lantry sat, or rather lay, in the front seat, his head back, his eyes faintly open, the glowing green light of the dash dials showing on his cheeks. His mouth was relaxed. He did not speak.

McClure talked quietly and logically, about life and moving, about death and not moving, about the sun and the great sun Incinerator, about the emptied tombyard, about hatred and how hate lived and made a clay man live and move, and how illogical it all was, it all was, it all was. One was dead, was dead, was dead, that was all, all, all. One did not try to be otherwise. The car whispered on the moving road. The rain spatted gently on the windshield. The men in the backseat conversed quietly. Where were they going, going? To the Incinerator, of course. Cigarette smoke moved slowly up on the air, curling and tying into itself in grey loops and spirals. One was dead and must accept it.

Lantry did not move. He was a marionette, the strings cut. There was only a tiny hatred in his heart, in his eyes, like twin coals, feeble, glowing, fading.

I am Poe, he thought. I am all that is left of Edgar Allan Poe, and I am all that is left of Ambrose Bierce and all that is left of a man named Lovecraft. I am a grey night bat with sharp teeth, and I am a square black monolith monster. I am Osiris and Bal and Set. I am the Necronomicon, the Book of the Dead. I am the house of Usher, falling into flame. I am the Red Death. I am the man mortared into the catacomb with a cask of Amontillado . . . I am a dancing skeleton. I am a coffin, a shroud, a lightning bolt reflected in an old house window. I am an autumn-empty tree, I am a rapping, flinging shutter. I am a yellowed volume turned by a claw hand. I am an organ played in an attic at midnight. I am a mask, a skull mask behind an oak tree on the last day of October. I am a poison apple bobbling in a water tub for child noses to bump at, for child teeth to snap . . . I am a black candle lighted before an inverted cross. I am a coffin lid, a sheet with eyes, a footstep on a black stairwell. I am Dunsany and Machen and I am the Legend of Sleepy Hollow. I am The Monkey's Paw and I am the Phantom Rickshaw. I am the Cat and the Canary, the Gorilla, the Bat. I am the ghost of Hamlet's father on the castle wall.

All of these things am I. And now these last things will be burned. While I lived they still lived. While I moved and hated and existed, *they* still existed. I am *all* that remembers them. I am all of them that *still* goes on, and will *not* go on after tonight. Tonight, all of us, Poe and Bierce and Hamlet's father, we burn together. They will make a big heap of us and burn us like a bonfire, like things of Guy Fawkes' Day, gasoline, torchlight, cries and all!

And what a wailing will we put up. The world will be clean of us, but in our going we shall say, oh what is the world like, clean of fear, where is the dark imagination from the dark time, the thrill and the anticipation, the suspense of old October, gone, never more to come again, flattened and smashed and burned by the rocket people, by the Incinerator people, destroyed and obliterated, to be replaced by doors that open and close and lights that go on or off without fear. If only you could remember how once we lived, what Hallowe'en was to us, and what Poe was, and how we gloried in the dark morbidities. One more drink, dear friends, of Amontillado, before the burning. All of this, all, exists but in one last brain on earth. A whole world dying tonight. One more drink, pray.

"Here we are," said McClure.

THE INCINERATOR WAS BRIGHTLY LIGHTED. There was quiet music nearby. McClure got out of the beetle, came around to the other side. He opened the door. Lantry simply lay there. The talking and the logical talking had slowly drained him of life. He was no more than wax now, with a small glow in his eyes. This future world, how the men talked to you, how logically they reasoned away your life. They wouldn't believe in him. The force of their disbelief froze him. He could not move his arms or his legs. He could only mumble senselessly, coldly, eyes flickering.

McClure and the two others helped him out of the car, put him in a golden box and rolled him on a roller table into the warm glowing interior of the building.

I am Edgar Allan Poe, I am Ambrose Bierce, I am Hallowe'en, I am a coffin, a shroud, a Monkey's Paw, a phantom, a Vampire . . .

"Yes, yes," said McClure, quietly, over him. "I know. I know."

The table glided. The walls swung over him and by him, the music played. You are dead, you are logically dead.

I am Usher, I am the Maelstrom, I am the MS Found In A Bottle, I am the Pit and I am the Pendulum, I am the Telltale Heart, I am the Raven nevermore, nevermore.

"Yes," said McClure, as they walked softly. "I know."

"I am in the catacomb," cried Lantry.

"Yes, the catacomb," said the walking man over him.

"I am being chained to a wall, and there is no bottle of Amontillado here!" cried Lantry weakly, eyes closed.

"Yes," someone said.

There was movement. The flame door opened.

"Now someone is mortaring up the cell, closing me in!"

"Yes, I *know*." A whisper.

The golden box slid into the flame lock.

"I'm being walled in! A very good joke indeed! Let us be gone!" A wild scream and much laughter.

"We know, we understand . . ."

The inner flame lock opened. The golden coffin shot forth into flame.

"For the love of God, Montresor! For the love of God!"

THE LIBRARY

THE PEOPLE POURED INTO THE ROOM. HEALTH OFFICIALS reeking of disinfectant, sprinklers in their hands. Police officials, fierce with blazing badges. Men with metal torches and roach exterminators, piling one on another, murmuring, shouting, bending, pointing. The books came down in avalanched thunders. The books were torn and rent and splintered like beams. Whole towns and towers of books collapsed and shattered. Axes beat at the windows, drapes fell in black sooty clouds of dust. Outside the door, the boy with the golden eyes looked in, stood silently, draped in his robin's egg sari, his rocket father and plastics mother behind him. The health official pronounced pronunciations. A doctor bent. "He's dying," was said, faintly, in the din. Antiseptic men lifted him on a stretcher, carried him through the collapsing room. Books were being piled into a portable incinerator; they were crackling and leaping and burning and twisting and vanishing into paper flame.

"No! No!" screamed A. "Don't do it! The last ones in the world! The last ones!"

"Yes, yes," soothed the health official mechanically.

"If you burn them, burn them, there are no other copies!"

"We know, we know. The law, the law," said the health official.

"Fools, idiots, dolts! Stop!"

The books climbed and stoned down into baskets which were carried out. There was the brisk suction of a vacuum cleaner.

"And when the books are burned, the last books"—A. was weakening—"then there will be only myself, and the memories in my mind. And when I die, then it will all be gone. All of it gone forever. All of us gone. All us dark nights and Halloweens and white bone masks and closeted skeletons, all the Bierces and the Poes, Anubis and Set and the Niebelungen, the Machens and the Lovecrafts and the Frankensteins and the black vampire bats hovering, the Draculas and the Golems, gone, all gone."

"We know, gone, gone," whispered the official.

He shut his eyes. "Gone. Gone. Tear my books, burn my books, cleanse, rip, clean away. Unearth the coffins, incinerate, do away with. Kill us, oh, kill us, for we are bleak castles on midnight mornings, we are blowing wind webs and scuttling spiders, and we are doors that swing unoiled and banging shutters banging, and we are darknesses so vast that ten million nights of darkness are held in one braincell. We are buried hearts in murdered bedrooms, hearts glowing under floorboards. We are clanking chains and gossamer veils, and vapors of enchanted and long dead and lovely ladies on grand castle stairs, float, afloat, windy and whispering and wailing. We are the Monkey's Paw, and the catacomb and the gurgling Amontillado bottle and the mortared brick, and the three wishes. We are the caped figure, the glass eye, the bloodied mouth, the sharp fang, the veined wing, the autumn leaf in the cold black sky, the wolf shining its white rimed morning pelt, we are the old days that come not again upon the earth, we are the red wild eye and the sudden instrument of knife or gun. We are all things violent and black. We are winds that keen and sad snows falling. We are October, burning down the lands into fused ruin, all flame, all blue and melancholy smoke. We are deep frozen winter. We are monumented mound yard, we are the chiseled marble name and the birth and death years. We are the tapping awake coffin and we are the scream in the night."

"Yes, yes," whispered the official.

"Carry me away, burn me up, let flames take me. Put me in a catacomb of books, brick me in with books, mortar me up with books and burn the whole of us together."

"Rest easily," whispered the official. "I'm dying," said Mr. A.

"No, no."

"Yes, I am. You're carrying me."

The stretcher was moving. His heart paled within him, fainter, fainter. "Dying. In a moment now—dead."

"Rest, please."

"All of it gone, forever, and nobody to know it ever lived, the dark nights, Poe, Bierce, the rest of us. Gone, all gone."

"Yes," said the official in the moving dark.

There was a crackle of flame. They were burning out the room scientifically, with controlled fire. There was a vast blowing wind of flame that tore away the interior of darkness. He could see the books explode like so many kernels of dark corn.

"For the love of God, Montresor!"

The sedge withered, the vast ancient lawn of the room sizzled and flumed.

"Yes, for the love of God," murmured the official.

"A very good joke indeed—an excellent jest! We will have many a rich laugh about it at the palazzo—over our wine! Let us be gone—"

In the dimness, the health official: "Yes. Let us be gone."

A. fell down in soft blackness. All black, all gone. He heard his own dry lips repeat, repeat the only thing thought of to repeat as he felt his old heart cease and grow cold within him:

"Requiescat in pace."

He dreamed that he was walling himself in with bricks and more bricks of books.

For the love of god, Montresor!

Yes, for the love of God!

HE WENT DOWN into the soft blackness, and before it was all black and all gone he heard his own dry lips repeating and repeating the only thing he could think of to repeat as he felt his heart cease and desist within him.

"Requiescat in pace."

BRIGHT PHOENIX

ONE DAY IN APRIL, 2022, THE GREAT LIBRARY DOOR slammed flat shut. Thunder. Hello, I thought.

AT THE BOTTOM STEP glowering up at my desk, in a United Legion uniform which no longer hung as neatly upon him as it had twenty years before, stood Jonathan Barnes.

Seeing his bravado momentarily in pause, I recalled ten thousand Veterans speeches sprayed from his mouth, the endless wind-whipped flag parades he had hustled, panted through, the grease-cold chicken and green-pea patriot banquets he had practically cooked himself; the civic drives stillborn in his hat.

Now Jonathan Barnes stomped up the creaking main library steps, giving each the full downthrust of his power, weight, and new authority. His echoes, rushed back from the vast ceilings, must have shocked even him into better manners, for when he reached my desk, I felt his warmly liquored breath stir mere whispers on my face.

"I'm here for the books, Tom."

I turned casually to check some index cards. "When they're ready, we'll call you."

"Hold on," he said. "Wait—"

"You're here to pick up the Veterans' Salvage books for hospital distribution?"

"No, no," he cried. "I'm here for *all* the books."

I gazed at him.

"Well," he said, "*most* of them."

"Most?" I blinked once, then bent to riffle the files. "Only ten volumes to a person at a time. Let's see. Here. Why, you let your card expire when you were twenty years old, thirty years ago. See?" I held it up.

Barnes put both hands on the desk and leaned his great bulk upon them. "I see you are interfering." His face began to color, his breath to husk and rattle. "*I* don't need a card for *my* work!"

So loud was his whisper that a myriad of white pages stopped butterflying under far green lamps in the big stone rooms. Faintly, a few books thudded shut.

Reading people lifted their serene faces. Their eyes, made antelope by the time and weather of this place, pleaded for silence to return, as it always must when a tiger has come and gone from a special freshwater spring, as this surely was. Looking at these upturned, gentle faces I thought of my forty years of living, working, even sleeping here among hidden lives and vellumed, silent, and imaginary people. Now, as always, I considered my library as a cool cavern or fresh, ever-growing forest into which men passed from the heat of the day and the fever of motion to refresh their limbs and bathe their minds an hour in the grass-shade illumination, in the sound of small breezes wandered out from the turning and turning of the pale soft book pages. Then, better focused, their ideas rehung upon their frames, their flesh made easy on their bones, men might walk forth into the blast-furnace of reality, noon, mob-traffic, improbable senescence, inescapable death. I had seen thousands career into my library starved and leave well-fed. I had watched lost people find themselves. I had known realists to dream and dreamers to come awake in this marble sanctuary where silence was a marker in each book.

"Yes," I said at last. "But it will only take a moment to re-register you, this new card. Give two reliable references—"

"I don't *need* references," said Jonathan Barnes, "to burn books!"

"Contrarily," said I. "You'll need even more, to do that."

"My men are my references. They're waiting outside for the books. They're dangerous."

"Men like that always are."

"No no, I mean the books, idiot. The *books* are dangerous. Good God, no two agree. All the damn double-talk. All the lousy Babel and slaver and spit. So, we're out to simplify, clarify, hew to the line. We need—"

"To talk this over," said I, taking up a copy of Demosthenes, tucking it under my arm. "It's time for my dinner. Join me, please—"

I was halfway to the door when Barnes, wide-eyed, suddenly remembered the silver whistle hung from his blouse, jammed it to his wet lips, and gave it a piercing blast.

The library doors burst wide. A flood of black charcoal-burnt uniformed men collided boisterously upstairs.

I called, softly.

They stopped, surprised.

"Quietly," I said.

Barnes seized my arm. "Are you opposing due process?"

"No," I said, "I won't even ask to see your property invasion permit. I only wish silence as you work."

The readers at the tables had leapt up at the storm of feet. I
patted the air. They sat back down and did not glance up again
at these men crammed into their tight dark char-smeared suits
who stared at my mouth now as if they disbelieved my cautions.
Barnes nodded. The men moved softly, on tip-toe, through
the big library rooms. With extra care, with proper stealth,
they raised the windows. Soundlessly, whispering, they col-
lected books from the shelves to toss down toward the evening
yard below. Now and again they scowled at the readers who
calmly went on leafing through their books, but made no move
to seize these volumes, and continued emptying the shelves.

"Good," said I.

"Good?" asked Barnes.

"Your men can work without you. Take five."

And I was out in the twilight so quickly he could only follow, bursting with unvoiced questions. We crossed the green
lawn where a huge portable Hell was drawn up hungrily, a fat
black tar-daubed oven from which shot red-orange and gaseous blue flames into which men were shoveling the wild birds,
the literary doves which soared crazily down to flop broken-
winged, the precious flights poured from every window to
thump the earth, to be kerosene-soaked and chucked in the
gulping furnace. As we passed this destructive if colorful industry, Barnes mused.

"Funny. Should be crowds, a thing like this. But . . . no crowd. How do you figure?"

I left him. He had to run to catch up.

In the small café across the street we took a table and Barnes, irritable for no reason he could say, called out, "Service! I've got to get back to work!"

Walter, the Proprietor, strolled over, with some dog-eared menus. Walter looked at me. I winked.

Walter looked at Jonathan Barnes.

Walter said, "'Come live with me and be my love; and we will all the pleasures prove.'"

"What?" Jonathan Barnes blinked.

"'Call me Ishmael,'" said Walter.

"Ishmael," I said. "We'll have coffee to start."

Walter came back with the coffee.

"'Tiger, Tiger, burning bright,'" he said. "'In the forests of the night.'" Barnes stared after the man who walked away casually. "What's eating him? Is he nuts?"

"No," I said. "But go on with what you were saying back at the library. Explain."

"Explain?" said Barnes. "My God, you're all sweet reason. All right, I will explain. This is a tremendous experiment. A test town. If the burning works here, it'll work anywhere. We don't burn everything, no no. You noticed, my men cleaned only certain shelves and categories? We'll eviscerate about 49 point 2 percent. Then we'll report our success to the overall government committee—"

"Excellent," I said.

Barnes eyed me. "How can you be so cheerful?"

"Any library's problem," I said, "is where to put the books. You've helped me solve it."

"I thought you'd be . . . afraid."

"I've been around Trash Men all my life."

"I beg pardon?"

"Burning is burning. Whoever does it is a Trash Man."

"Chief Censor, Green Town, Illinois, damn it!"

A new man, a waiter, came with the coffee pot steaming.

"Hello, Keats," I said.

"'Season of mists and mellow fruitfulness,'" said the waiter.

"Keats?" said the Chief Censor. "His name isn't Keats."

"Silly of me," I said. "This is a Greek restaurant. Right, Plato?"

The waiter refilled my cup. "'The people have always some champion whom they set over them and nurse into greatness . . . his and no other is the root from which a tyrant springs; when he first appears he is a protector.'"

Barnes leaned forward to squint at the waiter, who did not move. Then Barnes busied himself blowing on his coffee: "As I see it, our plan is simple as one and one make two . . ."

The waiter said, "'1 have hardly ever known a mathematician who was capable of reasoning.'"

"Damn it!" Barnes slammed his cup down. "Peace! Get away while we eat, you, Keats, Plato, Holdridge, *that's* your name. I remember now, *Holdridge!* What's all this *other* junk?"

"Just fancy," said I. "Conceit."

"Damn fancy, and to hell with conceit, you can eat alone, I'm getting out of this madhouse." And Barnes gulped his coffee as the waiter and proprietor watched and I watched him gulping and across the street the bright bonfire in the gut of the monster device burnt fiercely. Our silent watching caused Barnes to freeze at last with the cup in his hand and the coffee dripping off his chin. "Why? Why aren't you yelling? Why aren't you fighting me?"

"But I am fighting," I said, taking the book from under my arm. I tore a page from DEMOSTHENES, let Barnes see the name, rolled it into a fine Havana cigar shape, lit it, puffed it, and said, "'Though a man escape every other danger, he can never wholly escape those who do not want such a person as he is to exist.'"

Barnes was on his feet, yelling, the "cigar" was torn from my mouth, stomped on, and the Chief Censor was out of the door, almost in one motion.

I could only follow.

On the sidewalk, Barnes collided with an old man who was entering the café. The old man almost fell. I grabbed his arm.

"Professor Einstein," I said.

"Mr. Shakespeare," he said.

Barnes fled.

I found him on the lawn by the old and beautiful library where the dark men, who wafted kerosene perfume from their every motion, still dumped vast harvestings of gun-shot dead pigeon, dying pheasant books, all autumn gold and silver from the high windows. But . . . softly. And while this still, almost serene, pantomime continued, Barnes stood screaming silently, the scream clenched in his teeth, tongue, lips, cheeks, gagged back so none could hear. But the scream flew out of his wild eyes in flashes and was held for discharge in his knotted fists, and shuttled in colors about his face, now pale, now red as he glared at me, at the café, at the damned proprietor, at the terrible waiter who now waved amiably back at him. The Baal incinerator rumbled its appetite, spark-burnt the lawn. Barnes stared full at the blind yellow-red sun in its raving stomach.

"You," I called up easily at the men who paused. "City Ordinance. Closing time is nine sharp. Please be done by then. Wouldn't want to break the law— Good evening, Mr. Lincoln."

" 'Four score,' " said a man, passing, " 'and seven years—' "

"Lincoln?" The Chief Censor turned slowly. "That's Bowman. Charlie Bowman. I know you, Charlie, come back here, Charlie, Chuck!"

But the man was gone, and cars drove by, and now and again as the burning progressed men called to me and I called back, and whether it was, "Mr. Poe!" or hello to some small bleak stranger with a name like Freud, each time I called in good humor and they replied, Mr. Barnes twitched as if another arrow had pierced, sunk deep in his quivering bulk and he were dying slowly of a hidden seepage of fire and raging life. And still no crowd gathered to watch the commotion.

Suddenly, for no discernible reason, Mr. Barnes shut his eyes, opened his mouth wide, gathered air, and shouted, "Stop!"

The men ceased shoveling the books out of the window above.

"But," I said, "it's not closing time . . ."

"Closing time! Everybody out!" Deep holes had eaten away the centre of Jonathan Barnes' eyes. Within, there was no bottom. He seized the air. He pushed down. Obediently, all the windows crashed like guillotines, chiming their panes.

The dark men, bewildered, came out and down the steps.

"Chief Censor." I handed him a key which he would not take, so I forced his fist shut on it. "Come back tomorrow, observe silence, finish up."

The Chief Censor let his bullet-hole gaze, his emptiness, search without finding me.

"How . . . how long has this gone on . . . ?"

"This?"

"This . . . and . . . that . . . and *them.*"

He tried but could not nod at the café, the passing cars, the quiet readers descending from the warm library now, nodding as they passed into cold dark, friends, one and all. His blind man's rictal gaze ate holes where my face was. His tongue, anaesthetized, stirred:

"Do you think you can all fool me, me, *me?*"

I did not answer.

"How can you be sure," he said, "I won't burn people, as well as books?"

I did not answer.

I left him standing in the complete night.

Inside, I checked out the last volumes of those leaving the library now with night come on and shadows everywhere and the great Baal machinery churning smoke, its fire dying in the spring grass where the Chief Censor stood like a poured cement statue, not seeing his men drive off. His fist suddenly flew high. Something swift and bright flew up to crack the front-door glass. Then Barnes turned and walked after the Incinerator as it trundled off, a fat black funeral urn unraveling long tissues and scarves of black bunting smoke and fasTVanishing crepe.

I sat listening.

In the far rooms, filled with soft jungle illumination, there was a lovely autumnal turning of leaves, faint sifts of breathing, infinitesimal quirks, the gesture of a hand, the glint of a ring, the intelligent squirrel blink of an eye. Some nocturnal voyager sailed between the half-empty stacks. In porcelain serenity, the rest-room waters flowed down to a still and distant sea. My people, my friends, one by one, passed from the cool marble, the green glades, out into a night better than we could ever have hoped for.

At nine, I went out to pick up the thrown front door key. I let the last reader, an old man, out with me, and as I was locking up, he took a deep breath of the cool air, looked at the town, the spark-burnt lawn, and said:

"Will they come back again, ever?"

"Let them. We're ready for them, aren't we?"

The old man took my hand. "'The wolf also shall dwell with the lamb, and the leopard shall lie dawn with the kid; and the calf and the young lion and the fatling together.'"

We moved down the steps.

"Good evening, Isaiah," I said.

"Mr. Socrates," he said. "Good night."

And each walked his own way, in the dark.

THE MAD WIZARDS OF MARS

THEIR EYES WERE FIRE AND THE BREATH FLAMED FROM out the witches' mouths as they bent to probe the cauldron with greasy stick and bony finger.

> "When shall we three meet again
>   In thunder, lightning, or in rain?"
> "When the hurly burly's done,
>   When the battle's lost and won."

They danced most drunkenly on the shore of an empty sea, fouling the air with their three tongues and burning it with their cat's eyes all aglitter:

> "Round about the cauldron go;
>   In the poisoned entrails throw!
> Double, double, toil and trouble,
>   Fire burn and cauldron bubble!"

They paused and cast their glances round. "Where's the crystal? Where the needles?" "Here!" "Good!" "Is the yellow wax thickened?" "Yes!" "Pour it in the iron mold!" "Is the wax figure done?" They shaped the stuff like molasses adrip

on their green hands. "Shove the needle through the heart!"
"The crystal, the crystal, fetch it from the tarot bag, dust it off,
and have a look!"

They went to the crystal, their faces white.

"See, see, see—"

A ROCKET SHIP MOVED through space from the planet Earth
to the planet Mars. On the rocket ship, men were dying.

The captain raised his head, tiredly, "We'll have to use the
morphine."

"But, Captain—"

"You see yourself this man's condition." The captain lifted
the wool blanket and the man restrained beneath the wet sheet
moved and groaned. The air was full of sulphurous thunder.

"I saw it, I saw it!" The man opened his eyes and stared
at the port where there were only black spaces, reeling stars,
Earth far-removed, and the planet Mars rising large and red.
"I saw it, a bat, a huge thing, a bat with a man's face, spread
over the front port. Fluttering and fluttering, fluttering and
fluttering!"

"Pulse?" asked the captain.

The orderly measured it. "130."

"He can't go on with that. Use the morphine: Come along,
Smith."

They moved away. Suddenly the floorplates were laced
with bone and white skulls that screamed. The captain did not
dare look down, and over the screaming he said, "Is this where
Perse is?" turning in at a hatch.

A white-smocked surgeon stepped away from a body. "I
just don't understand it."

"How did Perse die?"

"We don't know, captain. It wasn't his heart, his brain, or shock. He just—died."

The captain felt the doctor's wrist which changed to a hissing snake and bit him. The captain did not flinch. "Take care of yourself. You've a pulse, too."

The doctor nodded. "Perse complained of pains, needles, he said, in his wrists and legs. Said he felt like wax, melting. He fell. I helped him up. He cried like a child. Said he had a silver needle in his heart. He died. Here he is. Everything's physically normal."

"That's impossible. He died of *some*thing."

The captain walked to a port. He smelled of menthol and iodine and green soap on his polished and manicured hands. His white teeth were very bright, and his ears scoured to a pinkness, as were his cheeks. His uniform was the color of new salt, and his boots were black mirrors shining below him. His crisp crew-cut hair smelled of sharp alcohol. Even his breath was antiseptic and new and clean. There was no spot to him. He was a fresh instrument, honed and ready, still hot from the surgeon's oven.

The men with him were from the same mold. One expected, but did not find, huge brass keys spiraling slowly from their backs. They were expensive, talented, well-oiled toys, obedient and quick.

The captain watched the planet Mars grow very large in space.

"We'll be landing in an hour on that blasted place. Smith, did you see any bats, or have other nightmares?"

"Yes, sir. The month before our rocket took off from New

York, sir. Felt rats biting my neck, drinking my blood. I didn't tell. I was afraid you wouldn't let me come on this trip."

"Never mind," sighed the captain. "I had dreams, too. In all of my fifty years I never had a dream until that week before we took off from Earth. And then, every night, I dreamed I was a white wolf. Caught on a snowy hill. Shot with a silver bullet. Buried with a stake in my heart." He moved his head toward Mars. "Do you think, Smith, *they* know we're coming?"

"We don't know if there *are* Martian people, sir."

"Don't we? They began frightening us off, eight weeks ago, before we started. They've killed Perse and Reynolds now. Yesterday, they made Grenville go blind. How? I don't know. Bats, needles, dreams, men dying for no reason. I'd call it witchcraft in another day. But this is the year 2120, Smith. We're rational men. This all can't be happening. But it is. Whoever they are, with their needles and their bats, they'll try to finish all of us." He swung about. "Smith, fetch those books from my file. I want them when we land."

Two hundred books were piled on the rocket deck.

"Thank you, Smith. Have you glanced at them? Think I'm insane? Perhaps. It's a crazy hunch. At the last moment, I ordered these books from the Historical Museum. Because of my dreams. Twenty nights I was stabbed, butchered, a screaming bat pinned to a surgical mat, a thing rotting underground in a black box; bad, wicked dreams. Our whole crew dreamed of witch-things and were-things, vampires and phantoms, things they *couldn't* know anything about. Why? Because books on such ghastly subjects were destroyed a century ago. By law. Forbidden for anyone to own the grisly volumes. These books you see here are the last copies, kept for historical purposes in the locked Museum vaults."

Smith bent to read the dusty titles:

Tales of Mystery and Imagination, by Edgar Allan Poe. *Dracula,* by Bram Stoker. *Frankenstein,* by Mary Shelley. *The Turn of the Screw,* by Henry James. *The Legend of Sleepy Hollow,* by Washington Irving. *Rappacini's Daughter,* by Nathaniel Hawthorne. *The Occurrence at Owl Creek Bridge,* by Ambrose Bierce. *Alice in Wonderland,* by Lewis Carroll. *The Willows,* by Algernon Blackwood. *The Wizard of Oz,* by L. Frank Baum. *The Weird Shadow over Innsmouth,* by H. P Lovecraft. And more! Books by Walter De La Mare, Wakefield, Harvey, Wells, Asquith, Huxley, all forbidden authors. All burned in the same year that Halloween was outlawed and Christmas was banned! But, sir, what good are these to us on the rocket?"

"I don't know," sighed the captain, "yet."

THE THREE HAGS LIFTED THE CRYSTAL where the captain's image flickered, tiny voice tinkling out of the glass:

"I don't know," sighed the captain, "yet."

The three witches glared redly into each other's faces.

"We haven't much time," said one.

"Better warn *Them* up at the House."

"They'll want to know about the books. It doesn't look good. That fool of a captain!"

"In an hour they'll land their rocket."

The three hags shuddered and blinked up at the castle by the edge of the dry Martian sea. In its highest window, a small man held a blood-red drape aside. He watched the wastelands where the three witches fed their cauldron and shaped the waxes. Farther along, ten thousand other blue fires and laurel incenses, black tobacco smokes and fir-weeds, cinnamons and bone-dusts rose soft as moths through the Martian night. The man counted the angry magical fires. Then, as the witches stared, he turned. The crimson drape, released, fell causing the distant portal to wink, like a yellow eye.

Mr. Edgar Allan Poe stood in the tower window, a faint vapor of spirits upon his breath. "Hecate's friends are busy tonight," he said, seeing the witches, far below.

A voice behind him said, "I saw Will Shakespeare on the shore, earlier, whipping them on. All along the sea, Shakespeare's army alone, tonight, numbers thousands; the three Witches, Oberon, Hamlet's father, Othello, Lear, all of them, thousands! Good Lord, a regular sea of people."

"Good William." Poe turned. He let the crimson drape fall shut. He stood for a moment to observe the raw stone room, the black-timbered table, the candle flame, the other man, Mr. Ambrose Bierce, seated peering desolately into the flame.

"We'll have to tell Mr. Hawthorne now," said Mr. Poe. "We've put it off too long. It's a matter of hours. Will you go down to his home with me, Bierce?"

Bierce glanced up. "What will happen to us? God save us!"

"If we can't kill the rocket men off, frighten them away, then we'll have to leave, of course. We'll go on to Jupiter, and when they come to Jupiter, we'll go to Saturn, and when they come to Saturn we'll go to Uranus, or Neptune, and then on out to Pluto—"

"Where then?"

Mr. Poe's face was weary, there were coals of fire remaining, fading, in his eyes, and a sad wildness in the way he talked, and a uselessness of his hands and the way his hair fell over his amazing white brow. He was like a satan of some lost dark cause, a general arrived from a derelict invasion. His silky soft black mustache was worn away by his musing lips. He was so small that his brow seemed to float, vast and phosphorescent by itself, in the dark room.

"We have the advantage of superior forms of travel," he said. "We can always hope for one of their atomic wars, dissolution, the dark ages come again. The return of superstition. We could go back then to Earth, all of us, in one night." Mr. Poe's black eyes brooded under his round and illuminant brow. He looked at the ceiling. "So they're coming to ruin this world, too? They won't leave anything undefiled, will they?"

"Does a wolf pack stop until it's killed its prey and eaten the guts?"

Poe swayed, faintly drunk with wine. "What did we do? Did we have a fair trial before a company of literary critics? No! Our books were plucked by neat, sterile surgeon's pliers, and flung into vats, to boil!"

They were interrupted by a hysterical shout from the tower stair.

"Mr. Poe, Mr. Bierce!"

"Yes, yes, we're coming!" Poe and Bierce descended to find a man gasping against the stone passage wall.

"HAVE YOU HEARD THE NEWS!" he cried, immediately, clawing at them like a man about to fall over a cliff. "In an hour they'll land! They're bringing books with them, old books, the witches said! What're you doing in the tower at a time like this? Why aren't you acting?"

Poe said, "We're doing everything we can, Blackwood. You're new to this. Come along, we're going to Mr. Hawthorne's place—"

"—to contemplate our doom, our *black* doom," said Mr. Bierce.

They moved down the echoing throats of the castle, level after dim, green level, down into mustiness and decay and spiders and dreamlike webbing.

"Don't worry," said Poe, his brow like a huge white lamp before them, descending, sinking. "All along the dead sea tonight I've called the Others. Your friends and mine, Blackwood, Bierce. They're all there. The animals and the old women and the tall men with the sharp white teeth. The traps are waiting, the pits, yes, and the pendulums. The Red Death." Here he laughed quietly.

"Yes, even the Red Death. I never thought, no, I never thought the time would come when a thing like the Red Death would actually *be*. But *they*—" he poked his finger at the sky "—asked for it, and they shall have it!"

"But are we strong enough?" wondered Blackwood. "How strong is strong? They won't be prepared for us, at least. They haven't the imagination. Those clean young rocket men with their antiseptic bloomers and fish-bowl helmets, with their new religion. About their necks, on gold chains, scalpels. Upon their heads, a diadem of microscopes. In their holy fingers, steaming incense urns which in reality are only germicidal ovens for steaming out superstition. The names of Poe, Bierce, Hawthorne, Blackwood blasphemy to their clean lips."

Outside the castle, they advanced through a watery space, a tarn that was not a tarn, which misted before them like the stuff of nightmares. The air filled with wing sounds and a whirring, a motion of winds and blacknesses. Voices changed, figures swayed at campfires. Mr. Poe watched the needles knitting, knitting, knitting, in the firelight, knitting pain and misery, knitting wickedness into wax marionettes, clay puppets. The cauldron smells of wild garlics and cayennes and saffron hissed up to fill the night with evil pungency.

"Get on with it!" cried Poe. "I'll be back!"

All down the empty seashore black figures spindled and waned, grew up and blew into black smokes on the wind. Bells rang in mountain towers and licorice ravens spilled out with the bronze sounds and spun away to ashes.

MR. HAWTHORNE WAS THE MAN who bolted doors and looked out at you from shuttered windows. You knew he was home by the smoke in his chimney, or you saw his footprints in the paths on an autumn afternoon after a drenching rain. You saw his pale breath on the winter windows of his house on mornings when the panes were blind with frost. Here was his house, away from the rest on Mars, in a land he had made for himself, a land where snows fell, rains cooled the hot sands, or spring and summer lingered in an instant if Mr. Nathaniel Hawthorne so much as blinked from his door.

As Mr. Poe, Mr. Bierce and Mr. Blackwood approached at a brisk pace, Mr. Hawthorne's front door, a moment before, open to a summer night's warmth and smell of red apples in distant trees, slammed shut. There was a skirl of raindrops, a flurry of snow as light as pollen; then all was still.

Mr. Poe gave a rap on the door.

"Who's there?" said a voice, at last.

"It's Mr. Poe."

"What do you want?" much later.

"We've come to tell you the latest."

"I know, I know. I saw it on the sky. The red mark."

"Open up, we need your help. We want you to meet the rocket."

"I don't like to meet people," said Hawthorne, hidden away. "I don't belong here, anyway. I'm not like you out there, you Poe, you Bierce!"

At last the door creaked wide and Hawthorne stood revealed, his mass of blowing white hair and his full animal-like mustache, and his deep, enquiring and lonely eyes.

"You'll be a delegate to greet the rocket men," said Poe. "When they're lulled and unsuspecting, we'll take care of them."

Mr. Hawthorne eyed the folds of the black cape which hid Poe's hands. From it, smiling, Mr. Poe drew forth a trowel.

"The Amontillado?" Hawthorne drew back.

"For *one* of our visitors." In his other hand now, Poe brought forth a cap and bells, which jingled softly and suggestively.

"And for the others?"

Poe smiled again, well pleased. "We finished digging the Pit this morning."

"And the Pendulum?"

"Is being installed."

"The Premature Burial?"

"That, too."

"You are a grim man, Mr. Poe."

"I am a frightened and an angry man. I am a god, Mr. Hawthorne, even as you are a god, even as we all are gods, and our inventions, our people, if you wish, have been not only threatened, but banished and burned, torn up and censored, ruined and done away with. The worlds we created are falling to ruin! Even gods must fight!"

"So." Hawthorne tilted his head a little. "Yes. Perhaps that explains why we are here. How did we come here?"

"War begets war. Destruction begets destruction. On Earth, a century ago, in the year 2067, they outlawed our books. Oh, what a horrible thing, to destroy our literary creations that way. It summoned us out of—what? Death? The Beyond? I don't like abstract things. I don't know. I only know that our worlds and our creations called us and we tried to save them and the only saving thing we could do was wait out the century here on Mars, hoping that Earth might overweight itself with these scientists and their doubtings, but now they're coming to clean us out of here, us and our dark thing, and all the alchemists, witches, vampires, and were-things that, one by one, retreated across space as science made inroads through every country on Earth and finally left no alternative at all but exodus. You must help us. You have a good speaking manner. We need you."

"But I'm not *of* you, I don't approve of you and the others," cried Hawthorne, indignantly. "I was no fantasist, no player with witches and vampires and midnight things."

"What of 'Rappacini's Daughter'?"

"Ridiculous! *One* story. Oh, I wrote a few others, perhaps, but what of that? My basic works had none of that nonsense!"

"Mistaken or not, they grouped you with us. They destroyed your works, too. You *must* hate them, Mr. Hawthorne."

"They are stupid and rude," reflected Mr. Hawthorne. He

looked at the immense crimson symbol on the sky where the rocket burned. "Yes," he said, finally, "I will help you."

THEY HURRIED ALONG the midnight shore of the dry sea. By fires and smokes, Mr. Poe hesitated, to shout orders, to check the bubbling poisons and chalked pentagrams. "Good!" He ran on. "Fine!" And he ran again, past shadowed armies, the armies of Oberon and Othello, the armies of Arthur and Macbeth, waiting in full armor. And there were serpents and angry demons and fiery bronze dragons and spitting vipers and trembling witches like the barbs and nettles and thorns and all the vile flotsams and jetsams of the retreating sea of imagination, left on the melancholy shore, whining and frothing and spitting.

Bierce stopped. He sat like a child on the cold sand. He began to sob. They tried to soothe him, but he would not listen. "I just thought," he said, "what happens to us on the day when the *last* copies of our books are destroyed?"

The air whirled.

"Don't speak of it!"

"We must," wailed Bierce. "Now, now as the rocket comes down, you, Hawthorne, Poe, Coppard, all of you, grow faint. Like wood smoke. Blowing away. Your faces thin and melt—"

"Death. *Real* death for all of us."

"We exist only through Earth's sufferance. If a final edict tonight destroyed our last few works we'd be like lights put out."

Hawthorne brooded gently. "I wonder who I am. In what Earth mind tonight do I exist? In some African hut? Some hermit, reading my tales? Is he the lonely candle in the wind of time and science? The flickering orb sustaining me here in rebellious exile? Is it he? Or some boy in a discarded attic, finding me, only just in time! Oh, last night I felt ill, ill, ill to the marrows of me, for there is a body of the soul as well as a body of the body, and this soul-body ached in all of its glowing parts, and last night I felt myself a candle, guttering. When suddenly I sprang up, given new light! As some child in some yellow garret on Earth once more found a worn, time-specked copy of me, sneezing with dust! And so I'm given a short respite."

A DOOR BANGED WIDE in a little hut by the shore. A thin short man, with flesh hanging from him in folds, stepped out and, paying no attention to the others, sat down and stared into his clenched hands.

"There's the one I'm sorry for," whispered Blackwood. "Look at him, dying away. He was once more real than we, who were men. They took him, a skeleton thought, and clothed him in centuries of pink flesh and snow-beard and red velvet suit and black boot, made him reindeers, tinsel, holly. And after centuries of manufacturing him they drowned him in a vat of Lysol, you might say."

The men were silent.

"What must it be on Earth," wondered Hawthorns, "without Christmas? No hot chestnuts, no tree, nor ornaments or drums or candies, nothing; nothing but the snow and the wind and the lonely, factual people—"

They all looked at the thin little old man with the scraggly beard and faded red velvet suit.

"Have you heard his story?"

"I can imagine it. The glitter-eyed psychologist, the clever sociologist, the resentful, froth-mouthed educationist, the antiseptic parents—"

"Has Dickens seen him?"

"Dickens!" Mr. Poe spat. "Him! He came for a visit! A *visit*, understand! How are you? he cried! A cozy place you have here! Dickens popped in and out of here. Why? Because the only book of his burned in the Great Fire was 'A Christmas Carol' and a few other of his ghost stories. He'll live forever on Earth. He wrote such a wealth of uncensorable material."

"It's not fair," protested Hawthorne. "For him to stay and me to be here."

"A dreadful mistake," agreed everyone.

"A man's remembered for his sensational things," observed Mr. Bierce. "Me for 'Owl-Creek Bridge,' Mr. Poe for his corpses and terrors instead of his serious essays. And—"

Bierce did not continue. He fell forward with a sigh. And as all watched, horrified, his body burned into blue dust and charred bone, the ashes of which fled through the air in black tatters, settling about their shocked faces like terrible snow.

"Bierce, Bierce!"

"Gone."

They looked up at the cold high clusters of stars.

"His last book gone. Someone, somewhere on Earth, just now, burned it."

"God rest him, nothing of him left now. For what are we but books, and when those are gone, nothing's to be seen."

A rushing sound filled the sky.

They cried out wildly and looked up. In the sky, dazzling it with sizzling fire-clouds, was the Rocket! Around the men

on the seashore, lanterns bobbed, there was a squealing and a
bubbling and an odor of cooking smells. Candle-eyed pump-
kins lifted into the cold clear air. Thin fingers clenched into
fists and a witch screamed from her withered mouth:

"Ship, ship, break, fall!
Ship, ship, burn all!
Crack, flake, shake, melt!
Mummy-dust, cat-pelt!"

"Time to go," murmured Hawthorne. "On to Jupiter, on to
Saturn or Pluto."

"Run away?" shouted Poe in the wind. "Never!"

"I'm a tired old man."

Poe gazed into the old man's face and believed him. He
climbed atop a huge boulder and faced the ten thousand grey
shadows and green lights and yellow eyes on the hissing wind.

"The needles!" he cried.

The rocket flashed over.

"The powders!" he shouted.

A thick hot smell of bitter almond, civet, cumin, wormseed
and orris!

The rocket came down—steadily down, with the shriek
of a damned spirit! Poe raged at it! He flung his fists up and
the orchestra of heat and smell and hatred answered in sym-
phony! Like stripped tree fragments, bats flew upward! Burning hearts, flung like missiles, burst in bloody fireworks on the
singed air. Down, down, relentlessly down, like a pendulum
the rocket came! And Poe howled furiously and shrank back
with every sweep and sweep of the rocket cutting and ravening
the air! All the dead sea seemed a pit in which, trapped, they

waited the sinking of the dread machinery, the glistening axe; they were people under the avalanche!

"The snakes!" screamed Poe.

And luminous serpentines of undulant green hurtled toward the rocket. But it came down, a sweep, a fire, a motion, and it lay panting out exhaustions of red plumage on the sand, a mile away.

"At it!" shrieked Poe. "The plan's changed! Only one chance! Run! At it! At it! Drown them with our bodies! Kill them!"

And as if he had commanded a violent sea to change its course, to suck itself free from primeval beds, the whirls and savage gouts of fire spread and ran like wind and rain and stark lightning over the sea sands, down the empty river deltas, shadowing and screaming, whistling and whining, sputtering and coalescing toward the rocket which, extinguished, lay like a clean metal torch in the furthest hollow. As if a great charred cauldron of sparkling lava had been overturned, the boiling people and snapping animals churned down the dry fathoms!

"Kill them!" screamed Poe, running.

"Perhaps," murmured Mr. Hawthorne, left behind, alone, at the edge of the ancient sea.

THE ROCKET MEN LEAPED OUT of their ship, guns ready. They stalked about, sniffing the air like hounds. They saw nothing. They relaxed.

The captain stepped forth last. He gave sharp commands. Wood was gathered, kindled, and a fire leapt up in an instant. The captain beckoned his men into a half circle about him.

"A new world," he said, forcing himself to speak deliberately, though he glanced nervously, now and again, over his shoulder at the empty sea. "The old world left behind. A new start. What more symbolic than that we here dedicate ourselves all the more firmly to science and progress." He nodded crisply to his lieutenant. "The books."

The ancient books were brought forth.

Firelight limned the faded gilt titles: *The Willows, The Outsider, Behold the Dreamer, Dr. Jekyll and Mr. Hyde, The Land of Oz, Pellucidar, The Land That Time Forgot, A Midsummer Night's Dream* and the monstrous names of Machen and Edgar Allan Poe and Cabell and Dunsany and Blackwood and Lewis Carroll; the names, the old names, the evil names, the black names, the blasphemous names.

"A new world. With a gesture, we burn the last of the old!"

The captain ripped pages from the books. Leaf by seared leaf, he fed them into the fire.

A scream!

Leaping back, the men stared beyond the firelight at the edges of the encroaching and uninhabited sea.

Another scream! A high and wailing thing, like the death of a dragon and the thrashing of a bronzed whale left gasping when the waters of a leviathan's sea drain down the shingles and evaporate.

It was the sound of air rushing in to fill a vacuum, where, a moment before, was something.

The clean rocket men faced the directions from which the scream had come rushing forward like a tide.

The captain neatly disposed of the last book.

The air stopped quivering.

Silence.

The rocket men leaned and listened.

"Captain, did you hear it?"

"No."

"Like a wave, sir. On the sea bottom! I thought I saw something. Over there. A black wave. Big. Running at us."

"You were mistaken."

"But the sound?"

"I say you heard *nothing*."

"There, sir!"

"What!"

"See it? There! The castle! Way over! That black castle, near that lake! It's splitting in half. It's falling!"

The men stared. "I don't see it."

"Yes, it's falling! It's all fire and rock."

The men squinted and shuffled forward.

Smith stood trembling among them. He put his hand to his head as if to find a thought there. "I remember. Yes, now I do. A long time back. When I was a child. A book I read. A story. Usher, I think it was. Yes, Usher. 'The Fall of the House of Usher'—"

"By whom?"

"I—I can't remember."

"Usher? Never heard of it."

"Yes, Usher, that's what it was. I saw it fall again, just now, like in the story."

"Smith!"

"Yes, sir?"

"Report for psychoanalysis tomorrow."

"Yes, sir!" A brisk salute.

"Be careful."

The men tiptoed, guns alert, beyond the ship's aseptic light to gaze at the long sea and the low hills.

"Why," whispered Smith, disappointed, "there's no one here at all, is there? No one here at all."

The wind blew sand over his shoes, whining.

CARNIVAL OF MADNESS

"DURING THE WHOLE OF A DULL, DARK AND SOUNDLESS day in the autumn of the year, when the clouds hung oppressively low in the heavens, I had been passing alone on horseback, through a singularly dreary tract of country, and at length found myself, as the shades of evening drew on, within view of the melancholy House of Usher . . ."

Mr. William Stendahl paused in his quotation. There, upon a low black hill, stood the house, its cornerstone bearing the inscription: 2249 A.D.

Mr. Bigelow, the architect said, "It's completed. Here's the key, Mr. Stendahl."

The two men stood together, silently, in the quiet autumn afternoon. Blueprints rustled on the raven grass at their feet.

"The House of Usher," said Mr. Stendahl, with pleasure. "Planned, built, bought, paid for. Wouldn't Mr. Poe be *delighted?*"

Mr. Bigelow squinted. "Is it everything you wanted, sir?"

"Yes!"

"Is its color right? Is it *desolate* and *terrible?*"

"*Very* desolate, *very* terrible!"

"The walls are—*bleak?*"

"Amazingly so!"

"The tarn, is it 'black and lurid' enough?"

"Most incredibly black and lurid."

"And the sedge—we've dyed it, you know—is it the proper gray and ebon?"

"Hideous!"

Mr. Bigelow consulted his architectural plans. From these he quoted in part: "Does the whole structure cause an 'iciness, a sickening of the heart, a dreariness of thought?' the House, the lake, the land, Mr. Stendahl?"

"Mr. Bigelow, your hand! Congratulations! It's worth every penny. My word, it's *beautiful!*"

"Thank you. I had to work in total ignorance. A puzzling job. You notice, it's always twilight here, this land, always October, barren, sterile, dead. It took a bit of doing. We killed everything! Ten thousand tons of DDT. Not a snake, frog, fly or anything left! Twilight, always, Mr. Stendahl, I'm proud of that. There are machines, hidden, which blot out the sun. It's always properly 'dreary'."

Stendahl drank it in, the dreariness, the oppression, the fetid vapors, the whole 'atmosphere,' so delicately contrived and fitted. And that House! That crumbling horror, that evil lake, the fungi, the extensive decay! Plastic or otherwise, who could guess?

He looked at the autumn sky. Somewhere, above, beyond, far off, was a sun. Somewhere it was the month of May, a yellow month with a blue sky. Somewhere above, the passenger rockets burned east and west across the continent in a modern land. The sound of their screaming passage was muffled and killed by this dim, sound-proofed world, this ancient autumn world.

"Now that my job's done," said Mr. Bigelow, uneasily, "I feel free to ask what you're going to do with all this?"

"With Usher? Haven't you guessed?"

"No."

"Does the name Usher mean nothing to you?"

"Nothing."

"Well, what about *this* name: Edgar Allan Poe?"

Mr. Bigelow shook his head.

"Of course." Stendahl snorted delicately, a combination of dismay and contempt. "How could I expect you to know blessed Mr. Poe? He died a long while ago, before Lincoln. That's four centuries back. All of his books were burned in The Great Fire."

"Ah," said Mr. Bigelow, wisely, "One of *those!*"

"Yes, one of those, Bigelow. He and Lovecraft and Hawthorne and Ambrose Bierce and all the tales of terror and fantasy and horror and, for that matter, tales of the future, were burned. Heartlessly. They passed a law. Oh, it started very small. Centuries ago it was a grain of sand. They began by controlling books and, of course, films, one way or another, one group or another, political bias, religious prejudice, union pressures, there was always a minority afraid of something, and a great majority afraid of the dark, afraid of the future, afraid of the past, afraid of the present, afraid of themselves and shadows of themselves."

"I see."

"Afraid of the word politics (which eventually became a synonym for communism among the more reactionary elements, so I hear, and it was worth your life to use the word!), and with a screw tightened here, a bolt fastened there, a push, a pull, a yank, Art and Literature were soon like a great twine of taffy strung all about, being twisted in braids and tied in knots, and thrown in all directions, until there was no more resiliency and no more savor to it. Then the film cameras chopped short and the theatres turned dark, and the print presses trickled down from a great Niagara of reading matter to a mere innocuous dripping of 'pure' material. Oh, the word "escape" was radical, too, I tell you!"

"Was it?"

"It was! Every man, they said, must face reality. Must face the Here and Now! Everything that was *not so* must go. All the beautiful literary lies and flights of fancy must be shot in midair! So, they lined them up against a library wall one Sunday morning twenty years ago, in 2229, they lined them up, Saint Nicholas and the Headless Horseman and Snow White and Rumpelstiltskin and Mother Goose, oh, what a wailing! and shot them down, and burned the paper castles and the fairy frogs and old kings and the people who lived happily ever after (for, of course, it was a fact that *nobody* lived happily ever after!) and Once Upon A Time became No More!

"And they spread the ashes of the Phantom Rickshaw with the rubble of The Land of Oz, they filleted the bones of Glinda the Good and Ozma and shattered Polychrome in a spectroscope and served Jack Pumpkinhead with meringue at the Biologist's Ball! The Beanstalk died in a bramble of red tape! Sleeping Beauty awoke at the kiss of a scientist and expired at the fatal puncture of his syringe. And they made Alice drink something from a bottle which reduced her to a size where she

could no longer cry Curioser and Curioser, and they gave the
Looking Glass one hammer blow to crash it and every Red
King and Oyster away!"

HE CLENCHED HIS FISTS. Lord, how immediate it was! His
face was red, and he was gasping for breath.

As for Mr. Bigelow, he was astounded at this long explosion. He blinked at Mr. Stendahl and at last said, "Sorry. I
don't know what you're talking about. Names, just names to
me. From what I hear, the Burning was a good thing."

"Get out!" screamed Mr. Stendahl. "Get the blazes out!
You've got your money, you've done your job, now let me
alone, you idiot!"

Mr. Bigelow summoned his workers and went away.

Mr. Stendahl stood alone before his House.

"Listen here," he said to the unseen rockets, flying over.
"I'm going to show you all. I'm going to teach you a fine lesson
for what you did to Mr. Poe. As of this day, beware. The House
of Usher is open for business!"

He pushed a fist at the sky.

THE ROCKET LANDED. A man stepped out. He looked at the
House and his gray eyes were displeased and vexed. He strode
across the moat and confronted the small man there.

"Your name Stendahl?

"I'm Mr. Stendahl, yes," said the small man.

"I'm Garrett, Investigator of Moral Climates." The irritated man waved a card at the House. "Suppose you tell me
about this place, Mr. Stendahl."

"Very well. It's a castle. A haunted castle, if you like."

"I don't like, Mr. Stendahl, I *don't* like. The sound of that word 'haunted'."

"Simple enough. In this year of Our Lord 2249 I have built a mechanical sanctuary. In it copper bats fly on electronic beams, brass rats scuttle in plastic cellars, robot skeletons dance; robot vampires, harlequins, wolves and white phantoms, compounded of chemical and ingenuity, live here."

"That's what I was afraid of," said Garrett, smiling quietly. "I'm afraid we're going to have to tear your place down."

"I knew you'd come out as soon as you discovered what went on."

"I'd have come sooner, but we at Moral Climates wanted to be sure of your intentions before we moved in. We can have the Dismantlers and Burning Crew here by supper. By midnight, your place will be razed to the cellar. Mr. Stendahl, I consider you somewhat of a fool, sir. Spending hard-earned money on a Folly. Why, it must have cost you three million dollars."

"Four million! But, Mr. Garrett, I inherited twenty-five million when very young. I can afford to throw it about. Seems a dreadful shame, though, to have the House finished only an hour and have you race out with your Dismantlers. Couldn't you possibly let me play with my Toy for just, well, twenty four hours?"

"You know the law. Strict to the letter. No books, no houses, nothing to be produced which in any way suggests ghosts, vampires, fairies, or any creatures of the imagination."

"You'll be burning Babbitts next!"

"You've caused us a lot of trouble, Mr. Stendahl. It's in the record. Twenty years ago. You and your library."

"Yes, me and my library. And a few others like me. Oh, Poe's been forgotten for many centuries, and Oz, and the other creatures. But I had *my* little cache. We had our libraries, a few private citizens, until you sent your men around with torches and incinerators and tore my fifty thousand books up and burned them. Just as you put a stake through the heart of Hallowe'en and told your film producers that if they made anything at all they would have to make and re-make Ernest Hemingway. My God, how many *times* have I seen *For Whom the Bell Tolls!* Thirty different versions! All realistic. Oh, realism! Oh, *here*, oh, now, oh *hell!*"

"It doesn't pay to be better!"

"Mr. Garrett, you must turn in a full report, mustn't you?"

"Yes."

"Then, for curiosity's sake, you'd better come in and look around. It'll take only a minute."

"All right. Lead the way. And no tricks. I've got a gun with me."

The door to the House of Usher creaked wide. A moist wind issued forth. There was an immense sighing and moaning, like a subterranean bellows breathing in the lost catacombs.

A rat pranced across the floorstones. Garrett, crying out, gave it a kick. It fell over, the rat did, and from its nylon fur streamed an incredible horde of metal fleas.

"Amazing!" Garrett bent to see.

An old witch sat in a niche, quivering her wax hands over some orange and blue cards. She jerked her head and hissed through her toothless mouth at Garrett, tapping her greasy cards.

"Death!" she cried.

"Now *that's* the sort of thing I mean," said Garrett. "Deplorable!"

"I'll let you burn her personally."

"Will you, *really?*" Garrett was pleased. Then he frowned. "I must say you're taking this all too well."

"It was enough just to be able to create this place. To be able to say I did it. To say I nurtured a medieval atmosphere in a modern, incredulous world."

"I've a somewhat reluctant admiration for your genius myself, sir." Garrett watched a mist drift by, whispering and whispering, shaped like a beautiful and nebulous woman. Down a moist corridor a machine whirled. Like the stuff from a cotton candy centrifuge, mists sprang up and floated, murmuring, in the silent halls.

An ape appeared out of nowhere.

"Hold on!" cried Garrett.

"Don't be afraid." Stendahl tapped the animal's black chest. "A robot. Copper skeleton and all, like the witch. See." He stroked the fur and under it metal tubing came to light.

"Yes." Garrett put out a timid hand to pet the thing. "But why, Mr. Stendahl, why all *this?* What obsessed you?"

"Bureaucracy, Mr. Garrett. But I haven't time to explain. The government will discover soon enough." He nodded to the ape. "All right. *Now.*"

The ape killed Mr. Garrett.

PIKES LOOKED UP from the table.

"Are we almost ready, Pikes?" Stendahl asked.

"Yes, sir."

"You've done a splendid job."

"Well, I'm paid for it, Mr. Stendahl," said Pikes, softly, as he lifted the plastic eyelid of the robot and inserted the glass eyeball to fasten the rubberoid muscles neatly. "There."

"The spitting image of Mr. Garrett."

"What do we do with *him?*" Pikes nodded at the slab where the real Mr. Garrett lay dead.

"Better burn him, Pikes. We wouldn't want *two* Mr. Garretts, would we?"

Pikes wheeled Mr. Garrett to the brick incinerator. "Goodby." He pushed Mr. Garrett in and slammed the door.

Stendahl confronted the robot Garrett. "You have your orders, Garrett?"

"Yes, sir." The robot sat up. "I'm to return to Moral Climates. I'll file a complementary report. Delay action for at least forty-eight hours. Say I'm investigating more fully."

"Right, Garrett. Good-by."

The robot hurried out to Garrett's rocket, got in, and flew away.

Stendahl turned. "Now, Pikes, we send the remainder of the Invitations for tonight. I think we'll have a jolly time, don't you?"

"Considering we waited twenty years, quite jolly!"

They winked at each other.

SEVEN O'CLOCK. Stendahl studied his watch. Almost time. He twirled the sherry glass in his hand. He sat quietly. Above him, among the oaken beams, the bats, their delicate copper bodies hidden under rubber flesh, blinked at him and shrieked. He raised his glass to them. "To our success." Then he leaned back, closed his eyes and considered the entire affair. Now he would *savor* this in his old age. This paying back of the antiseptic government for their literary terrors and conflagrations. Oh, how the anger and hatred had grown in him through the years. Oh, how the plan had taken a slow shape in his numbed mind, until that day, three years ago, when he had met Pikes.

Ay, yes, Pikes. Pikes, with the bitterness in him as deep as a black, charred well of green acid. Who was Pikes? Only the greatest of them all! Pikes, the man of ten thousand faces, a fury, a smoke, a blue fog, a white rain, a bat, a gargoyle, a monster, that was Pikes! A whisper, a scream, a terror, a witch, a puppet, all things was Pikes! Better than Lon Chaney, the father?

Stendahl ruminated. Night after night he had watched Chaney in the old films. Yes, better than Chaney. Better than that other ancient mummer? What was his name? Karloff? Far better! Lugosi? The comparison was odious! No, there was only one Pikes, and he was a man stripped of his fantasies, now, no place on earth to go, no one to show off to. Forbidden even to perform for himself, before a mirror!

Poor impossible, defeated Pikes! How must it have felt, Pikes, the night they seized your films, like entrails yanked from the camera, out of your guts, clutching them in rolls and wads to stuff them up a stove to burn away! Did it feel as bad as having some fifty thousand books annihilated with no recompense? Yes. Yes. Stendahl felt his hands grow cold with the senseless anger. So what more natural than they would one day talk over endless coffee-pots into innumerable midnights, and out of all the talk and the bitter brewings would come—the House of Usher.

A great church bell rang. The guests were arriving.

Smiling, he went to greet them.

FULL GROWN WITHOUT MEMORY the robots waited. In green silks the color of forest pools, in silks the color of frog and fern they waited. In yellow hair the color of the sun and sand, the robots waited. Oiled, with tube-bones cut from bronze and sunk in gelatin, the robots lay. In coffins for the not dead and not alive, in planked boxes, the metronomes waited to be set in motion. There was a smell of lubrication and lathed brass. There is a silence of the tombyard. Sexed but sexless, the robots. Named but unnamed, and borrowing from humans everything but humanity, the robots stared at the nailed lids of their labeled F.O.B. boxes, in a death that was not even a death for there had never been a life. And now there was a vast screaming of yanked nails. Now there was a lifting of lids. Now there were shadows on the boxes, and the pressure of a hand squirting oil from a can. Now one clock was set in motion, a faint ticking. Now another and another, until this was an immense clock shop, purring. The marble eyes rolled wide their rubber lids. The nostrils winked.

The robots, clothed in hair of ape and white rabbit arose, Tweedledum following Tweedledee, Mock-Turtle, Dormouse, drowned bodies from the sea compounded of salt and white-weed, swaying; hung, blue-throated men with turned up, clam-flesh eyes, and creatures of ice and burning tinsel, loam-dwarves and pepper-elves, Tik-Tok, Ruggedo, Saint Nicholas with a self-made snow flurry blowing on before him, Bluebeard with whiskers like acetylene flame, and sulphur clouds from which green fire snouts protruded, and in scaly and gigantic serpentine, a dragon, with a furnace in its belly, reeled out the door with a scream, a tick, a bellow, a silence, a rush, a wind.

Ten thousand lids fell back. The clock shop moved out into Usher. The night was enchanted.

A WARM BREEZE CAME OVER THE LAND. The guest rockets, burning the sky and turning the weather from autumn to spring, arrived.

The men stepped out in evening clothes and the women stepped out after them, their hair coifed up in elaborate detail.

"So that's Usher!"

"But where's the door?"

At this moment, Stendahl appeared. The women laughed and chattered. Mr. Stendahl raised a hand to quiet them. Turning, he looked up to a high castle window and called:

"Rapunzel, Rapunzel, let down your hair."

And from above, a beautiful maiden leaned out upon the night wind and let down her golden hair. And the hair twined and blew and became a ladder upon which the guests might ascend, laughing, into the House.

What eminent sociologists! What clever psychologists! What tremendously important politicians, bacteriologists, and neurologists! There they stood, within the dank walls.

"Welcome, all of you!"

Mr. Tryon, Mr. Owen, Mr. Dunne, Mr. Lang, Mr. Steffens, Mr. Fletcher, and a double-dozen more.

"Come in, come in!"

Miss Gibbs, Miss Pope, Miss Churchill, Miss Blunt, Miss Drummond, and a score of other women, glittering.

Eminent, eminent people, one and all, members of the Society for the Prevention of Fantasy, advocators of the banishment of Hallowe'en and Guy Fawkes, killers of bats, burners of books, bearers of torches; good clean citizens, every one! And what is more, friends! Yes, carefully, carefully, he had met and befriended each, in the last year!

"Welcome to the vasty halls of Death!" he cried.

"Hello, Stendahl, what *is* all this?"

"You'll see. Everyone off with your clothes. You'll find booths to one side there. Change into costumes you find there. Men on this side, women that."

The people stood uneasily about.

"I don't know if we should stay," said Miss Pope. "I don't like the looks of this. It verges on—blasphemy."

"Nonsense, a costume ball!"

"This seems quite illegal," said Mr. Steffens, sniffing about.

"Oh, come off it," said Stendahl, laughing. "Enjoy yourselves. Tomorrow, it'll be a ruin. Get in there, all of you. The booths!"

The House blazed with life and color, harlequins rang by with belled caps and white mice danced miniature quadrilles to the music of dwarves who tickled tiny fiddles with tiny bows, and flaps rippled from scorched beams while bats flew in clouds about the gargoyle turrets and the gargoyles spouted down red wine from their mouths, cool and wild and foaming. There was a creek which wandered through the seven rooms of the masked ball, and the guests were bade to sip of it and found it to be sherry.

The guests poured forth from the booths transformed from one age into another, their faces covered with dominoes, the very act of putting on a mask revoking all their licenses to pick and quarrel with fantasy and horror. The women swept about in red gowns, laughing.

The men danced them attendance. And on the walls were shadows with no people to throw them, and here or there were mirrors in which no image showed.

"All of us vampires!" laughed Mr. Fletcher. "Dead!"

There were seven rooms, each a different color, one blue, one purple, one green, one orange, another white, the sixth violet, and the seventh shrouded in black velvet. And in the black room was an ebony clock which struck the hour loud. And through these rooms the guests ran, drunk at last, among the robot fantasies, amid the Dormice and Mad Hatters, the trolls and giants, the Black Cats and White Queens, and under their dancing feet the floor gave off the massive pumping beat of a hidden telltale heart.

"Mr. Stendahl!"

A whisper.

"Mr. Stendahl!"

A MONSTER WITH THE FACE OF DEATH stood at his elbow. It was Pikes. "I must see you alone."

"What is it?"

"Here." Pikes held out a skeleton hand. In it were a few half-melted, charred wheels, nuts, cogs, bolts.

Stendahl looked at them for a long moment. Then he drew Pikes into a corridor.

"Garrett?" he whispered.

Pikes nodded. "He sent a robot in his place. Cleaning out the incinerator a moment ago, I found these."

They both stared at the fateful cogs for a time.

"This means the police will be here any minute," said Pikes. "Our plan will be ruined."

"I don't know." Stendahl glanced in at the whirling yellow and blue and orange people. The music swept through the misting halls. "I should have guessed Garrett wouldn't be fool enough to come in person. But wait!"

"What's the matter?"

"Nothing. There's nothing the matter. Garrett sent a robot to us. Well, we sent one back. Unless he checks closely he won't notice the switch."

"Of course!"

"Next time, he'll come *himself*. Now that he thinks it's safe. Why, he might be at the door any minute, in *person!* More wine, Pikes!"

The great bell rang.

"There he is now, I'll bet you. Go let Mr. Garrett in."

Rapunzel let down her golden hair.

"Mr. Stendahl?"

"Mr. Garrett. The *real* Mr. Garrett?"

"The same." Garrett eyed the dank walls and the whirling people. "I thought I'd better come see for myself. You can't depend on robots. Other people's robots, especially. I also took the precaution of summoning the Dismantlers. They'll be here in one hour to knock the props out from under this horrible place."

Stendahl bowed. "Thanks for telling me." He waved his hand. "In the meantime, you might as well enjoy this. A little wine?"

"No thank you. What's going on? How low can a man sink?"

"See for yourself, Mr. Garrett."

"Murder," said Garrett.

"Murder most foul," said Stendahl.

A woman screamed. Miss Pope ran up, her face the color of a cheese. "The most horrid thing just happened! I saw Miss Blunt strangled by an ape and stuffed up a chimney!"

They looked and saw the long yellow hair trailing down from the flue. Garrett cried out.

"Horrid!" sobbed Miss Pope, and then ceased crying. She blinked and turned. "Miss Blunt!"

"Yes," said Miss Blunt, standing there.

"But I just saw you crammed up the flue!"

"No," laughed Miss Blunt. "A robot of myself. A clever facsimile!"

"But, but—"

"Don't cry, darling. I'm quite all right. Let me look at myself. Well, so there I *am!* Up the chimney, like you said. Isn't that funny?"

Miss Blunt walked away, laughing softly.

"Have a drink, Garrett?"

"I believe I will. That unnerved me. My God, what a place. This *does* deserve tearing down. For a moment there . . ." Garrett drank.

ANOTHER SCREAM. Mr. Steffens, borne upon the shoulders of four white rabbits, was carried down a flight of stairs which magically appeared in the floor. Into a pit went Mr. Steffens, where, bound and tied, he was left to face the advancing razor steel of a great pendulum which now swept down, coming closer and closer to his outraged body.

"Is that me down there?" said Mr. Steffens, appearing at Garrett's elbow. He bent over the pit. "How strange, how odd, to see yourself die."

The pendulum made a final stroke.

"How realistic," said Mr. Steffens, turning away.

"Another drink, Mr. Garrett?"

"Yes, please."

"It won't be long. The Dismantlers will be here."

"Thank God!"

And for a third time, a scream.

"What now?" said Garrett, apprehensively.

"It's my turn," said Miss Drummond. "Look."

And a second Miss Drummond, shrieking, was nailed into a coffin and thrust into the raw earth under the floor.

"Why I remember *that*," gasped the Investigator of Moral Climates. "From the old forbidden books. The Premature Burial. And the others. The Pit, the Pendulum, and the ape; the chimney, the Murders in the Rue Morgue. In a book I burned, yes!"

"Another drink, Garrett. Here, hold your glass steady."

"My Lord, you have an imagination, haven't you?"

They stood and watched five others die, one in the mouth of a dragon, the others thrown off into the black tarn, sinking and vanishing.

"Would you like to see what we have planned for you?" asked Stendahl.

"Certainly," said Garrett. "What's the difference? We'll blow the whole thing up, anyway. You're nasty."

"Come along then. This way."

And he led Garrett down into the floor, through numerous

passages and down again upon spiral stairs into the earth, into the catacombs.

"What do you want to show me down here?" said Garrett.

"Yourself killed."

"A duplicate?"

"Yes. And also something else."

"The Amontillado," said Stendahl, going ahead with a blazing lantern which he held high. Skeletons froze half out of coffin lids. Garrett held his hand to his nose, face disgusted.

"The what?"

"Haven't you ever heard of the Amontillado?"

"No!"

"Don't you recognize this?" Stendahl pointed to a cell.

"Should I?"

"Or this?" Stendahl produced a trowel from under his cape, smiling.

"What's that thing?"

"Come," said Stendahl.

They stepped into the cell. In the dark, Stendahl affixed the chains to the half-drunken man.

"For God's sake, what are you doing?" shouted Garrett, rattling about.

"I'm being ironic. Don't interrupt a man in the midst of being ironic. It's not polite. There!"

"You've locked me in chains!"

"So I have."

"What are you going to do?"

"Leave you here."

"You're joking."

"A very good joke."

"Where's my duplicate? Don't we see him killed?"

"There is no duplicate."

"But, the *others!*"

"The others are dead. The ones you saw killed were the real people. The duplicates, the robots, stood by and watched." Garrett said nothing.

"Now you're supposed to say 'For the love of God, Montresor!'" said Stendahl. "And I will reply 'Yes, for the love of God.' Won't you say it? Come on. *Say* it."

"You fool."

"Must I coax you? Say it. Say 'For the love of God, Montresor!'"

"I won't, you idiot. Get me out of here." He was sober now.

"Here. Put this on." Stendahl tossed in something that belled and rang.

"What is it?"

"A cap and bells. Put it on and I might let you out."

"Stendahl!"

"Put it on, I said!"

Garrett obeyed. The bells tinkled.

"Don't you have a feeling that this has all happened before?" inquired Stendahl, setting to work with trowel and mortar and brick now.

"What're you doing?"

"Walling you in. Here's one row. Here's another."

"You're insane!"

"I won't argue that point."

"You'll be prosecuted for this!"

He tapped a brick and placed it on the wet mortar, humming.

Now there was a thrashing and pounding and a crying out from within the darkening place. The bricks rose higher. "More thrashing, please," said Stendahl. "Let's make it a good show."

"Let me out, let me out!"

There was one last brick to shove into place. The screaming was continuous.

"Garrett?" called Stendahl softly. Garrett silenced himself. "Garrett," said Stendahl. "Do you know why I've done this to you? Because you burned Mr. Poe's books without really reading them. You took other people's advice that they needed burning. Otherwise you'd have realized what I was going to do to you when we came down here a moment ago. Ignorance is fatal, Mr. Garrett."

Garrett was silent.

"I want this to be perfect," said Stendahl, holding his lantern up so its light penetrated in upon the slumped figure. "Jingle your bells, softly." The bells rustled. "Now, if you'll please say 'For the love of God, Montresor,' I might let you free."

The man's face came up in the light. There was a hesitation. Then, grotesquely, the man asked, "For the love of God, Montresor."

"Ah," said Stendahl, eyes closed. He shoved the last brick into place and mortared it tight. "*Requiescat in pace,* dear friend."

He hastened from the catacomb.

In the seven rooms, the sound of midnight clock brought everything to a halt.

The Red Death appeared.

Stendahl turned for a moment, at the door, to watch. And then he ran out of the great House, across the moat, to where a helicopter waited.

"Ready, Pikes?"

"Ready."

"There it goes!"

They looked at the great House, smiling. It began to crack down the middle, as with an earthquake, and as Stendahl watched the magnificent sight, he heard Pikes reciting behind him in a low, cadenced voice:

"'—my brain reeled as I saw the mighty walls rushing asunder—there was a long tumultuous shouting sound like the voice of a thousand waters—and the deep and dank tarn at my feet closed sullenly and silently over the fragments of the House of Usher.'"

The helicopter rose over the steaming lake and flew into the west.

BONFIRE

THE THING THAT BOTHERED WILLIAM PETERSON MOST was Shakespeare and Plato, and Aristotle, and Jonathan Swift and William Faulkner and the poems of Weller, Robert Frost perhaps and John Donne and Robert Herrick. All of these, mind you, tossed into the Bonfire. Then he got to thinking of certain paintings at the museum, or in the books in his den, the good Picassos, not the bad ones, but the really rare good ones; the good Dalís (there had been some, you know); and the best of Van Gogh; the lines in certain Matisses, not to mention color, and the way Monet had with rivers and streams, and the rare haze that moved upon the Renoir peach-women's faces in the summer shadows. Or, to go back, there were the wonderful El Grecos in lightning illumination, the saints' bodies elongated by some heavenly gravity toward white, sulphurous thunderclouds. After he thought of these bits of kindling (for that's what they would become) he thought of the massive Michelangelo sculptures, the boy David with his youth-swelled wrists and tendoned neck, the sensitive hands and eyes, the soft mouth; the passionately combined Rodins; the soft dimple in the back of the nude female statue in the rear of the Museum of Modern Art, that cool dimple where he might in passing press his hand to congratulate Lembroocke for his artistry. . .

William Peterson lay with the lights out in his study very late at night, with only the soft pinkish glow of his record player touching upon his bony face. The music filtered across the room with the softest motion, a locust chorus from Beethoven's *Jena*, a raining pizzicato amidst Tchaikovsky's *Fourth*, a brass charge across Shostakovich's *Sixth*, a ghost from *La Valse*. Sometimes William Peterson would touch his face with his hand and discover a wetness beneath each lower eyelid. It's not really self-pity is it? he thought. It's just not being able to do anything about all this. For centuries their thoughts had gone on and on, living. For tomorrow, they would be dead. Shakespeare, Frost, Huxley, Dalí, Picasso, Beethoven, Swift, really dead. Until now they had never died, even though their bodies had been with the worms. Tomorrow that would be attended to.

The phone rang. William Peterson put his hand through the dark air and picked up the receiver.

"Bill?"

"Oh. Hello, Mary."

"What're you doing?"

"Listening to music."

"Aren't you going to do anything special tonight?"

"What's there to do?" he said.

"God knows where we'll all be tomorrow night, I just thought—"

"There won't be any tomorrow night," he interrupted. "There'll just be the Bonfire is all."

"What an odd way to put it. What a shame," she said, remotely. "I've been thinking, what a waste. Here my mother goes and has me and raises me and my father puts me through school. The same with you, Bill. The same with all 2 billion of us on Earth tonight. And then this has to happen."

"Not only that," he thought, eyes shut, the phone to his mouth. "But all the million years it took for us to get here. Oh, you might ask, 'What have we got, where did we go? Did we arrive? And where are we?' But here we are anyway, for better or worse. And it took millions of years for man to creep up. It simply galls me that a few men in high places can snap their fingers and raze it all. The only consolation is that they'll burn too." He opened his eyes. "Do you believe in Hell, Mary?"

"I didn't. I do now. They say that once started, Earth should burn for a billion years, like a small sun."

"Yes, that's Hell all right, and us in it. I never thought about it, but our souls will be roasted in the air here, kept on Earth long after it's nothing else but a bonfire."

She began to cry, across the city, in her apartment.

"Don't cry, Mary," he said. "It hurts me more to hear you do that than any other thing about the mess."

"I can't help it," she said. "I'm really in a rage. To think that we've all *wasted* our lives, spent our time, you to write three of the finest books of our age, and it comes to nothing. And all the other people, the thousands of hours of writing and building and thinking we've put in, my God, the total is frightening, and then to have someone to strike a match.

He allowed her a long minute of silent hysteria.

"Do you think everyone hasn't thought of it," he said. "We all have our little stake. We think, 'Jesus, is this what grandfather crossed the plains for, is this what Columbus discovered America for, is this what Galileo dropped the weights off Pisa for, is this what Moses crossed the Red Sea for?' Suddenly this erases the whole equation and makes everything we ever did silly because it totals up to CANCEL, CANCEL on the machine."

"Isn't there anything we can do?"

"I belonged to every organization, I talked, I banged tables, I voted, I was thrown in jail, and now I'm silent," he said. "We've done everything. It got away from us all. Someone threw the steering wheel out the window back in the 1940s somewhere, and no one thought to check the brakes."

"Why did we bother doing anything?" she said.

"I don't know. I want to go back now and tell myself in the year 1939, 'Look, young fellow, don't rush, don't hurry, don't be excited, don't rack your brain, don't create your stories or your books, it's no good, it's for nothing, in 1960 they'll poke you and it in the incinerator!' And I'd like to tell Mr. Matisse, 'Stop making those beautiful lines,' and Mr. Picasso, 'Don't bother with *Guernica*,' and Mr. Franco, 'Don't bother with conquering your own people, everyone don't bother about anything!' "

"But we had to bother, we had to go on."

"Yes," he said. "That's the wonderful and the silly part of it. We went on even when we knew we were walking into the kiln. That's one thing we can say right up to the last, almost, we were fiddling and painting and reproducing and talking and acting as if this might go on forever. Once I kidded myself that, somehow, part of Earth might remain, that a few fragments might carry over, Shakespeare, Blake, a few busts, a few tidbits, perhaps one of my short stories, remnants. I thought we'd go and leave the world to the Islanders or the Asiatics. But this is different. This is *en toto*."

"What time do you think it will happen?"

"Any hour now."

"They don't even know what the bomb'll do, do they?"

"There's an even chance either way. Forgive my pessimism, I happen to think they have miscalculated."

"Why don't you come over to my place?" she asked.

"Why?"

"We could at least talk—"

"Why?"

"It would be something to do—"

"Why?"

"It would give us something to talk about."

"Why, why, why!"

She waited a minute.

"Bill?"

Silence.

"Bill!"

No answer.

He was thinking of a poem by Thomas Lovell Beddoes, he was thinking of a scrap of film from an old picture called *Citizen Kane*, he was thinking of the white feather-soft haze in which the Degas ballerinas poised, he was thinking of a Braque mandolin, a Picasso guitar, a Dalí watch, a line from Houseman, he was thinking of a thousand mornings splashing cold water on his face, he was thinking of a billion mornings and a billion people splashing cold water on their faces and going out to their work in the last ten thousand years. He was thinking of fields of grass and wheat and dandelions. He was thinking of women.

"BILL, ARE YOU THERE?"

No answer.

At last, swallowing, he said, "Yes, I'm here."

"I—" she said.

"Yes?"

"I want—" she said.

The earth blew up and burned steadily for a thousand million centuries. . .

THE CRICKET ON THE HEARTH

THE DOOR SLAMMED AND JOHN MARTIN WAS OUT OF HIS hat and coat and past his wife as fluently as a magician en route to a better illusion. He produced the newspaper with a dry whack as he slipped his coat into the closet like an abandoned ghost and sailed through the house, scanning the news, his nose guessing at the identity of supper, talking over his shoulder, his wife following. There was still a faint scent of the train and the winter night about him. In his chair he sensed an unaccustomed silence resembling that of a birdhouse when a vulture's shadow looms; all the robins, sparrows, mockingbirds quiet. His wife stood whitely in the door, not moving.

"Come sit down," said John Martin. "What're you doing? God, don't stare as if I were dead. What's new? Not that there's ever anything new, of course. What do you think of those fathead city councilmen today? More taxes, more every goddamn thing."

"John!" cried his wife. "Don't!"

"Don't what?"

"Don't talk that way. It isn't safe!"

"For God's sake, not safe? Is this Russia or is this our own house?!"

"Not exactly."

"Not exactly?"

"There's a bug in our house," she whispered.

"A bug?" He leaned forward, exasperated.

"You know. Detective talk. When they hide a microphone somewhere you don't know, they call it a bug, I think," she whispered even more quietly.

"Have you gone nuts?"

"I thought I might have when Mrs. Thomas told me. They came last night while we were out and asked Mrs. Thomas to let them use her garage. They set up their equipment there and strung wires over here, the house is wired, the bug is in one or maybe all of the rooms."

She was standing over him now and bent to whisper in his ear.

He fell back. "Oh, no!"

"Yes!"

"But we haven't done anything—"

"Keep your voice down!" she whispered.

"Wait!" he whispered back, angrily, his face white, red, then white again. "Come on!"

Out on the terrace, he glanced around and swore. "Now say the whole damn thing again! They're using the neighbor's garage to hide their equipment? The FBI?"

"Yes, yes, oh it's been awful! I didn't want to call, I was afraid your wire was tapped, too."

"We'll see, dammit! Now!"

"Where are you going?"

"To stomp on their equipment! Jesus! What've we done?"

"Don't!" She seized his arm. "You'd just make trouble. After they've listened a few days they'll know we're okay and go away."

"I'm insulted, no, outraged! Those two words I've never used before, but, hell, they fit the case! Who do they think they are? Is it our politics? Our studio friends, my stories, the fact I'm a producer? Is it Tom Lee, because he's Chinese and a friend? Does that make him dangerous, or us? What, what?!"

"Maybe someone gave them a false lead and they're searching. If they really think we're dangerous, you can't blame them."

"I know, I know, but us! It's so damned funny I could laugh. Do we tell our friends? Rip out the microphone if we can find it, go to a hotel, leave town?"

"No, no, just go on as we have done. We've nothing to hide, so let's ignore them."

"Ignore!? The first thing I said tonight was political crap and you shut me up like I'd set off a bomb."

"Let's go in, it's cold out here. Be good. It'll only be a few days and they'll be gone, and after all, it isn't as if we were guilty of something."

"Yeah, okay, but damn, I wish you'd let me go over and kick the hell out of their junk!"

They hesitated, then entered the house, the strange house, and stood for a moment in the hall, trying to manufacture some appropriate dialogue. They felt like two amateurs in a shoddy out-of-town play, the electrician having suddenly turned on too much light, the audience, bored, having left the theater, and, simultaneously, the actors having forgotten their lines. So they said nothing.

He sat in the parlor trying to read the paper until the food was on the table. But the house suddenly echoed. The slightest crackle of the sports section, the exhalation of smoke from his pipe, became like the sound of an immense forest fire or a wind blowing through an organ. When he shifted in the chair the chair groaned like a sleeping dog, his tweed pants scraped and sandpapered together. From the kitchen there was an ungodly racket of pans being bashed, tins falling, oven doors cracking open, crashing shut, the fluming full-bloomed sound of gas jumping to life, lighting up blue and hissing under the inert foods, and then when the foods stirred ceaselessly under the commands of boiling water, they made a sound of washing and humming and murmuring that was excessively loud. No one spoke. His wife came and stood in the door for a moment, peering at her husband and the raw walls, but said nothing. He turned a page of football to a page of wrestling and read between the lines, scanning the empty whiteness and the specks of undigested pulp.

Now there was a great pounding in the room, like surf, growing nearer in a storm, a tidal wave, crashing on rocks and breaking with a titanic explosion again and again, in his ears.

My God, he thought, I hope they don't hear my heart!

His wife beckoned from the dining room, where, as he loudly rattled the paper and plopped it into the chair and walked, padding, padding on the rug, and drew out the protesting chair on the uncarpeted dining-room floor, she tinkled and clattered last-minute silverware, fetched a soup that bubbled like lava, and set a coffeepot to percolate beside them. They looked at the percolating silver apparatus, listened to it gargle in its glass throat, admired it for its protest against silence, for saying what it felt. And then there was the scrape and click of the knife and fork on the plate. He started to say some-thing, but it stuck, with a morsel of food, in his throat. His eyes bulged. His wife's eyes bulged. Finally she got up, went to the kitchen, and got a piece of paper and a pencil. She came back and handed him a freshly written note: *Say something!*

He scribbled a reply:

What?

She wrote again: *Anything! Break the silence. They'll think something's wrong!*

They sat staring nervously at their own notes. Then, with a smile, he sat back in his chair and winked at her. She frowned. Then he said, "Well, dammit, say something!"

"What?" she said.

"Dammit," he said. "You've been silent all during supper. You and your moods. Because I won't buy you that coat, I sup-pose? Well, you're not going to get it, and that's final!"

"But I don't want—"

He stopped her before she could continue. "Shut up! I won't talk to a nag. You know we can't afford mink! If you can't talk sense, don't talk!"

She blinked at him for a moment, and then she smiled and winked this time.

"I haven't got a thing to wear!" she cried.

"Oh, shut up!" he roared.

"You never buy me anything!" she cried.

"Blather, blather, blather!" he yelled.

They fell silent and listened to the house. The echoes of their yelling had put everything back to normalcy, it seemed. The percolator was not so loud, the clash of cutlery was soft-ened. They sighed.

"Look," he said at last, "don't speak to me again this evening. Will you do me that favor?"

She sniffed.

"Pour me some coffee!" he said.

Along about eight-thirty the silence was getting unbearable again. They sat stiffly in the living room, she with her latest library book, he with some flies he was tying up in preparation for going fishing on Sunday. Several times they glanced up and opened their mouths but shut them again and looked about as if a mother-in-law had hove into view.

At five minutes to nine he said, "Let's go to a show."

"This late?"

"Sure, why not?"

"You never like to go out weeknights, because you're tired. I've been home all day, cleaning, and it's nice to get out at night."

"Come on, then!"

"I thought you were mad at me."

"Promise not to talk mink and it's a go. Get your coat."

"All right." She was back in an instant, dressed, smiling, and they were out of the house and driving away in very little time. They looked back at their lighted house.

"Hail and farewell, house," he said. "Let's just drive and never come back."

"We don't dare."

"Let's sleep tonight in one of those motels that ruin your reputation," he suggested.

"Stop it. We've got to go back. If we stayed away, they'd be suspicious."

"Damn them. I feel like a fool in my own house. Them and

their cricket."

"Bug."

"Cricket, anyway. I remember when I was a boy a cricket got in our house somehow. He'd be quiet most of the time, but in the evening he'd start scratching his legs together, an ungodly racket. We tried to find him. Never could. He was in a crack of the floor or the chimney somewhere. Kept us awake the first few nights, then we got used to him. He was around for half a year, I think. Then one night we went to bed and some-one said, 'What's that noise?' and we all sat up, listening. 'I know what it is,' said Dad. 'It's silence. The cricket's gone.' And he was gone. Dead or went away, we never knew which. And we felt sort of sad and lonely with that new sound in the house."

They drove on the night road.

"We've got to decide what to do," she said.

"Rent a new house somewhere."

"We can't do that."

"Go to Ensenada for the weekend, we've been wanting to make that trip for years, do us good, they won't follow us and wire our hotel room, anyway."

"The problem'd still be here when we come back. No, the only solution is to live our life the way we used to an hour before we found out what was going on with the microphone."

"I don't remember. It was such a nice little routine. I don't remember how it was, the details, I mean. We've been married ten years now and one night's just like another, very pleasant, of course. I come home, we have supper, we read or listen to the radio, no television, and go to bed."

"Sounds rather drab when you say it like that."

"Has it been for you?" he asked suddenly.

She took his arm. "Not really. I'd like to get out more, occasionally."

"We'll see what we can do about that. Right now, we'll plan on talking straight out about everything, when we get back to the house, politically, socially, morally. We've nothing to hide. I was a Boy Scout when I was a kid, you were a Camp Fire Girl; that's not very subversive, it's as simple as that. Speak up. Here's the theater."

They parked and went into the show.

ABOUT MIDNIGHT THEY DROVE into the driveway of their house and sat for a moment looking at the great empty stage waiting for them. At last he stirred and said, "Well, let's go in and say hello to the cricket."

They garaged the car and walked around to the front door, arm in arm. They opened the front door and the feel of the atmosphere rushing out upon them was a listening atmosphere. It was like walking into an auditorium of one thousand invisible people, all holding their breath.

"Here we are!" said the husband loudly.

"Yes, that was a wonderful show, wasn't it?" said his wife.

It had been a pitiable movie.

"I liked the music especially!"

They had found the music banal and repetitive.

"Yes, isn't that girl a terrific dancer!"

They smiled at the walls. The girl had been a rather club-footed thirteen-year-old with an immensely low IQ.

"Darling!" he said. "Let's go to San Diego Sunday, for just the afternoon."

"What? And give up your fishing with your pals? You always go fishing with your pals," she cried.

"I won't go fishing with them this time. I love only you!" he said, and thought, miserably, We sound like Gallagher and Sheen warming up a cold house.

They bustled about the house, emptying ashtrays, getting ready for bed, opening closets, slamming doors. He sang a few bars from the tired musical they had seen in a lilting off-key baritone, she joining in.

In bed, with the lights out, she snuggled over against him, her hand on his arm, and they kissed a few times. Then they kissed a few more times. "This is more like it," he said. He gave her a rather long kiss. They snuggled even closer and he ran his hand along her back. Suddenly her spine stiffened.

Jesus, he thought, what's wrong now.

She pressed her mouth to his ear.

"What if," she whispered, "what if the cricket's in our bedroom, here?"

"They wouldn't dare!" he cried.

"Shh!" she said.

"They wouldn't dare," he whispered angrily. "Of all the nerve!"

She was moving away from him. He tried to hold her, but she moved firmly away and turned her back. "It would be just like them," he heard her whisper. And there he was, stranded on the white cold beach with the tide going out.

Cricket, he thought, I'll never forgive you for this.

The next day being Tuesday, he rushed off to the studio, had a busy day, and returned, on time, flinging open the front door with a cheery "Hey there, lovely!"

When his wife appeared, he kissed her solidly, patted her rump, ran an appreciative hand up and down her body, kissed her again, and handed her a huge green parcel of pink carnations.

"For me?" she said.

"You!" he replied.

"Is it our anniversary?"

"Nonsense, no. I just got them because, that's all, because."

"Why, how nice." Tears came to her eyes. "You haven't brought me flowers for months and months."

"Haven't I? I guess I haven't!"

"I love you," she said.

"I love you," he said, and kissed her again. They went, holding hands, into the living room.

"You're early," she said. "You usually stop off for a quick one with the boys."

"To hell with the boys. You know where we're going Saturday, darling? Instead of my sleeping in the backyard on the lounge, we're going to that fashion show you wanted me to go see."

"I thought you hated—"

"Anything you want, peaches," he said. "I told the boys I won't make it Sunday for the fishing trip. They thought I was crazy. What's for supper?"

He stalked smiling to the kitchen, where he appreciatively ladled and spooned and stirred things, smelling, gasping, tasting everything, "Shepherd's pie!" he cried, opening the oven and peering in, gloriously, "My God! My favorite dish. It's been since last June we had that!"

"I thought you'd like it!"

He ate with relish, he told jokes, they ate by candlelight,

the pink carnations filled the immediate vicinity with a cinnamon scent, the food was splendid, and, topping it off, there was black-bottom pie fresh from the refrigerator.

"Black-bottom pie! It takes hours and genius to make a really good black-bottom pie."

"I'm glad you like it, dear."

After dinner he helped her with the dishes. Then they sat on the living-room floor and played a number of favorite symphonies together, they even waltzed a bit to the *Rosenkavalier* pieces. He kissed her at the end of the dance and whispered in her ear, patting her behind, "Tonight, so help me God, cricket or no cricket."

The music started over. They swayed together.

"Have you found it yet?" he whispered.

"I think so. It's near the fireplace and the window."

They walked over to the fireplace. The music was very loud as he bent and shifted a drape, and there it was, a beady black little eye, not much bigger than a thumbnail. They both stared at it and backed away. He went and opened a bottle of champagne and they had a nice drink.

The music was loud in their heads, in their bones, in the walls of the house. He danced with his mouth up close to her ear.

"What did you find out?" she asked.

"The studio said to sit tight. Those damn fools are after everyone. They'll be tapping the zoo telephone next."

"Everything's all right?"

"Just sit tight, the studio said. Don't break any equipment, they said. You can be sued for breaking government property."

They went to bed early, smiling at each other.

On Wednesday night he brought roses and kissed her a full minute at the front door. They called up some brilliant and witty friends and had them over for an evening's discussion, having decided, in going over their phone list, that these two friends would stun the cricket with their repertoire and make the very air shimmer with their brilliance. On Thursday afternoon he called her from the studio for the first time in months, and on Thursday night he brought her an orchid, some more roses, a scarf he had seen in a shop window at lunchtime, and two tickets for a fine play. She in turn had baked him a chocolate cake from his mother's recipe, on Wednesday, and on Thursday had made Toll House cookies and lemon chiffon pie, as well as darning his socks and pressing his pants and sending everything to the cleaners that had been neglected previous times. They rambled about the town Thursday night after the play, came home late, read Euripides to one another out loud, went to bed late, smiling again, and got up late, having to call the studio and claim sickness until noon, when the husband, tiredly, on the way out of the house, thought to himself, This can't go on. He turned and came back in. He walked over to the cricket near the fireplace and bent down to it and said:

"Testing, one, two, three. Testing. Can you hear me? Testing."

"What're you doing?" cried his wife in the doorway.

"Calling all cars, calling all cars," said the husband, lines under his eyes, face pale. "This is me speaking. We know you're there, friends. Go away. Go away. Take your microphone and get out. You won't hear anything from us. That is all. That is all. Give my regards to J. Edgar. Signing off."

His wife was standing with a white and aghast look in the door as he marched by her, nodding, and thumped out the door.

She phoned him at three o'clock.

"Darling," she said, "it's gone!"

"The cricket?"

"Yes, they came and took it away. A man rapped very politely at the door and I let him in and in a minute he had unscrewed the cricket and taken it with him. He just walked off and didn't say boo."

"Thank God," said the husband. "Oh, thank God."

"He tipped his hat at me and said thanks."

"Awfully decent of him. See you later," said the husband.

This was Friday. He came home that night about six-thirty, having stopped off to have a quick one with the boys. He came in the front door, reading his newspaper, passed his wife, taking off his coat and automatically putting it in the closet, went on past the kitchen without twitching his nose, sat in the living room and read the sports page until supper, when she served him plain roast beef and string beans, with apple juice to start and sliced oranges for dessert. On his way home he had turned in the theater tickets for tonight and tomorrow, he informed her; she could go with the girls to the fashion show, he intended to bake in the backyard.

"Well," he said, about ten o'clock. "The old house seems different tonight, doesn't it?"

"Yes."

"Good to have the cricket gone. Really had us going there."

"Yes," she said.

They sat awhile. "You know," she said later, "I sort of miss it, though, I really sort of miss it. I think I'll do something subversive so they'll put it back."

"I beg your pardon?" he said, twisting a piece of twine around a fly he was preparing from his fishing box

"Never mind," she said. "Let's go to bed."

She went on ahead. Ten minutes later, yawning, he followed after her, putting out the lights. Her eyes were closed as he undressed in the semi-moonlit darkness. She's already asleep, he thought.

THE PEDESTRIAN

TO ENTER OUT INTO THAT SILENCE THAT WAS THE CITY AT eight o'clock of a misty evening in November, to put your feet upon that buckling concrete walk, to step over grassy seams and make your way, hands in pockets, through the silences, that was what Mr. Leonard Mead most dearly loved to do. He would stand upon the corner of an intersection and peer down long moonlit avenues of sidewalk in four directions, deciding which way to go, but it really made no difference; he was alone in this world of A.D. 2131, or as good as alone, and with a final decision made, a path selected, he would stride off, sending patterns of frosty air before him like the smoke of a cigar.

Sometimes he would walk for hours and miles and return only at midnight to his house. And on his way he would see the cottages and homes with their dark windows, and it was not unequal to walking through a graveyard, because only the faintest glimmers of firefly light appeared in flickers behind the windows. Sudden gray phantoms seemed to manifest themselves upon inner walls where a curtain was still undrawn against the night, or there were whisperings and murmurs where a window in a tomblike building was still open.

MR. LEONARD MEAD WOULD PAUSE, cock his head, listen, look, and march on, his feet making no noise on the lumpy walk. For a long while now the sidewalks had been vanishing under flowers and grass. In ten years of walking by night or day, for thousands of miles, he had never met another person walking, not one in all that time.

He now wore sneakers when strolling at night, because the dogs in intermittent squads would parallel his journey with barkings if he wore hard heels, and lights might click on and faces appear, and an entire street be startled by the passing of a lone figure, himself, in the early November evening.

On this particular evening he began his journey in a westerly direction toward the hidden sea. There was a good crystal frost in the air; it cut the nose going in and made the lungs blaze like a Christmas tree inside; you could feel the cold light going on and off, all the branches filled with invisible snow. He listened to the faint push of his soft shoes through autumn leaves with satisfaction, and whistled a cold quiet whistle between his teeth, occasionally picking up a leaf as he passed, examining its skeletal pattern in the infrequent lamplights as he went on, smelling its rusty smell.

"Hello, in there," he whispered to every house on every side as he moved. "What's up tonight on Channel 4, Channel 7, Channel 9? Where are the cowboys rushing, and do I see the United States Cavalry over the next hill to the rescue?"

The street was silent and long and empty, with only his shadow moving like the shadow of a hawk in mid-country. If he closed his eyes and stood very still, frozen, he imagined himself upon the center of a plain, a wintry, windless Arizona country with no house in a thousand miles, and only dry river-beds, the streets, for company.

"What is it now?" he asked the houses, noticing his wrist-watch. "Eight-thirty p.m. Time for a dozen assorted murders? A quiz? A revue? A comedian falling off the stage?"

Was that a murmur of laughter from within a moon-white house? He hesitated, but went on when nothing more happened. He stumbled over a particularly uneven section of walk as he came to a cloverleaf intersection which stood silent where two main highways crossed the town. During the day it was a thunderous surge of cars, the gas stations open, a great insect rustling and ceaseless jockeying for position as the scarab beetles, a faint incense puttering from their exhausts, skimmed homeward to the far horizons. But now these highways too were like streams in a dry season, all stone and bed and moon radiance.

HE TURNED BACK on a side street, circling around toward his home. He was within a block of his destination when the lone car turned a corner quite suddenly and flashed a fierce white cone of light upon him. He stood entranced, not unlike a night moth, stunned by the illumination and then drawn toward it.

A metallic voice called to him:

"Stand still. Stay where you are! Don't move!"

He halted.

"Put up your hands."

"But—" he said.

"Your hands up! Or we'll shoot!"

The police, of course, but what a rare, incredible thing; in a city of three million, there was only one police car left. Ever since a year ago, 2130, the election year, the force had been cut down from three cars to one. Crime was ebbing; there was no need now for the police, save for this one lone car wandering and wandering the empty streets.

"Your name?" said the police car in a metallic whisper. He couldn't see the men in it for the bright light in his eyes.

"Leonard Mead," he said.

"Speak up!"

"Leonard Mead!"

"Business or profession?"

"I guess you'd call me a writer."

"No profession," said the police car, as if talking to itself. The light held him fixed like a museum specimen, needle thrust through chest.

"You might say that," said Mr. Mead. He hadn't written in years. Magazines and books didn't sell any more. Everything went on in the tomblike houses at night now, he thought, continuing his fancy. The tombs, ill-lit by television light, where the people sat like the dead, the gray or multicolored lights touching their expressionless faces but never really touching them.

"No profession," said the phonograph voice, hissing. "What are you doing out?"

"Walking," said Leonard Mead.

"Walking!"

"Just walking," he said, simply, but his face felt cold.

"Walking, just walking, walking?"

"Yes, sir."

"Walking where? For what?"

"Walking for air. Walking to see."

"Your address!"

"Eleven South St. James Street."

"And there is air in your house, you have an air-conditioner, Mr. Mead?"

"Yes."

"And you have a viewing screen in your house to see with?"

"No."

"NO?" THERE WAS A CRACKLING quiet that in itself was an accusation.

"Are you married, Mr. Mead?"

"No."

"Not married," said the police voice behind the fiery beam. The moon was high and clear among the stars and the houses were gray and silent.

"Nobody wanted me," said Leonard Mead, with a smile.

"Don't speak unless you're spoken to!"

Leonard Mead waited in the cold night.

"Just walking, Mr. Mead?"

"Yes."

"But you haven't explained for what purpose."

"I explained: for air and to see, and just to walk."

"Have you done this often?"

"Every night for years."

The police car sat in the center of the street with its radio throat faintly humming.

"Well, Mr. Mead," it said.

"Is that all?" he asked politely.

"Yes," said the voice. "Here." There was a sigh, a pop. The back door of the police car sprang wide. "Get in."

"Wait a minute, I haven't done anything!"

"Get in."

"I protest!"

"Mr. Mead."

He walked like a man suddenly drunk. As he passed the front window of the car he looked in. As he had expected, there was no one in the front seat, no one in the car at all.

"Get in."

He put his hand to the door and peered into the back seat, which was a little cell, a little black jail with bars. It smelled of riveted steel. It smelled of harsh antiseptic; it smelled too clean and hard and metallic. There was nothing soft there.

"Now if you had a wife to give you an alibi," said the iron voice. "But—"

"Where are you taking me?"

The car hesitated, or rather gave a taint whirring click, as if information, somewhere, was dropping card by punch-slotted card under electric eyes. "To the psychiatric Center for Research on Regressive Tendencies."

He got in. The door shut with a soft thud. The police car rolled through the night avenues, flashing its dim lights ahead.

They passed one house on one street a moment later, one house in an entire city of houses that were dark, but this one particular house had all its electric lights brightly lit, every window a loud yellow illumination, square and warm in the cool darkness.

"That's my house," said Leonard Mead.

No one answered him.

The car moved down the empty river bed streets and off away, leaving the empty streets with the empty sidewalks, and no sound and no motion all the rest of the chill November night.

THE GARBAGE COLLECTOR

THIS IS HOW HIS WORK WAS: HE GOT UP AT FIVE IN THE cold dark morning and washed his face with warm water if the heater was working and cold water if the heater was not working. He shaved carefully, talking out to his wife in the kitchen, who was fixing ham and eggs or pancakes or whatever it was that morning. By six o'clock he was driving on his way to work alone, and parking his car in the big yard where all the other men parked their cars as the sun was coming up. The colors of the sky that time of morning were orange and blue and violet and sometimes very red and sometimes yellow or a clear color like water on white rock. Some mornings he could see his breath on the air and some mornings he could not. But as the sun was still rising he knocked his fist on the side of the green truck, and his driver, smiling and saying hello, would climb in the other side of the truck and they would drive out into the great city and go down all the streets until they came to the place where they started work. Sometimes, on the way, they stopped for black coffee and then went on, the warmness in them. And they began the work which meant that he jumped off in front of each house and picked up the garbage cans and brought them back and took off their lids and knocked them against the bin edge, which made the orange peels and canta- loupe rinds and coffee grounds fall out and thump down and begin to fill the empty truck. There were always steak bones and the heads of fish and pieces of green onion and stale cel- ery. If the garbage was new it wasn't so bad, but if it was very old it was bad. He was not sure if he liked the job or not, but it was a job and he did it well, talking about it a lot at some times and sometimes not thinking of it in any way at all. Some days the job was wonderful, for you were out early and the air was cool and fresh until you had worked too long and the sun got hot and the garbage steamed early. But mostly it was a job significant enough to keep him busy and calm and look- ing at the houses and cut lawns he passed by and seeing how everybody lived. And once or twice a month he was surprised to find that he loved the job and that it was the finest job in the world.

It went on just that way for many years. And then suddenly the job changed for him. It changed in a single day. Later he often wondered how a job could change so much in such a few short hours.

HE WALKED INTO THE APARTMENT and did not see his wife or hear her voice, but she was there, and he walked to a chair and let her stand away from him, watching him as he touched the chair and sat down in it without saying a word. He sat there for a long time.

"What's wrong?" At last her voice came through to him. She must have said it three or four times.

"Wrong?" He looked at this woman and yes, it was his wife

all right, it was someone he knew, and this was their apartment with the tall ceilings and the worn carpeting.

"Something happened at work today," he said.

She waited for him.

"On my garbage truck, something happened." His tongue moved dryly on his lips and his eyes shut over his seeing until there was all blackness and no light of any sort and it was like standing alone in a room when you got out of bed in the middle of a dark night. "I think I'm going to quit my job. Try to understand."

"Understand!" she cried.

"It can't be helped. This is all the strangest damned thing that ever happened to me in my life." He opened his eyes and sat there, his hands feeling cold when he rubbed his thumb and forefingers together. "The thing that happened was strange."

"Well, don't just *sit* there!"

He took part of a newspaper from the pocket of his leather jacket. "This is today's paper," he said. "December 10, 1951. Los Angeles *Times*. Civil Defense Bulletin. It says they're buying radios for our garbage trucks."

"Well, what's so bad about a little music?"

"No music. You don't understand. No music."

He opened his rough hand and drew with one clean fingernail, slowly, trying to put everything there where he could see it and she could see it. "In this article the mayor says they'll put sending and receiving apparatus on every garbage truck in town." He squinted at his hand. "After the atom bombs hit our city, those radios will talk to us. And then our garbage trucks will go pick up the bodies."

"Well, that seems practical. When—"

"The garbage trucks," he said, "go out and pick up all the bodies."

"You can't just leave bodies around, can you? You've got to take them and—" His wife shut her mouth very slowly. She blinked, one time only, and she did this very slowly also. He watched that one slow blink of her eyes. Then, with a turn of her body, as if someone else had turned it for her, she walked to a chair, paused, thought how to do it, and sat down, very straight and stiff. She said nothing.

He listened to his wristwatch ticking, but with only a small part of his attention.

At last she laughed. "They were joking!"

He shook his head. He felt his head moving from left to right and from right to left, as slowly as everything else had happened. "No. They put a receiver on my truck today. They said, at the alert, if you're working, dump your garbage anywhere. When we radio you, get *in* there and haul out the dead."

Some water in the kitchen boiled over loudly. She let it boil for five seconds and then held the arm of the chair with one hand and got up and found the door and went out. The boiling sound stopped. She stood in the door and then walked back to where he still sat, not moving, his head in one position only.

"It's all blueprinted out. They have squads, sergeants, captains, corporals, everything," he said. "We even know where to *bring* the bodies."

"So you've been thinking about it all day," she said.

"All day since this morning. I thought: Maybe now I don't want to be a garbage collector anymore. It used to be Tom and me had fun with a kind of game. You got to do that. Garbage is bad. But if you work at it you can make a game. Tom and me did that. We watched people's garbage. We saw what kind they had. Steak bones in rich houses, lettuce and orange peel in poor ones. Sure it's silly, but a guy's got to make his work as good as he can and worthwhile or why in hell do it? And you're your own boss, in a way, on a truck. You get out early in the morning and it's an outdoor job, anyway; you see the sun come up and you see the town get up, and that's not bad at all. But now, today, all of a sudden it's not the kind of job for me anymore."

His wife started to talk swiftly. She named a lot of things and she talked about a lot more, but before she got very far he cut gently across her talking. "I know, I know, the kids and school, our car, I know," he said. "And bills and money and credit. But what about that farm Dad left us? Why can't we move there, away from cities? I know a little about farming. We could stock up, hole in, have enough to live on for months if anything happened."

She said nothing.

"Sure, all of our friends are here in town," he went on reasonably. "And movies and shows and the kids' friends, and. . ."

She took a deep breath. "Can't we think it over a few more days?"

"I don't know. I'm afraid of that. I'm afraid if I think it over, about my truck and my new work, I'll get used to it. And, oh Christ, it just doesn't seem right a man, a human being, should ever let himself get used to any idea like that."

She shook her head slowly, looking at the windows, the gray walls, the dark pictures on the walls. She tightened her hands. She started to open her mouth.

"I'll think tonight," he said. "I'll stay up awhile. By morning I'll know what to do."

"Be careful with the children. It wouldn't be good, their knowing all this."

"I'll be careful."

"Let's not talk anymore, then. I'll finish dinner!" She jumped up and put her hands to her face and then looked at her hands and at the sunlight in the windows. "Why, the kids'll be home any minute."

"I'm not very hungry."

"You got to eat, you just got to keep on going." She hurried off, leaving him alone in the middle of a room where not a breeze stirred the curtains, and only the gray ceiling hung over him with a lonely bulb unlit in it, like an old moon in a sky. He was quiet. He massaged his face with both hands. He got up and stood alone in the dining-room door and walked forward and felt himself sit down and remain seated in a dining-room chair. He saw his hands spread on the white tablecloth, open and empty.

"All afternoon," he said, "I've thought."

She moved through the kitchen, rattling silverware, crashing pans against the silence that was everywhere.

"Wondering," he said, "if you put the bodies in the trucks lengthwise or endwise, with the heads on the right, or the *feet* on the right. Men and women together, or separated? Children in one truck, or mixed with men and women? Dogs in special trucks, or just let them lie? Wondering how *many* bodies one garbage truck can hold. And wondering if you stack them on top of each other and finally knowing you must just have to. I can't figure it. I can't work it out. I try, but there's no guessing, no guessing at all how many you could stack in one single truck."

He sat thinking of how it was late in the day at his work, with the truck full and the canvas pulled over the great bulk of garbage so the bulk shaped the canvas in an uneven mound. And how it was if you suddenly pulled the canvas back and looked in. And for a few seconds you saw the white things like macaroni or noodles, only the white things were alive and boiling up, millions of them. And when the white things felt the hot sun on them they simmered down and burrowed and were gone in the lettuce and the old ground beef and the coffee grounds and the heads of white fish. After ten seconds of sunlight the white things that looked like noodles or macaroni were gone and the great bulk of garbage silent and not moving, and you drew the canvas over the bulk and looked at how the canvas folded unevenly over the hidden collection, and underneath you knew it was dark again, and things beginning to move as they must always move when things get dark again.

He was still sitting there in the empty room when the front door of the apartment burst wide. His son and daughter rushed in, laughing, and saw him sitting there, and stopped.

Their mother ran to the kitchen door, held to the edge of it quickly, and stared at her family. They saw her face and they heard her voice:

"Sit down, children, sit down!" She lifted one hand and pushed it toward them. "You're just in time."

THE SMILE

IN THE TOWN SQUARE THE QUEUE HAD FORMED AT FIVE IN the morning, while cocks were crowing far out in the rimed country and there were no fires. All about, among the ruined buildings, bits of mist had clung at first, but now with the new light of seven o'clock it was beginning to disperse. Down the road, in twos and threes, more people were gathering in for the day of marketing, the day of festival.

The small boy stood immediately behind two men who had been talking loudly in the clear air, and all of the sounds they made seemed twice as loud because of the cold. The small boy stomped his feet and blew on his red, chapped hands, and looked up at the soiled gunny-sack clothing of the men, and down the long line of men and women ahead.

"Here, boy, what're you doing out so early?" said the man behind him.

"Got my place in line, I have," said the boy.

"Whyn't you run off, give your place to someone who appreciates?"

"Leave the boy alone," said the man ahead, suddenly turning.

"I was joking." The man behind put his hand on the boy's

head. The boy shook it away coldly. "I just thought it strange, a boy out of bed so early."

"This boy's an appreciator of arts, I'll have you know," said the boy's defender, a man named Grigsby. "What's your name, lad?"

"Tom."

"Tom here is going to spit clean and true, right, Tom?"

"I sure am!"

Laughter passed down the line.

A man was selling cracked cups of hot coffee up ahead. Tom looked and saw the little hot fire and the brew bubbling in a rusty pan. It wasn't really coffee. It was made from some berry that grew on the meadowlands beyond town, and it sold a penny a cup to warm their stomachs; but not many were buying, not many had the wealth.

TOM STARED AHEAD to the place where the line ended, beyond a bombed-out stone wall.

"They say she *smiles*," said the boy.

"Aye, she does," said Grigsby.

"They say she's made of oil and canvas, and she's four centuries old."

"Maybe more. Nobody knows what year this is, to be sure."

"It's 2251!"

"That's what they say. Liars. Could be 3000 or 5000 for all we know, things were in a fearful mess there for a while. All we got now is bits and pieces."

They shuffled along the cold stones of the street.

"How much longer before we see her?" asked Tom, uneasily.

"Oh, a few minutes, boy. They got her set up with four

brass poles and velvet rope, all fancy, to keep people back. Now mind, no rocks, Tom, they don't allow rocks thrown at her."

"Yes, sir."

They shuffled on in the early morning which grew late, and the sun rose into the heavens bringing heat with it which made the men shed their grimy coats and greasy hats.

"Why're we all here in line?" asked Tom at last. "Why're we all here to spit?"

Grigsby did not glance down at him, but judged the sun. "Well, Tom, there's lots of reasons." He reached absently for a pocket that was long gone, for a cigarette that wasn't there. Tom had seen the gesture a million times. "Tom, it has to do with hate. Hate for everything in the Past. I ask you, Tom, how did we get in such a state, cities all junk, roads like jigsaws from bombs, and half the cornfields glowing with radioactivity at night? Ain't that a lousy stew, I ask you?"

"Yes, sir. I guess so."

"It's this way, Tom. You hate whatever it was that got you all knocked down and ruined. That's human nature. Unthinking, maybe, but human nature anyway."

"There's hardly nobody or nothing we don't hate," said Tom.

"Right! The whole blooming kaboodle of them people in the Past who run the world. So here we are on a Thursday morning with our guts plastered to our spines, cold, live in caves and such, don't smoke, don't drink, don't nothing except have our festivals, Tom, our festivals."

AND TOM THOUGHT OF THE FESTIVALS in the past few years. The year they tore up all the books in the square and burned

them and everyone was drunk and laughing. And the festival
of science a month ago when they dragged in the last motor car
and picked lots and each lucky man who won was allowed one
smash of a sledge-hammer at the car.

"Do I remember *that*, Tom? Do I *remember?* Why, I got
to smash the front window, the window, you hear? My god, it
made a lovely sound! *Crash!*"

Tom could hear the glass falling in glittering heaps.

"And Bill Henderson, he got to bash the engine. Oh, he did
a smart job of it, with great efficiency. Wham!"

But best of all, recalled Grigsby, there was the time they
smashed a factory that was still trying to turn out airplanes.

"Lord, did we feel good blowing it up," said Grigsby. "And
then we found that newspaper plant and the munitions depot
and exploded them together. Do you understand, Tom?"

Tom puzzled over it. "I guess."

It was high noon. Now the odors of the ruined city stank on
the hot air and things crawled among the tumbled buildings.

"Won't it ever come back, mister?"

"What, civilization? Nobody wants it. Not me!"

"I could stand a bit of it," said the man behind another
man. "There were a few spots of beauty in it."

"Don't worry your heads," shouted Grigsby. "There's no
room for that, either."

"Ah," said the man behind the man. "Someone'll come
along some day with imagination and patch it up. Mark my
words. Someone with a heart."

"No," said Grigsby.

"I say yes. Someone with a soul for pretty things. Might

give us back a kind of limited sort of civilization, the kind we could live in in peace."

"First thing you know there's war!"

"But maybe next time it'd be different."

At last they stood in the main square. A man on horseback was riding from the distance into the town. He had a piece of paper in his hand. In the center of the square was the roped-off area. Tom, Grigsby, and the others were collecting their spittle and moving forward—moving forward prepared and ready, eyes wide. Tom felt his heart beating very strongly and excitedly, and the earth was hot under his bare feet.

"Here we go, Tom, let fly!"

Four policemen stood at the corners of the roped area, four men with bits of yellow twine on their wrists to show their authority over other men. They were there to prevent rocks being hurled.

"This way," said Grigsby at the last moment, "everyone feels he's had his chance at her, you see, Tom? Go on, now!"

Tom stood before the painting and looked at it for a long time.

"Tom, spit!"

His mouth was dry.

"Get on, Tom! Move!"

"But," said Tom, slowly, "she's BEAUTIFUL!"

"Here, I'll spit for you!" Grigsby spat and the missile flew in the sunlight. The woman in the portrait smiled serenely, secretly, at Tom, and he looked back at her, his heart beating, a kind of music in his ears.

"She's beautiful," he said.

"Now get on, before the police—"

"Attention!"

The line fell silent. One moment they were berating Tom for not moving forward, now they were turning to the man on horseback.

"What do they call it, sir?" asked Tom, quietly.

"The picture? *Mona Lisa*, Tom, I think. Yes, the *Mona Lisa*."

"I have an announcement," said the man on horseback. "The authorities have decreed that as of high noon today the portrait in the square is to be given over into the hands of the populace there, so they may participate in the destruction of—"

Tom hadn't even time to scream before the crowd bore him, shouting and pummeling about, stampeding toward the portrait. There was a sharp ripping sound. The police ran to escape. The crowd was in full cry, their hands like so many hungry birds pecking away at the portrait. Tom felt himself thrust almost through the broken thing. Reaching out in blind imitation of the others, he snatched a scrap of oily canvas, yanked, felt the canvas give, then fell, was kicked, sent rolling to the outer rim of the mob. Bloody, his clothing torn, he watched old women chew pieces of canvas, men break the frame, kick the ragged cloth, and rip it into confetti.

ONLY TOM STOOD APART, silent in the moving square. He looked down at his hand. It clutched the piece of canvas close to his chest, hidden. "Hey there, Tom!" cried Grigsby.

Without a word, sobbing, Tom ran. He ran out and down the bomb-pitted road, into a field, across a shallow stream, not looking back, his hand clenched tightly, tucked under his coat.

At sunset he reached the small village and passed on through. By nine o'clock he came to the ruined farm dwelling. Around back, in the half silo, in the part that still remained upright, tented over, he heard the sounds of sleeping, the family—his mother, father and brother. He slipped quickly, silently, through the small door and lay down, panting

"Tom?" called his mother in the dark.

"Yes."

"Where've you been?" snapped his father. "I'll beat you in the morning."

Someone kicked him. His brother, who had been left behind to work their little patch of ground.

"Go to sleep," cried his mother, faintly.

Another kick.

Tom lay getting his breath. All was quiet. His hand was pushed to his chest, tight, tight. He lay for half an hour this way, eyes closed. Then he felt something, and it was a cold white light. The moon rose very high and the little square of light moved in the silo and crept slowly over Tom's body. Then, and only then, did his hand relax. Slowly, carefully, listening to those who slept about him, Tom drew his hand forth. He hesitated, sucked in his breath, and then, waiting, opened his hand and uncrumpled the tiny fragment of painted canvas.

ALL THE WORLD WAS ASLEEP in the moonlight.

And there on his hand was the Smile.

He looked at it in the white illumination from the midnight sky. And he thought, over and over to himself, quietly, *the Smile, the lovely Smile.*

An hour later he could still see it, even after he had folded it carefully and hidden it. He shut his eyes and the Smile was there in the darkness. And it was still there, warm and gentle, when he went to sleep and the world was silent and the moon sailed up and then down the cold sky toward morning.

LONG AFTER MIDNIGHT

MR. MONTAG DREAMED.

He was an old man hidden with six million dusty books. His hands crawled, trembling, over yellow pages, and his face was a smashed mirror of wrinkles by candlelight.

Then, an eye at the keyhole!

In his dream, Mr. Montag yanked the door. A boy fell in.

"Spying!"

"You got books!" cried the boy. "It's against the law! I'll tell my father!"

He grabbed the boy, who writhed, screaming.

"Don't, boy," pleaded Mr. Montag. "Don't tell. I'll give you money, books, clothes, but don't tell!"

"I seen you reading!"

"Don't!"

"I'll tell!" The boy ran, shrieking.

A crowd rushed up the street. Health officials burst in, followed by police, fierce with silver badges. And then himself! Himself as a young man, in a Fire uniform, with a torch. The room swarmed while the old man pleaded with himself as a young man. Books crashed down. Books were stripped and torn. Windows crashed inward, drapes fell in sooty clouds.

Outside, staring in, was the boy who had turned him in.

"No! Please!"

Flame crackled. They were charring out the room, with controlled, scientific fire. A vast wind of flame devoured the walls. Books exploded in a million live kernels.

"For the love of God!"

The ancient lawn of the room sizzled.

The hooks became black ravens, fluttering.

Mr. Montag fell shrieking to the far end of the dream.

He opened his eyes.

"Blackjack," said Mr. Leahy.

Mr. Montag stared at the playing cards in his cold hand. He was awake. He was in the Fire House. And they were dealing Blackjack at one-thirty in the dark morning.

"You're doing badly, Montag."

"What?" Montag shivered.

"What's eating him?" Everyone raised their black eyebrows.

A radio was playing in the smoky ceiling over their heads. "War may be declared any hour. This country is ready to defend its destiny. War may be declared . . ."

The room shook. Some planes were flying over, filling the sky with invisible vibration. The men played their cards.

They sat in their black uniforms, trim men, with the look of thirty years in their blue-shaved faces and their receding hair, and the blue veins on the back of their hands becoming more prominent. On the table in the corner in neat rows lay auxiliary helmets and thick overcoats. On the walls, in precise sharpness, hung gold-plated hatchets, with inscriptions under them from famous fires. Under their nervous feet, under the wooden floor, stood the silent huge fire apparatus, the boa-constrictor hoses, the pumps, the glittery brass and silver, the crimson and gold. The brass pole, distorting their game, stood mirror-shiny through the floor-hole.

"I've been thinking about that last job," said Mr. Montag.

"Don't," said Mr. Leahy, putting down the cards.

"That poor man, when we burned his library."

"He had it coming to him," said Black.

"Right," said Stone.

The four men played another game. Montag watched the calendar on the wall which was mechanical and which now read five minutes after one A.M. Thursday October 4th, in the year 2052 A.D.

"I was wondering how it'd feel if Firemen broke in my house and burned my books."

"You haven't any books." Leahy smiled.

"But if I did have some."

"You got some?" The men turned their faces to him.

"No," he said.

Yes, Mr. Montag's mind said. He had some books, hidden away, unread. In the last year, in the crashing and breaking, in burning confusion, his hand, like a separate thief, had snatched a volume here, a volume there, hid it in his fat coat, or under his pompous helmet, and, trembling, he had gone home to hide it before drinking his nightly glass of milk, and so to bed with Mildred, his wife.

"No," he said, looking at his cards, not the men. He glanced at the wall suddenly. And there hung the long lists of a million forbidden books. The names leaped out in fire, he saw the names burning down the years, under his ax, under his hose that sprayed not water but kerosene!

"Was it always like this?" asked Mr. Montag. "The Fire House, our duties, the city, was it?"

"I don't know," said Leahy. "Do you, Black?"

"No. Do you, Stone?"

Stone smiled at Mr. Montag.

"I mean," said Montag, "that once upon a time—"

"Once upon a time?" said Leahy, quietly. "What kind of language is that?"

Fool! cried Mr. Montag to himself. You'll give it away. That book. The last fire. A book of fairy tales. He had dared to read a line or so . . .

"Old fancy language here," said Leahy, looking at the ceiling.

"Yeah," said Black.

"I mean, once there were fires in the town, houses burnt down. That was before houses were completely fireproof, I guess. And Fire Men went to fires to put them out, not start them."

"Oh?" said Leahy.

"I never knew that." Stone drew forth a rule card from his shirt pocket and laid it on the table where Montag, though knowing its message by heart, could read it:

RULE ONE: ANSWER THE ALARM QUICKLY.

TWO: START THE FIRE SWIFTLY.

THREE: BE SURE YOU BURN EVERYTHING.

FOUR: REPORT BACK TO THE FIRE HOUSE RAPIDLY.

FIVE: STAY ALERT FOR ANOTHER ALARM.

"Well, well," said Mr. Stone.

They watched Montag.

Montag said, "What will they do to that old man we caught last night?"

"Thirty years in the insane asylum."

"But he wasn't insane."

"Any man's insane to think he can fool the government or us." Leahy began to shuffle the cards.

The alarm sounded.

The bell kicked itself thirty times in five seconds. The next thing Mr. Montag knew there were three empty chairs, the cards in a kind of snow flurry on the air, the brass pole trembling and empty, the men gone, their hats gone with them. He still sat. Below, the mighty engine coughed to life.

Mr. Montag slid down the pole like a man returning to a dream.

"Hey, Montag, you forgot your hat!"

And they were off, the night wind hammering about their siren noise and their mighty metal thunder.

IT WAS A TWO-STORY HOUSE in the old district of town. A century old it was, if it was a day, but it, like many others had been given a thin fireproof coating fifty years ago, and as a result the thin preservative layer seemed to be holding it up. One sneeze and . . .

"Here we are, boys!"

Leahy and Stone and Black clubbered across the sidewalk making the ridiculous wet rubber sounds of men in thick soft boots, suddenly odious and fat because of their thick coats, suddenly childlike and full of games because of the thick huge hats on their heads. Mr. Montag followed.

"Is this the right place?"

"Voice on the phone said 757 Oak Knoll, name of Skinner."

"This is it."

They walked through the front door.

A woman was running. They caught her.

"I didn't do anything," she said. "What did I do? I didn't harm anyone!"

"Where is it?" Leahy glared about as if the walls were poisonous. "Come on now, fessup, where are they?"

"You wouldn't take an old woman's pleasures from her."

"Save that. It'll go easier with you if you tell."

She said nothing but simply swayed before them.

"Let's have the report, Stone." Stone produced the telephone alarm card with the complaint signed in telephone duplicate on the back. "It says here, you've an attic full of books. All right, men!"

Next thing they were up in the musty blackness, clumping with their boots and swinging hatchets at doors that were unlocked, tumbling through like children at a playpool in summer, all rollick and shout. "Hey!" A fountain of books leaped down upon Montag as he climbed shuddering up the steep stair well. Books struck his head, his shoulders, his upturned, lined, pale face. He held his hands up and a book landed obediently in them, like an open flower! In the dim light a page fell open and it was like a petal with words delicately flourished there. In all the fervor and rushing he had only time to read a line, but it blazed in his mind for the next minute, as if he had been stamped with a hot bronze iron. He dropped the book, but almost immediately another fell into his hand.

"Hey, there, you, come on!"

Montag closed his hand like a trap on the book, he crushed it to his breast. Another fount descended, a gush of books, a torrent of literature, Stone and Black seizing and hurling them down in shovelfuls from above, down down through dusty space, through the echoing house toward Montag and the woman who stood like a small girl under the collecting ruin. "Come on, Montag!"

And he was forced to clump up and in to lend a hand, though he fell twice.

"In here!"

"This too shall pass away."

"What?" Leahy glared at him.

Montag stopped, blinking, in the dark.

"Did I say something?"

"Don't stand there, idiot, move!"

The books lay in piles like fishes left to dry, and the air was so thick with a gunpowdery dust that at any instant it might blow them through the roof into the stars. "Trash! Trash!" The men kicked books. They danced among them. Titles glittered like golden eyes, gone, falling.

"Kerosene!"

Stone and Black pumped out the fluid from the white hose they had carried up the stairs. They coated each remaining book with the shining stuff. They pumped it into rooms.

"This is better than the old man's place last night, eh?"

That had been different. The old man had lived in an apartment house with other people. They had had to use controlled fire there. Here, they could rampage the whole house.

When they ran downstairs, with Montag reeling after them, the house was aflame with kerosene. The walls were drenched.

"Come on, woman!"

"My books," she said, quietly. She stood among them now, kneeling down to touch them, to run fingers over the leather, reading the golden titles with fingers instead of eyes, by touch in this instant, while her eyes accused Montag. "You can't take my books. They're my whole life."

"You know the law," said Leahy.

"But . . ."

"Confusion. People who never existed. Fantasy, pure fantasy all of it. No two books alike, none agreeing. Come on now, lady, out of your house, it'll burn."

"No," she said.

"The whole thing'll go up in one bloom."

"No."

The three men went to the door. They looked at Montag who stood near the woman. "Okay, Montag."

"You're not going to leave her here?" he protested.

"She won't come."

"But you must force her!"

Leahy raised his hand. It contained the concealed igniter to start the fire. "No time. Got to get back to the station. Besides, she'd cost us a trial, money, months, jail, all that." He examined his wristwatch. "Got to get back on the alert."

Montag put his hand on the woman's arm. "You can come with me. Here, let me help you."

"No." She actually saw him for a moment. "Thank you, anyway."

"I'm counting to ten," said Leahy. "Outside, Montag! Stone. Black." He began counting. "One. Two."

"Lady," said Montag.

"Go on," she said.

"Three," said Leahy.

"Come on," said Montag, tugging at her.

"I like it here," she said.

"Four. Five," said Leahy.

He tried to pull her, but she twisted, he slipped and fell. She ran up the stairs and stood there, with the books at her feet.

"Six. Seven. Montag," said Leahy.

Montag did not move. He looked out the door at that man there with the apparatus in his hand. He felt the book hidden against his chest.

"Go get him," said Leahy.

Stone and Black dragged Montag yelling from the house.

Leahy backed out after them, leaving a kerosene trail down the walk. When they were a hundred feet from the house, Montag was still kicking at the two men. He glanced back wildly.

In the front door where she had come to look out at them quietly, her quietness a condemnation, staring straight into Mr. Leahy's eyes, was the woman. She had a book in one hand.

Leahy reached down and ignited the kerosene.

People ran out on their porches all down the street.

"WHO IS IT?"

"Who would it be?" said Mr. Montag, now leaning against the closed door in the dark.

His wife said, at last. "Well, put on the light."

"No."

"Why not? Turn it on."

"I don't want the light."

The room was black.

"Take off your clothes. Come to bed."

"What?"

He heard her roll impatiently; the springs squeaked. "Are you drunk?"

He took off his clothes. He worked out of his coat and let it slump to the floor. He removed his pants and held them in the air and let them drop.

His wife said, "What are you doing?"

He balanced himself in the room with the book in his sweating, icy hand.

A minute later she said, "Just don't stand there in the middle of the room."

He made a sound.

"What?" she asked.

He made more sounds. He walked to the bed and shoved the book clumsily under the pillow. He fell into the bed and his wife called out at this. He lay separate from her. She talked to him for a long while and when he didn't answer but only made sounds, he felt her hand creep over, up along his chest, his throat, his chin. Her hand brushed his cheeks. He knew that she pulled her hand away from his cheeks wet.

A long time later, when he was at last drifting into sleep, he heard her say, "You smell of kerosene . . ."

Late in the night he looked over at Mildred. She was awake. Many nights in the past ten years he had come awake and found her with her eyes open in the dim room. She would look that way, blankly, for an hour or more, and then rise and go into the bathroom. You could hear the water run into the glass, the tinkle of the sedatives bottle, and Mildred gulping hungrily, frantically, at sleep.

She was awake now. In a minute she would rise and go for the barbiturate.

And suddenly she was so strange to him that he couldn't believe that he knew her at all. He was in someone else's house, with a woman he had never seen before, and this made him shift uneasily under the covers.

"Awake?" she whispered.

"Yes. Millie?"

"What?"

"Mildred, when did we meet? And where?"

"For what?" she asked.

"I mean, originally."

She was frowning in the dark.

He clarified it. "The first time we met, where, when?"

"Why it was at—"

She stopped.

"I don't know."

"Neither do I," he said, frightened. "Can't you remember?"

They both tried to remember.

"It's been so long."

"We're only thirty!"

"Don't get excited—I'm trying to think!"

"Think, then!"

She laughed. "Wait until I tell Rene! How funny, not to remember where or when you met your wife or husband!"

He did not laugh, but lay there with his eyes tight, his face screwed up, pressing and massaging his brow, tapping and thumping his blind head again and again.

"It can't be very important." She was up, in the bath now, the water running, the swallowing sound.

"No, not very," he said.

And he wondered, did she take two tablets now, or twenty, like a year ago, when we had to pump her stomach at the hospital, and me shouting to keep her awake, walking her, asking her why she did it, why she wanted to die, and she said she didn't know, she didn't know, she didn't know anything about anything. But he thought he had known for her . . . She didn't belong to him. He didn't belong to her. She didn't know herself, or him, or anyone. The world didn't need her. She didn't need herself. And in the hospital looking down at her he had realized that if she should die in the next minute, he wouldn't cry. For it was the dying of a stranger. And it was suddenly so very wrong that he had cried not at death but at the thought of not crying at death, a silly man, empty, beside an empty woman while the doctors emptied her stomach still more.

And why are we empty and lonely and not in love, he had asked himself, a year ago. Why are we strangers in the same house? That was the first time he had begun to think about the world and how it was made, and his job, all of it.

And then he realized what it was. They were never together. There was always something between. A radio, a television set, a car, a plane, nervous exhaustion, a mad rushing, or, simply, a little pheno-barbitol. They didn't know each other. They knew things. They knew inventions. They had both applauded while science had built a beautiful glass structure, a fine glittering wonder, so precise and mechanical and wonder-ful that it was glorious, and, too late, discovered that it was a glass wall, through which they could not shout, through which they gestured empty pantomime silently, never touching, never hearing, never seeing really, never smelling or tasting one another.

Looking at her in the hospital he had thought, I don't know you, who are you, does it matter if we live or die?

That might not have been enough, if the people had not moved next door, with their beautiful daughter. Twelve months ago it had been, hadn't it, he had first seen the dark young girl?

PERHAPS THAT HAD BEEN THE START of his awareness. One night, as had become his custom over the years, he had gone out for a long walk. Two things happened as he strolled along in the moonlight. One, he realized that he had gone out to escape the crash of the television set, whereas always before he had put it down to nervous tension. Second, he noted what he had often seen but never thought about, that he was the only pedestrian in the entire city. He passed street after empty street. At a distance cars moved like fire-bugs in the misting darkness, faintly hooting. But no other man ventured upon the earth to test the concrete with foot or cane, in fact it had been so long since the sidewalks were steadily used that they were beginning to lump up and crack and become overgrown with hardy flowers and grass.

And so he walked alone, suddenly realizing his loneliness, exhaling a powdery vapor from his mouth and watching the pattern.

That was the night the police stopped him and searched him.

"What're you doing?"

"Out for a walk?"

"He says he's out for a walk, Jim."

The laughter. The cold precise turning over of his identity cards, the careful noting of his home address.

"Okay, mister, you can walk now."

He had gone on, hands in pockets, in such a rage at being questioned for being a simple pedestrian, that he had to stop and hold onto himself, for his rage was all out of proportion to the incident.

And then the girl had turned a corner and walked by.

"Hello," she said, half turning. "Aren't you my neighbor?"

"Of course," he said. She was smiling at him.

"We're the only live ones, aren't we?" she said. She waved at the streets. "Did they stop you, too?"

"Walking is a misdemeanor."

"They flashed their lights on me for a minute and saw I was a woman and went on," she said. She looked no more than sixteen. "I'm Clarisse McClellan. And you're Mr. Montag, the fireman."

They walked along together.

"Isn't it like a city of the dead," she said. "I like to come out and walk around just to keep my franchise on the sidewalks."

He looked, and the city was like a tombyard, houses dark for television. He did not know what to say.

"Have you ever noticed all the cars rushing," she said. "On the streets down there, the big ones, day and night. I sometimes think they don't know what grass is or flowers, because they never see them slowly. If you showed them a green blur, oh yes they'd say, that's grass. Or a pink blur, yes, that's roses." She laughed to herself. "And a white blur, that's a house. And quick brown blurs, those are cows. My uncle drove slow on a highway once and they threw him in jail. Isn't that funny and sad, too?"

"You think about a lot of things for a girl," said Montag, looking over at her.

"I have to. I have so much time to think. I never watch TV or go to the races or the fun parks or any of that. So I have time to think lots of crazy things. Have you noticed the elongated billboards in the country, two hundred feet long. Did you know that once those billboards were only 25 feet long? But cars started going by them so swiftly they had to stretch them out so they could be seen?"

"I didn't know that." Montag laughed.

"I bet I know something else you don't know," she said.

"What?"

"There's dew on the grass in the morning."

"Is there?" He couldn't remember, and it suddenly frightened him.

"And there's a man in the moon if you look."

He had never looked. His heart began to beat rapidly.

They walked silently from there on. When they reached her house the lights were all on, it was the only house on the street with bright lights.

"What's going on?" said Montag. He had never seen that many lights.

"Oh just my mother and father and my uncle and aunt. They're sitting around talking. It's like being a pedestrian, only rarer. Come over some time and try the water."

"But what do you talk about?"

She laughed at this and said good night and was gone.

At three o'clock in the morning he got out of bed and looked out the window. The moon was rising and there was a man in the moon, and upon the broad lawn, a million jewels of dew sparkled and glittered. "I'll be damned," he said, and went back to bed.

He saw Clarisse many afternoons sitting on her green lawn, studying the autumn leaves, or returning from the woods with wild flowers, or looking at the sky, even while it was raining.

"Isn't it nice?" she said.

"What?"

"The rain, of course."

"I hadn't noticed."

"Believe me, it *is* nice."

He always laughed embarrassedly, whether at her, or at himself, he was never certain. "I believe you."

"Do you really? Do you ever smell old leaves? Don't they smell like cinnamon."

"Well—"

"Here, smell."

"Why, it is cinnamon, yes!"

She gazed at him with her clear grey eyes. "My gosh, you don't really know very much do you." It was not unkind, but concerned with him.

"I don't suppose any of us do."

"I do," she said. "Because I've time to look."

"Don't you attend school?"

"Oh, no, they say I'm anti-social. I don't mix. And the yelling extrovert is the thing this season, you know."

"It's been a long season," observed Mr. Montag, and stood shocked at his own perception.

"Then you've noticed?"

"Where are your friends?" he asked.

"I haven't any."

"None?"

"No. That's supposed to mean I'm abnormal. But they're always packed around the TV, or rushing in cars, or shouting or hurting each other. Do you notice how people hurt people nowadays?"

"You sound ancient."

"I am. I know about rain. That makes me ancient to them. They kill each other. It didn't used to be that way, did it? Children killing each other all the time. Four of my friends have been shot in the past year. I'm afraid of *them*."

"Maybe it was always this way."

"My father says no, says his grandfather remembers when children didn't kill each other, when children were seen and not heard. But that was a long time ago when they had discipline. When they had responsibility. Do you know, *I'm* disciplined. I'm beat when I need it. And I've responsibility, I tend to the whole house three days a week."

"And you know about rain," said Mr. Montag.

"Yes. It tastes good if you lean back and open your mouth. Go on!"

He leaned back and gaped.

"Why," he said, "it's wine!"

THAT HAD NOT BEEN THE END OF IT. The girl, while only 16, was always about, it seemed, and he caught himself looking for her. She was the only one who had ever given him the dandelion test.

"It proves you're in love or not.

That was the day he knew he didn't love Mildred.

Clarisse passed the dandelion under his chin.

"Oh, you're not in love with anyone. What a shame!"

And he thought, when did I stop loving Mildred, and the answer was never! For he had never known her. She was the pale sad goldfish that swam in the subterranean illumination of the TV set, her natural habitat the yeasty chairs especially placed for viewing.

"It's the dandelion you used," he protested. "Use another."

"No," said Clarisse. "You're not in love. A dandelion won't help." She got up. "Well, I've got to go see my psychiatrist. The school sends me to him. So I can go back to school, he's trying to make me normal."

"I'll kill him if he does!"

He didn't see Clarisse for a month. He watched for her each day. And after some forty days had passed, one afternoon, he mentioned it to his wife.

"Oh, her," said Mildred, with the radio music jarring the table plates. "Why, she was killed by an auto a month ago."

"A month!" He leaped up. "But why didn't you tell me!"

"Didn't I? A car hit her."

"Did they find whose car it was?"

"No. You know how those things are. What do you want for supper, dear, frozen steak or an omelet?"

And so with the death of the girl, 1 percent of the world died. And the other 99 percent was on the instant revealed to him for what it was. He saw what she had been and what

Mildred had been, was, and always would be, what he himself was but didn't want to be any more, what Millie's friends were and would forever be. And he saw that it was no idle, separate thing, Mildred's suicide attempts, the lovely dark girl with the flowers and the leaves being ground under a motor-car, it was a thing of the world they lived in, it was all a parcel of the world, it was part of the screaming average, of the pressing down of people into electric moulds, it was the vacuum of civilization in its meaningless cam-shaft rotations down a rotary track to smash against its own senseless tail. Suddenly Millie's attempts at death were a symbol. She was trying to escape from Nothingness. Whereas the girl had been fighting nothingness with something, with being aware instead of forgetting, with walking instead of sitting, with going to get life instead of having it brought to her. And the civilization had killed her for her trouble, not purposely no, but with a fine ironic sense, for no purpose at all, simply the blind rushing destruction of a car driven by a vanilla-faced idiot going nowhere for nothing, and very irritated that he had been detained for 120 seconds while the police investigated and released him on his way to some distant base that he must tag before running for home.

Mildred. Clarisse. Life. And his own work, growing aware for the first time of what he was doing. And now, tonight. Burning that woman. And last night, the man's book, and him into an asylum. It was all such a nightmare that only a nightmare could be used as an escape from it.

He lay there all night, thinking, smelling the smoke on his hands, in the dark.

He awoke with chills and fever in the morning.

"You can't be sick," said Mildred.

He looked at his wife. He closed his eyes upon the hotness and the trembling. "Yes."

"But you were all right, last night."

"I'm sick now." He heard the radio shouting in the parlor.

She stood over the bed, curiously. He felt her there, looking at him but he didn't open his eyes. He felt his body shake as if there was another person in it somewhere pounding away at his ribs, someone pulling at the bars of a prison screaming, with no one to hear. Did Mildred hear?

"Will you bring me some water and aspirin."

"You've got to get up," she said. "It's noon. You've slept five hours later than usual."

There she lay with her hair burnt to straw, her eyes with a kind of cataract far behind the pupils unseen but suspect, and the reddened, pouting lips, and the body as thin as a praying mantis from diet, and the flesh like thin milk, and the voice with that metallic ferocity that came from imitating radio voices. He could remember her no other way.

"Will you turn the radio off?"

"That's my program."

"Will you turn it off for a sick man?"

"I'll turn it down," she said.

She went out of the room and did nothing to the radio. She came back. "Is that better?"

He opened his eyes and wondered at her. "Thanks."

"That's my favorite program," she said.

"What about the aspirin?" he said.

"You've never been sick before." She went away again.

"Well, I'm sick now. I'm not going to work this evening. Call Healy for me."

"You acted funny last night," she said, coming back, humming.

"Where's the aspirin," he said, looking at the glass of water she handed him.

"Oh," she said, and went off again. "Did something happen?"

"A fire, is all."

"I had a nice evening," she said, in the bathroom.

"What doing?"

"Television."

"What was on."

"Programs."

"What programs?"

"Some of the best ever."

"Who?"

"Oh, you know, the bunch."

"Yes, the bunch, the bunch, the bunch." He pressed at the pain in his eyes and suddenly the odor of kerosene was so strong that he vomited.

She came back, humming. She was surprised. "Why'd you do that?"

He looked with dismay at what he had done. "We burned an old woman with her books."

"It's a good thing the rug's washable." She fetched a mop and worked on it. "I went to Helen's last night."

"What for?"

"Television."

"Couldn't you get it on your own set."

"Sure, but it's nice visiting."

"How's Helen?"

"All right."

"Did she get over that infection in her hand?"

"I didn't notice."

She went out into the living room. He heard her by the radio humming.

"Mildred," he called.

She came back, singing, snapping her fingers softly.

"Aren't you going to ask me about last night?" he said.

"What about it?"

"We burned a thousand books and a woman."

"Forbidden books."

The radio was exploding in the parlor.

"Yes," he said. "Copies of Edgar Allan Poe and William Shakespeare and Plato."

"Wasn't he a European?"

"Something like that."

"Wasn't he a radical?"

"I don't know, I never read him."

"He was a radical." Mildred fiddled with the telephone. "You don't expect me to call Mr. Leahy, do you?"

"You must!"

"Don't shout."

"I wasn't shouting!" he cried. He was up in bed, enraged and flushed, trembling. The radio roared in the tight air. "I can't call him. I can't tell him I'm sick. You've got to do it."

"Why?"

"Because . . ."

Because you're afraid, he thought. A child pretending illness. Afraid to call Leahy, because after only a moment's discussion the conversation would run like this: "Yes, Mr. Leahy, I feel better already. I'll be in at six o'clock. I'm fine."

"You're not sick," she said.

Mr. Montag propped himself up in bed and felt, secretly, for the book under his warm pillow. It was still there. "Millie?"

"What?"

"How would it be if, well, maybe, I went away for a little rest. Quit my job awhile."

Her mouth was open and now she had pivoted to stare at him.

"You *are* sick, aren't you?"

"Don't take it that way!"

"You want to give up everything. You need your head examined. Why your father was a fireman, and his father before him."

"Mildred."

"After all these years of working hard, to give it all up because one night, one morning you're sick, lying to me, all because of some woman."

"You should have seen her, Millie."

"She's nothing to me, she shouldn't have had books. It was her responsibility, she should've thought of that. I hate her. She's got you going and next you know we'll be out, no job, no house, nothing."

"Shut up."

"I won't."

"I'll shut you up in a moment," he cried, almost out of bed. "You weren't there. You didn't see. There must be something in books, whole worlds we don't dream about, to make a woman stay in a burning house, there must be something fine there, you don't stay for nothing."

"She was simple-minded."

"She was as rational as you or I, and we *burned* her!"

"That's water under the bridge."

"No, not water, Millie, but fire. You ever see a burnt house? It smolders for days. Well, this fire'll last me half a century. My God, I was trying to put it out all night, and I was crazy in trying!"

"You should've thought of that before becoming a fireman."

"Thought!" he cried. "Was I given a choice? I was raised to think the best thing in the world is not to read. The best thing is listening to radios, watching television sets, filling your mind with pap and swill. My God, it's only now I realize what I've done. I went into this job because it was just a job."

The radio was playing a dance tune.

"I've been killing the brain of the world for ten years, pouring kerosene on it. My God, Millie, a book is a brain, it isn't only that woman we killed, or others like her, in these years, but it's the thoughts I burned with fire reckless abandon."

He got out of bed.

"It took a man a lifetime to put some of his thoughts on paper, looking after all the beauty and goodness in life, and then we come along in five minutes and toss it in the incinerator!"

"I'm proud to say," said Mildred, eyes wide. "I never read a book in my life."

"And look at you!" he said. "Turn you on and I get predigested news, gossip, tidbits from daytime serials. Why even the music you hum is some deodorant commercial!"

"Let me alone," she said.

"Let you alone is what you don't need. That's what's wrong.

You need to be bothered. No one's bothered any more. No-body thinks. Let a baby alone, why don't you? What would you have in twenty years, if you let a baby alone, a gangling idiot!"

A motor sounded outside the house. Mildred went to the window, "Now you've done it," she wailed. "Look who's here."

"I don't give a damn." He stood up and he was feeling bet-ter, but he didn't know why. He stalked to the window.

"Who is it?"

"Mr. Leahy!"

The elation drained away. Mr. Montag slumped.

"Go open the door," he said, at last. "I'll get back to bed. Tell him I'm sick."

"Tell him yourself."

He hurried back, cold and suddenly shaking again, as if lightning had struck just beyond the window. In the white glare, he found the pillow, made sure the terrible book was hid-den, climbed in, and had made himself uneasily comfortable, when the door opened and Mr. Leahy strolled in.

"SHUT THE RADIO OFF," said Leahy, abstractedly.

This time, Mildred obeyed.

Mr. Leahy sat down in a comfortable chair and folded one knee over another, not looking at Mr. Montag.

"Just thought I'd come by and see how the sick man is."

"How'd you guess!"

"Oh." Leahy smiled his pink smile and shrugged. "I'm an old hand at this. I've seen it all. You were going to call me and tell me you needed a day off."

"Yes."

"Take a day off," said Leahy. "Take two. But *never* take

three. Not, that is, unless, you're really ill. Remember that."
He took a cigar from his pocket and cut off a little piece to
chew. "When will you be well?"

"Tomorrow, the next day, first of the week."

"We've been talking about you," said Leahy. "Every man
goes through this. They only need a little understanding. They
need to be told how the wheels run."

"And how do they?"

"Mr. Montag, you don't seem to have assimilated the history of your honorable trade. They don't give it to rookies any
more. Only fire chiefs remember it now. I'll let you in on it."
He chewed a moment.

"Yes," said Montag. Mildred fidgeted.

"You ask yourself why, how, and when. About the books."

"Maybe."

"It started in the early 1900s, I'd say. After the Civil War
maybe. Photography invented. Fast print presses. Films. Television. Things began to have mass, Montag, mass."

"I see."

"And because they had mass, they had to become simpler.
Books now. Once they appealed to various bits of people here
and there. They could afford to be different. The world was
roomy. Plenty of room for elbows and differentness, right?"

"Right."

"But then the world got full of mass and elbows. And
things for lots of millions of people had to be simple. Films
and radio and TV and big big magazines had to be a sort of
paste-pudding norm, you might say. Follow me?"

"I think."

"Picture it. The nineteenth century man with his horses

and books and leisure. You might call him the Slow Motion man. Everyone taking a year to sit down, get up, jump a fence. Then, in the Twentieth Century you speed up the camera."

"A good simile."

"Splendid. Books get shorter. Condensations appear. Tabloids. Radio programs simplify. The exquisite pantomime of great actors become the pratfall. Everything sublimates itself to the joke, the gag, the snap ending. Everything is sacrificed for pace."

"Pace." Mildred smiled.

"Great classics are cut to fit a fifteen minute show, then a two minute Book column, then a two line Dictionary resume. Magazines become picture books! Out of the nursery to the college back to the nursery, in a few short centuries!"

Mildred got up. She was losing the thread of the talk, Montag knew, and when this happened, she began to fiddle with things. She went about the room, cleaning up. Leahy ignored her.

"Faster and faster the film, Mr. Montag, quick! Men over hurdles, dogs over stiles, horses over fences! CLICK? PIC, LOOK, EYE, NOW? FLICK, HERE, THERE? QUICK, WHY, HOW, WHO, EH?, Mr. Montag! The world's political affairs become one paper column, a sentence, a headline. Then, in mid-air, vanishes. Look at your man now, quick over hurdles, over stile, horse over fence so swift you can't see the blur. And the mind of man, whirling so fast under the pumping hands of publishers, exploiters, broad-casters that the centrifuge throws off all ideas! He is unable to concentrate."

Mildred was smoothing the bed now. Montag felt panic as she approached his pillow to straighten it. The book was behind the pillow! And she would pull it out, not knowing, of course, in front of Leahy!

"School is shortened. Short cuts are made, philosophies and languages dropped. English dropped. Spelling dropped. Life is immediate. The job is what counts. Why learn anything except how to work your hands, press a button, pull a switch, fit a bolt?"

"Yes," quavered Montag.

"Let me fix your pillow," said Mildred, smiling.

"No," whispered Montag.

"The button is replaced by the zipper. Does a man have time to think while he dresses, a philosophical time, in the morning."

"He does not," said Montag, automatically.

Mildred pulled at the pillow.

"Get away," said Montag.

"Life becomes one Big Prat Fall, Mr. Montag. No more of the subtleties, everything is bang and boff and wow!"

"Wow," said Mildred, yanking at the pillow.

"For God's sake, leave me alone," said Montag. Leahy stared at him.

Mildred's hand was thrusting behind him.

"The theatres are empty, Mr. Montag. Something that was getting meaningless is replaced by something evermore massive and meaningless, the television set, and after that The Clam."

"What's this?" said Mildred. Montag crushed back against her hand. "What've you got hidden here?"

"Go sit down," he screamed at her. She drew back, her hand empty. "We're talking."

"As I was saying," said Leahy. "Cartoons everywhere. Books become cartoons. The mind drinks in less and less. Impatience. Nervous impatience. Time to kill. No work. Highways full of crowds going somewhere, anywhere, nowhere. Impatience to be somewhere they are not, not where they are. The gasoline refugee, towns becoming almost exclusively motels. And people in vast nomadic moves from city to city, impatient, following the moon tides, living tonight in the room where you slept last night and I slept the night before."

Mildred went in the other room and shut the door. She turned on the radio.

"Go on," said Montag.

"Along with the technological rush, there was the minority problem. The bigger a population, the more minorities. It's hard to find a majority in a big mass. And since the Mass Market was with us there were ten thousand minorities, union minorities, church minorities, racial minorities, dog lovers, cat lovers."

"Professional Irishmen, Texans, Brooklynites," suggested Mr. Montag, sweating. He leaned back hard on the hidden book.

"Right. Swedes, Britons, French, people from Oregon, Illinois, Mexico. You couldn't have doctors as villains, or lawyers, or merchants or chiefs. The UN prevented your doing films on past wars. The Dog Protectors had to be pleased and bull fights were banished. All the minorities with their own little navels that had to be kept clean. Intelligent men gave up in disgust.

"Pictures became puddings. Magazines were tapioca. The book buyer, the ticket buyer bored by dishwater, his brain spinning, quit buying, the trades died a slow death. There you have it. Don't blame the government. Technology coupled with mass exploitation, coupled with censorship from minorities. All you've got today to read is comic books, confessions, and trade journals."

"I know," said Montag.

"The psychologists killed off Edgar Allan Poe, said his stories were bad for the mind. They killed off fairy tales, too. Fantasy. Not facing facts, they said."

"But why the firemen," said Montag at last. "Why all the fear and the prejudice and the burning and killing now?"

"Ah," said Leahy, leaning forward to finish. "Books went out of fashion. Minority groups in order to insure their security made sure the censorship was fastened tight. Psychiatrists helped. They needn't have bothered. By that time people were uneducated. They stayed away from books, and, in ignorance, hated and feared them. You always fear something you don't know. Men have been burned at the stake for centuries, for knowing too much."

"Yes," said Montag. "The worst thing you can call a man today is a 'professor' or 'intellectual.' It's a swear word."

"Intelligence is suspect, for good reason. The little man fears someone'll put something over on him as does the big man. So the best thing is to keep everybody as dumb as everybody else. The little man wants you and me to be like him. Rewrite the slogan. Not everyone born free and equal, but everyone *made* equal. Crush the IQs down to the sub-norm. A book is a loaded gun in the house next door. Burn it. Take the shout out of the weapon. Unbreach men's minds. Who knows who might be the target of the well-read man. And so, the Fire Men came into being. You, Mr. Montag, and me."

Leahy stood up. "I've got to go."

"Thanks for talking to me."

"You needed to be put straight. Now that you understand it, you'll see our civilization, because it's so big, has to be placid. We can't have minorities stirred and upset. People must be content, Mr. Montag. Books upset them. Colored people who don't like *Little Black Sambo* are unhappy. So we burn *Little Black Sambo*. White people who read *Uncle Tom's Cabin* are unhappy. We burn that, too. Keep everyone calm and happy. That's the trick."

Leahy walked over and shook Mr. Montag's hand.

"One more thing."

"Yes."

"Every fireman gets curious."

"I imagine."

"What do the books say, he wonders. A good question. They say nothing, Mr. Montag, nothing you can touch or believe in. They're about people who never existed. Figments of the mind. Can you trust figments? No. Figments and confusion. But anyway, a fireman steals a book at a fire, almost by accident, a copy of the Bible, perhaps. A natural thing."

"Natural."

"We allow for that. We let him keep it 24 hours. If he hasn't burned it by then, we burn it for him."

"Thanks," said Mr. Montag.

"I think you have a special edition of this one book the Bible, haven't you?"

Montag felt his mouth move. "Yes."

"You'll be at work tonight at six o'clock?"

"No," said Montag.

"What!"

Montag shut his eyes and opened them. "I'll be in later, maybe."

"See that you do," said Leahy, smiling. "And bring the book with you, then, eh, after you've looked it over?"

"I'll never come in again," yelled Montag, in his mind.

"Get well," said Leahy, and went out.

He watched Leahy drive away in his gleaming beetle the color of the last fire they had set.

Mildred was listening to the radio in the front room.

Montag cleared his throat in the door. She didn't look up, but laughed at something the radio announcer said.

"It's only a step," said Montag. "From not going to work today to not going tomorrow, and then not for a year."

"What do you want for lunch?" asked Mildred.

"How can you be hungry at a time like this!"

"You're going to work tonight, aren't you?"

"I'm doing more than that," he said. "I'm going to start killing people and raving and buying books!"

"A one man revolution?" she said, lightly. "They'd put you in jail."

"That's not a bad idea." He put his clothes on, furiously, walking about the bedroom. "But I'd kill a few people before I did get locked up. There's a real bastard, that Leahy, did you *hear* him? Knows all the answers, but does nothing about it!"

"I won't have anything to do with all this junk," she said.

"No?" he said. "This is your house, isn't it, as well as mine?"

"Yes."

"Then look at this!"

She watched as he ran into the hall, peered up at a little ceiling vent. He got a chair and climbed up and opened the vent. Reaching in, he began tossing books, big books, little books, red, yellow, green, black-covered books, ten, thirty, forty of them into the parlor at her feet. "There," he cried. "So you're not in this with me? You're in it up to your neck!"

"Leonard!" She stood looking at them. She looked at the house, the furniture. "They'll burn our house down if they find these, and put us in jail for life or kill us." She edged away, wailing.

"Let them try!"

She hesitated, and then in one motion bent and threw a book at the fireplace.

He caught her, shrieking, and took another book from her hand. "Oh, no, Millie, no. Never touch these books. If you do I'll give you the beating of your life." He shook her. "Listen." He held her very firmly and her face bobbed; tears streaked down her rouged cheeks. "You're going to help me. You're in it now. You're going to read a book, one of these. Sit down. I'll help you. You're going to do something with me about men like Leahy and this city we live in. Do you hear me?"

"Yes, I hear." Her body was sagging.

The door bell rang.

They both jerked about to glance at the door and the books strewn about in heaps.

The door bell rang again.

"Sit down." Montag pushed his wife gently into the chair. He handed her a book.

The bell rang a third time.

"Read." He pointed to a page. "Out loud."

"The tongue of the wise useth knowledge aright."

The bell sounded.

"Go on."

"But the mouth of fools poureth out foolishness."

Another ring.

"They'll go away after a while," said Montag.

"A wholesome tongue is a tree of life."

In the distance, Montag thought he heard a fire siren.

The Sieve and the Sand

THEY READ THE LONG AFTERNOON THROUGH, WHILE THE
fire flickered and blew the hearth and the rain fell from the sky
over the house. Now and again, Mr. Montag would quietly
light a cigarette and puff it, or go bring in a bottle of cold beer
and drink it easily or say, "Will you read that part over again?
Isn't that an idea now?" And Mildred's voice, as colorless as a
beer bottle which contains a beautiful wine but does not know
it, went on enclosing the words in plain glass, pouring forth the
beauties with a loose mouth, while her drab eyes moved over
the words and over the words and the cigarette smoke idled,
and the hour grew late. They read a man named Shakespeare
and a man named Poe and part of a book by a man named
Matthew and one named Mark. On occasion, Mildred glanced
fearfully at the window.

"Go on," said Mr. Montag.

"Someone might be watching. That might've been Mr. Leahy at our door a while back."

"Whoever it was went away. Read that last section again, I want to think on that."

She read from the works of Jefferson and Lincoln.

When it was five o'clock, her hands dropped open. "I'm tired. Can I stop now?" Her voice was hoarse.

"How thoughtless of me," he said, taking the book. "But isn't it beautiful, Millie, the words, and the thoughts, aren't they exciting!"

"I don't understand any of it."

"But surely . . ."

"Just words," she said.

"But you remember some of it."

"Nothing."

"Try."

She tried to remember and tell it. "Nothing."

"You'll learn, in time. Doesn't some of the beauty get through to you?"

"I don't like books, I don't understand them, they're over my head, they're for professors and radicals and I don't want to read any more. Please, promise you won't make me!"

"Mildred!"

"I'm afraid," she said, putting her face into her shaking hands. "I'm so terribly frightened by these ideas, by Mr. Leahy, and having these books in our house. They'll burn our books and kill us. Now, I'm sick."

"Poor Millie," he said, at last, sighing. "I've put you on trial, haven't I? I'm way out front, trying to drag you, when I should be walking beside you, barely touching. I expect too much. It'll take months to put you in the frame of mind where you can receive the ideas in these books. It's not fair of me. All right, you won't have to read again."

"Thanks."

"But you must *listen*. I'll explain. And one day you'll understand why these books are so fine."

"I'll never learn."

"You must, if you want to be free."

"I'm free already, I couldn't be freer."

"But aware, no. You're like the moth that got caught in the interior of a bell at midnight. Numb with concussion, drunk on sound. Thirty years of that confounded blatting radio, no ideas, no beauty, just noise. A moth in a bell. And we've got to—"

"You're not going to forbid me my radio, are you?" Her voice rose.

"Well, to start—"

She was up in a fury, raging at him. "I'll sit and listen to this for a while every day," she cried. "But I've got to have my radio, too. You can't take that away from me!"

"Millie."

The telephone rang. They both started. She snatched it up, and was almost immediately laughing. "Hello, Ann, yes, yes! Of course. Tonight. Yes. You come here. Yes, the Clown's on tonight, yes and the Terror, it'll be nice."

Mr. Montag shuddered. He left the room. He walked through the house, thinking. Leahy. The Fire House. These books.

"I'll shoot him, tonight," he said, aloud. "I'll kill Leahy. That'll be one censor out of the way. No." He laughed coldly.

"For I'll have to shoot most of the people in the world. How does one start a revolution? What can a single lonely man do?"

Mildred was chattering. The radio was back on again, thundering.

And then he remembered, about a year ago, walking through a park alone he had come upon a man in a black suit unawares. The man had been reading something. Montag hadn't seen a book, he had seen the man move hastily, and his face was flushed, and he had jumped up as if to run, and Montag had said, "Sit down."

"I didn't do anything."

"No one said you did."

They had sat in the park all afternoon. Montag had drawn the man out. He was a retired professor of English literature, who had lost his job forty years before when the last college of arts had been closed. His name was William Faber, and yes, shyly, fearfully, he produced a little book of American Poems he had been reading, "Just to know I'm alive," said Mr. Faber. "Just to know where I am and what things are. To be aware. Most of my friends aren't aware. Most of them can't talk. They stutter and halt and hunt words. And what they talk is sales and profits and what they saw on television the hour before."

What a nice afternoon that had been. Professor Faber had read some of the poems to him, none of which he understood, but the sounds were good, and slowly the meaning crept in. When it was over, Montag said, "I'm a fireman."

Faber had almost died on the spot from a heart attack.

"Don't be afraid. I won't turn you in," said Montag. "I've stopped being mean about it years ago. I take long walks. No one walks anymore. Do you have the same trouble? Are you stopped by the police as a robbery or burglary suspect simply because you're on foot?"

He and Faber had laughed, exchanged addresses verbally, and parted. He had never seen Faber again. It wouldn't be safe to know a former English lit. professor. But now . . . ?

He dialed the call through.

"Hello?"

"Hello, Professor Faber?"

"Yes. Who is this?"

"This is Mr. Montag. Remember, in the park, a year ago."

"Oh yes, Mr. Montag. Can I help you?"

"Mr. Faber . . ."

"Yes?"

"How many copies of Shakespeare are there left in the world?"

"I'm afraid I don't know what you're talking about." The voice grew cold.

"I want to know if there are any copies at all."

"I can't talk to you now, Montag."

"This telephone line is closed, there's no one listening."

"Is this some sort of trap? I can't talk to just anyone on the phone."

"Tell me. Are there any copies left?"

"None!" And Faber hung up.

None. Montag fell back in his chair, gasping. None! None in all the world, none left, none anywhere, all of them destroyed, torn apart, burnt. Shakespeare at last dead for all time to the world! He got up shakily and walked across the room and bent down among the books. He took hold of one and lifted it.

"The plays of Shakespeare, Millie! One last copy and I own it!"

"Fine," she said.

"If anything should happen to this copy he'd be lost forever. Do you realize what that means, the importance of this copy here in our house."

"And you have to hand it back to Mr. Leahy tonight to be burned, don't you?" she said. She was not being cruel. She merely sounded relieved that the book was going out of her life.

"Yes."

He could see Leahy turning the book over with slow appreciation. "Sit down, Montag, I want you to watch this. Delicately, like an eggplant, see?" Ripping one page after another from the book. Lighting the first page with a match. And when it had curled down into a black butterfly, lighting the second page, and so on, chain-smoking the entire volume page by printed page. When it was all finished, with Montag seated there sweating, the floor would look like a swarm of black moths had died in a small storm. And Leahy smiling, washing his hands.

"My God, Millie, we've got to do something, we've got to copy this, there must be a duplicate made, this can't be lost!"

"You haven't time."

"No, not by hand, but photographed."

"No one would do it for you."

He stopped. She was right. There was no one to trust. Except, perhaps, Faber. Montag started for the door.

"You'll be here for the television party, won't you?" she called after him. "It wouldn't be fun without you!"

"You'd never miss me." But she was looking at the daylight

TV program and didn't hear. He went out and slammed the door.

Once as a child he had sat upon the yellow sands in the middle of the blue and hot summer day trying to fill a sieve with sand. The faster he poured it in, the faster it sifted through, with a hot whispering. He tried all day because some cruel cousin had said, "Fill this sieve with sand and you'll get a dime!"

Seated there in the midst of July, he had cried. His hand was tired, the sand was boiling. The sieve was empty.

And now, as the underground jet-tube roared him through the lower cellars of town, rocking him, he remembered the sieve. And he held the copy of Shakespeare, trying to pour the words into his mind. But the words fell through! And he thought, in a few hours I must hand this book to Leahy, but I must remember every word, none must escape me, each line can be memorized. I must remember, I must.

"But I don't." He shut the book and tried to repeat the lines.

"Try Denham's Dentifrice tonight," said the jet-radio in the bright wall of the swaying car. Trumpets blared.

"Shut up," thought Mr. Montag. "To be or not to be—"

"Denham's Dentifrice is only surpassed by Denham's Dentifrice."

"—that is the question. Shut up, shut up, let me remember."

He tore the book open feverishly and jerked the pages about, tearing at the lines with his eyes, staring until his eyelashes were wet and quivering. His heart pounded.

"Denham's Dentifrice, spelled D-E-N-H . . ."

"Whether it is nobler—"

A whispering of hot yellow sand through empty sieve.

"Denham's, Denham's, Denham's does it! No dandier, dental detergent!"

"Shut up!" It was a cry so loud that the radio seemed stunned. Mr. Montag found himself on his feet, the shocked inhabitants of the loud car staring at him, recoiling from a man with an insane face, a gibbering mouth, a terrible book in his hand. These rabbit people who hadn't asked for music and commercials on their public vehicles, but who had got it by the sewerful, the air drenched and sprayed and pummeled and kicked by voices and music every instant. And here was an idiot man, himself, suddenly scrabbling at the wall, beating at the loud-speaker, at the enemy of peace, at the killer of Shakespeare!

"Mad man!"

"Call the conductor!"

"Denham's, Denham's Double Dentifrice for dingy dentures!"

"Fourteenth Street."

Only that saved him. The car stopped. Mr. Montag, suddenly shocked by the lack of motion, swayed back, dropped from the seat, ran past the pale faces, screaming in his mind soundlessly, the voice crying like a sea-gull on a lonely shore after him, "Denham's, Denham's . . ." fading.

Professor Faber opened the door and when he saw the book, seized it. "My God, man, I haven't seen Shakespeare in years!"

"We burned a house last night. I stole this."

"What a chance to take."

"I was curious."

"Of course. It's beautiful. There were a lot of lovely books once. Before we let them go." He turned the pages hungrily, a thin man, bald, with slender hands, as light as chaff. He sat down and put his hand over his eyes. "You are looking at a coward, Mr. Montag. When they burned the last of the evil books, as they called them, forty years back, I made only a few grunts and subsided. I've damned myself ever since."

"It's not too late. There are still books."

"And there is still life in me, but I'm afraid of dying. Civilizations fall because men like myself fear death."

"I have a plan. I'm in a position to do things. I'm a fireman, I can find books and hide them."

"True."

"I lay awake last night, thinking. We might publish many books privately when we have copies to print from."

"It's been tried. A good many thousand men have sat in the electric chair for that. Besides, where will you get a press?"

"Can't we build one? I have a little money."

"If we can find a skilled craftsman who cares."

"But here's the really fine part of my plan." Montag almost laughed. He leaned forward. "We'll print extra copies of each book and plant them in firemen's houses!"

"What!"

"Yes! Ten copies, twenty copies in each house, plenty, more than plenty of evidence, criminal intent. Books on philosophy, politics, religion, fantasy!"

"My God!" Faber jumped up and paced the room, looking back at Montag, beginning to smile. "That's incredible."

"Do you like my plan?"

"Insidious!"

"Would it work?"

"It'd be *fun*, wouldn't it?"

"That's the word. Christ, to hide the books in houses and phone the alarm and see the engines roar up, the hoses uncoil, the door battered down, the windows crashed in, and the fireman himself accused, his house burnt and himself in jail!"

"Positively insidious." The professor almost danced. "The dragon eats his tail!"

"I've a list of all firemen's homes here and across the continent. With an underground organization we could sow books and reap fire for every bastard in the industry."

"But how will you start?"

"A few books here and there. And build the organization."

"Who can you trust?"

"Former professors like yourself, former actors, directors, writers, historians, linguists. There must be thousands boiling under the skin."

"Ancient, most of them. There've been no new crops lately."

"All the better. They'll have fallen from public notice."

"I know a few."

"We could start with those, spread slowly in a network. Think of the actors who never have a chance to play Shakespeare, or Pirandello or Shaw anymore. We would use their anger, my God, to good purpose! Think of the historians who haven't written a line of history for forty years, and the writers who've written pap half a century now, who go home nights and vomit to forget. There must be a million such people!"

"At least."

"And perhaps we could get small classes in reading started, build an interest in the people."

"Impossible."

"But we must try."

"The whole structure must come down. This isn't a façade job, we can't change the front. We've got to kick down the skeleton. The whole works is so shot through with mediocrity. I don't think you realize, Montag, that the burning was almost unnecessary, forty years back."

"Oh?"

"By that time the great mass had been so pulverized by comic books, quick digests of digests, that public libraries were like the great Sahara, empty and silent. Except, of course, for the science dept."

"But we can bring libraries back."

"Can you shout louder than the radio, dance faster than the freak dancers, are your books enough to interest this population breast-fed from infancy through senility? Look at your magazine stands. Half naked women on every cover. Your billboards, your films, sex. Can you get the American man from under his crankcase, the woman out of her beauty salon, both of them away from their friend, the TV?"

"We can try."

"You're a fool. They don't want to think. They're having fun."

"They only think they are. My wife has everything. She, like a million others, tried to commit suicide last week."

"All right, they're lying to themselves, but if you try to show them to themselves, they'll crush you like a bug."

A flight of warplanes shook the house, going west.

"There's our hope," said Faber, pointing up. "Let's hope for a good long bad war, Montag. Let the war take away the TVs and radio and comics and true confessions. This civilization is flinging itself to pieces. Wait for the centrifuge to break the wheel."

"I can't wait. There has to be another structure, anyway, ready and waiting when this one falls. That's us."

"A few men quoting Shakespeare or saying I remember Sophocles? It would be funny if it weren't so tragic."

"We must be there to remind them that there is a little more to man besides machines, that the right kind of work is happiness, rather than the wrong kind of leisure. Man must have something to *do*. He feels useless. We must tell him about things like honesty and beauty and poetry and art, which they lost along the wayside."

"All right, Montag." The professor sighed. "You're wrong, but you're right. We'll do a little, anyway. How much money could you get me today?"

"Five thousand dollars."

"Bring it here then. I know a man who once printed our college paper years ago. I remember that year very well. I came to my class one morning and there was only one student there to sign up for my Ancient Greek Drama. You see, that's how it went. Like a block of ice melted on an August afternoon. Nobody passed a law. It happened. And when the people had censored themselves into a living idiocy, the Government, realizing it was to their advantage that the public read only pap and swill, stepped in and froze the situation. Newspapers were dying as far back as the nineteen fifties. They were dead by the year 2000. So nobody cared if the government said no more newspapers. No one wanted them back anyway. The world is full of half-people. They don't know how to be happy because they know neither how to work, nor how to relax. But enough of that. I'll contact the printer. We'll get the books started. That part'll be fun. I'm going to really enjoy it."

"And we'll plan the reading classes."

"Yes, and wait for the war," said Faber. "That's one fine thing about war. It destroys machines so beautifully." Montag stood up. "I'll get the money to you some time today or tomorrow. You'll have to give me back that Shakespeare, though. It's to be burned tonight."

"No!" Faber held it out before him, turning the pages.

"I've tried to memorize it, but I forget. It's driven me crazy trying to remember."

"Jesus God, if only we had time."

"I keep thinking that. Sorry." He took the book and went to the door. "Good night."

The door shut. He was in the street again, looking at the real world.

You could feel the war getting ready in the sky that night. The way the clouds moved aside and came back, and the way the stars looked, a million of them between the clouds, like the enemy planes, and the feeling that the sky might fall upon the city and turn the houses to dust, and the moon turn to fire, that was how the night felt. Montag walked from the bus stop, with the money in his pocket. He was listening abstractedly to the Sea-Shell radio which you could stopper in your left ear "Buy a Sea-Shell and hear the ocean of Time"—and a voice was talking to him and only him as he put his feet down toward his home: "Things took a sudden turn for the worse today. War threatens at any hour."

A flight of jet-bombers, like the whistle of a scythe, went over the sky in one second. It was less than a radio impulse.

Montag felt of the money in one pocket, the Shakespeare in the other. He had given up trying to memorize it now, he was simply reading it for the enjoyment it gave, the simple pleasure of good words on the tongue and in the mind. He unscrewed the Seashell Ear Radio and read another page of *Lear* by moonlight.

AT EIGHT O'CLOCK the front door scanner recognized three women and opened, letting them in with laughter and loud, empty talk. Mrs. Masterson, Mrs. Phelps, and Mrs. Bowles, drinking the martinis Mildred handed them, laughing like a crystal chandelier that someone has pushed, tinkling upon themselves in a million crystal chimes, flashing the same white smiles, their echoes repeated into empty corridors. Mr. Montag found himself in the middle of a conversation the main subject of which was how nice everybody looked.

"Doesn't everyone look nice?"

"Nice."

"You look fine, Alma."

"You look fine, too, Mildred."

"Everybody looks nice and fine," said Montag. He had given up the book. None of it would stay in his mind. The harder he tried to remember *Hamlet*, the quicker it vanished. He was in a mood to walk, but he never did that any more. Somehow he was always afraid he might meet Clarisse, or not meet her, on his strolls, so that kept him in, standing here upon the blond tenpins, blasting back at them with leers and blatherings, and somehow the television set was put on before they had finished saying how nice everyone looked, and there was a man selling orange soda pop and a woman drinking it with a Cheshire cat smile, how in hell did a person drink and smile simultaneously? A real advertising stunt! Following this, a demonstration of how to bake a certain new cake, followed by a rather inane domestic comedy, a news analysis that did not analyze the news. "There may be war in 24 hours. Nobody knows." And an intolerable a quiz show naming the capitols of states.

Abruptly, Montag walked to the televisor and switched it off.

"Hey!" said everyone as if this were a joke.

"Leonard," said Mildred, nervously.

"I thought we might enjoy a little silence."

They thought about it and blinked.

"I thought we might try a little conversation for a change."

Conversation!

A flight of bombers going East shook the house and trembled up through their bodies to shake the drinks in their hands. Mr. Montag followed the sound with his eyes.

"There they go," he said.

Everyone glanced at him.

"When do you suppose the war will be?"

Silence.

At last: "What war?"

"There isn't going to be any war."

"What about your husbands? I notice they're not here tonight."

Mrs. Masterson looked sidewise at the empty TV screen. "Oh. My husband'll be back in a week or so. The Army called him. But they have these things every month or so." She laughed.

"Don't you worry? About the war?"

"Well, even if there was one, heavens, it's got to be fought and got over with, we can't just sit, can we?"

"No, but we can think about it."

She sipped her drink charmingly. "Who wants to think about war. I'll let Bob think of all that."

"And die."

"It's always someone else's husband dies, isn't that the joke?" The women all tittered. "Bob can take care of himself."

Yes, thought Montag, and if he doesn't, what'll it matter, we've learned the magic of the replaceable part from factories. A man after all is just a man. You can't tell one from another these days. As for these women. His wife, the others, with their barbarously bright faces, the neon lipstick, the doll-lash eyes. Why worry about Bob or Mary or Tom, if there is a Joe or Helen or Roger to replace them, just as vacuous. In the land of television pallor, where the tanned face? In the land of the spread gluteus maximus, where the muscular thigh? In the land of blanc mange and vanilla pudding where the crisp bacon, the sharp roquefort? Where in this world of dull paring knives the mind like a machete to cut to the heart of the matter! Why these women couldn't peel the rind from a bit of small-talk without lopping their arms off at the elbow!

The silence in the room was like a cotton batting.

"Did you see the Clarence Dove film last night, wasn't he funny."

"He's funny!"

"He sure is funny."

"But what if Bob should be killed, or your husband, Mrs. Phelps . . ."

"He's already dead," said Mrs. Phelps. "He died a week ago, didn't you know? Jumped off a building."

"I didn't know." He fell silent, embarrassed.

"But back to Clarence Dove, he's really funny," said Mildred.

"Why did you marry Mr. Phelps?" said Montag.

"Why?"

"Yes, what did you have in common."

The poor woman waved her hands helplessly. "Why, because he had such a nice sense of humor, and we liked the same TV programs, and things like that. He danced nice."

He had seen other widows at funerals, dry-eyed, even as this woman was dry-eyed because the dead man was a robot turned out on assembly belt, gay, casual, but replaceable by another gay casual chap who would pop up like the clap pipe so mistakable for the one you just blew to bits at the shooting gallery.

"And you? Mrs. Masterson, have you any children?"

"Don't be ridiculous."

"Come to think of it, no one here has any children," said Montag. "Except you, Mrs. Bowles."

"Four, by Caesarian section. It's so easy."

"The Caesarians weren't physically necessary?"

"No. But I always said I'll be damned if I'll go through all that agony just for a baby. Four Caesarians." She held up her fingers.

Yes, everything easy. To mistake the easy way for the right way, how delicious the temptation, but it wasn't living. A woman who wouldn't have a baby, or a man who wouldn't work didn't belong. They were passing through, they were expendables. They belonged to nothing and did nothing.

"Have you ever thought, ladies," he said, growing more contemptuous of them by the minute, "that perhaps this isn't the best of all possible worlds? That perhaps the Negroes and Jews and civil rights and every damned other thing is still where it was a hundred years ago, maybe worse?"

"Why that can't be true," said Mrs. Phelps. "We'd have heard about it."

"On that pap-dispenser?" said Montag, jerking his thumb at the TV. "On that censoring machine?"

"You're lying," said Mrs. Phelps.

He drew a paper from his pocket, shaking with irritation.

"What's that?" Mrs. Masterson squinted.

"A poem from a book, I want you to hear it."

"I don't like poetry."

"Have you ever heard any?"

"I detest it."

Mildred jumped up, but Montag said, "Sit down." The women all lit cigarettes nervously, twisting their mouths, their nicotined hands gesturing in the smoky air. "Well, go on," said Mrs. Masterson, impatiently "Let's get this junk over with."

Mrs. Phelps was squealing. "This is illegal, isn't it? I'm afraid. I'm going home."

"Sit down, we'll talk about that later." He cleared his throat. The room was quiet. He glanced up and the women were all looking with expectation at the television set, as if looking would turn it back on.

"Listen," he said. "This is a poem by Matthew Arnold, titled 'Dover Beach.'" He waited. He wanted very much to speak it right, and he was afraid that he might stumble. He read:

"*The sea is calm tonight.*
The tide is full, the moon lies fair
Upon the straits—on the French coast the light
Gleams and is gone; the cliffs of England stand,
Glimmering and vast, out in the tranquil bay.
Come to the window, sweet in the night air!
Only, from the long line of spray
Where the sea meets the moon-blanched land
Listen! You hear the grating roar
Of pebbles which the waves draw back, and fling,
At their return, up the high strand,
Begin, and cease, and then again begin,
With tremulous cadence slow, and bring
The eternal note of sadness in.

"*Sophocles long ago*
Heard it on the Aegean, and it brought
Into his mind the turbid ebb and flow
Of human misery; we
Find also in the sound a thought,
Hearing it by this distant northern sea.

"*The Sea of Faith*
Was once, too, at full, and round earth's shore
Lay like the folds of a bright girdle furled.
But now I only hear
Its melancholy, long, withdrawing roar,
Retreating, to the breath
Of the night wind, down the vast edges drear
And naked shingles of the world.

"Ah, love, let us be true

To one another! for the world, which seems

To lie before us like a land of dreams,

So various, so beautiful, so new,

Hath really neither joy, nor love, nor light,

Nor certitude, nor peace, nor help for pain;

And we are here as on a darkling plain

Swept with confused alarms of struggle and flight,

Where ignorant armies clash night."

He stopped reading.

Mildred got up. "Can I turn on the TV now?"

"No, god damn it, no!"

Mildred sat down.

Mrs. Masterson said, "I don't get it."

"What was it about?" said Mrs. Phelps, her eyes frightened.

"Don't you see the beauty?" asked Montag, much too loudly.

"Hardly worth getting excited about," said Mrs. Masterson.

"That's just it. Because it is such a little thing, it's big. We don't have time for poetry or anything anymore. We don't like rain. We seed clouds to make it rain away from our cities. On Christmas we dump the snow in the sea. Trees are trouble, rip them out! Grass needs cutting, pour cement over it! We can't be troubled to live anymore."

"Mr. Montag," said Mrs. Masterson. "It's only because you're a fireman that we haven't turned you in for reading this to us tonight. This is illegal. But it's silly. The poem was silly."

"Of course, because you can't plug it in anywhere, it isn't practical."

"Ladies, let's get out of here."

"We don't want to get caught here with him and his poem," said Mrs. Phelps, running.

"Don't," said Mildred.

Not speaking, the ladies ran. The door slammed.

"Go home and plug in your blankets and fry!" yelled Montag. "Go home and think of your first husband, Mrs. Masterson, in the insane asylum, and you Mrs. Phelps of Mr. Phelps jumping off a building!"

The house was quiet.

He went to the bedroom where Mildred had locked herself in the bath. He heard the water running. He heard her shaking the sleeping tablets out into her hand.

He walked out of the house, slamming the door.

"THANK YOU, MONTAG." Mr. Leahy took the copy of Shakespeare and without even looking at it, tore it slowly apart and threw it into a wall slot. "Now, let's have a game of blackjack and forget all about it, Montag. Glad to see you're back." They walked upstairs in the fire house.

They sat and played cards.

In Leahy's sight, he felt the guilt of his hands. His hands were like ferrets that had done some evil deed in Leahy's sight, and now were never at rest, were always stirring and picking and hiding in pockets, or moving out from under his alcohol-flame gaze. If Leahy so much as breathed on them, Montag felt his hands might turn upon their backs and die and he might never shake them to life again, they would be frozen cold, to be buried forever in his coat-sleeves, forgotten. For these were the hands that acted on their own, that were no part of him, that snatched books, tore pages, hid paragraphs and sentences in little wads to be opened later, at home, by match-light, read, and burned. These were the hands that ran off with Shakespeare and Job and Ruth and packed them away next to his crashing heart, over the beating ribs and the hot, pouring blood of a man excited by his theft, appalled by his temerity, betrayed by ten fingers which at times he held up and looked upon as if they were covered with fresh blood. He washed the hands continually. He found it impossible to smoke, not only because of having to use his hands in front of Leahy, but because the drifting cigarette clouds made him think of the old man and the old woman and the fire that he and these others had set with their brass machines.

"You're not smoking any more, Montag?"

"No. I've a cigarette cough. Got to stop."

And when he played cards he hid his hands under the table so that Leahy wouldn't see him fumble. "Let's have our hands on the table," said Leahy. "Not that we don't trust you. You got extra cards under there." And they all laughed. While Montag drew forth the guilty hands, the stealers and the seekers, shaking, to place his cards during the long game.

The phone rang.

Mr. Leahy, carrying his cards in his quiet hand, walked over and stood by it, let it ring once more, and then picked up the receiver.

"Yes?"

Mr. Montag listened.

"Yes," said Leahy.

The clock ticked in the room.

"I see," said Leahy. He looked at Mr. Montag and smiled

and winked Montag looked away. "Better give me that address again."

Mr. Montag got up and walked around the room, hands in pockets. The other two men were standing, now, ready. Leahy gave them a nod of his head, toward their hats and coats, as if to say, on the double. They shoved their arms in their coats and pushed on their helmets, joking.

Mr. Montag waited.

"I understand perfectly," said Leahy. "Yes. Yes. Perfectly. No, that's all right. Don't you worry. We'll be right out."

Mr. Montag put down the phone. "Well, well," he said.

"A call?"

"Yes."

"Books to be burned?"

"So it seems."

Mr. Montag sat down. "I don't feel well."

"What a shame, for this is a special case," said Leahy, coming forward slowly, putting on his slicker.

"I think I'm tendering my resignation."

"Please wait. One more fire, eh, Montag. And then I'll be agreeable, you can hand in your papers and we'll all be happy."

"Do you mean that?"

"Have I ever lied to you."

Mr. Leahy fetched Montag his helmet. "Put it on. It'll all be over in an hour. I understand you, Montag, really I do. And soon everything will be hunky-dory."

"All right." Montag arose. They slid down the brass pole. "Where's the fire this time?"

"I'll direct you, Mr. Brown," shouted Leahy up at the man on the engine.

The engine blasted itself to life and in gaseous thunder they all climbed aboard.

They rounded the corner in thunder and siren, with concussion of tires, with scream of rubber, with a shifting of kerosene bulk in the glittery brass tank, like the food in the stomach of a giant, with Mr. Montag's fingers jolting off the silver rail, swinging into cold space, with the wind tearing his hair back from his bleak face, with the wind whistling in his teeth, and him all the while thinking of the women, the chaff women, with the kernels blown out from under them by a neon wind, and his reading the book to them, what a silly thing it was now, for what was a book, a bit of paper, a bit of type, why should he care about one book, ten books, five thousand books, he was the only one in the world who cared about books, really. Why not forget it all, let it drop, let the books lie?

"Turn here!" said Leahy.

"Elm Street?"

"Right!"

He saw Leahy up ahead, with his massive black slicker flapping out about him. He seemed to be a black bat flying over the engine, over the brass numbers, taking the wind. His phosphorescent face glimmered in the high darkness, pressing forward, and he was smiling.

"Here we go to keep the world happy!" he shouted.

And Mr. Montag thought, no, I won't let the books die. I won't let them burn. As long as there are men like Leahy, I can't quit. But what can I do. I can't kill everyone. It's me against the world, and the odds are too big for one man. What can I do? Against fire, what water is best?

He didn't know.

"Now over on Park Terrace!" That was Leahy.

The Fire Engine blundered to a stop, throwing the men forward on themselves. Mr. Montag stood there, looking at the cold rail under his loose fingers, trembling.

"I can't do it," he murmured. "I can't go in there. I can't burn another book."

Leahy jumped down from his perch, smelling of the fresh wind that had hammered at him. "All right, Montag, fetch the kerosene!"

The hoses were being reeled out. The men were running on soft bootheels, as clumsy as cripples, as quiet as spiders.

Mr. Montag at last looked up.

Mr. Leahy said, "What's wrong, Montag?"

"Why," said Montag. "That house. It's my house."

"So it is," said Leahy.

"That's my house!"

All the lights were on. Down the street, lights were burning yellow in every house. People were coming out on porches, as on to stages. The door of Montag's house stood wide. In it, with two suitcases at her feet, was Mildred. When she saw her husband she stooped, picked up the suitcases, and came down the steps with dream-like rigidity, looking at the third button on his jacket.

"Mildred!"

She didn't speak.

"Okay, Montag, up with the hoses and the axes."

"Just a moment, Mr. Leahy. Mildred, you didn't telephone this call in, did you?"

She walked past him with her arms rigid and at the ends of

them, in the sharp fingers, the valise handles. Her mouth was bloodless.

"Mildred!"

She put the valises into a waiting cab and climbed in and sat there, staring straight ahead.

Montag started toward her, but Leahy held his arm. Leahy jerked his head toward the house. "Come on, Montag."

The cab drove away slowly among the lighted houses.

There was a crystal tinkling as the windows of the house were broken to provide fine drafts for fire.

Mr. Montag walked but did not feel his feet touch the sidewalk, nor the hose in his cold fingers, nor did he hear Leahy talking continually as they reached the door.

"Pour it on, Montag."

"What?"

"The kerosene."

Montag stood looking in at the strange house, made strange by the hour of the night, by the murmur of neighbor voices, by the broken glass and the lights burning in each room, and there on the floor, their covers torn off, the pages spilled about like pigeon feathers, were his incredible books, and they looked so pitiful and silly and not worth bothering with there, for they were nothing but type and paper and raveled binding.

But he knew what he must do to quench the fire that was burning everything even before set ablaze. He stepped forward in a huge silence, and he picked up one of the pages of the books and he read what it had to say.

"I'll memorize it," he told himself. "And some day I'll write it down and make another book from what I remember."

He had read three lines when Leahy snatched the paper away from him, wadded it into a ball, and tossed it over his shoulder.

"Oh, no, no," said Leahy, smiling. "Because then we'd have to burn your mind, too. Mustn't have that."

"Ready!" said Leahy, stepping back.

"Ready," said Montag, snapping the valve lock on the fire-thrower.

"Aim," said Leahy.

"Aim."

"Fire!"

"Fire!"

He burnt the television set and he burnt the radio and he burnt the motion picture projector and he burnt the films and the gossip papers and the litter of cosmetics on the table, and he took pleasure in it, and he burned the walls because he wanted to change everything, the chairs, the tables, the paintings, he didn't want to remember that he had lived here with that strange woman who was an interchangeable part, who would forget him tomorrow, and who was, really, to be pitied, for she did not know anything about the world or the way it was run.

So he burned the room.

"The books, Montag, the books!"

He directed the fire at the books. The books leaped up and danced about, like roasted birds, their wings ablaze in red and yellow feathers. They fell in charred lumps. They twisted and went up in founts of spark and soot.

"Get Shakespeare there, get him!" said Leahy.

He burned Mr. Shakespeare to a turn.

He burned books, he burned them by the dozen, he burned books, with water dripping from his eyes.

"When you're all done, Montag," said Leahy. "You're under arrest."

Books Without Pages

THE HOUSE FELL INTO RED RUIN. IT BEDDED ITSELF DOWN to sleepy pink ashes and a smoke pall hung over it, rising straight to the sky. It was ten minutes after one in the morning. The crowd was going back into their houses, the fun was over.

Mr. Montag stood with the fire-thrower in his hands, great islands of perspiration standing out under his arms, his face dirty with soot. The three other firemen stood there in the darkness, their faces illumined faintly by the burnt house, by the house which Mr. Montag had just burned down so efficiently with kerosene, fire-thrower, and especial aim.

"All right, Montag," said Leahy. "Come along. You've done your duty. Now you're under arrest."

"What've I done?'

"You know what you done, don't ask. The books."

"Why so much fuss over a few bits of paper?"

"We won't stand here arguing, it's cold."

"Was it my wife called you, or one of her friends."

"It doesn't matter."

"Was it my wife?'

Leahy nodded. "But her friends called about an hour ago.

One way or the other, you'd have got it. That was pretty silly, quoting poetry around free and easy, Montag. Come on, now."

"No," said Montag.

He felt the fire-thrower in his hand. Leahy glanced at Montag's trigger finger and saw what he intended before Montag himself had even considered it. After all, murder is always a new thing, and Montag knew nothing of murder, he knew only burning and burning things that people said were evil.

"But I know what's really wrong with the world," said Montag.

"Don't!" screamed Leahy.

And then he was a shrieking blaze, a jumping sprawling, babbling thing, all aflame, writhing on the grass as Montag shot three more blasting squirts of liquid fire at him. The sounds Leahy made were horrible. He twisted in on himself, like a ridiculous black wax image and was silent.

The other two men stood appalled.

"Montag!"

He pointed the weapon at them. "Turn around!"

They turned. He beat them over the head with the weapon, he didn't want to burn them, too. Then he turned the fire-thrower on the fire engine itself, set the trigger, and ran. The engine blew up, a hundred gallons of kerosene in one great flower of heat.

He ran away down the street and into an alley, thinking, that's the end of you, Leahy, that's the end of you and what you are.

He kept running.

He remembered the books and turned back.

"You're a fool, a damned fool, an awful fool, but definitely a fool," he told himself. "You idiot, you and your stinking temper. And you've ruined it all. At the very start, you ruin. But those women, those stupid women, they drove me to it with their nonsense!" he protested, in his mind.

"A fool, nevertheless, no better than them! We'll save what we can, we'll do what has to be done."

He found the books where he had left them, beyond the garden fence. He heard voices yelling in the night and flash-beams jerked about. Other Fire Engines wailed from far off and police cars were arriving.

Mr. Montag took as many books as he could carry under each arm, ten on a side and staggered away down the alley. He hadn't realized what a shock the evening had been to himself, but suddenly he fell and lay sobbing, weak, his legs folded. At a distance he heard running feet. Get up, he told himself. But he lay there. Get up, get up. But he cried like a child. He hadn't wanted to kill anybody, not even Leahy, killing did nothing but kill something of yourself when you did it, and suddenly he saw Leahy again, a torch, screaming, and he shut his eyes and crawled his sooty fingers over his wet face. "I'm sorry, I'm sorry."

Everything at once. In one 24 hour period, the burning of a woman, the burning of books, the trip to the professor's, Leahy, Shakespeare, trying to memorize, the sand and the sieve, the bank money, the printing press, the plan, the rage, the alarm, Mildred's departure, the fire, Leahy into a torch, too much for any one day in any one life. Too much.

At last he was able to get to his feet, but the books were impossibly heavy. He staggered along the alley and the voices and sound faded behind him. He moved in darkness, panting.

"You must remember," he said. "You must burn them or they'll burn you. Burn them or they'll burn you."

Six blocks away the alley opened out onto a wide empty thoroughfare, that looked like an amphitheatre, so broad, so quiet, so clean, and him, alone, running across it, easily seen, easily shot down. He hid back in the shadows. There was a gas station nearby. First he must go there, clean up, wash, comb his hair, become presentable. Then, with books under arm, stroll calmly across that wide boulevard to get where he was going.

"Where am I going?"

He didn't know.

THERE WAS THE WIDE BOULEVARD, a game for him to win, there was the vast bowling alley at two in the morning, and him dirty, his lungs like burning brooms in his chest, his mouth sucked dry from running, all of the lead in the world poured into his empty feet, and the gas station nearby like a big white metal flower open for the long night ahead.

The moon had set and a mist was come to shelter him and drive away the police helicopters. He saw them wavering, indecisive, a half mile off, like butterflies puzzled by autumn, dying with winter, and then they were landing, one by one, dropping softly to the streets where, turned into police cars, they would scream along the boulevard, continuing their search.

Approaching from the rear, Mr. Montag entered the men's wash room. Through the tin wall he could hear a voice crying, "War has been declared! War has been declared. Ten minutes ago—" But the sound of washing his hands and rinsing his face and toweling himself dry cut the announcer's voice away.

Emerging from the washroom a cleaner, newer man, less suspect, having left ashes and dirt behind down the drain, Mr.
Montag returned to his bundle of books, picked them up and
walked as casual as a man looking for a bus, out upon the boulevard. He looked north and south. The boulevard was as clean
as a pinball machine, but, underneath, one could feel the electrical energy, the readiness to dart lights, flash red and blue,
and out of nowhere, rolling like a silver ball, might flash the
searchers. Two blocks away, there were a few headlights. He
took a deep breath, and kept walking. He would have to chance
it. A hundred yards across the boulevard in the open, plenty of
time for a police car to run him down if one came.

There was a car coming. Its headlights leaped out and
caught him in mid-stride. He faltered, got a new hold on his
books, and forced himself not to run. He was now one third of
the way across. There was a growl from the car motor as it put
on more speed.

The police! thought Montag. They see me. Careful man,
careful.

The car was coming at a terrific speed. A good one hundred miles an hour, if anything. Its horn was blaring. Its lights
flushed the concrete and the heat of them, it seemed, burned
his cheeks and eyelids and brought the sweat coursing from
his body.

He began to shuffle and then run. The horn hooted. The
sound of the motor went higher, higher. He ran. He dropped
a book, hesitated, let it lie, and plunged on, babbling to himself, he was in the middle of the street, the car was a hundred
yards away, closer, closer, hooting, pushing, rolling, screeching, the horn frozen, him running, his legs up and down, his

eyes blind in the flashing hot light, the horn nearer, upon him.

They're going to run me down, they know who I am, it's all over, it's all done! said Mr. Montag. But he held to the books and kept racing.

He stumbled and fell.

That saved him. Just an instant before reaching him the wild, hysterical car swerved to one side, went around him and was gone like a bullet away. Mr. Montag lay where he had fallen. Wisps of laughter trailed back with the blue exhaust.

That wasn't the police, thought Mr. Montag.

It was a carful of high school children, yelling, whistling, hurrahing, laughing. And they had seen a man, a pedestrian, a rarity, and they had said to themselves, Let's get him! They didn't know he was wanted, that he was Montag, they were out for a night of howling and roaring here and there covering five hundred miles in a few moonlit hours, their faces icy with the wind, their hair flowing.

"They would have killed me," thought Montag, lying there. "For no reason. They would have killed me."

He got up and walked unsteadily to the far curb. Somehow he had remembered to pick up the spilled books. He looked at them, oddly, in his hands.

"I wonder," he said, "If they were the ones who killed Clarisse." His eyes watered, standing there. The thing that had saved him was self-preservation. If he had remained upright, they'd have hit him, like a domino, sent him spinning. But the fact that he was prone had caused the driver to consider the possibility that running over a body at one hundred miles an hour might turn the car over and spill them all out to their deaths.

Montag glanced down the avenue. A half mile away, the car full of kids had turned and was coming back, picking up speed.

Montag hurried into an alley and was gone long before the car returned.

The house was silent.

Mr. Montag approached it from the back, creeping through the scent of daffodils and roses and wet grass. He touched the screen door, found it open, slipped in, tiptoed across the porch, and, behind the ice-box, beyond another door, in the kitchen, deposited five of the books. He waited, listening to the house.

"Billett, are you asleep up there?" he asked of the second floor in a whisper. "I hate to do this to you, but you did it to others, never asking, never wondering, never worrying. Now it's your house, and you in jail awhile, all the houses you've burned and people you've killed."

The ceiling did not reply.

Quietly, Montag slipped from the house and returned to the alley. The house was still dark, no one had heard him come or go.

He walked casually down the alley, around a block to an all night druggist's, where he closed himself in a booth and dialed a number.

"Hello?"

"I want to report an illegal ownership of books," he said.

The voice sharpened on the other end. "The address?"

"11 South Grove Glade."

"Who are you?"

"A friend, no name. Better get there before he burns them."

"We'll get there, thanks." Click.

Montag stepped out and walked down the street. Far away, he heard sirens coming, coming to burn Mr. Billett's house, and him upstairs, not knowing, deep in sleep.

"Good night, Mr. Billett," said Montag.

A RAP AT THE DOOR.

"Professor Faber!"

Another rap and a long silence. And then, from within, the lights flickering on as the Professor sat up in bed, cutting the selenium rays in his room, all about the house the lights winked on, like eyes opening up.

Professor Faber opened the door. "Who is it?" he said, for the man who catered was scarcely recognizable. "Oh, Montag!"

"I'm going away," said Montag, stumbling to a chair. "I've been a fool."

Professor Faber stood at the door half a minute, listening to the distant sirens wailing off like animals in the morning. "Someone's been busy."

"It worked."

"At least you were a fool about the right things." Faber shut the door, came back, and poured a drink for each of them. "I wondered what had happened to you."

"I was delayed. But the money is here." He took it from his pocket and laid it on the desk, then sat there and tiredly sipped his drink. "How do you feel?"

"This is the first night I've fallen right to sleep in years," said Faber. "That must mean I'm doing the correct thing. I think we can trust me, now. I didn't."

"People never trust themselves, but they never let others know. I suppose that's why we do rash things, to expose ourselves in such a position we do not dare retreat. Unconsciously, we fear that we may give in, quit the fight, and so we do a foolish thing, like read poetry to women." He laughed at himself. "So I guess I'll be on the run now. It's up to you to keep things moving."

"I'll do my damndest," Faber sat down. "Tell me about it. What you did just now, I mean."

"I hid the books in three houses, in different places in each house so it would not look planned. Then I telephoned the firemen."

Faber shook his head. "God, I'd like to have been there. Did the places burn!"

"Yes, they burned very well."

"Where are you going now?"

"I don't know. I'll keep in touch with you. You can leave some books for me to use, from time to time, in vacant lots. I'll call you."

"Of course. Do you want to sleep here for a while?"

"I'd better get going, I wouldn't want you to be held responsible for my being here."

"Just a moment. Let's listen." Faber waved his hand three times at the radio and it came on, with a voice talking rapidly.

"—this evening. Montag has escaped but will be found. Citizens are alerted to watch for this man. Five foot ten, 170 pounds, blond-brown hair, blue eyes, healthy complexion. Here's a bulletin. The Electric Dog is being transported here from Albany."

Montag and Faber glanced at each other, eyebrows up.

"—you may recall the stories recently of this new invention, a machine so delicate that it can follow a trail, much in the way bloodhounds have done for centuries. But this machine always finds its quarry, without fail!"

Montag put his drink down and he was cold.

"The machine is self-operating, on a miniature cell motor, weighs about sixty pounds, and is propelled on a series of seven rubber wheels. The front part of this machine is a nose which, in reality, is a thousand noses, so sensitive they can distinguish ten thousand foods, five thousand flower smells, and remember the identity index odors of 15,000 men without resetting."

Faber began to tremble. He looked at his house, at the door, the floor, the chair in which Montag sat. Montag interpreted this look. They both looked together at the invisible trail of footprints leading to this house, coming across this room, the fingerprints on the door knob, and the smell of his body in the air and on this chair.

"The Electric Hound is now landing, by helicopter, at the burned Montag house, we take you there by TV control!"

And there was the burned house, the crowd, and something with a sheet over it, Mr. Leahy, yes, Mr. Leahy, and out of the sky, fluttering, came the red helicopter, landing like a grotesque flower while the police pushed back the crowd and the wind blew the women's dresses.

Mr. Montag watched the scene with a solid fascination, not wanting to move, ever. If he wished, he could sit here, in comfort, and follow the entire hunt on through its phases, down alleys, up streets, across empty running avenues, with the sky lightening to dawn, up other alleys to burned houses, so on to this place here, this house, with Faber and himself seated here at their leisure, smoking idly, drinking good wine, while the

Electric Hound sniffed down the paths, wailing, and stopped outside that door right there, and then, if he wished, Montag could rise, go to the door, keeping one eye on the television screen, open the door, and look out, and look back, and see himself standing there, limned in the bright screen, from out-side, a drama to be watched objectively, and he would watch himself, for an instant before oblivion, being killed for the benefit of a TV audience that was thousands bigger now, for the TV stations across the country were probably beeping-beeping to waken the viewer to a Scoop!

"There it is," said Faber.

Out of the helicopter came something that was not a machine, not an animal, not dead, not alive, just moving. It glowed with a green light, like phosphorescence from the sea, and it was on a long leash, and behind it came a man, dressed lightly, with earphones on his shaven head.

"I can't stay here," said Montag, getting up, his eyes still fixed to the scene. The Electric Hound shot forward to the ruins, the man running after it. A coat was brought forward. Montag recognized it as his own, dropped in the back yard during flight. The Electric Hound studied this implacably. There was a clicking and whirring of dials and meters.

"You can't escape," Faber sighed and turned away. "I've heard about that damned Hound. No one has ever escaped."

"I'll try anyway. I'm sorry, Professor."

"About me, about this house? Don't be. I'm only sorry we didn't have time to do more."

"Wait a minute." Montag moved forward. "There's no use your being discovered. We can wipe out the trail here. First the chair. Get me a knife."

Faber ran and brought a knife. With it, Montag attacked the chair where he had been sitting. He cut the upholstery out, into bits, then he shoved it, bit by bit, into the wall incinerator. "Now," he said, "After I leave, rip up the carpet, it has my footprints on it, cut it up, burn it, leave the floor bare. Rub the doorknobs with alcohol, and after I've left here, turn the garden sprinkler on full. That'll wash away every trace."

Faber shook his hand vigorously. "Thank you, thank you! You don't know what this means. I'll do anything to help you in the future. The plan can go on then, if they don't burn my house."

"Of course. Do as I say. And one more thing. A suitcase, get it, fill it with your dirty laundry, the dirtier the better, some denim pants, a shirt, some old sneakers and socks."

"I understand." Faber was gone, and back in a minute with a suitcase which they sealed with scotch tape. "To keep the odor in," said Montag, breathlessly. He swabbed the suitcase with a thick pouring of cognac and whiskey. "I won't want that Hound to pick up two odors at once. When I get a safe distance away, at the river, I'll change clothes."

"And identities. From Montag to Faber."

"Christ, I hope it works! If your clothes are strong enough, which God knows they seem to be, I might at least confuse the Hound."

"Try it, anyway."

"Now, no more talk. I'll run."

They shook hands again and looked at the screen. The Electric Hound was on its way, followed by mobile camera TV units, through alleys and across empty morning streets,

silently, silently, sniffing the great night wind for Mr. Leonard
Montag, going on through the town to bring him to justice.

"We'll show the Hound a thing or two," said Montag.

"Good luck."

"Be seeing you."

And he was out the door, lightly, running with the suitcase.
Behind him, he saw and felt and heard the garden sprinkler
system jump up, filling the dark air with moisture to wash
away the smell of a man named Montag. Through the back
window, the last thing he saw was Faber tearing up the carpet
and cramming it in the wall incinerator.

Montag ran.

Behind him, in the city, ran the electric Hound.

HE STOPPED NOW AND AGAIN, across town, to watch through
the dimly lighted windows of wakened houses. He peered in
at silhouettes of people before television screens, and there on
the screens saw where the Electric Hound was, now at Elm
Terrace, now at Lincoln Avenue, now at 34th Avenue, now up
the alley toward Mr. Faber's, now at Faber's!

Montag held his breath.

Now passing on! Leaving Faber's behind. For a moment
the TV camera scanned Faber's. The house was dark. In the
garden, the water was sprinkling in the cool air, softly.

The Electric hound jumped ahead, down the alley.

"Sleep tight, professor." And Montag was gone, again, racing toward the distant river.

As he ran, he put the Thimble in his ear and a voice ran
with him every step of the way with the beat of his heart and

the sound of his shoes on the gravel: "Look for the pedestrian, look for the pedestrian, citizens, look for the pedestrian. Any one on the sidewalks or in the street, walking or running, is suspect, look for the pedestrian!" How simple, of course, in a city where no one walked. Look, look for the Walking Man, the man who proves his legs. Thank god for good dark alleys where men can walk or run in peace. House lights flashed on all about, porch lights. Montag saw faces peering streetward as he passed behind them, faces hid by curtains, pale, night-frightened faces like animals peering from electric caves, faces with grey eyes and grey souls, and then he hurried on, panting, leaving them to their tasks, and in another minute was at the black, moving river.

The boat floated easily on a long silence of river and went down stream away from the town, bobbing and whispering, while he stripped in darkness down to the flesh, and splashed his body, his arms, legs, and face with raw alcohol. Then he changed into Faber's old clothing and shoes. Whether the stratagem would work or not, there was no way of telling. There could be a delay while they rode the electric Hound up and down river to see where a man named Montag had stepped ashore. Whether or not the smell of Faber would be strong enough, with the aid of raw alcohol, to cover the familiar scent of Montag, was something else again. He must remember to cover his mouth with an alcohol soaked rag after stepping ashore, the particles of his breathing might remain in an invisible cloud for hours after he had passed on.

He saw the distant black butterflies in the sky, three police helicopters bumbling in the air, throwing down great legs of yellow light with which they strode over the earth ahead of the Electric Hound. They were as remote as autumn moths now, but in a few minutes . . . ? He couldn't wait any longer. He was below the town now, in a lonely place of weeds and old rail tracks. He rowed the boat in toward shore, poured the rest of the alcohol on his handkerchief, tied it over his nose and mouth, and leaped out as the boat touched briefly upon the shore.

The current took the boat and the clothes away from him, turning slowly. "Farewell to Mr. Montag," he said. "Hello, Mr. Faber."

He ran into the woods as the sun was rising.

IT WAS AN OLD SECTION OF TOWN. He found his way along railroad tracks that had not been used in a dozen years, crusted with brown rust and overgrown with weeds. He listened to his feet moving in the long grass. He paused now and then and checked behind to see if he was followed, but there was nothing.

Firelight shone ahead, and as he came into its illumination he saw a half dozen figures gathered about the light, their hands out to the flames, conversing quietly. In the distance, a train rolled along a track and was gone.

Montag waited half an hour in the shadows. And then a voice called to him. "All right, you can come out now."

He shrank back. "It's okay," said the voice. "You're welcome."

He let himself stand forth and then he walked toward the fire, peering at the men there.

"Sit down," said the man who seemed to be the leader of the little group. "Have some coffee."

He watched the dark steaming mixture poured into a collapsible cup which was handed him straight-off. He sipped it gingerly and felt the scald on his lips. "Thanks."

"Don't mention it. We don't want to know who you are or where you're from. We're all named Smith. That's the way it is."

"A good way." Montag sipped again and winced.

"Take this," said the man, holding out a small bottle.

"What is it?"

"Take it. Whoever you are now, a few hours from now you'll be someone else. It does something to the perspiratory system. It changes the content of your sweat. Drink it and stay here, otherwise you'll have to move on. If there's a Hound after you you'll be bad company."

Montag hesitated, then drank. The fluid stung and was bitter on its way. He was sick for a moment, a blackness in his eyes, and a roaring in his head. Then it passed.

"That's better." The man took back the empty bottle. "Later, if you want, we can use plastic surgery on your face. Until then, you'll have to stay out of sight."

"How did you know you could trust me?"

The man gestured to the small radio beside the fire.

"We've been listening."

"Quite a chase."

They turned the radio up. "The chase is now veering south along the river. On the eastern shore the police helicopters are converging on Avenue 87 and Elm Grove Park."

"You're safe," said the stranger. "They're faking. You threw them off at the river, but they can't admit it. Must be a million people listening and watching that bunch hound after you. They'll catch you in five minutes. Watch."

"But if they're ten miles away, how can they . . ."

"Look."

He turned the TV up.

"Up that street somewhere is a poor son-of-a-bitch, out for an early morning walk, maybe, having a smoke, taking it easy. Call him Billings or Brown or Baumgartner, but the search is getting near him every minute. There! See!"

In the video screen a man turned a corner. The Hound rushed forward, screeching.

"There's Montag now!" shouted the radio voice.

"The search is over!"

The innocent man stood watching the crowd come on. In his hand was a cigarette, half smoked. He looked at the Hound and his jaw dropped and he opened his mouth to say something, then a God-like voice boomed. "All right, Montag, don't move. We've got you, Montag!"

By the quiet fire, with six other men, Montag sat ten miles away, the light of the video screen on his face.

"Don't run, Montag!"

The man turned and bolted. The crowd roared. The Hound leaped ahead.

"The poor son-of-a-bitch."

A dozen shots rattled out. The man crumpled.

"Montag is dead, the search is over, a criminal is given his due!" cried the announcer.

The camera panned up near the dead man. Just before it showed his face, however, the screen went black.

"We now switch you to the Sky room of the Hotel Lux in Pittsburg for a half hour of dance music by—"

The stranger cut it off. "They couldn't show the man's

face, naturally. Better if everyone thinks it's Montag."

The man put out his hand. "Welcome back from the dead, Mr. Montag." Montag took the hand a moment. The man said, "My name is Stewart, former occupant of the T.S. Eliot Chair at Cambridge. That was before it became an Electrical Engineering school. This gentleman here is Dr. Simmons from U.C.L.A., wasn't it, Doctor?" A nod.

"I don't belong here," said Montag. "I've been an idiot."

"Rage makes idiots of us all, you can only be angry so long and then you blow up and do the wrong things, and it can't be helped now."

"I shouldn't have come here, it might endanger you."

"We're used to that. We all made mistakes, too, or we wouldn't be here. When we were separate individuals, all we had was rage. I struck a fireman who had come to demand my library in 2010. I had to run. I've been running ever since. And Dr. Simmons here . . ."

"I started quoting Donne in the midst of a genetics lecture one afternoon. You see? Fools, all of us."

They looked into the fire for a moment.

"So you want to join us, Mr. Montag?'

"Yes."

"What have you to offer."

"The book of Job, no more, no less, I'm afraid."

"The Book of Job will do very well. Where is it?"

"Here." Montag touched his head.

"Ah-ha!" said Stewart. Simmons smiled.

"WHAT'S WRONG, ISN'T IT ALL RIGHT?" asked Montag.

"Better than all right, perfect. Mr. Montag, you have hit

upon the secret of our organization. Living books, Mr. Montag, living books. Inside the old skull where no one can see." He turned to Simmons. "Do we have a book of Job?"

"Only one. A man named Harris in Youngstown."

"Mr. Montag." The man reached out and held Montag's shoulder firmly. "Walk slowly, and carefully, and take care of yourself. If anything should happen to Harris, you are the book of Job. Do you see how important you are?"

"It scares the hell out of me. At first I didn't remember, and then, tonight, on the river, it suddenly came back, all of it."

"Good. Many people are fast studies but don't know it. Some of God's simplest creatures have the ability called eidetic memory, the ability to remember entire pages of print at one glance. It has nothing to do with IQ. No offense, Mr. Montag. It varies. Would you like, one day, to read Plato's *Republic?*"

"Of course."

Stewart gestured to a man who had been sitting to one side. "Mr. Plato, if you please."

The man began to talk. He stared into the fire idly, his hands filling a corncob pipe, unaware of the words tumbling from his lips. He talked for two minutes without a pause.

Stewart made the smallest move of his hand and the man stopped. "Perfect word for word memory, every word important, every word Plato's," said Stewart.

"And," said the man who was Plato, "I don't understand a damned word of it. I just say it. It's up to you to understand."

"None of it?"

"None. But I can't get it out. Once it's in, it's like glue in a bottle, there for good. Mr. Stewart says it's important, that's good enough for me."

"We're old friends," said Stewart. "Grew up together. Met a few years ago on that track, somewhere between here and Seattle, walking, me running away from the firemen, him away from cities."

"Never liked cities. I always felt that cities owned men, that was all, and used men to keep themselves going, to keep machines oiled and dusted, so I got out. And then I met Stewart and he found out I had this eidetic memory as he calls it, and he gave me a book to read and then we burned the book so we wouldn't be caught with it, and now I'm Plato, that's what I am."

"He is also Socrates."

The man bowed.

"And Schopenhauer."

The man nodded again.

"And Nietzsche."

"All that in one bottle," said the man. "You wouldn't think there was room. But I can open my mind up like a concertina, and play it. There's plenty of room if you don't try to think about what you read, it's when you start thinking that all of a sudden it's crowded. I don't think about anything except eating and sleeping and traveling. There's plenty of room."

"So here we are, Plato and his confreres in this man, Mr. Simmons in really Mr. Donne, Mr. Darwin and Mr. Aristophanes. These other gentlemen are Matthew, Mark, Luke and John, we are not without humor, despite this melancholy age, and I'm bits and pieces, snatches of Byron and Shaw and Washington and Galileo and DaVinci and Washington Irving. A kaleidoscope. Hold me up to the sun and give me a shake. And you are Mr. Job, and in half an hour or more, a war will begin, while those people in the anthill across the river have been busy with chasing Montag, the war has been getting underway. By this time tomorrow the world will belong to the little green towns and the rusted railroad tracks and the men walking the ties, that's us. The cities will be soot and ash and baking powder."

The TV set rang a bell. "Final negotiations are now arranged for a conference tomorrow with the leaders of the enemy government, too—"

Stewart switched it off.

"Well, what do you think, Mr. Montag?"

"It's amazing, it's not to be believed. I was pretty blind, trying to go at it the way I did, planting books and calling firemen."

"You did what you thought you had to do. But our way simply is better to keep the knowledge intact and not get excited or mad, but just wait quietly until the machines are dented junk, and then step up and say, here we are, we've been waiting and now you've come to your senses, civilized man, perhaps a book will do you good."

"How many of you are there?"

"Thousands on the road, on the rails, just bums on the outside, libraries on the inside. It wasn't really planned, it grew. Each man had a book he wanted to remember. He did. Then we discovered each other and made the plan. Some of us live in small towns across the country. Chapter one of *Walden* in Nantucket, chapter two in Rhode Island, chapter three in Waukesha, chapter four and five in Tucson, each according to his ability, some people can memorize a lot, some only a few lines."

"The books are safe then."

"Couldn't be safer. Why, there's one little village of 200 people in North Carolina, no bomb'll ever touch it, which is the complete *Meditations* of Marcus Aurelius. You could pick the people up and flip them like pages, almost, a page to a person. People who wouldn't dream of being seen with a book, gladly memorized a page. You couldn't be caught with that. And when the war's over and we have the time and need, the books will be written again, the people will be called in one by one to recite what they know and it'll be in print again until another Dark Age when maybe we'll have to do the whole damned thing over again, man being the fool he is."

"What do we do tonight?" asked Montag.

"Just wait, that's all."

"Not anymore," said Simmons. "Look."

But even as he said it, it was over and done, the war.

Montag glanced up.

THE BOMBS BEGAN TO FALL ON THE CITY. They stood in the sky as if someone had thrown up a handful of wheat grains and they were balanced there for a moment between the buildings and the stars, and then they fell down. They picked the buildings apart, separated windows from doors, beams from jousts, roofs from walls, and people from bricks, then put them all back together again in a powdery heap. The sound came after this.

"Isn't it funny," said Mr. Bedloe at the fire, watching. "Man comes along and throws stones and cement and water into a concrete mixer and pours it and it's a city, then he comes along with the biggest damn concrete mixer of all time and throws the city back into it and grinds it around and you've got stones and dust and water again."

"My wife's somewhere in that city," said Montag.

"I'm sorry to hear that."

The city took another flight of bombs. Now it was burning.

"As I was saying," said Mr. Bedloe. "It all has to come down. There it is, coming down fast. And here we are, waiting for it to finish falling."

"I wonder if she's all right," said Montag.

"Whatever she is now she's better than she was," said Bedloe. "Being dead is better than being dull, being dead is better than not being aware."

"I hope she's alive."

"She'll be fretting tomorrow because the television isn't on. Not because the city's dead, no, or the people, but because she'll be missing Zack Zack, the greatest comedian of all time."

The bombardment was finished and over, even while the seeds were in the windy sky, even while they drifted with dreadful slowness down upon a city where all of the people looked up at their destiny coming upon them like the lid of a dream shutting tight and becoming an instant later a red and powdery nightmare, the bombardment to all intents and purposes was finished, for once the ships had sighted their target and alerted their bombardier at three thousand miles an hour, as quick as the whisper of a knife through the sky, the war was finished; once the trigger was pulled, once the bombs took flight, it was over. Now, a full three seconds, all of the time in history, before the bombs struck, the enemy ships themselves were gone, around the visible world, it seemed, like bullets a caveman might not believe in because they remain unseen, but nevertheless the heart is suddenly struck, the body falls into separate divisions, the blood is astounded to be free on the air, and the brain gives up all its precious memories, and still puzzled, dies.

This war was not to be believed. It was a gesture. It was the flirt of a great metal hand over the city and a voice saying, "Disintegrate. Leave not one stone upon another. Perish. Die."

Montag held the bombs in the sky for a precious moment, with his mind and his hands. "Run," he cried to Faber. To Clarisse: "Run, get out, get out!" But Faber was out. There, in the deep valleys of the country, went the dawn train on its way from one desolation to another. Though the desolation had not yet arrived, was still in the air, it was as certain as man could make it. Before the train had gone another fifty yards on the track, its destination would be meaningless, its point of departure made from a metropolis into a yard, and in that metropolis now, in the half second left, as the bombs perhaps were three inches, three small inches shy of her hotel building, Montag could see Mildred, leaning into the TV set as if all of the hunger of looking would find the secret of her sleepless unease there, leaning anxiously, nervously into that tubular world as into a crystal ball to find happiness. The first bomb struck. Perhaps the television station went first into oblivion. Montag saw the screen go dark in Mildred's face and her screaming, because, in the next millionth part of time remaining, Mildred would see her own face reflected there, hungry and alone, in a mirror instead of a crystal, and it would be such a wildly empty face that she would at last recognize it, and stare at the ceiling almost with welcome as it and the entire structure of the hotel blasted down upon her and carried her with a million pounds of brick, metal and people down into the cellar, there to dispose of them in its unreasonable way.

Montag found himself on his face. The concussion had knocked the air across the river, and turned the men down like dominoes in a line, blown out the fire like a last candle, and caused the trees to mourn with a great voice of wind passing away south. Montag raised his head. Now the city, instead of the bombs, was in the air, they had displaced each other. For another of those impossible instants the city stood, rebuilt and unrecognizable, taller than it had ever hoped to be, taller than man had built it, erected at last in gusts of dust and sparkles of torn metal into a city not unlike the shakings of a kaleidoscope in a giant hand, now one pattern, now another, but all of it formed of flame and steel and stone, a door where a window ought to be, a top for a bottom, a side for a back, and then the city rolled over and fell down dead. The sound of its death came after.

"THERE," SAID THE STRANGER.

The men lay like gasping fish on the grass.

They did not get up for a long time, but held to the earth as children hold to a familiar thing, no matter how cold or dead, no matter what has happened or will happen, their fingers were clawed into the soil, and they were all shouting to keep their ears in balance and open, Montag shouting with them, a protest against the wind that swept over them and made their noses bleed. Montag watched the blood drip into the earth with such an abstraction that the city was forgotten.

The wind died.

The city was flat as if one took a heaping tablespoon of

baking powder and passed one finger over it, smoothing it to an even level.

The man said nothing. They lay awhile like people on the dawn edge of sleep, not yet ready to arise and begin the day with its obligations, its fires and foods, its thousand details of putting foot after foot, hand after hand, its deliveries and functions and minute obsessions. They lay blinking their stunned eyelids. You could hear them breathing faster, then slower, then slow.

Montag sat up but did not move farther. The other men did likewise, sun was touching the horizon with a faint red tip. The air was cool and sweet and smelled of rain. In a few minutes it would smell of dust and pulverized iron, but now it was sweet.

Silently, the leader of the small group arose, felt his arms and legs, touched his face to see if everything was in its place, then shuffled over to the blown-out fire and bent over it. Montag watched. Striking a match, the man touched it to a piece of paper and shoved this under a bit of kindling, placed together tiny bits of straw and dry kindling, and after a while, drawing the men slowly, awkwardly to it, the fire was licking up, coloring their faces pink and yellow, while the sun rose slowly to color their backs.

There was no sound except the low and secret talk of men at morning, and the talk was this:

"How many strips?"

"Two each."

The bacon was counted out on a wax paper. The frying pan was set to the fire and the bacon laid in it. After a moment it began to flutter and dance in the pan and the sputter of it filled the morning air with its aroma. Eggs were cracked in upon the bacon and the men watched this ritual, for the leader was a participant, as were they, in a religion of early rising, a thing man had done for many centuries, and Montag felt at ease, among them, as if during the night the walls of a great jail had vaporized around them and they were on the land again and only the birds sang on or off as they pleased, no schedule, and no insistence.

"Here," said the old man, dishing out the bacon and eggs to each from the hot pan.

And then, without looking up, breaking fresh eggs into the pan, the leader, slowly, and with a concern both for what he said, recalling it, rounding it, but careful of making the food also began to recite snatches and rhythms, even while the day brightened all about as if a pink lamp had been given more wick, and Montag listened and they all looked at the tin plates in their hands, waiting a moment for the eggs to cool, while the leader started the routine, and others took it up, here or there, about, and when it was Montag's turn he spoke, too:

"Thy days are as grass . . ."

"To be or not to be, that is the question . . ."

The bacon sputtered.

"She walks in beauty like the night . . ."

"Behold, the lilies of the fields . . ."

The forks moved in the pink light.

"They, oil not, neither do they spin . . ."

The sun was fully up.

"Oh, do you remember Sweet Alice, Ben Bolt . . . ?"

Montag felt fine.

THE FIREMAN

Fire, Fire, Burn Books

THE FOUR MEN SAT SILENTLY PLAYING BLACKJACK UNDER a green drop-light in the dark morning. Only a voice whispered from the ceiling:

"One thirty-five a.m. Thursday morning, October 4th, 2052, A.D. . . . One forty a.m. . . . one fifty . . ."

Mr. Montag sat stiffly among the other firemen in the fire house, heard the voice-clock mourn out the cold hour and the cold year, and shivered.

The other three glanced up.

"What's wrong, Montag?"

A radio hummed somewhere. "War may be declared any hour. This country is ready to defend its destiny and . . ."

The fire house trembled as five hundred jet-planes screamed across the black morning sky.

The firemen slumped in their coal-blue uniforms, with the look of thirty years in their blue-shaved, sharp, pink faces and their burnt-colored hair. Stacked behind them were glittering piles of auxiliary helmets. Downstairs in concrete dampness the fire monster itself slept, the silent dragon of nickel and tangerine colors, the boa-constrictor hoses, the twinkling brass.

"I'm thinking of our last job," said Mr. Montag.

"Don't," said Leahy, the fire chief.

"That poor man, when we burned his library. How would it feel if firemen burned *our* houses and *our* books?"

"We haven't any books."

"But if we *did* have some."

"You *got* some?"

"No."

Montag gazed beyond them to the wall and the typed lists of a million forbidden books. The titles cringed in fire, burning down the years under his ax and his fire hose spraying not water but—kerosene!

"Was it always like this?" asked Mr. Montag. "The fire house, our duties. I mean, well, once upon a time . . ."

"Once upon a time?" Leahy crowed. "What kind of language is *that?*"

Fool! cried Mr. Montag to himself. You'll give yourself away! The last fire. A book of fairy tales. He had dared to read a line or so. "I mean," he said quickly, "in the old days, before homes were completely fireproof, didn't firemen ride to fires to put them out, instead of *start* them."

"I never knew that." Stoneman and Black drew forth their rule books and laid them where Montag, though long familiar with them, might read:

1. Answer the alarm quickly.
2. Start the fire swiftly.
3. Be sure you burn everything.

4. Report back to the fire house.

5. Stand alert for another alarm.

EVERYONE WATCHED MONTAG.

He swallowed. "What will they do to that old man we caught last night with his books?"

"Insane asylum."

"But he wasn't insane!"

"Any man's insane who thinks he can hide books from the government or us." Leahy blew a great fiery cloud of cigar smoke from his thin mouth. He idled back.

The alarm sounded.

The bell kicked itself two hundred times in a few seconds. Suddenly there were three empty chairs. The cards fell in a snow flurry. The brass pole trembled. The men were gone, their hats with them. Montag still sat. Below, the orange dragon coughed to life.

Montag slid down the pole like a man in a dream.

"Montag, you forgot your hat!"

He got it and they were off, the night wind hammering about their siren noise and their mighty metal thunder.

It was a flaking three-story house in the old section of town. A century old if it was a day, but, like every house, it had been given a thin fireproof plastic coat fifty years ago, and this preservative shell seemed to be holding it up.

"Here we are!"

The engine slammed to a stop. Leahy, Stoneman, and Black ran up the sidewalk, suddenly odious and fat in their plump slickers. Montag followed.

They crashed the front door and caught a woman, running.

"I didn't hurt anyone," she cried.

"Where are they?" Leahy twisted her wrist.

"You wouldn't take an old woman's pleasures from her, would you?"

Stoneman produced the telephone alarm card with the complaint signed in facsimile duplicate on the back. "Says here, Chief, the books are in the attic."

"All right, men, let's get 'em!"

Next thing they were up in musty blackness, swinging silver hatchets at doors that were, after all, unlocked, tumbling through like boys all rollick and shout.

"Hey!"

A fountain of books sprayed down on Montag as he climbed shuddering up the steep stair well. Books bombarded his shoulders, his pale face. A book lit, almost obediently, like a white pigeon, in his hands, wings fluttering. In the dim wavering light a page hung open and it was like a snowy feather, the words delicately painted thereon. In all the rush and fervor, Montag had only an instant to read a line, but it blazed in his mind for the next minute as if stamped there with a fiery iron. He dropped the book. Immediately, another fell into his arms.

"Montag, come on up!"

Montag's hand closed like a trap, crushed the book with wild devotion, with an insanity of mindlessness to his chest. The men above were hurling shovelfuls of literature into the dusty air. They fell like slaughtered birds and the woman stood like a small girl among the bodies.

"Montag!"

He climbed up into the attic.

"This too shall pass away."

"What?" Leahy glared at him.

Montag froze, blinking. "Did I *say* something?"

"Move, you idiot!"

THE BOOKS LAY IN PILES like fishes left to dry.

"Trash! Trash!" The men danced on the books. Titles glittered their golden eyes, falling, gone.

"Kerosene!"

They pumped the cool fluid from the white snake they had twined upstairs. They coated every book; they pumped rooms full of it.

"This is better than the old man's place last night, eh?"

That had not been as much fun. The old man had lived in an apartment house with other people. They had had to use controlled fire there. Here, they could ravage the entire house.

They ran downstairs, Montag reeling after them in the kerosene fumes.

"Come on, woman!"

"My books," she said, quietly. She knelt among them to touch the drenched leather, to read the gilt titles with her fingers instead of her eyes, while her eyes accused Montag.

"You can't take my books," she said.

"You know the law," said Leahy. "Pure nonsense, all of it. No two books alike, none agreeing. Confusion. Stories about people who never existed. Come on now."

"No," she said.

"The whole house'll burn."

"I won't go."

The three men walked clumsily to the door. They glanced back at Montag, who stood near the woman.

"You're not leaving her *here?*" he protested.

"She won't come."

"But she's got to!"

Leahy raised his hand. It contained the concealed igniter to start the fire. "Got to get back to the station. Besides, she'd cost us a trial, money, jail."

Montag placed his hand around the woman's elbow. "You can come with me."

"No." She actually focused her eyes on him for a moment. "Thank you, anyway."

"I'm counting to ten," said Leahy. "One, two . . ."

"Please," said Montag.

"Go on," said the woman.

"Three," said Leahy.

"Come." Montag pulled at her.

"I want to stay here," she replied, quietly.

"Four, five . . ." said Leahy.

The woman twisted. Montag slipped on an oily book and fell. The woman ran up the stairs half way and stood there with the books at her feet.

"Six . . . seven . . . Montag," said Leahy.

Montag did not move. He looked out the door at that man there with the pink face, pink and burned and shiny from too many fires, pink from night excitements, the pink face of Mr. Leahy with the igniter poised in his pink fingers.

Montag felt the book hidden against his pounding chest.

"Go get him!" said Leahy.

THE MEN DRAGGED MONTAG yelling from the house.

Leahy backed out after them, leaving a kerosene trail down the walk. When they were a hundred feet away, Montag was still shouting and kicking. He glanced back wildly.

In the front door where she had come to gaze out at them quietly, her quietness a condemnation, staring straight into Mr. Leahy's eyes, was the woman.

Leahy twitched his finger to ignite the fuel.

He was too late. Montag gasped.

The woman in the door, reaching with contempt toward them all, struck a match against the saturated wood.

People ran out of houses all down the street.

"WHO IS IT?"

"Who would it be?" said Mr. Montag, leaning back against the closed door in the dark.

His wife said, at last. "Well, put on the light."

"I don't want the light," he said.

"Come to bed."

He heard her roll impatiently; the springs squeaked. "Are you drunk?"

He worked out of his coat and let it slump to the floor. He held his pants out into an abyss and let them fall forever and forever into darkness.

His wife said, "What *are* you doing?"

He balanced in space with the book in his sweating, icy hand.

A minute later, she said, "Well, don't just stand there in the middle of the room."

He made a small sound.

"What?" she asked.

He made more soft sounds. He stumbled toward the bed and shoved the book clumsily under the cold pillow. He fell into bed and his wife cried out, startled. He lay separate from her. She talked to him for what seemed a long while and when he didn't reply but only made sounds, he felt her hand creep over, up along his chest, his throat, his chin. Her hand brushed his cheeks. He knew that she pulled her hand away from his cheeks wet.

A long time later, when he was finally floating into sleep, he heard her say, "You smell of kerosene."

"I always smell of kerosene," he mumbled.

Late in the night he looked over at Mildred. She was awake. There was a tiny dance of melody in the room. She had her thimble-radio tamped into her ear, listening, listening to far people in far places, her eyes peeled wide at deep ceilings of blackness. Many nights in the last ten years he had found her with her eyes open, like a dead woman. She would lie that way, blankly, hour upon hour, and then rise and go soundlessly to the bath. You could hear faucet water run, the tinkle of the sedatives bottle, and Mildred gulping hungrily, frantically, at sleep.

She was awake now. In a minute she would rise and go for the barbiturates.

"Mildred," he thought.

And suddenly she was so strange to him that he couldn't believe that he knew her at all. He was in someone else's house, like those jokes men told about the gentleman, drunk on life, who had come home late at night, unlocked the wrong door, entered a wrong room. And now here Montag lay in the strange night by this unidentified body he had never seen before.

"Millie?" he called.

"What?"

"I didn't mean to startle you. What I want to know is, when did we meet? And *where?*"

"For what?" she asked.

"I mean, originally."

She was frowning in the dark.

He clarified it. "The first time we met, where was it, and when?"

"Why, it was at . . ."

She stopped.

"I don't know."

He was frightened. "Can't you remember?"

They both tried.

"It's been so long."

"Only ten years. We're only thirty!"

"Don't get excited, I'm trying to think!" She laughed a strange laugh. "How funny, not to remember where or when you met your husband or wife!"

He lay with his eyes tight, pressing, massaging his brow. It was suddenly more important than any other thing in a lifetime that he knew where he had met Mildred.

"It doesn't matter." She was up, in the bathroom now. He heard the water rushing, the swallowing sound.

"No, I guess not," he said.

And he wondered, did she take twenty tablets now, like a year ago, when we had to pump her stomach, and me shouting to keep her awake, walking her, asking her why she did it, why she wanted to die, and she saying she didn't know, she didn't know, she didn't know anything about anything!

She didn't belong to him; he didn't belong to her. She didn't know herself, him, or anyone; the world didn't need her, she didn't need herself, and in the hospital he had realized that if she died he would not cry. For it was the dying of an unknown, a street face, a face in the newspaper, and it was suddenly so wrong that he had begun to cry, not at death but at the thought of *not* crying at death, a silly empty man beside an empty woman while the doctors emptied her still more.

And why are we empty, lonely, and not in love? he had asked himself, a year ago.

They were never together. There was always something between, a radio, a televisor, a car, a plane, a game, nervous exhaustion, or, simply, a little pheno-barbitol. They didn't know each other; they knew things, inventions. They had both applauded science while it had built a beautiful glass structure, a glittering miracle of contraptions about them, and, too late, they had found it to be a glass wall. They could not shout through the wall; they could only pantomime silently, never touching, hearing, barely seeing each other.

Looking at Mildred at the hospital, he had thought, does it matter if we live or die?

That might not have been enough if the people had not moved next door with their daughter.

Perhaps that had been the start of his awareness of his job, his marriage, his life.

ONE NIGHT—IT WAS SO LONG AGO—he had gone out for a long walk. In the moonlight, he realized that he had come out to get away from the nagging of his wife's television set. He walked, hands in pockets, blowing steam from his mouth into the cold air.

"Alone." He looked at the avenues ahead. "By God, I'm alone. Not another pedestrian in miles." He walked swiftly down street after street. "Why, I'm the only pedestrian in the entire city!" The streets were empty and long and quiet. Distantly, on crosstown arteries, a few cars moved in the dark. But no other man ventured upon the earth to test the use of his legs. In fact, it had been so many years since the sidewalks were used that they were buckling, becoming obscured with grass.

So he walked alone, aware of his loneliness, until the police car pulled up and flashed its cold white light upon him.

"What're you doing?" shouted a voice.

"I'm out for a walk."

"He says he's out for a walk."

The laughter, the cold, precise turning over of his identity cards, the careful noting of his address.

"Okay, mister, you can *walk* now."

He had gone on, stomping his feet, jerking his mouth and hands, eyes blazing, gripping his elbows. "The nerve! The nerve! Is there a law against pedestrians?"

The girl turned a corner and walked toward him.

"Why, hello," she said, and put out her hand. "You're my neighbor, aren't you?"

"Am I?" he said.

She was smiling quietly. "We're the only live ones, aren't we?" She waved at the empty sidewalks. "Did the police stop you, too?"

"Walking's a crime."

"They flashed their lights on me, but saw I was a woman—" She was no more than sixteen, Montag estimated, with eyes and hair as dark as mulberries, and a paleness about her that was not illness but radiance. "Then they drove away. I'm Clarisse McClellan. And you're Mr. Montag, the fireman."

They walked together. And she began to talk for both of them.

"Isn't it a graveyard, this town," she said. "I like to walk just to keep my franchise on the sidewalks."

He looked, and it was true. The city was like a dark tomb, every house deep in television dimness, not a sound or move anywhere.

"HAVE YOU EVER NOTICED all the cars rushing?" she asked. "On the big boulevards down that way, day and night. I sometimes think they don't know what grass is, or flowers, because they never see them slowly. If you showed them a green blur, oh yes! They'd say, that's grass! A pink blur, yes, that's *roses!*" She laughed to herself. "And a white blur's a house. Quick brown blurs are cows. My uncle drove slow on a highway once. They threw him in jail. Isn't that funny and sad, too?"

"You think about a lot of things for a girl," said Montag, uneasily.

"That's because I've got time to think. I never watch TV or go to games or races or funparks. So I've lots of time for crazy thoughts, I guess. Have you seen the two-hundred-foot-long billboards in the country? Well, did you know that once billboards were only twenty-five feet long? But cars started going by so quickly, they had to stretch the advertising out so it could be seen."

"I didn't know that." Montag laughed abruptly.

"I bet I know something else you don't."

"What?"

"There's dew on the grass in the morning."

He couldn't remember, and it suddenly frightened him.

"And, if you look, there's a man in the moon."

He had never looked. His heart beat rapidly.

They walked the rest of the way in silence. When they reached her house, its lights were all blazing. It was the only house, in a city of a million houses, with its lights burning brightly.

"What's going on?" Montag had never seen that many house lights.

"Oh, just my mother and father and uncle sitting around, talking. It's like being a pedestrian, only rarer."

"But what do they *talk* about?"

She laughed at this, said good night, and was gone.

At three o'clock in the morning, he got out of bed and stuck his head out the front window. The moon was rising and there was a man in the moon. Over the broad lawn, a million jewels of dew sparkled.

"I'll be damned," said Montag, and went back to bed.

HE SAW CLARISSE MANY AFTERNOONS and came to hope he would be seeing her, found himself watching for her sitting on her green lawn, studying the autumn leaves with a fine casual air, or returning from a distant woods with wild yellow flowers, or looking at the sky, even while it was raining.

"Isn't rain nice?" she said.

"I hadn't noticed."

"Believe me, it *is* nice."

He always laughed embarrassedly. Whether at her, or at himself, he wasn't sure. "I believe you."

"Do you really? Do you ever smell old leaves? Don't they smell like cinnamon? Here."

"Why, it is cinnamon, yes!"

She gazed at him with her clear dark eyes. "My gosh, you don't really know very much, do you?" She was not unkind, just concerned for him.

"I don't suppose any of us know much."

"I do," she said, quietly, "because I've time to look."

"Don't you attend school?"

"Oh, no. They say I'm anti-social. I don't mix. And the yelling bully is the thing among kids this season, you know."

"It's been a long season," observed Mr. Montag, and stood somewhat shocked at his own perception.

"Then you've noticed?"

"Yes. But what about your friends?"

"I haven't any. That's supposed to prove I'm abnormal. But they're always packed around the TV, or racing in cars, or shouting or beating one another. Do you notice how people hurt one another nowadays?"

"You sound ancient."

"I am. I know about rain. That makes me ancient to them. They kill each other. It didn't used to be that way, did it? Children killing each other all the time? Four of my friends have been shot in the past year. I'm afraid of children."

"Maybe it was always this way."

"My father says his grandfather remembered when children didn't kill each other, when children were seen and not heard. But that was a long time ago, when they had discipline and responsibility. Do you know, I'm disciplined. I'm spanked when I need it, and I've responsibility. I do all the shopping and housecleaning. By hand."

"And you know about rain," said Mr. Montag, with the rain beating on his hat and coat.

"It tastes good if you lean back and open your mouth. Go on."

He leaned back and gaped.

"Why," he said, "it's *wine*."

THAT HAD NOT BEEN THE END OF IT. The girl had talked to him one bright afternoon and given him the dandelion test.

"It proves you're in love or not."

She brushed a dandelion under his chin.

"What a shame! You're not in love with anyone."

And he thought, when did I stop loving Mildred? and the answer was never! For he had never known her. She was the pale, sad goldfish that swam in the subterranean illumination of the television parlor, her natural habitat.

"It's the dandelion you use," protested Montag.

"No," said Clarisse, solemnly. "You're not in love. A dandelion won't help." She tossed the flower away. "Well, I've got to go see my psychiatrist. My teachers are sending me to him. He's trying to make me normal."

"I'll throttle him if he does!"

"Right now he's trying to figure out why I go away from the city and walk in the forests once a day. Have you ever walked in a forest? No? It's so quiet and lovely, and nobody rushing. I like to watch the birds and the insects. They don't rush."

Before she left him to go inside, she looked at him suddenly and said, "Do you know, Mr. Montag, I can't believe you're a fireman."

"Why not?"

"Because you're so nice. Do you mind if I ask one last question?"

"I don't mind."

"Why do you do what you *do?*"

But before he knew what she meant or could make a reply, she had run off, embarrassed at her own frankness.

"What did she mean, why do I do what I do?" he said to himself. "I'm a fireman, of course. I burn books. Is *that* what she meant?"

He didn't see Clarisse for a month. He watched for her each day, but made no point of her absence to his wife. He wanted to go rap on her parents' door, but decided against it; he didn't want them misunderstanding his interest in the child. But after thirty-six days had passed, he brought Clarisse's name up offhand.

"Oh, her?" said Mildred, with the radio music jarring the table plates. "Why, didn't you know?"

"Know what?"

"She was killed by an automobile a month ago."

"A month! But why didn't someone tell me!"

"Didn't I? I suppose it slipped my mind. Yes, a car hit her."

"Did they find whose car it was?"

"No. You know how those things are. What do you want for supper, frozen steak or chops?"

And so Clarisse was dead. No, disappeared! For in a large city you didn't die, you simply vanished. No one missed you, no one saw you go; your death was as insignificant as that of a butterfly carried secretly away, caught in the radiator grille of a speeding car.

And with Clarisse's death, half of the world was dead, and the other half was instantly revealed to him for what it was.

He saw what Mildred was and always would be, what he himself was but didn't want to be any more. And he saw that it was no idle thing, Mildred's suicide attempts, the lovely dark girl with the flowers being ground under a car; it was a thing of the world they lived in. It was a part of the screaming, pressing down of people into electric molds. It was the meaningless flight of civilization down a rotary track to smash its own senseless tail. Mildred's flight was trying to die and escape nothingness, whereas Clarisse had been fighting nothingness with something, with being aware instead of forgetting, with walking instead of sitting, with going to get life instead of having it brought to her.

And the civilization had killed her for her trouble. Not purposely, no, but with a fine ironic sense, for no purpose at all. Killed by a vanilla-faced idiot racing nowhere for nothing and irritated that he had been detained 120 seconds while the police investigated and released him on his way to some distant base that he must tag frantically before running for home.

Montag felt the slow gathering of awareness. Mildred, Clarisse. The firemen. The murdering children. Last night, the old man's books burned and him in an asylum. Tonight, that woman burned before his eyes. It was such a nightmare that only another nightmare, less horrible, could be used to escape from it, and Clarisse had died weeks ago and he had not seen her die, which made it somehow crueler and yet more bearable.

"Clarisse. Clarisse."

Montag lay all night long, thinking, smelling the smoke on his hands, in the dark.

HE HAD CHILLS AND FEVER IN THE MORNING.

"You can't be sick," said Mildred.

He closed his eyes upon the hotness. "Yes."

"But you were all right last night."

"No, I wasn't all right." He heard the radio in the parlor.

Mildred stood over his bed, curiously. He felt her there; he saw her without opening his eyes, her hair burned by chemicals to a brittle straw, her eyes with a kind of mental cataract unseen but suspect far behind the pupils, the reddened pouting lips, the body as thin as a praying mantis from dieting, and her flesh like raw milk. He could remember her no other way.

"Will you bring me an analgesic and water?"

"You've got to get up," she said. "It's noon. You've slept five hours later than usual."

"Will you turn the radio off?" he asked

"That's my favorite program."

"Will you turn it off for a sick man?"

"I'll turn it down."

She went out of the room and did nothing to the radio and came back. "Is that better?"

"Thanks."

"That's my favorite program," she repeated, as if she had not said it a thousand times before.

"What about the analgesic?"

"You've never been sick before." She went away again.

"Well, I'm sick now. I'm not going to work tonight. Call Leahy for me."

"You acted funny last night." She returned, humming.

"Where's the analgesic?" He glanced at the water glass.

"Oh." She walked to the bath again. "Did something happen?"

"A fire, that's all."

"I had a nice evening," she said, in the bathroom.

"What doing?"

"Television."

"What was on."

"Programs."

"What programs?"

"Some of the best ever.

"Who?"

"Oh, you know, the big shows."

"Yes, the big shows, big, big, big." He pressed at the pain in his eyes and suddenly the odor of kerosene made him vomit.

Mildred came in, humming. She was surprised. "Why'd you do that?"

He looked with dismay at the floor. "We burned an old woman with her books."

"It's a good thing the rug's washable." She fetched a mop and swabbed clumsily at it. "I went to Helen's last night."

"Couldn't you get the shows on your own TV?"

"Sure, but it's nice visiting."

"Did Helen get over that finger infection?"

"I didn't notice."

SHE WENT OUT INTO THE LIVING ROOM. He heard her by the radio, singing.

"Mildred," he called.

She returned, singing, snapping her fingers softly.

"Aren't you going to ask me about last night?" he said.

"What about it?"

"We burned a thousand books and a woman."

"*Forbidden* books."

The radio was exploding in the parlor.

"Yes: copies of Plato and Socrates and Marcus Aurelius."

"Foreigners?"

"Something like that."

"Then they were radicals?"

"All foreigners can't be radicals."

"If they wrote books, they were." Mildred fiddled with the telephone. "You don't expect me to call Mr. Leahy, do you?"

"You must!"

"Don't shout."

"I wasn't shouting!" he cried. He was up in bed, suddenly, enraged and flushed, shaking. The radio roared in the hot air. "I can't call him. I can't tell him I'm sick."

"Why?"

"Because . . ."

Because you're afraid, he thought, pretending illness, afraid to call Leahy because after a moment's discussion the conversation would run so: "Yes, Mr. Leahy, I feel better already. I'll be in at ten o'clock tonight."

"You're not sick," she said.

Montag fell back in bed. He reached under his pillow and groped for the hidden book. It was still there.

"Mildred, how would it be if—well, maybe I quit my job a while?"

"You want to give up everything? After all these years of working, because, one night, some woman and her books—"

"You should have seen her, Millie!"

"She's nothing to me. She shouldn't have had books. It was her responsibility; she should've thought of that. I hate her. She's got you going and next you know we'll be out, no house, no job, nothing."

"You weren't there. You didn't see," he said. "There must be something in books, whole worlds we don't dream about, to make a woman stay in a burning house. There must be something fine there. You don't stay and burn for nothing."

"She was simple-minded."

"She was as rational as you or I, and we burned her!"

"That's water under the bridge."

"No, not water, Millie, but fire. You ever see a burned house? It smolders for days. Well, this fire'll last me half a century. My God, I've been trying put it out, in my mind, all night, and I'm crazy with trying!"

"You should've thought of that before becoming a fireman."

"THOUGHT!" HE SAID. "Was I given a choice? I was raised to think the best thing in the world *is not* to read. The best thing is television and radio and ball games and a home I can't afford and, Good Lord, now, only now I realize what I've done. My grandfather and father were firemen. Walking in my sleep, I followed them."

The radio was playing a dance tune.

"I've been killing the brain of the world for ten years, pouring kerosene on it. Millie, a book is a brain. It isn't only that woman we destroyed, or others like her, in these years, but it's the thoughts I burned and never knew it."

He got out of bed.

"It took some man a lifetime to put some of his thoughts on paper, looking after all the beauty and goodness in life, and then we come along in two minutes and heave it in the incinerator!"

"Let me alone," said Mildred.

"Let *you* alone!" He almost cried out with laughter. "Letting you alone is easy, but how can I leave *myself* alone? That's what's wrong. We need *not* to be let alone. We need to be upset and stirred and bothered, once in a while, anyway. Nobody bothers any more. Nobody thinks. Let a baby alone, why don't you? What would you have in twenty years? A savage, unable to think or talk—like us!"

Mildred glanced out the window. "Now you've done it. Look who's here."

"I don't give a damn." He was feeling better but didn't know why.

"It's Mr. Leahy."

The elation drained away. Mr. Montag slumped.

"Go open the door," he said, at last. "Tell him I'm sick."

"Tell him yourself."

He made sure the book was hidden behind the pillow, climbed back into bed, and had made himself tremblingly comfortable, when the door opened and Mr. Leahy strolled in, hands in pockets.

"Shut the radio off," said Leahy, abstractedly.

This time, Mildred obeyed.

Mr. Leahy sat down in a comfortable chair with a look of strange peace in his pink face. He did not look at Montag.

"Just thought I'd come by and see how the sick man is."

"How'd you guess?"

"Oh." Leahy smiled his pink smile, and shrugged. "I'm an old hand at this. I've seen it all. You were going to call me and tell me you needed a day off."

"Yes."

"WELL, TAKE A DAY OFF," said Leahy, looking at his hands. He carried an eternal match with him at times in a little case which said, *Guaranteed: One Million Cigarettes Can Be Lit with this Match,* and kept striking this abstractedly against its case as he talked. "Take a day off. Take two. But *never* take three." He struck the match and looked at the flame and blew it out. "When will you be well?"

"Tomorrow, the next day, first of the week. I . . ."

"We've been wondering about you." Leahy put a cigar in his mouth. "Every fireman goes through this. They only need understanding, need to know how the wheels run, what the history of our profession is. They don't give it to rookies any more. Only fire chiefs remember it now. I'll let you in on it." He lit the cigar leisurely.

Mildred fidgeted.

"You ask yourself about the burning of books, why, how, when." Leahy exuded a great gray cloud of smoke.

"Maybe," said Montag.

"It started around about the Civil War, I'd say. Photography discovered. Fast printing presses coming up. Films at the early part of the Twentieth Century. Radio. Television. Things began to have mass, Montag, *mass*."

"I see."

"And because they had mass, they became simpler. Books now. Once they appealed to various small groups of people, here and there. They could afford to be different. The world was roomy. But then the world got full of mass and elbows. Films and radios and magazines and books had to level down to a sort of paste-pudding norm. Do you follow me?"

"I think so."

Leahy looked through a veil of smoke, not at Montag, but at the thing he was describing. "Picture it. The nineteenth-century man with his horses, dogs, and slow living. You might call him a slow motion man. Then in the Twentieth Century you speed up the camera."

"A good analogy."

"Splendid. Books get shorter. Condensations appear. Digests. Tabloids. Radio programs simplify. Everything sublimates itself to the gag, the snap ending."

"Snap ending." Mildred nodded approvingly. "You should have heard last night—"

"Great classics are cut to fit fifteen minute shows, then two minute book columns, then two line digest resumes. Magazines become picture books! Out of the nursery to the college, back to the nursery, in a few short centuries!"

MILDRED AROSE. She was losing the thread of the talk, Montag knew, and when this happened she began to fiddle with things. She went about the room, picking up.

"Faster and faster the film, Mr. Montag! *Quick, Click, Pic, Look, Eye, Now! Flick, Flash, Here, There, Swift, Up, Down, Why, How, Who, Eh?* Mr. Montag, digest-digests, political affairs in one column, a sentence, a headline, and then, in mid-air, vanish! The mind of man, whirling so fast under the pumping hands of publishers, publicists, ad men, broadcasters that the centrifuge throws off all ideas! He is unable to concentrate!"

Mildred was smoothing the bed now. Montag felt panic as she approached his pillow to straighten it. In a moment, with sublime innocence, she would be pulling the hidden book out from behind the pillow and displaying it as if it were a reptile!

Leahy blew a cumulus of cigar smoke at the ceiling. "School is shortened, discipline relaxed, philosophies, histories, languages dropped, English and spelling neglected, finally ignored. Life is immediate. The job counts. Why learn anything save pressing buttons, pulling switches, fitting bolts?"

"Let me fix your pillow," said Mildred, being the video housewife.

"No," whispered Montag.

"The zipper replaces the button. Does a man have time to think while dressing in the morning, a philosophical time?"

"No," said Montag, automatically.

Mildred tugged at the pillow.

"Get away," said Montag.

"Life becomes one big Prat Fall, Mr. Montag. No more subtleties. Everything is bang and boff and wow!"

"Wow," reflected Mildred, yanking the pillow edge.

"For God's sake, let me be!" said Montag, passionately.

Leahy stared.

Mildred's hand was frozen behind the pillow. Her hand was on the book, her face stunned, her mouth opening to ask a question . . .

"Theaters stand empty, Mr. Montag, replaced by television and baseball and sports where nobody has to think at all, not at all, at all." Now Leahy was almost invisible, a voice somewhere back of a choking screen of cigar smoke.

"What's this?" asked Mildred, with delight, almost. Montag crushed and heaved back against her hands. "What've you hid here?"

"Sit down!" Montag screamed. She jumped back, her hands empty. "We're talking!"

LEAHY CONTINUED, MILDLY. "Cartoons everywhere. Books become cartoons. The mind drinks less and less. Impatience. Time to kill. No work, all leisure. Highways full of crowds going somewhere, anywhere, nowhere. The gasoline refugee, towns becoming motels, people in nomadic surges from city to city, impatient, following the moon tides, living tonight in the room where you slept last night and I the night before."

Mildred went in the other room and slammed the door. She turned on the radio.

"Go on," said Montag.

"Intelligent writers gave up in disgust. Magazines were vanilla tapioca. The book buyer, bored by dishwater, his brain spinning, quit buying. Everyone but the comic-publisher died a slow publishing death. There you have it. Don't blame the Government. Technology, mass exploitation, and censorship from frightened officials did the trick. Today, thanks to them, you can read comic books, confessions, or trade journals, nothing else. All the rest is dangerous."

"Yes, but why the firemen?" asked Montag.

"Ah," said Leahy, leaning forward in the clouds of smoke to finish. "With schools turning out doers instead of thinkers, with non-readers, naturally in ignorance, they hated and feared books. You always fear an unfamiliar thing. 'Intellectual' became a swear word. Books were snobbish things.

"The little man wants you and me to be like him. Not everyone born free and equal, as the Constitution says, but everyone *made* equal. A book is a loaded gun in the house next door. Burn it. Take the shot out of the weapon. Un-breach men's minds. Who knows who might be the target of the well-read man? And so, when houses became all fireproof and there was no longer need of firemen for protection, they were given the new job, as official censors, judges, jurors, punishers. That's you, Mr. Montag, and me."

Leahy stood up. "I've got to get going."

Montag lay back in bed. "Thanks for explaining it to me."

"You must understand our civilization is so vast that we can't have our minorities upset and stirred. People must be contented. Books bother them. Colored people don't like *Little Black Sambo*. We burn it. White people don't like to read *Uncle Tom's Cabin*. Burn it, too. Anything for serenity."

Leahy shook Montag's limp hand.

"Oh, one last thing. Once in his career, every fireman gets curious. What do the books say, he wonders. A good question. Well, they say nothing, Mr. Montag. Nothing you can touch or believe in. They're about non-existent people, figments. Not to be trusted. But anyway, say, a fireman 'takes' a book, at a fire, almost by 'accident.' A natural error."

"Natural."

"We allow that. We let him keep it 24 hours. If he hasn't burned it by then, we burn it for him."

"I see," said Montag. His throat was dry.

"You'll be at work tonight at six o'clock?"

"No."

"What!"

Montag shut his eyes. "I'll be in later, maybe."

"See that you do."

"I'll never come in again!" yelled Montag, but only in his mind.

"Get well."

Leahy, trailing smoke, went out.

MONTAG WATCHED THROUGH THE FRONT window as Leahy drove away in his gleaming beetle which was the color of the last fire they had set.

Mildred had turned on the afternoon television show and was staring into the shadow screen.

Montag cleared his throat, but she didn't look up.

"It's only a step," he said, "from not working today, to not working tomorrow, to not working ever again."

"You're going to work tonight, though?"

"I'm doing more than that," he said. "I'm going to start to kill people and rave, and buy books!"

"A one man revolution," said Mildred, lightly, turning to look at him. "They'd put you in jail, wouldn't they?"

"That's not a bad idea. The best people are there." He put

his clothes on, furiously, walking about the bedroom. "But I'd kill a few people before I did get locked up. There's a real bastard, that Leahy. Did you *hear* him! Knows all the answers, but does nothing about it!"

"I won't have anything to do with all this junk," she said.

"No?" he said. "This is your house as well as mine, isn't it?"

"Yes."

"Then I have something I want you to see, something I put away and never looked at again during the past year, not even knowing why I put them away and hid them and kept them and never told you."

He dragged a chair into the hall, climbed up on it, and opened an air-vent. Reaching up, he began throwing books, big ones, little ones, red, yellow, green books, twenty, thirty, fifty books, one by one, swiftly, into the parlor at her feet. "There!"

"Leonard Montag! You *didn't!*"

"So you're not in this with me? You're in it up to your neck!"

She backed away as if she were surrounded by a pack of terrible rats. Her face was paled out and her eyes were fastened wide and she was breathing as if someone had struck her in the stomach. "They'll burn our house. They'll kill us."

"Let them try."

She hesitated, then, moaning, she seized a book and ran toward the fireplace.

He caught her. "No, Millie! No! Never touch my books. Never. Or, by God, if you do, touch just one of them meaning to burn it, believe me, Millie, I'll kill you."

"Leonard Montag! You *wouldn't!*"

HE SHOOK HER. "Listen," he pleaded down into her face. He held her shoulders firmly, while her face bobbed helplessly, and tears sprang from her eyes.

"You must help me," he said, slowly, trying to find his way into her thinking. "You're in this now, whether you like it or not. I've never asked for anything in my life of you, but I ask it now, I plead it. We just start somewhere. We're going to read books. It's a thing we haven't done and must do. We've got to know what these books are so we can tell others, and so that, eventually, they can tell everyone. Sit down now, Millie, there, right there. I'll help you, we'll help each other. Between us, we'll do something to destroy men like Leahy and Stoneman and Black and myself, and this world we live in, and put it all back together a different way. Do you *hear* me?"

"Yes." Her body sagged.

The doorbell rang.

They jerked about to stare at the door and the books toppled everywhere, everywhere in heaps.

"Leahy!"

"It can't be him!"

"He's come back!" sobbed Mildred.

The bell rang again.

"Let him stand out there. We won't answer." Montag reached blindly for a book on the floor, any book, any beginning, any start, any beauty at all would do. He put the book into Mildred's shaking hands.

The bell rang a third time, insistently.

"Read." He quivered a hand to a page. "Out loud."

Mildred's eyes were on the door and the bell rang angrily, loudly, again and again. "He'll come in," she said, "Oh, God, and set fire to everything, and us."

But at last she found the line, with Montag standing over her, swaying, any line in the book, and after trying it four times, she began to fumble out the words of a poem printed there on the white, unburned paper:

> *"And evening vanish and no more*
> *The low pale light across that land—"*

The bell rang.

> *"Nor now the long light on the sea:*
> *And here face downward in the sun . . ."*

Another ring.
Montag whispered. "He'll go away in a minute."
Mildred's lips trembled:

> *"To feel how swift, how secretly*
> *The shadow of the night comes on . . ."*

Near the ceiling, smoke from Leahy's cigar still lingered.

The Sieve and the Sand

THEY READ THE LONG AFTERNOON THROUGH, WHILE THE
fire flickered and blew on the hearth and the October rain fell
from the sky upon the strangely quiet house. Now and again,
Mr. Montag would silently pace the room, or bring in a bottle
of cold beer and drink it easily or say, "Will you read that part
over again? Isn't *that* an idea now?"

Mildred's voice, as colorless as a beer bottle which contains a rare and beautiful wine but does not know it, went on
enclosing the words in plain glass, pouring forth the beauties
with a loose mouth, while her drab eyes moved over the words
and over the words and the rain rained and the hour grew
late.

They read a man named Shakespeare and a man named
Poe and part of a book by a man named Matthew and one
named Mark. On occasion, Mildred glanced fearfully at the
window.

"Go on," said Mr. Montag.

"Someone might be watching. That might've been Mr.
Leahy at our door a while back."

"Whoever it was went away. Read that last section again. I
want to understand that."

She read from the works of Jefferson and Lincoln.

When it was five o'clock her hands dropped open. "I'm
tired. Can I stop now?" Her voice was hoarse.

"How thoughtless of me." He took the book from her. "But
isn't it beautiful, Millie? The words, and the thoughts, aren't
they exciting!"

"I don't understand any of it."

"But surely . . ."

"Just words."

"But you remember some of it."

"Nothing."

"You'll learn. It's difficult at first."

I don't like books," she said. "I don't understand books. They're over my head. They're for professors and radicals and I don't want to read any more. Please, promise you won't make me."

"Mildred!"

"I'm afraid," she said, putting her face into her shaking hands. "I'm so terribly frightened by these ideas, by Mr. Leahy, and having these books in the house. They'll burn our books and kill us. Now, I'm sick."

"I'm sorry," he said, at last, sighing. "I've put you on trial, haven't I? I'm way out front, trying to drag you, when I should be walking beside you, barely touching. I expect too much. It'll take months to put you in the frame of mind where you can receive the ideas in these books. It's not fair of me. All right, you won't have to read aloud again."

"Thanks."

"But you must *listen*. I'll explain."

"I'll never learn. I just know I won't."

"You must if you want to be free."

"I'm free already. I couldn't be freer."

"You can't be free if you're not aware."

"Why do you want to ruin us with all this?" she asked.

"Listen," he said.

SHE LISTENED.

Jet-bombers were crossing the sky over their house.

Those quick gasps in the heavens, as if a running giant had drawn his breath. Those sharp, almost quiet whistles, here and gone in so much less than an instant that one almost believed one had heard nothing. And seeing nothing in the sky, if you *did* look, was worse than seeing something. There was a feeling as if a great invisible fan was whirring blade after hostile blade across the stars, with giant murmurs and no motion, perhaps only a faint trembling of starlight. All night, every night of their lives, they had heard those jet sounds and seen nothing, until, like the tick of a clock or a timebomb, it had come to be unnoticed, for it was the sound of today and the sound of today dying, the Cheyne-Stokes respiration of civilization.

"I want to know why and how we are where we are," said Montag. "How did those bombers get in the sky every instant? Why have there been three semi-atomic wars since 1960? Where did we take the wrong turn? What can we do about it? Only the books know this. Maybe the books can't solve my problem, but they can bring me out in the light. And they might stop us from going on with the same insane mistakes—"

"You can't stop wars. There've always been wars."

"No, I can't. War's so much a part of us now that in the last three days, though we're on the very rim of war, people hardly mention it. Ignoring it, at least, isn't the answer. But now, about us. We must have a schedule of reading. An hour in the morning. An hour or so in the afternoon. Two hours in the evening—"

"You're not going to forbid me my radio, are you?" Her voice rose.

"Well, to start . . ."

She was up in a fury, raging at him. "I'll sit and listen if you want me to for a while every day," she cried. "But I've got to have my radio programs, too, and every night on the TV—you can't take that away from me!"

"But don't you see? That's the very thing I'd like to counteract—"

The telephone rang. They both started. Mildred snatched it up and was almost immediately laughing. "Hello, Ann. Yes, oh, yes! Tonight, you come here. Yes, the White Clown's on tonight and the Terror will be fun."

Mr. Montag shuddered, sick. He left the room. He walked through the house, thinking.

Leahy, the firehouse, these dangerous books.

"I'll shoot him tonight," he said, aloud. "I'll kill Leahy. That'll be one censor out of the way. No." He laughed coldly. "I'd have to shoot most of the people in the world. How does one start a revolution? I'm alone. My wife, as the saying goes, does not understand me. What can a single lonely man do?"

MILDRED WAS CHATTERING. The radio was thundering, turned on again.

And then Mr. Montag remembered; about a month ago, walking through the park alone, he had come upon a man in a black suit, unaware. The man had been reading something. Montag hadn't seen a book; he had only seen the man move hastily, face flushed. The man had jumped up as if to run, and Montag had said, simply, "Sit down."

"I didn't do anything."

"No one said you did."

They had sat in the park all afternoon. Montag had drawn the man out. He was a retired professor of English literature, who had lost his job forty years before when the last college of fine arts had been closed. His name was William Faber, and shyly, fearfully, he admitted he had been reading a little book of American poems, forbidden poems which he now produced from his coat pocket.

"Just to know I'm alive," said Mr. Faber. "Just to know where I am and what things are. To sense things. Most of my friends sense nothing. Most of them can't talk. They stutter and halt and hunt words. And what they talk is sales and profits and what they saw on television the hour before."

What a nice afternoon that had been. Professor Faber had read some of the poems to Montag, none of which Montag understood, but the sounds were good, and slowly the meaning crept in. When it was all over, Montag said, "I'm a fireman."

Faber had looked as if he might die on the spot.

"Don't be afraid. I won't turn you in," said Montag, hastily. "I stopped being mean about it years ago. You know, the way you talk reminds me of a girl I knew once, name of Clarisse. She was killed a few months ago by a car. But she had me thinking, too. We met each other because we took long walks. No one walks anymore. I haven't seen a pedestrian in ten years on our street. Are you ever stopped by police simply because you're a pedestrian?"

He and Faber had smiled, exchanged addresses orally, and parted. He had never seen Faber again. It wouldn't be safe to know a former English literature professor. But now . . . ?

He dialed the call.

"Hello, Professor Faber?"

"Who is this?"

"This is Montag. You remember? The park? A month ago?"

"Yes, Mr. Montag. Can I help you?"

"Mr. Faber." He hesitated. "How many copies of the Bible are left in the world?"

"I'm afraid I don't know what you're talking about." The voice grew cold.

"I want to know if there *are* any copies at all."

"I can't discuss such things, Montag."

"This line is closed. There's no one listening."

"Is this some sort of trap? I can't talk to just anyone on the phone."

"Tell me, are there any copies?"

"None!" And Faber hung up

None.

Montag fell back in his chair. None! None in all the world, none left, none anywhere, all, all of them destroyed, torn apart, burned. The Bible at last dead for all time to the world.

He got up shakily and walked across the room and bent down among the books. He took hold of one and lifted it.

"The old and new testaments, Millie! One last copy and we have it here!"

"Fine," she said vaguely.

"Do you realize what it means, the importance of this copy here in our house? If anything should happen to this book, it would be lost forever."

"And you have to hand it back to Mr. Leahy tonight to be burned, don't you?" said Mildred. She was not being cruel.

She was merely relieved that the one book, at least, was going out of her life.

"Yes."

He could see Leahy turning the book over with slow appreciation. "Sit down, Montag. I want you to watch this. Delicately, like a head of lettuce, see?" Ripping one page after another from the binding. Lighting the first page with a match. And when it had curled down into black wings, lighting the second page from the first and the third from the second, and so on, chain-smoking the entire volume chapter by printed chapter. When it was finished, with Montag seated there sweating, the floor would resemble a swarm of black moths that had fluttered and died in one small storm. And Leahy smiling, washing his hands.

"My God, Millie, we've got to do something! We've got to copy this. There must be a duplicate made. This *can't* be lost!"

"You haven't time."

"No, not by hand. But if we could photograph it."

"No one would do it for you."

He stopped. She was right. There was no one to trust, except, perhaps, Professor Faber. Montag started for the door.

"You'll be here for the TV party, won't you?" Mildred called after him. "It wouldn't be fun without you."

"You'd never miss me." But she was looking at the late afternoon TV show and didn't hear. He went out and slammed the door, the book in his hand.

Once as a child, he had sat upon the yellow dunes by the sea in the middle of the blue and hot summer day, trying to fill a sieve with sand. The faster he poured, the faster it sifted through with a hot whispering. He tried all day because some cruel cousin had said, "Fill this sieve with sand and you'll get a dime!"

Seated there in the middle of July, he had cried. His hands were tired, the sand was boiling, the sieve was empty.

And now, as the jet-underground car roared him through the lower cellars of town, rocking him, jolting him, he remembered that frustrating sieve and he held this precious copy of the old and new testaments fiercely in his hands, trying to pour the words into his mind. But the words fell through, and he thought, in a few hours I must hand this book to Leahy, but I must remember each word, no phrase must escape me, each line can be memorized. I must remember, I *must*.

"But I do not remember." He shut the book and pressed it with his fists and tried to force his mind.

"Try Denham's Dentifrice tonight!" screamed the radio in the bright, shuddering wall of the jet-train. Trumpets blared.

"Shut up," thought Mr. Montag in panic. "Behold the lilies of the field—"

"Denham's Dentifrice!"

"They toil not—"

"Denham's Dentifrice!"

"Behold the lilies of the field, shut up, let me remember!"

"Denham's Dentifrice!"

He tore the book open furiously and flicked the pages about as if blind, tearing at the lines with raw eyes, staring until his eyelashes were wet and quivering.

"Denham's, Denham's, Denham's! D-E-N—"

"They toil not, neither do they . . ."

A whisper, a faint sly whisper of yellow sand through empty, empty sieve.

"Denham's does it!"

"Behold the lilies—"

"No dandier dental detergent!"

"Shut up!" It was a shriek so loud, so vicious that the loud-speaker seemed stunned. Mr. Montag found himself on his feet, the shocked inhabitants of the loud car looking at him, recoiling from a man with an insane, gorged face, a gibbering wet mouth, a flapping book in his fist. These rabbit people who hadn't asked for music and commercials on their public trains but who had got it by the sewerful, the air drenched and sprayed and pummeled and kicked by voices and music every instant. And here was an idiot man, himself, suddenly scrabbling at the wall, beating at the loudspeaker, at the enemy of peace, at the killer of philosophy and privacy!

"Mad man!"

"Call the conductor!"

"Denham's, Denham's Double Dentifrice!"

"Fourteenth Street!"

Only that saved him. The car stopped. Montag, thrown into the aisle by the grinding halt, rolled over, book in hand, leaped past the pale, frightened faces, screamed in his mind soundlessly, and was out the opening door of the train and running on the white tiles up and up through tunnels, alone, that voice still crying like a seagull on a lonely shore after him, "Denham's, Denham's . . ."

PROFESSOR FABER OPENED THE DOOR, saw the book, seized it. "My God, I haven't held a copy in years!"

"We burned a house last night. I stole this."

"What a chance to take!"

Montag stood catching his breath. "I was curious."

"Of course. It's beautiful. Here, come in, shut the door, sit down." Faber walked with the book in his fingers, feeling it, flipping the pages slowly, hungrily, a thin man, bald, with slender hands, as light as chaff. "There were a lot of lovely books once. Before we let them go." He sat down and put his hand over his eyes. "You are looking at a coward, Mr. Montag. When they burned the last of the evil books, as they called them, forty years back, I made only a few feeble protestations and subsided. I've damned myself ever since."

"It's not too late. There are still books."

"And there is still life in me, but I'm afraid of dying. Civilizations fall because men like myself fear death."

"I've a plan," said Montag. "I'm in a position to do things. I'm a fireman; I can find and hide books. Last night I lay awake, thinking. We might publish many books privately when we have copies to print from."

"How many have been killed for that?"

"We'll get a press."

"We? Not we. You, Mr. Montag."

"You must help me. You're the only one I know. You *must*."

"Must? What do you mean, *must?*"

"We could find someone to build a press for us."

"Impossible. The books are dead."

"We can bring them back. I have a little money."

"No, no." Faber waved his hands, his old hands, blotched with liver freckles.

"But let me tell you my plan."

"I don't want to hear. If you insist on telling me, I must ask you to leave."

"We'll have extra copies of each book printed and hide them in firemen's houses!"

"What?" The professor raised his brows and gazed at Montag as if a bright light had been switched on.

"Yes, and put in an alarm."

"Call the fire engines?"

"Yes, and see the engines roar up. See the doors battered down on firemen's houses for a change. And see the planted books found and each fireman, at last, accused and thrown in jail!"

The professor put his hand to his face. "Why, that's absolutely sinister."

"Do you like it?"

"The dragon eats his tail."

"You'll join me?"

"I didn't say that. No, no."

"But you see the confusion and suspicion we could spread?"

"Yes, plenty of trouble there."

"I've a list of firemen's homes all across the states. With an underground, we could reap fire and chaos for every blind bastard in the industry."

"You can't trust anyone, though."

"What about professors like yourself, former actors, directors, writers, historians, linguists?"

"Dead or ancient, all of them."

"Good. They'll have fallen from public notice. You know hundreds of them. I know you must."

"Nevertheless, I can't help you, Montag. I'll admit your

idea appeals to my sense of humor, to my delight in striking back. A temporary delight, however. I'm a frightened man; I frighten easily."

"Think of the actors alone, then, who haven't acted Shakespeare or Pirandello. We could *use* their anger, and the rage of historians who haven't written for forty years. We could start small classes in reading . . ."

"Impractical."

"We could try."

"The whole civilization must fall. We can't change just the front. The framework needs melting and remolding. Don't you realize, young man, that the Great Burning forty years back was almost unnecessary? By that time the public had stopped reading. Libraries were Saharas of emptiness. Except the Science Department."

"But—"

"Can you shout louder than radio, dance faster than TV? People don't want to think. They're having fun."

"Committing suicide."

"Let them commit it."

"Murdering."

"Let them murder. The fewer fools there will be."

"A war is starting, perhaps tonight, and no one will even talk about it."

The house shook. A bomber flight was moving south. It had slowed to five hundred miles an hour and was trembling the two men standing there across from each other.

"Let the war take away the TVs and radio, and bomb the true confessions."

"I can't wait," said Montag.

"Patience. The civilization is flinging itself to pieces. Stand back from the centrifuge."

"There has to be another structure ready when this one falls," insisted Montag. "That's us."

"A bunch of men quoting Shakespeare and saying I remember Sophocles? It would be funny if it were not tragic."

"We've got to be there. We've got to remind those who are left that there are things more urgent than machines. We must remember that the right kind of work is happiness, instead of the wrong kind of leisure. We must give people things to do. We must make them feel wanted again."

"They will only war again. No, Montag, go on home and go to bed. It was nice seeing you. But it's a lost cause."

MONTAG PACED ABOUT the room for a few moments, chafing his hands, then he returned and picked up the book and held it toward the other man.

"Do you see this book? Would you like to own it?"

"My God, yes! I'd give my right arm for it."

"Watch." Montag began ripping the pages out, one by one, dropping them to the floor, tearing them in half, spitting on them and rolling them into wads.

"Stop it!" cried Faber. "You idiot, stop it!" He sprang forward. Montag warded him off and went on tearing at the pages.

"Do you see?" he said, a fistful of pages in his tightening fist, flourishing them under the chin of the old man. "Do you see what it means to have your heart torn out? Do you see what *they* do?"

"Don't tear any more, please," said the old man.

"Who can stop me? You? I'm a fireman. I can do anything I want to do. Why, I could burn your house now, do you know that? I could burn everything. I have the power."

"You wouldn't!"

"No. I wouldn't."

"Please. The book; don't rip it any more. I can't stand that." Faber sank into a chair, his face white, his mouth trembling. "I see; I understand. My God, I'm old enough so it shouldn't matter what happens to me. I'll help you. I can't take any more of this. If I'm killed it won't make any difference. I'm a terrible fool of an old man and it's too late, but I'll help you."

"To print the books?"

"Yes."

"To start classes?"

"Yes, yes, anything, but don't ruin that book, don't. I never thought a book could mean so much to me." Faber sighed. "Let us say that you have my limited cooperation. Let us say that part of your plan, at least, intrigues me, the idea of striking back with books planted in firemen's homes. I'll help. How much money could you get me today?"

"Five thousand dollars."

"Bring it here when you can. I know a man who once printed our college paper. That was the year I came to class one morning and found only two students there to sign up for Ancient Greek Drama. You see, that's how it went. Like an ice-block melting in the sun. And when the people had censored themselves into a living idiocy with their purchasing power, the Government, which of course represents the people's will, being composed of representative people, froze the situation. Newspapers died. No one cared if the government said they couldn't come back. No one *wanted* them back. Do they now? I doubt it, but I'll contact a printer, Montag. We'll get the books started, and wait for the war. That's one fine thing; war destroys machines so beautifully."

MONTAG WENT TO THE DOOR. "I'm afraid I'll have to take the Bible along."

"No!"

"Leahy guessed I have a book in the house. He didn't come right out and accuse me, or name the book . . ."

"Can't you substitute another book for this?"

"I can't chance it. It might be a trap. If he expects me to bring a Bible and I've brought something else, I'd be in jail very quickly. No, I'm afraid this Bible will be burned tonight."

"That hard to accept." Faber took it for a moment and turned the pages, slowly, reading.

"I've tried to memorize it," said Montag. "But I forget. It's driven me crazy, trying to remember."

"Oh, God, if we only had a little time."

"I keep thinking that. Sorry." He took the book. "Good night."

The door shut. Montag was in the darkening street again, looking at the real world.

You could feel the war getting ready in the sky that night. The way the clouds moved aside and came back, and the way the stars looked, a million of them hovering between the clouds, like the enemy discs, and the feeling that the sky might fall upon the city and turn the homes to chalk dust, and the moon turn to red fire; that was how the night felt.

Montag walked from the subway stop with his money in

his pocket—he had been to the bank which stayed open until all hours with mechanical tellers doling out the money—and as he walked he was listening abstractedly to the Seashell radio which you could cup to your ear (Buy a Seashell and hear the Ocean of Time!) and a voice was talking to him and only him as he turned his feet toward home. "Things took another turn for the worse today. War threatens at any hour."

Always the same monologue. Nothing about causes or effects, no facts, no figures, nothing but sudden turns for the worse.

Seven flights of jet-rockets went over the sky in a breath. Montag felt the money in his pocket, the Bible in his hand. He had given up trying to memorize it now; he was simply reading it for the enjoyment it gave, the simple pleasure of good words on the tongue and in the mind. He uncapped the Seashell radio from his ear and read another page of the Book of Job by moonlight.

AT EIGHT O'CLOCK, the front door scanner recognized three women and opened, letting them in with laughter and loud, empty talk. Mrs. Masterson, Mrs. Phelps, and Mrs. Bowles drank the martinis Mildred handed them, rioting like a crystal chandelier that someone has pushed, tinkling upon themselves in a million crystal chimes, flashing the same white smiles, their echoes repeated into empty corridors. Mr. Montag found himself in the middle of a conversation the main topic of which was how nice everyone looked.

"Doesn't everyone look nice?"

"Real nice."

"You look fine, Alma."

"You look fine, too, Mildred."

"Everybody looks nice and fine," said Montag.

He had put the book aside. None of it would stay in his mind. The harder he tried to remember Job, for instance, the quicker it vanished. He wanted to be out paying this money to Professor Faber, getting things going, and yet he delayed himself. It would be dangerous to be seen at Faber's twice within a few hours, just in case Leahy was taking the precaution of having Montag watched.

Like it or not, he must spend the rest of the evening at home, and be ready to report to work at eleven so that Leahy wouldn't be suspicious. Most of all, Montag wanted to walk, but he rarely did this anymore. Somehow he was always afraid that he might meet Clarisse, or not meet her again, on his strolls, so that kept him here standing among these blonde tenpins, bowling back at them with socially required leers and wisecracks.

Somehow the television set was turned on before they had even finished saying how nice everyone looked, and there on the screen was a man selling orange soda pop and a woman drinking it with a smile; how could she drink and smile simultaneously? A real stunt! Following this, a demonstration of how to bake a certain new cake, followed by a rather dreary domestic comedy, a news analysis that did not analyze anything and did not mention the war, even though the house was shaking constantly with the flight of new jets from four directions, and an intolerable quiz show naming the state capitols.

Montag sat tapping his fingers on his knee and exhaling.

Abruptly, he walked to the televisor and snapped it off.

"I thought we might enjoy a little silence."

Everyone blinked.

"Perhaps we might try a little conversation . . ."

"Conversation?"

THE HOUSE SHOOK with successive waves of jet bombers which splashed the drinks in the ladies' hands.

"There they go," said Montag, watching the ceiling. "When do you suppose the war will start?"

"What war? There won't be a war."

"I notice your husbands aren't here tonight."

Mrs. Masterson glanced nervously at the empty TV screen. "Oh, Dick'll be back in a week or so. The Army called him. But they have these things every month or so." She beamed.

"Don't you worry about the war?"

"Well, heavens, if there is one, it's got to be over with. We can't just sit and worry, can we?"

"No, but we can think about it."

"I'll let Dick think of it." A nervous giggle.

"And die maybe."

"It's always someone else's husband dies, isn't that the joke?" The women all tittered.

Yes, thought Montag, and if Dick does die, what does it matter. We've learned the magic of the replaceable part from machines. You can't tell one man from another these days. And women, like so many plastic dolls—

Everyone was silent, like children with a schoolmaster.

"Did you see the Clarence Dove film last night?" said Mildred, suddenly.

"He's hilarious."

"But what if Dick should die, or *your* husband, Mrs. Phelps?" Montag insisted.

"He's dead. He died a week ago. Didn't you know? He jumped from the tenth floor of the State Hotel."

"I didn't know." Montag fell silent, embarrassed.

"But to get back to Clarence Dove . . ." said Mildred.

"Wait a minute," said Montag, angrily. "Mrs. Phelps, why did you marry your husband? What did you have in common?" said Montag.

The woman waved her hands helplessly. "Why, he had such a nice sense of humor, and we liked the same TV shows and—"

"Did you have any children?"

"Don't be ridiculous."

"Come to think of it, no one here has children," said Montag. "Except Mrs. Bowles."

"Four, by Caesarian section. It's easy that way."

"The Caesarians weren't necessary?"

"I always said I'd be damned if I'd go through all that agony just for a baby. Four Caesarians. Nothing to it, really."

Yes, everything easy. Montag clenched his teeth. To mistake the easy way for the right way, how delicious a temptation. But it wasn't living. A woman who wouldn't bear, or a shiftless man didn't belong; they were passing through. They belonged to nothing and did nothing.

"Have you ever thought, ladies," he said, growing more contemptuous of them by the minute, "that perhaps this isn't the best of all possible worlds? That perhaps our civil rights and other previous possessions haven't been taken away in the past century, but have, if anything, been given away by us?"

"Why, that can't be true! We'd have heard about it."

"On that pap-dispenser?" cried Montag, jerking his hand at the TV. Suddenly he shoved his hand in his pocket and drew forth a piece of printed paper. He was shaking with rage and irritation and he was half blind, staring down at the twitching sheet before his eyes.

"What's that?" Mrs. Master squinted.

"A poem I tore from a book."

"I don't like poetry."

"Have you ever *heard* any?"

"I detest it."

Mildred jumped up, but Montag said, coldly, "Sit down." The women all lit cigarettes nervously, twisting their red mouths.

"This is illegal, isn't it?" squealed Mrs. Phelps. "I'm afraid. I'm going home."

"Sit down and shut up," said Montag.

The room was quiet.

"This is a poem by a man named Matthew Arnold," said Montag. "Its title is 'Dover Beach.'"

The women were all glancing with expectation at the television set, as if it might save them from this moment.

Montag cleared his throat. He waited. He wanted very much to speak the poem right, and he was afraid that he might stumble. He read.

His voice rose and fell in the silent room and he found his way through to the final verses of the poem:

> "*The Sea of Faith*
> *Was once, too, at full, and round earth's shore*
> *Lay like the folds of a bright girdle furled.*

But now I only hear
Its melancholy, long, withdrawing roar,
Retreating, to the breath
Of the night wind, down the vast edges drear
And naked shingles of the world."

The four women twisted in their chairs.
Montag finished it out:

"Ah, love, let us be true
To one another! for the world, which seems
To lie before us like a land of dreams,
So various, so beautiful, so new,
Hath really neither joy, nor love, nor light,
Nor certitude, nor peace, nor help for pain;
And we are here as on a darkling plain
Swept with confused alarms of struggle and flight,
Where ignorant armies clash by night."

Montag let the white piece of paper fall slowly to the floor.
The women watched it flutter and settle.

Mildred said, "Can I turn the TV on now?"

"No, God damn it, no!"

Mildred sat down.

Mrs. Masterson said, "I don't get it. The poem, I mean."

"What was it about?" said Mrs. Phelps, her eyes darting fearfully in flashes of white and dark.

"Don't you *see?*" shouted Montag.

"Nothing to get upset about," said Mrs. Masterson, casually.

"But it is, it is."

"Just silly words," said Mrs. Masterson. "But, Mr. Montag, I don't mind telling you—it's only because you're a fireman that we haven't called in an alarm on you for reading this to us. It's illegal. But it's also very silly. It was nonsense." She got to her feet and mashed out her cigarette. "Ladies, don't you think it's time for us to leave?"

"I don't want to come back here, ever," said Mrs. Phelps, hurrying for the door.

"Please stay!" cried Mildred.

The door slammed.

"Go home and think of your first husband, Mrs. Masterson, in the insane asylum, and of Mr. Phelps jumping off a building!"yelled Montag through the shut door.

The house was completely abandoned. He stood alone.

In the bathroom, water was running. He heard Mildred shaking the sleeping tablets out into her palm.

"You fool," he said to himself. "You idiot. Now you've done it. Now you've ruined it all, you and your poem, you and your righteous indignation."

He went into the kitchen and found the books where Mildred had stacked them behind the refrigerator. He carried a selection of them into the back yard, hid them in the weeds near the fence. "Just in case," he thought, "Mildred gets a passion for burning things during the night. The best books out here; the others in the house don't matter."

He went back through the house. "Mildred?" he called at the bedroom door but there was no sound.

He shut the front door quietly and left for work.

"THANK YOU, MONTAG." Mr. Leahy accepted the copy of the Bible and, without even looking at it, dropped it into the wall incinerator. "Let's forget all about it. Glad to see you back, Montag."

They walked upstairs.

They sat and played cards at one minute after midnight.

In Leahy's sight, Montag felt the guilt of his hands. His fingers were like ferrets that had done some evil deed, and now were never at rest, always stirring and picking and hiding in pockets, or moving out from under Leahy's alcohol-flame gaze. If Leahy so much as breathed on them, Montag felt that they might wither upon his wrists and die and he might never shake them to life again; they would be buried forever in his coat-sleeves, forgotten.

For these were the hands that had acted on their own, that were no part of him, that were his swift and clever conscience, that snatched books, tore pages, hid paragraphs and sentences in little wads to be opened later, at home, by match-light, read, and burned. They were the hands that in the last year had darted off with Shakespeare and Job and Ruth and shelved them away next to his crashing heart, over the throbbing ribs and the hot, roaring blood of a man excited by his theft, appalled by his temerity, betrayed by ten fingers which at times he held up to watch as if they were gloved with blood.

The game proceeded. Twice in half an hour, Montag got up and went to the latrine to wash his hands. He came back. He sat down. He held his cards. Leahy watched his fingers fumble the cards.

"Not smoking, Montag?"

"I've a cigarette cough."

And then, of course, the smoke reminded him of old men and old women screaming and falling into wild cinders, and it was not good any more to hold fire in your hand.

He put his hands under the table. "Let's have your hands in sight," said Leahy, casually. "Not that we don't trust you."

They all laughed.

The phone rang.

MR. LEAHY, CARRYING HIS CARDS in one pink hand, walked slowly over and stood by the phone, let it ring twice more, and then picked it up.

"Yes?"

Mr. Montag listened, eyes shut.

The clock ticked in the room.

"I see," said Leahy. He looked at Montag. He smiled. He winked. Montag glanced away. "Better give me that address again."

Mr. Montag got up. He walked around the room, hands in pockets. The other two men were standing ready. Leahy jerked his head toward their coats, as if to say, "On the double!" They shoved their arms in their coats and pushed on their helmets, joking in whispers.

Mr. Montag waited.

"I understand perfectly," said Leahy into the phone. "Yes. Yes. Perfectly. No, that's all right. Don't you worry. We'll be right out."

Leahy deposited the receiver. "Well, well."

"A call? Books to be burned?"

"So it seems."

Mr. Montag sat down heavily. "I don't feel well."

"What a shame; this is a special case," said Leahy, coming forward slowly, putting on his slicker.

"I think I'm handing in my resignation."

"Not yet, Montag. One more fire, eh? Then I'll be agreeable; you can hand in your papers. We'll all be happy."

"Do you mean that?"

"Have I ever lied to you?"

Leahy fetched a helmet. "Put this on. The job'll be over in an hour. I understand you, Montag, really I do. Everything will be just as you want it."

"All right."

They slid down the brass pole.

"Where's the fire?"

"I'll drive!" shouted Leahy. "I've got the address."

The engine blasted to life and in the gaseous tornado they all leaped aboard.

THEY ROUNDED A CORNER in thunder and siren, with concussion of tires, with scream of rubber, with a shift of kerosene bulk in the glittery brass tank, like the food in the stomach of a giant, with Mr. Montag's fingers jolting off the silver rail, swinging into cold space, with the wind tearing his hair back from his bleak face, with the wind whistling in his teeth, and he all the while thinking of the women, the chaff women, with the kernels blown out from under them by a neon wind, and his reading the book to them.

What a silly thing it was now! For what was a book? Sheets of paper, lines of type. Why should he fret for books—one, two, or ten thousand of them, really? He was the only inhabitant of a burning world that cared, so why not drop it all, forget it, let the now-meaningless books lie?

"Here we go!" shouted Leahy.

"Elm Street?"

"Right!"

He saw Leahy up on his driver's throne, with his massive black slicker flapping out behind. He seemed to be an immense black bat flying above the engine, over the brass numbers, taking the wind. His pink, phosphorescent face glimmered in the high darkness, pressing forward, and he was smiling furiously.

"Here we go to keep the world happy!"

And Mr. Montag thought, "No, I can't let the books rot; I can't let them burn. As long as there are souls like Leahy, I can't hold my breath. But what can I do? I can't kill everyone. It's me against the world, and the odds too big for one man. What can I do? Against fire, what water is best?"

"Now over on Park Terrace!"

The fire engine boomed to a halt, throwing the men off in skips and clumsy hops. Mr. Montag stood fixing his raw eyes to the cold bright rail under his gripped fingers.

"I can't do it," he murmured. "I can't go in there. I can't rip another book."

Leahy jumped from his throne, smelling of the wind that had hammered him about. "Okay, Montag, fetch the kerosene!"

The hoses were snaked out. The men ran on soft boots, as clumsy as cripples, as quiet as deadly black spiders.

Mr. Montag turned his head.

"What's wrong, Montag?" Leahy asked, solicitously.

"Why," protested Montag, "that is *my* house."

"So it is," agreed Leahy, heartily.

All the lights were lit. Down the street, more lights were flicking on, people were standing on porches, as the door of Montag's house opened. In it, with two suitcases in her hands, stood Mildred. When she saw her husband she came down the steps quickly, with a dream-like rigidity, looking at the third button on his coat.

"Mildred!"

She said nothing.

"Okay, Montag, up with the hose and ax."

"Just a moment, Mr. Leahy. Mildred, you didn't telephone this call in, did you?"

SHE WALKED PAST HIM with her arms stiff and at the ends of them, in the sharp, red-nailed fingers, the valise handles. Her mouth was bloodless.

"You didn't!"

She shoved the valises into a waiting taxi-beetle and climbed in and sat there, staring straight ahead

Montag started toward her. Leahy caught his arm.

"Come on, Montag."

The cab drove away slowly down the lighted street.

There was a crystal tinkling as Stoneman and Black chopped the windows to provide fine drafts for fire.

Mr. Montag walked but did not feel his feet touch the walk, nor the hose in his icy hands, nor did he hear Leahy talking continually as they reached the door.

"Pour the kerosene on, Montag."

Montag stood gazing in at the queer house, made strange

by the hour of the night, by the murmur of neighbor voices, by the littered glass, the lights blazing, and there on the floor, their covers plucked off, the pages spilled about like pigeon feathers, were his incredible books, and they looked so pitiful and silly and not worth bothering with, for they were nothing but type and paper and raveled binding.

Montag stepped forward in a huge silence and picked up one of the pages of the books and read what it had to say.

He had read only three lines when Leahy snatched the paper from him.

"Oh, no," he said, smiling. "Because then we'd have to burn your mind, too. Mustn't have that." He stepped back. "Ready?"

"Ready." Montag snapped the valve lock on the fire-thrower.

"Aim," said Leahy.

"Aim."

"Fire!"

He burned the television set first and then the radio and he burned the motion picture projector and he burned the films and the gossip magazines and the litter of cosmetics on a table, and he took pleasure in it all, and he burned the walls because he wanted to change everything, the chairs, the table, the paintings. He didn't want to remember that he had lived here with some strange woman who would forget him tomorrow, who had gone and forgotten him already and was listening to a radio as she rode across town. So he burned the room with a precise fury.

"The books, Montag, the books!"

He directed the fire at the books. The books leaped and

danced, like roasting birds, their wings frantically ablaze in red and yellow feathers. They fell in charred lumps.

"Get that one there, get it!" directed Leahy, pointing.

Montag burned the indicated book.

He burned books, he burned them by the dozen, he burned books with sweat pouring down his cheeks.

"When you're all done, Montag," said Leahy behind him, "you're under arrest."

Water, Water, Quench Fire

THE HOUSE FELL INTO RED RUIN. IT BEDDED ITSELF DOWN to sleepy pink ashes and a smoke pall hung over it, rising straight to the sky. It was ten minutes after one in the morning. The crowd drew back into their houses: The fun was over.

Mr. Montag stood with the fire-thrower in his stiff hands, great islands of perspiration standing out under his arms, his face smeared with soot. The three other firemen waited behind him in the darkness, their faces illumined faintly by the burnt house, by the house which Mr. Montag had just charred and crumpled so efficiently with kerosene, flame-gun, and deliberate aim.

"All right, Montag," said Leahy. "Come along. You've done your duty. Now you're in custody."

"What've I done?"

"You know what you did. Don't ask."

"Why so much fuss over a few bits of paper?"

"We won't stand here arguing; it's cold."

"Was it my wife called you, or one of her friends."

"It doesn't matter."

"Was it my wife?'

Leahy nodded. "But her friends turned in an alarm earlier. I let it ride. One way or the other, you'd have got it. That was pretty silly, quoting poetry around free and easy, Montag. Very silly. Come on, now."

"I think not," said Montag.

He twitched the fire-trigger in his hand. Leahy glanced at Montag's fingers and saw what he intended before Montag himself had even considered it. In that instant, Montag was stunned by the thought of murder, for murder is always a new thing, and Montag knew nothing of murder; he knew only burning and burning things that people said were evil.

"I know what's really wrong with the world," said Montag.

"Look here, Montag—" cried Leahy.

And then he was a shrieking blaze, a jumping, sprawling, gibbering thing, all aflame, writhing on the grass as Montag shot three more blazing pulses of liquid fire over him. There was a hissing and bubbling like a snail upon which salt has been poured. There was a sound like spittle on a red-hot stove. Montag shut his eyes and yelled and tried to get his hands to his ears to cut away the sounds. Leahy twisted in upon himself like a ridiculous black wax doll and lay silent.

The other two firemen stood appalled.

"Montag!"

Montag jerked the weapon at them. "Turn around!"

They turned stiffly. He beat them over the head with the gun shaft; he didn't want to burn any other thing ever again.

They fell. Then Montag turned the fire-thrower on the fire engine itself, set the trigger, and ran. Voices screamed in several houses. The engine blew up, hundreds of gallons of kerosene in one great flower of heat.

Montag ran away down the street and into an alley, thinking, "That's the end of you, Leahy! That's the end of you and what you were!"

He kept running.

HE REMEMBERED THE BOOKS and turned back.

"You're a fool, a damned fool, an awful fool, but most of all a fool." He stumbled and fell. He got up. "You blind idiot, you and your pride and your stinking temper and your righteousness, you've ruined it all, at the very start, you fumbler. But those women, those stupid women, they drove me to it with their nonsense!" he protested to himself.

"A fool, nevertheless, no better than they! We'll save what we can. We'll do what has to be done. We'll take a few more firemen with us if we burn!"

He found the books where he had left them, beyond the garden fence. He heard voices yelling in the night and flash-beams were swirling about. Other fire engines wailed from far off and police cars were arriving.

Mr. Montag took as many books as he could carry under each arm and staggered away down the alley. He hadn't realized what a shock the evening had been to him, but suddenly he fell and lay sobbing, weak, his legs folded, his face in the gravel. At a distance he heard running feet. Get up, he told himself. But he lay there. Get up, get up! But he cried like a child. He hadn't wanted to kill anyone, not even Leahy. Killing did nothing but kill something of yourself when you did it, and suddenly he saw Leahy again, a torch, screaming, and he shut his hand over his wet face, gagging. "I'm sorry, I'm sorry."

Everything at once. In twenty-four hours the burning of a woman, the burning of books, the trip to the professor's, Leahy, the Bible, memorizing, the sieve and the sand, the bank money, the printing press, the plan, the rage, the alarm, Mildred's departure, the fire, Leahy into a torch—too much for any one day in any one life.

At last he was able to get to his feet, but the books seemed impossibly heavy. He fumbled along the alley and the voices and sirens faded behind him. He moved in darkness, panting.

"You must remember," he said, "that you've go to burn them or they'll burn you. Burn them or they'll burn you."

He searched his pockets. The money was there. In his shirt pocket he found the Seashell radio and slapped it to his ear.

"Attention! Attention, all police alert. Special alarm. Wanted: Leonard Montag, fugitive, for murder and crimes against the State. Description . . ."

Six blocks away the alley opened out onto a wide empty thoroughfare. It looked like a clean stage, so broad, so quiet, so well lit, and him alone, running across it, easily seen, easily shot down.

"Beware of the pedestrian, watch for the pedestrian!" The Seashell stung his ear.

Montag hid back in the shadows. He must use only alleys. There was a gas station nearby. It might give him the slightest extra margin of safety if he were clean and presentable. He must get to the station rest room and wash up, comb his hair, then, with books under arm, stroll calmly across that wide boulevard to get where he was going.

"Where *am* I going?"

NOWHERE. THERE WAS NOWHERE to go, no friend to turn to. Faber couldn't take him in; it would be murder to even try; but he had to see Faber for a minute or two, to give him this money. Whatever happened, he wanted the money to go on after him. Perhaps he could make it to open country, live on the rivers and near highways, in the meadows and hills, the sort of life he had often thought about but never tried.

Something caught at one corner of his vision and he turned to look at the sky.

The police helicopters were rising, far away, like a flight of gray moths, spreading out, six of them. He saw them wavering, indecisive, a half mile off, like butterflies puzzled by autumn, dying with winter, and then they were landing, one by one, dropping softly to the streets where, turned into cars, they would shriek along the boulevards or, just as suddenly, hop back into the air, continuing their search.

And here was the gas station. Approaching from the rear, Mr. Montag entered the men's wash room. Through the tin wall he heard a radio voice crying, "War has been declared! Repeat—war has been declared! Ten minutes ago—" But the sound of washing his hands and rinsing his face and toweling himself dry cut the announcer's voice away. Emerging from the washroom a cleaner, newer man, less suspect, Mr. Montag walked as casually as a man looking for a bus, to the edge of the empty boulevard.

There it lay, a game for him to win, a vast bowling alley in the dark morning. The boulevard was as clean as a pinball machine, but underneath, somewhere, one could feel the electrical energy, the readiness to dark lights, flash red and blue, and out of nowhere, rolling like a silver ball, might thunder the searchers! Three blocks away, there were a few headlights. Montag drew a deep breath. His lungs were like burning brooms in his chest; his mouth was sucked dry from running. All of the iron in the world lay in his dragging feet.

He began to walk across the empty avenue.

A hundred yards across. He estimated. A hundred yards in the open, more than plenty of time for a police car to appear, see him, and run him down.

He listened to his own loud footsteps.

A car was corning. Its headlights leaped and caught Montag in full stride.

"Keep going."

Montag faltered, got a new hold on his books, and forced himself not to freeze. Nor should be draw suspicion to himself by running. He was now one third of the way across. There was a growl from the car's motor as it put on speed.

THE POLICE, THOUGHT MONTAG. They see me, of course. But walk slowly, quietly, don't turn, don't look, don't seem concerned. Walk, that's it, walk, walk.

The car was rushing at a terrific speed. A good one hundred miles an hour. Its horn blared. Its light flushed the concrete. The heat of the lights, it seemed, burned Montag's cheeks and eyelids and brought the sweat coursing from his body.

He began to shuffle idiotically, then broke and run. The horn hooted. The motor sound whined higher. Montag sprinted. He dropped a book, whirled, hesitated, left it there, plunged on, yelling to himself, in the middle of concrete emptiness, the car a hundred feet away, closer, closer, hooting, pushing, rolling, screeching, the horn hunting, himself running, his legs up, down, out, back, his eyes blind in the flashing glare, the horn nearer, now on top of him!

They'll run me down, they know who I am, it's all over, thought Montag, it's done!

He stumbled and fell.

An instant before reaching him, the wild car swerved around him and was gone. Falling had saved him.

Mr. Montag lay flat, his head down. Wisps of laughter trailed back with the blue car exhaust.

That wasn't the police, thought Mr. Montag.

It was a carful of high school children, yelling, whistling, hurrahing. And they had seen a man, a pedestrian, a rarity, and they had yelled "Let's get him!" They didn't know he was the fugitive Mr. Montag; they were simply out for a night of roaring five hundred miles in a few moonlit hours, their faces icy with wind.

"They would have killed me," whispered Montag to the shaking concrete under his bruised cheek. "For no reason at all in the world, they would have killed me."

He got up and walked unsteadily to the far curb. Somehow, he had remembered to pick up the spilled books. He shuffled them, oddly, in his numb hands.

"I wonder if they were the ones who killed Clarisse."

His eyes watered.

The thing that had saved him was falling flat. The driver of that car, seeing Montag prone, considered the possibility that running over a body at one hundred miles an hour might turn the car over and spill them all out. Now, if Montag had remained upright, things would have been far different. . .

Montag gasped. Far down the empty avenue, four blocks away, the car of laughing children had turned. Now it was racing back, picking up speed.

Montag dodged into an alley and was gone in the shadow long before the car returned.

THE HOUSE WAS SILENT.

Mr. Montag approached it from the back, creeping through the scent of daffodils and roses and wet grass. He touched the screen door, found it open, slipped in, tiptoed across the porch, and, behind the refrigerator in the kitchen, deposited three of the books. He waited, listening to the house.

"Mrs. Black, are you asleep up there?" he asked of the second floor in a whisper. "I hate to do this to you, but your husband did just as bad to others, never asking, never wondering, never worrying. You're a fireman's wife, Mrs. Black, and now it's your house, and you in jail a while, for all the houses your husband has burned and people he's killed."

The ceiling did not reply.

Quietly, Montag slipped from the house and returned to the alley. The house was still dark; no one had heard him come or go.

He walked casually down the alley, and came to an all night, dimly lighted phone booth. He closed himself in the booth and dialed a number.

"I want to report an illegal ownership of books," he said.

The voice sharpened on the other end. "The address?" He

gave it and added, "Better get there before they burn them. Check the kitchen."

Montag stepped out and stood in the cold night air, waiting. At a great distance he heard the fire sirens coming, coming to burn Mr. Black's house while he was away at work, and make his wife stand shivering in the morning air while the roof dropped down. But now she was upstairs, deep in sleep.

"Good night, Mrs. Black," said Montag. "You'll excuse me—I have several other visits to make."

A RAP AT THE DOOR.

"Professor Faber!"

Another rap and a long waiting. Then, from within, lights flickered on about the small house. After another pause, the front door opened.

"Who is it?" Faber cried, for the man who staggered in was in the dark for a moment and then rushing past. "Oh, Montag!"

"I'm going away," said Montag, stumbling to a chair. "I've been a fool."

Professor Faber stood at the door listening to the distant sirens wailing off like animals in the morning. "Someone's been busy."

"It worked."

"At least you were a fool about the right things." Faber shut the door, came back, and poured a drink for each of them. "I wondered what had happened to you."

"I was delayed." Montag patted his inside pocket. "The money's here." He took it out and laid it on the desk, then sat tiredly sipping his drink. "How do you feel?"

"This is the first night in many years I've fallen right to

sleep," said Faber. "That must mean I'm doing the right thing. I think we can trust me, now. Once, I didn't think so."

"People never trust themselves, but they never let others know. I suppose that's why we do rash things, expose ourselves to positions from which we don't dare retreat. Unconsciously, we fear we might give in, quit the fight, and so we do a foolish thing, like reading poetry to women." Montag laughed at himself. "So I guess I'm on the run. It'll be up to you to keep things moving."

"I'll do my damndest." Faber sat down. "Tell me about it. What you did just now, I mean."

"I hid my remaining books in four firemen's homes. Then I telephoned an alarm. I figured I might be dead by morning, and I wanted to have done something before then.

"God, I'd like to have been there."

"Yes, the places burned very well."

"Where are you going now?"

"I don't know."

"Try the factory section, follow the old rail lines, look up some of the hobo camps. I didn't tell you this before—maybe I didn't quite trust you yet, I don't know—but they were in touch with me last year, wanting me to go underground with them."

"With *tramps?*"

"There are a lot of Harvard degrees on the tracks between here and Los Angeles. What else can they do? Most of them are wanted and hunted in cities. They survive. I don't think they have a plan for a revolution, though; I never heard them speak of it. They simply sit by their fires. Not a very lively group. But they might hide you now."

"I'll try. I'm heading for the river, I think, then the old factory district. I'll keep in touch with you."

"In Boston, then. I'm leaving on the three o'clock train tonight—or, rather, this morning. That's not long from now. There's a retired printer in Boston that I want to see with this money."

"I'll contact you there," said Montag. "And get books from you when I need them, to plant in firemen's houses across the country."

MONTAG DRAINED HIS DRINK.

"Do you want to sleep here a while?" Faber asked.

"I'd better get going. I wouldn't want you held responsible."

"Let's check." Faber switched on the televisor. A voice was talking swiftly:

"—this evening. Montag has escaped, but we expect his arrest in 24 hours. Here's a bulletin. The Electric Hound is being transported here from Green Town—"

Montag and Faber glanced at each other.

"—You may recall the interviews recently on TV concerning this incredible new invention, a machine so delicate in sense perception that it can follow trails much as bloodhounds did for centuries. But this machine, without fail, *always* finds its quarry!"

Montag put his empty glass down and he was cold.

"The machine is self-operating, weighs only forty pounds, is propelled on seven rubber wheels. The front is a nose, which in reality is a thousand noses, so sensitive that they can distinguish 10,000 food combinations, 5,000 flower smells, and remember identity index odors of 15,000 men without the bother of resetting."

Faber began to tremble. He looked at his house, at the door, the floor, the chair in which Montag sat. Montag interpreted this look. They both stared together at the invisible trail of his footprints leading to this house, the odor of his hand on the brass doorknobs; the smell of his body in the air and on this chair.

"The Electric Hound is now landing, by helicopter, at the burned Montag home. We take you there by TV control!"

So they must have a game, thought Montag. In the midst of a time of war, they must play the game out.

There was the burned house, the crowd, and something with a sheet over it, Mr. Leahy—yes, Mr. Leahy—and out of the sky, fluttering, came the red helicopter, landing like a grotesque and menacing flower.

MONTAG WATCHED THE SCENE with a solid fascination, not wanting to move, ever. If he wished, he could linger here, in comfort, and follow the entire hunt on through its quick phases, down alleys, up streets, across empty running avenues, with the sky finally lightening with dawn, up other alleys to burned houses, and so on to this place here, this house, with Faber and himself seated at their leisure, smoking idly, drinking good wine, while the Electric Hound sniffed down the fatal paths, whirring and pausing with finality outside that door there.

Then, if he wished, Montag could rise, walk to the door, keep one eye on the TV screen, open the door, look out, look back, and see himself, dramatized, described, made over, standing there, limned in the bright television screen, from outside, a drama to be watched objectively, and he would catch himself, an instant before oblivion, being killed for the benefit of a million televiewers who had been wakened from their sleeps a few minutes ago by the frantic beep-beeping of their receivers to watch the big game, the big hunt, the Scoop!

"There it is," whispered Faber, hoarsely.

OUT OF THE HELICOPTER glided something that was not a machine, not an animal, not dead, not alive, just gliding. It glowed with a green phosphorescence, and it was on a long leash. Behind it came a man, dressed lightly, with earphones on his shaven head.

"I can't stay here," Montag leaped up, his eyes still fixed to the scene. The Electric Hound shot forward to the smoking ruins, the man running after it. A coat was brought forward. Montag recognized it as his own, dropped in the back yard during flight. The Electric Hound studied it for only a moment. There was a shirring and clicking of dials and meters.

"You can't escape." Faber mourned over it, turning away. "I've heard about that damned monster. No one has ever escaped."

"I'll try, anyway. I'm sorry about this, Professor."

"About me? About my house? Don't be. I'm the one to be sorry I didn't act years ago. Whatever I get out of this, I deserve. You run, now; perhaps I can delay them here somehow—"

"Wait a minute." Montag moved forward. "There's no use your being discovered. We can erase the trail here. First the chair. Get me a knife."

Faber ran and fetched a knife. With it, Montag attacked the chair where he had sat. He cut the upholstery free, then shoved

it, bit by bit, without touching the lid, into the wall incinerator. "Now," he said, "after I leave, rip up the carpet. It has
my footprints on it. Cut it up, burn it, air the house. Rub the
doorknobs with alcohol. After I go, turn your garden sprinkler
on full. That'll wash away the sidewalk traces."

Faber shook his hand vigorously. "You don't know what
this means. I'll do anything to help you in the future. Get in
touch with me in Boston, then."

"One more thing. A suitcase. Get it, fill it with your dirty
laundry, an old suit, the dirtier the better, denim pants maybe,
a shirt, some old sneakers and socks."

Faber was gone and back in a minute. Montag sealed the
full suitcase with scotch tape. "To keep the odor in," he said,
breathlessly. He poured a liberal amount of cognac over the
exterior of the case. "I don't want that Hound picking up two
odors at once. Mind if I take this bottle of whisky? I'll need it
later. When I get to the river, I'll change clothes."

"And identities; from Montag to Faber."

"Christ, I hope it works! If your clothes smell strong
enough, which God knows they seem to, we might confuse the
Hound, anyway."

"Good luck."

They shook hands again and glanced at the TV. The Electric Hound was on its way, followed by mobile camera units,
through alleys, across empty morning streets, silently, silently,
sniffing the great night wind for Mr. Leonard Montag.

"Be seeing you."

And Montag was out the door, running lightly, with the
half empty case. Behind him, he saw and felt and heard the
garden sprinkler system jump up, filling the dark air with

synthetic rain to wash away the smell of Montag. Through the back window, the last thing he saw of Faber was the old man tearing up the carpet and cramming it in the wall incinerator.

Montag ran.

Behind him, in the night city, the Electric Hound followed.

HE STOPPED NOW AND AGAIN, panting, across town, to watch through the dimly lighted windows of wakened houses. He peered in at silhouettes before television screens and there on the screens saw where the Electric Hound was, now at Elm Terrace, now at Lincoln Avenue, now at 34th, now up the alley toward Mr. Faber's, now *at* Faber's!

"No, no!" thought Montag. "Go on past! Don't turn in, don't!"

He held his breath.

The Electric Hound hesitated, then plunged on, leaving Faber's house behind. For a moment the TV camera scanned Faber's home. The windows were dark. In the garden, the water sprinkled the cool air, softly.

THE ELECTRIC HOUND jumped ahead, down the alley.

"Good going, professor." And Montag was gone, again, racing toward the distant river, stopping at other houses to see the game on the TV sets, the long running game, and the Hound drawing near behind. "Only a mile away now!"

As he ran he put the Seashell at his ear and a voice ran with every step, with the beat of his heart and the sound of his shoes on the gravel. "Watch for the pedestrian! Look for the pedestrian! Anyone on the sidewalks or in the street, walking or running, is suspect! Watch for the pedestrian!"

How simple in a city where no one walked. Look, look for the walking man, the man who proves his legs. Thank God for good dark alleys where men could run in peace. House lights flashed on all about. Montag saw faces peering streetward as he passed behind them, faces hid by curtains, pale, night-frightened faces, like odd animals peering from electric caves, faces with grey eyes and grey minds, and he plunged ahead, leaving them to their tasks, and in another minute was at the black, moving river.

He found what he was looking for after five minutes of running along the bank. It was a rowboat drawn and staked to the sand. He took possession.

The boat slid easily on the long silence of river and went away downstream from the city, bobbing and whispering, while Montag stripped in darkness down to the skin, and splashed his body, his arms, his legs, his face with raw liquor. Then he changed into Faber's old clothing and shoes. He tossed his own clothing into the river with the suitcase.

He sat watching the dark shore. There would be a delay while the pursuit rode the Electric Hound up and down stream to see where a man named Montag had stepped ashore.

Whether the smell of Faber would be strong enough, with the aid of the alcohol, was something else again. He pulled out a handkerchief he had saved over, doused it with the remainder of the liquor. He must hold this over his mouth when stepping ashore.

The particles of his breathing might remain in an electronically detectable invisible cloud for hours after he had passed on.

He couldn't wait any longer. He was below the town now, in a lonely place of weeds and old railway tracks. He rowed the boat toward shore, tied the handkerchief over his face, and leaped out as the boat touched briefly.

The current swept the boat away, turning slowly.

"Farewell to Mr. Montag," he said. "Hello, Mr. Faber."

He went into the woods.

HE FOUND HIS WAY along railroad tracks that had not been used in years, crusted with brown rust and overgrown with weeds. He listened to his feet moving in the long grass. He paused now and then, checking behind to see if he was followed, but was not.

Firelight shone far ahead. "One of the camps," thought Montag. "One of the places where the hobo intellectuals cook their meals and talk!" It was unbelievable.

Half an hour later he came out of the weeks and the forest into the half light of the fire, for only a moment, then he hid back and waited, watching the group of seven men, holding their hands to the small blaze, murmuring. To their right, a quarter mile away, was the river. Up the stream a mile, and still apparent in the dark, was the city, and no sound except the voices and the fire crackling.

Montag waited ten minutes in the shadows. Finally a voice called: "All right, you can come out now."

He shrank back.

It's okay," said the voice. "You're welcome here."

He let himself stand forth and then he walked tiredly toward the fire, peering at the men and their dirty clothing.

"We're not very elegant," said the man who seemed to be the leader of the little group. "Sit down. Have some coffee."

He watched the dark steaming mixture poured into a collapsible cup which was handed him straight off. He sipped it gingerly. He felt the scald on his lips. The men were watching him. Their faces were unshaved but their beards were much too neat, and their hands were clean. They had stood up, as if to welcome a guest, and now they sat down again. Montag sipped. "Thanks," he said.

The leader said, "My name is Granger, as good a name as any. You don't have to tell us your name at all." He remembered something. "Here, before you finish the coffee, better take this." He held out a small bottle of colorless fluid.

"What is it?"

"Drink it. Whoever you are, you wouldn't be here unless you were in trouble. Either that, or you're a Government spy, in which case we are only a bunch of men traveling nowhere and hurting no one. In any event, whoever you are, an hour after you've drunk this fluid, you'll be someone else. It does something to the perspiratory system—changes the sweat content. If you want to stay here you'll have to drink it, otherwise you'll have to move on. If there's a Hound after you, you'd be bad company."

"I think I took care of the Hound," said Montag, and drank the tasteless stuff. The fluid stung his throat. He was sick for a moment; there was a blackness in his eyes, and roaring in his head. Then it passed.

"THAT'S BETTER, MR. MONTAG," said Granger, and snorted at his social error. "I beg your pardon—" He poked his thumb at a small portable TV beyond the fire. "We've been watching. They videoed a picture of you, not a very good resemblance. We hoped you'd head this way."

"It's been quite a chase."

"Yes." Granger snapped the TV on. It was no bigger than a handbag, weighing some seven pounds, mostly screen. A voice from the set cried:

"The chase is now veering south along the river. On the eastern shore the police helicopters are converging on Avenue 87 and Elm Grove Park."

"You're safe," said Granger. "They're faking. You threw them off at the river, but they can't admit it. Must be a million people watching that bunch of scoundrels hound after you. They'll catch you in five minutes."

"But if they're ten miles away, how can they . . . ?"

"Watch."

He turned the TV picture brighter.

"Up that street there, somewhere, right now, out for an early morning walk. A rarity, an odd one. Don't think the police don't know the habits of queer ducks like that, men who walk early in the morning just for the hell of it. Anyway, up that street the police know that every morning a certain man walks alone, for the air, to smoke. Call him Billings or Brown or Baumgartner, but the search is getting nearer to him every minute. See?"

In the video screen, a man turned a corner. The Electric Hound rushed forward, screeching. The police converged upon the man.

The TV voice cried, "There's Montag now! The search is over!"

The innocent man stood watching the crowd come on. In his hand was a cigarette, half smoked. He looked at the Hound and his jaw dropped and he started to say something when a godlike voice boomed, "All right, Montag, don't move! We've got you, Montag!"

By the small fire, with seven other men, Mr. Montag sat, ten miles removed, the light of the video screen on his face.

"Don't run, Montag!"

The man turned, bewildered. The crowd roared. The Hound leaped up.

"The poor son-of-a-bitch," said Granger, bitterly.

A dozen shots rattled out. The man crumpled.

"Montag is dead, the search is over, a criminal is given his due," said the announcer.

The camera trucked forward. Just before it showed the dead man's face, however, the screen went black.

"We now switch you to the Sky Room of the Hotel Lux in San Francisco for a half hour of dance music by—"

GRANGER TURNED IT OFF. "They didn't show the man's face, naturally. Better if everyone thinks it's Montag.

Montag said nothing, but simply looked at the blank screen. He could not move or speak.

Granger put out his hand. "Welcome back from the dead, Mr. Montag." Montag took the hand, numbly. The man said, "My real name is Clement, former occupant of the T.S. Eliot Chair at Cambridge. That was before it became an Electrical Engineering school. This gentleman here is Dr. Simmons from U.C.L.A."

"I don't belong here," said Montag, at last, slowly. "I've been an idiot, all the way down the line, bungled and messed and tripped myself up."

"Anger makes idiots of us all, I'm afraid. You can only be

angry so long, then you explode and do the wrong things. It can't be helped now."

"I shouldn't have come here. It might endanger you."

"We're used to that. We all make mistakes, or we wouldn't be here ourselves. When we were separate individuals, all we had was rage. I struck a fireman in the face, once. He'd come to burn my library back about 40 years ago. I had to run. I've been running ever since. And Simmons here . . ."

"I quoted Donne in the midst of a genetics lecture one afternoon. For no reason at all. Just started quoting Donne. You see? Fools, all of us."

They glanced at the fire, self-consciously.

"So you want to join us, Mr. Montag?"

"Yes."

"What have you to offer?"

"Nothing. I thought I had the Book of Job, but I haven't even got that."

"The Book of Job would do very well. Where was it?"

"Here." Montag touched his head.

"Ah," said Granger-Clement. He smiled and nodded.

"What's wrong, isn't it all right?" said Montag.

"Better than all right—perfect! Mr. Montag, you have hit upon the secret of, if you want to give it a term, our organization. Living books, Mr. Montag, living books. Inside the old skull where no one can see." He turned to Simmons. "Do we have a Book of Job?"

"Only one. A man named Harris in Youngstown."

"Mr. Montag." The man reached out and held Montag's shoulder firmly. "Walk slowly, be careful, take your health seriously. If anything should happen to Harris, you are the Book of Job. Do you see how important you are?"

"But I've forgotten it!"

"Nonsense, nothing is ever forgotten. Mislaid, perhaps, but not forgotten. We have ways, several new methods of hypnosis, to shake down the clinkers there. You'll remember, don't fear."

"I've been *trying* to remember."

"Don't try. Relax. It'll come when we need it. Some people are quick studies but don't know it. Some of God's simplest creatures have the ability called eidetic or photographic memory, the ability to memorize entire pages of print at a glance. It has nothing to do with IQ. No offense, Montag. It varies. Would you like, one day, to read Plato's *Republic?*"

"Of course."

Stewart nodded to a man who had been sitting to one side. "Mr. Plato, if you please."

THE MAN BEGAN TO TALK. He looked at Montag idly, his hands filling a corncob pipe, unaware of the words tumbling from his lips. He talked for two minutes without a pause or stumble.

Granger made the smallest move of his fingers. The man cut off. "Perfect word-for-word memory, every word important, every word Plato's," said Granger.

"And," said the man who was Plato, "I don't understand a damned word of it. I just say it. It's up to you to understand."

"Don't you understand *any* of it?"

"None of it. But I can't get it out. Once it's in, it's like solidified glue in a bottle, there for good. Mr. Granger says it's important. That's good enough for me."

"We're old friends," said Granger. "We hadn't seen each other since we were boys. We met a few years ago on that track, somewhere between here and Seattle, walking, me running away from firemen, he running from cities."

"Never liked cities," said the one who was Plato. "Always felt that cities owned men, that was all, and used men to keep themselves going, to keep machines oiled and dusted. So I got out. And then I met Granger and he found out that I had this eidetic memory, as he calls it, and he gave me a book to read and then we burned the book ourselves so we wouldn't be caught with it. And now I'm Plato; that's what I am."

"He is also Socrates."

The man nodded.

"And Schopenhauer."

Another nod.

"And John Dewey."

"All that in one bottle. You wouldn't think there was room. But I can open my head like a concertina and play it. There's plenty of room if you don't try to think about what you've memorized. It's when you start thinking that all of a sudden it's crowded. I don't think about anything except eating, sleeping, and traveling. I let you people do the thinking when you hear what I recite. Oh, there's *plenty* of room, believe me."

"So here we are, Mr. Montag. Mr. Simmons is really Mr. John Donne and Mr. Darwin and Mr. Aristophanes. These other gentlemen are Matthew, Mark, Luke and John. And *I* am Ruth."

Everyone laughed quietly.

"You see, we are not without humor in this melancholy age. I'm also bits and pieces, Mr. Montag, snatches of Byron and Shelley and Shaw and Washington Irving and Shakespeare. I'm one of those kaleidoscopes. Hold me up to the sun, give a shake, watch the patterns. And you are Mr. Job, and in half an hour or less, a war will begin. While those people in the anthill across the river have been busy chasing Montag, as if he were the cause of all their nervous anxiety and frustration, the war has been getting underway. By this time tomorrow the world will belong to the little green towns and the rusted railroad tracks and the men walking on them; that's us. The cities will be soot and ash and baking powder."

The TV rang a bell. Granger switched it on.

"Final negotiations are arranged for a conference today with the enemy government—"

Granger snapped it off.

"Well, what do you think Montag?"

"I think I was pretty blind and ferocious trying to go at it the way I did, planting books and calling firemen."

"You did what you thought you had to do. But our way is simpler and better and the thing we wish to do is keep the knowledge intact and safe and not to excite or anger anyone; for then, if we are destroyed, the knowledge is most certainly dead. We are model citizens in our own special way—we walk the tracks, we lie in the hills at night, we bother no one, and the city have none, and our faces have been changed by plastic surgery, as have our fingerprints. So we wait quietly for the day when the machines are dented junk and then we hope to walk by and say 'Here we are,' to those who survived this war, and we'll say 'Have you come to your senses now? Perhaps a few books will do you some good.'"

"But will they listen to you?"

"Perhaps not. Then we'll have to wait some more. Maybe a few hundred years. Maybe they'll never listen; we can't *make* them. So we'll pass the books on to our children in their minds, and let them wait in turn, on other people. *Some* day someone will need us. This can't last forever."

"How many of you are there?"

"Thousands on the road, on the rails, bums on the outside, libraries on the inside. It wasn't really planned; it grew. Each man had a book he wanted to remember and did. Then we discovered each other and over twenty years or so got a loose network together and made a plan. The important thing we had to learn was that we were not important, we were not to be pedants, we were not to feel superior, we were nothing more than covers for books, of no individual significance whatever. Some of us live in small towns—chapter one of *Walden* in Nantucket, chapter two in Reading, chapter three in Waukesha, each according to his ability. Some can learn a few lines, some a lot."

"The books are safe then."

"Couldn't be safer. Why there's one village in North Carolina, some 200 people, no bomb'll ever touch their town, which is the complete *Meditations* of Marcus Aurelius. You could pick up that town, almost, and flip the pages, a page to a person. People who wouldn't dream of being seen with a book gladly memorized a page. You can't be caught with that. And when the war's over and we've time and need, the books can be written again. The people will be called in one by one to recite what they know and it'll be in print again until another Dark Age, when maybe we'll have to do the whole damned thing over again, man being the fool he is."

"What do we do tonight?" asked Montag.

"Just wait, that's all."

MONTAG LOOKED AT THE MEN'S FACES, old, all of them, in the firelight, and certainly tired. Perhaps he was looking for a brightness, a resolve, a triumph over tomorrow that wasn't really there. Perhaps he expected these men to be proud with the knowledge they carried, to glow with the wisdom as lanterns glow with the fire they contain.

But all the light came from the campfire here, and these men seemed no different than any other man who has run a long run, searched a long search, seen precious things destroyed, seen old friends die, and now, very late in time, were gathered together to watch the machines die, or hope they might die, even while cherishing a last paradoxical love for those very machines which could spin out a material with happiness in the warp and terror in the woof, so interblended that a man might go insane trying to tell the design to himself, and his place in it.

They weren't at all certain that what they carried in their heads might make every future dawn dawn brighter. They were sure of nothing save that the books were on file behind their solemn eyes and that if man put his mind to them properly, something of dignity and happiness might be regained.

Montag looked from one face to another.

"Don't judge a book by its cover," said someone.

A soft laughter moved among them.

Montag turned to look at the city across the river.

"My wife's in that city now," he said.

"I'm sorry to hear that."

"Look," said Simmons.

Montag glanced up.

The bombardment was finished and over, even while the seeds were in the windy sky. The bombs were there, the jet-planes were there, for the merest trifle of an instant, like grain thrown across the heavens by a great hand, and the bombs drifted with a dreadful slowness down upon the morning city where all of the people looked up at their destiny coming upon them like the lid of a dream shutting tight and become an instant later a red and powdery nightmare.

The bombardment to all military purposes was finished. Once the planes had sighted their target, alerted their bombardier at five thousand miles an hour, as quick as the whisper of a knife through the sky, the war was finished. Once the trigger was pulled, once the bombs took flight, it was over.

Now, a full three seconds, all of the time in history, before the bombs struck, the enemy ships themselves were gone, half around the visible world, it seemed, like bullets in which an island savage might not believe because they were unseen, yet the heart is struck suddenly, the body falls into separate divisions, the blood is astounded to be free on the air, and the brain gives up all its precious memories and, still puzzled, dies.

THIS WAR WAS NOT TO BE BELIEVED. It was merely a gesture. It was the flirt of a great metal hand over the city and a voice saying, "Disintegrate. Leave not one stone upon another. Perish. Die."

Montag held the bombs in the sky for a precious moment, with his mind and his hands. "Run!" he cried to Faber. To Clarisse: "Run!" To Mildred, "Get out, get out of there!" But Clarisse, he remembered, was dead. And Faber *was* out; there, in the deep valleys of the country, went the dawn train on its way from one desolation to another. Though the desolation had not yet arrived, was still in the air, it was as certain as man could make it. Before the train had gone another fifty yards on the track, its destination would be meaningless, its point of departure made from a metropolis into a junkyard.

And Mildred!

"Get out, run!" he thought.

He could see Mildred in that metropolis now, in the half second remaining, as the bombs were perhaps three inches, three small inches shy of her hotel building. He could see her leaning into the TV set as if all of the hunger of looking would find the secret of her sleepless unease there. Mildred, leaning anxiously, nervously into that tubular world as into a crystal ball to find happiness.

The first bomb struck.

"Mildred!"

Perhaps the television station went first into oblivion.

Montag saw the screen go dark in Mildred's face, and heard her screaming, because in the next millionth part of time left, she would see her own face reflected there, hungry and alone, in a mirror instead of a crystal ball, and it would be such a wildly empty face that she would at last recognize it, and stare at the ceiling almost with welcome as it and the entire structure of the hotel blasted down upon her, carrying her with a million pounds of brick, metal and people down into the cellar, there to dispose of them in its unreasonable way.

"I remember now," thought Montag, "where we first met. It was in Chicago. Yes, now I remember."

Montag found himself on his face. The concussion had knocked the air across the river, turned the men down like dominoes in a line, blown out the fire like a last candle, and caused the trees to mourn with a great voice of wind passing away south.

Montag lay with his face toward the city. Now it, instead of the bombs, was in the air. They had displaced each other. For another of those impossible instants the city stood, rebuilt and unrecognizable, taller than it had ever hoped or strived to be, taller than man had built it, erected at last in gouts of dust and sparkles of torn metal into a city not unlike a reversed avalanche, formed of flame and steel and stone, a door where a window ought to be, a top for a bottom, a side for a back, and then the city rolled over and fell.

The sound of its death came after.

AND MONTAG LYING THERE, his eyes shut, gasping and crying out, suddenly thought, "Now I remember another thing. Now I remember the Book of Job." He said it over to himself, lying tight to the earth; he said the words of it many times and they were perfect without trying. "Now I remember the Book of Job. Now I *do* remember . . ."

"There," said a voice, Granger's voice.

The men lay like gasping fish on the grass.

They did not get up for a long time, but held to the earth as children hold to a familiar thing, no matter how cold or dead, no matter what has happened or will happen. Their fingers were clawed into the soil, and they were all shouting to keep their ears in balance and open, Montag shouting with them, a protest against the wind that swept them, shaking their hair, tearing at their lips, making their noses bleed.

Montag watched the blood drip into the earth with such an absorption that the city was effortlessly forgotten.

The wind died.

The city was flat, as if one had taken a heaping tablespoon of flour and passed one finger over it, smoothing it to an even level.

The men said nothing. They lay a while like people on the dawn edge of sleep, not yet ready to arise and begin the day's obligations, its fires and foods, its thousand details of putting foot after foot, hand after hand, its deliveries and functions and minute obsessions. They lay blinking their stunned eyelids. You could hear them breathing faster, then slower, then with the slowness of normality.

Montag sat up. He did not move any farther, however. The other men did likewise. The sun was touching the black horizon with a faint red tip. The air was cool and sweet and smelled of rain. In a few minutes it would smell of dust and pulverized iron, but now it was sweet.

And across the world, thought Montag, the cities of the other nations are dead, too, almost in the same instant.

Silently, the leader of the small group, Granger, arose, felt of his arms and legs, touched his face to see if everything was in its place, then shuffled over to the blown-out fire and bent over it. Montag watched.

Striking a match, Granger touched it to a piece of paper

and shoved this under a bit of kindling, and shoved together bits of straw and dry wood, and after a while, drawing the men slowly, awkwardly to it by its glow, the fire licked up, coloring their faces pink and yellow, while the sun rose slowly to color their backs.

THERE WAS NO SOUND except the low and secret talk of men at morning, and the talk was no more than this:

"How many strips?"

"Two each."

"Good enough."

The bacon was counted out on a wax paper. The frying pan was set to the fire and the bacon laid in it. After a moment it began to flutter and dance in the pan and the sputter of it filled the morning air with its aroma. Eggs were cracked in upon the bacon and the men watched this ritual, for the leader was a participant, as were they, in a religion of early rising, a thing man had done for many centuries, thought Montag, a thing man had done over and over again, and Montag felt at ease among them, as if during the long night the walls of a great prison had vaporized around them and they were on the land again and only the birds sang on or off as they pleased, with no schedule, and with no nagging human insistence.

"Here," said Granger, dishing out the bacon and eggs to each from the hot pan. They each held out the scratched tin plates that had been passed around.

Then, without looking up, breaking more eggs into the pan for himself, Granger slowly and with a concern both for what he said, recalling it, rounding it, and for making the food also, began to recite snatches and rhythms, even while the day brightened all about as if a pink lamp had been given more wick, and Montag listened and they all looked at the tin plates in their hands, waiting a moment for the eggs to cool, while the leader started the routine, and others took it up, here or there, round about.

WHEN IT WAS MONTAG'S TURN, he spoke too:

> "To everything there is a season,
> And a time to every purpose under the heaven. . .
> A time to be born, and a time to die. . .
> A time to kill, and a time to heal . . ."

ORKS MOVED IN THE PINK LIGHT. Now each of the men remembered a separate and different thing, a bit of poetry, a line from a play, an old song. And they spoke these little bits and pieces in the early morning air:

> "Man that is born of a woman
> Is of few days and full of trouble . . ."

A WIND BLEW IN THE TREES.

> "To be or not to be, that is the question . . ."

THE SUN WAS FULLY UP.

> "Oh, do you remember Sweet Alice, Ben Bolt . . . ?"

Montag felt fine.

Bonus Stories

THE DRAGON WHO ATE HIS TAIL

SOMETIME BEFORE DAWN

TO THE FUTURE

THE DRAGON WHO ATE HIS TAIL

WHAT DID THEY WISH MOST? DID THEY WISH TO LINGER IN old Chicago, to smell the grit and grime, to touch the strange buildings, to inhabit the reeking subways of Manhattan, to taste the lime popsicles of some forgotten summer, to listen to scratchy phonographs in 1910, would they board the ships of Nelson for Trafalgar, would they have a day with Socrates prior to the hemlock, would they stroll Athens on the busiest day and see the flash of knees in the sunlit gas, in what idea and magnificent fashion would they most dearly love to spend the next hour, the next day, the next month, the next year. The rates were extremely reasonable, as on any excursion! So much down, so much a day, and you could fetch yourself home any time antiquity annoyed or bored or frightened you. Here was a way to learn your history! Here was a frontier for you, ready, waiting, alive, fresh and new.

Come along, now!

"Do you think you'd like it, Alice?"

"I hadn't thought. I imagine."

"Would you like to go?"

"Where?"

"Paris, 1940. London, 1870. Chicago, 1895? Or the Saint Louis exposition around 1900, I hear it was naïve and tremendous."

The husband and wife sat at their mechanical breakfast table being fed exact portions of magnificently browned toast adrip with synthetic and therefore absolutely guaranteed pure butter.

Oh, that empty future, when the dragon has devoured his radioactive tail, when the people of that time, dismayed and utterly discouraged, their faces blanched by explosions and their hair burned to the root, and their hope scorched and twisted to a shapeless mass in their hearts, when those people turn backward, turn backward, oh time in thy flight, makes us a child again just for tonight!

And so they were picking up, picking up and going, the law couldn't stop, the law-makers couldn't stop them, the police, the tribunals, the silly senates and corruptible congresses, the talkers and pounders and wavers of lists couldn't stop them, the world was emptying. The plug was pulled, and the people were gushing down the drain of time into yesterday.

Alice and John Weathers stood outside their door. The houses on their street were empty and silent. The children were gone from the trees, their stomachs no longer distended with green and hideous fruit. The curbs were empty of cars and the sky of ships, and the windows of light motion.

"Did you forget to turn off the bath tap?"

"It's off?"

"The gas?"

"Off."

"The electricity?"

"Why must you worry?"

"Now, lock the door."

"No one's going to come in."

"The wind might."

"Oh, the wind, that's different."

"But lock it anyway, please, John."

And so they locked it and walked off down the lawn with their clothes left behind and all the furniture neatly sheeted. Everything in its place.

"Do you think we'll ever come back?"

"No."

"Never at all."

"Never."

"I wonder if we'll ever remember this house on Elm Terrace, the furniture, the electric lights, the parties, all of it, and, in the past, remember that there was such a time or place?"

"No, we'll never remember. They put you in a machine that takes memory away. And gives you a new memory. I'm going to be John Sessions, accountant in the city of Chicago in the year 1920, and you're my wife."

They walked along the twilight street.

"And just think," she said, quietly, "someday we'll meet Edgar and his wife on the street, in Chicago, and they'll look at us, and we'll look at them and think, Where've I seen those faces before, but walk on, strangers, never guessing we met a hundred and ninety years in the future."

"Yes, strangers, that is an odd thought."

"And all of us, a million or more, hiding in the Past, not knowing each other, but fitting into the pattern, never guessing that we are all from another age."

"We're running away," he said, stopping, and looking at the dead houses. "I don't like running away from a problem."

"What else can we do?"

"Stay and fight it out."

"Against the hydrogen bomb?"

"Make laws against it."

"And have them broken."

"Keep trying, keep trying, that's what we ought to do, instead of run."

"It's no use."

"No, of course it isn't," he said. "I realize now that as long as there is one unscrupulous scientist and one dirty politician they'll get together and make the bomb for whatever silly reason they have. It used to be we had weapons, the little man, to fight back with, a musket, the minute men, a revolution of the people against tyranny, there were always spears to throw or guns to point, but we can't point a gun at the hydrogen explosion nor any of its keepers for fear of reprisal. The thing is so vast, we are like currants lost in a great yeast, baked before we know it. Come on, it's no use talking."

They went on away from the dead street, into the silence of the business section of town.

BUT OFTEN NIGHTS, when the great El rounds the corner near their sixth story room and for an instant flashes their bed with yellow and mechanical light, and trembles and jounces their bones in their sleeping flesh, she shudders and cries out to her husband's back in his slumber, and he, waking turns to whisper, "Now, now, what was it?"

"Oh, Charles," she tells him in the now silent, now dark

and empty and lost room, "I dreamt we were at breakfast in another time, with a mechanical table feeding us, and rockets in the air, and all sorts of strange things and inventions."

"There, there, a nightmare," he says.

And a minute later, clutched very tight together, they are tremblingly asleep once more.

SOMETIME BEFORE DAWN

IT WAS THE CRYING LATE AT NIGHT, PERHAPS, THE HYSTE-
ria, and then the sobbing violently, and after it had passed
away into a sighing, I could hear the husband's voice through
the wall. "There, there," he would say, "there, there."

I would lie upon my back in my night bed and listen and
wonder, and the calendar on my wall said August 2002. And
the man and his wife, young, both about thirty, and fresh-
looking, with light hair and blue eyes, but lines around their
mouths, had just moved into the rooming house where I took
my meals and worked as a janitor in the downtown library.

Every night and every night it would be the same thing, the
wife crying, and the husband quieting her with his soft voice
beyond my wall. I would strain to hear what started it, but I
could never tell. It wasn't anything he said, I was positive of
this, or anything he did. I was almost certain, in fact, that it
started all by itself, late at night, about two o'clock. She would
wake up, I theorized, and I would hear that first terrorized
shriek and then the long crying. It made me sad. As old as I
am, I hate to hear a woman cry.

I remember the first night they came here, a month ago, an

August evening here in this town deep in Illinois, all the houses dark and everyone on the porches licking ice-cream bars. I remember walking through the kitchen downstairs and standing in the old smells of cooking and hearing but not seeing the dog lapping water from the pan under the stove, a nocturnal sound, like water in a cave. And I walked on through to the parlor in the dark, with his face devilish pink from exertion, Mr. Fiske, the landlord, was fretting over the air conditioner, which, damned thing, refused to work. Finally in the hot night he wandered outside onto the mosquito porch—it was made for mosquitoes only, Mr. Fiske averred, but went there anyway.

I went out onto the porch and sat down and unwrapped a cigar to fire away my own special mosquitoes, and there were Grandma Fiske and Alice Fiske and Henry Fiske and Joseph Fiske and Bill Fiske and six other boarders and roomers, all unwrapping Eskimo pies.

It was then that the man and his wife, as suddenly as if they had sprung up out of the wet dark grass, appeared at the bottom of the steps, looking up at us like the spectators in a summer night circus. They had no luggage. I always remembered that. They had no luggage. And their clothes did not seem to fit them.

"Is there a place for food and sleep?" said the man, in a halting voice. Everyone was startled. Perhaps I was the one who saw them first, then Mrs. Fiske smiled and got out of her wicker chair and came forward. "Yes, we have rooms."

"Twenty dollars a day, with meals."

They did not seem to understand. They looked at each other.

"Twenty dollars," said Grandma.

"We'll move into here," said the man.

"Don't you want to look first?" asked Mrs. Fiske

They came up the steps, looking back, as if someone was following.

That was the first night of the crying.

BREAKFAST WAS SERVED every morning at seven-thirty, large, toppling stacks of pancakes, huge jugs of syrup, islands of butter, toast, many pots of coffee, and cereal if you wished. I was working on my cereal when the new couple came down the stairs, slowly. They did not come into the dining room immediately, but I had a sense they were just looking at everything. Since Mrs. Fiske was busy I went in to fetch them, and there they were, the man and wife, just looking out the front window, looking and looking at the green grass and the big elm trees and the blue sky. Almost as if they had never seen them before.

"Good morning," I said.

They ran their fingers over antimacassars or through the bead-curtain-rain that hung in the dining room doorway. Once I thought I saw them both smile very broadly at some secret thing. I asked them their name. At first they puzzled over this but then said,

"Smith."

I introduced them around to everyone eating and they sat and looked at the food and at last began to eat.

They spoke very little, and only when spoken to, and I had an opportunity to remark the beauty in their faces, for they had fine and graceful bone structures in their chins and cheeks and brows, good straight noses, and clear eyes, but always that tiredness about the mouths.

Half through the breakfast, an event occurred to which I

must call special attention. Mr. Britz, the garage mechanic, said, "Well, the president has been out fund-raising again today, I see by the paper."

The stranger, Mr. Smith, snorted angrily. "That terrible man! I've always hated Westercott."

Everyone looked at him. I stopped eating.

Mrs. Smith frowned at her husband. He coughed slightly and went on eating.

Mr. Britz scowled momentarily, and then we all finished breakfast, but I remember it now. What Mr. Smith had said was, "That terrible man! I've always hated Westercott."

I never forgot.

THAT NIGHT SHE CRIED AGAIN, as if she was lost in the woods, and I stayed awake for an hour, thinking.

There were so many things I suddenly wanted to ask them. And yet it was almost impossible to see them, for they stayed locked in the room constantly.

The next day, however, was Saturday. I caught them momentarily in the garden looking at the pink roses, just standing and looking, not touching, and I said, "A fine day!"

"A wonderful, wonderful day!" they both cried, almost in unison, and then laughed embarrassedly.

"Oh, it can't be *that* good." I smiled.

"You don't know how good it is, you don't know how wonderful it is—you can't possibly guess," she said, and then quite suddenly there were tears in her eyes.

I stood bewildered. "I'm sorry," I said. "Are you all right?"

"Yes, yes." She blew her nose and went off a distance to pick a few flowers. I stood looking at the apple tree hung with red fruit, and at last I got the courage to inquire, "May I ask where you're from, Mr. Smith?"

"The United States," he said slowly, as if piecing the words together.

"Oh, I was rather under the impression that—"

"We were from another county?"

"Yes."

"We are from the United States."

"What's your business, Mr. Smith?"

"I *think*."

"I see," I said, for all the answers were less than satisfactory. "Oh, by the way, what's Westercott's first name?"

"Lionel," said Mr. Smith, and then stared at me. The color left his face. He turned in a panic. "Please," he cried, softly. "Why do you ask these questions?" They hurried into the house before I could apologize. From the stair window they looked out at me as if I were the spy of the world. I felt contemptible and ashamed.

ON SUNDAY MORNING I helped clean the house. Tapping on the Smiths' door I received no answer. Listening, for the first time, I heard the tickings, the little clicks and murmurs of numerous clocks working away quietly in the room. I stood entranced. Tick-tick-tick-tick-tick! Two, no, *three* clocks. When I opened their door to fetch their wastepaper basket, I saw the clocks, arrayed, on the bureau, on the windowsill, and by the nightstand, small and large clocks, all set to this hour of the late morning, ticking like a roomful of insects.

So *many* clocks. But why? I wondered. Mr. Smith had *said* he was a *thinker*.

I took the wastebasket down to the incinerator. Inside the basket, as I was dumping it, I found one of her handkerchiefs. I fondled it for a moment, smelling the flower fragrance. Then I tossed it onto the fire.

It did not burn.

I poked at it and pushed it far back in the fire.

But the handkerchief would not burn.

In my room I took out my cigar lighter and touched it to the handkerchief. It would not burn, nor could I tear it.

And then I considered their clothing. I realized why it had seemed peculiar. The cut was regular for men and women in this season, but in their coats and shirts and dresses and shoes, there was not one blessed seam anywhere!

They came back out later that afternoon to walk in the garden. Peering from my high window I saw them standing together, holding hands, talking earnestly.

It was then that the terrifying thing happened.

A roar filled the sky. The woman looked into the sky, screamed, put her hands to her face, and collapsed. The man's face turned white, he stared blindly at the sun, and he fell to his knees calling to his wife to get up, but she lay there, hysterically.

By the time I got downstairs to help, they had vanished. They had evidently run around one side of the house while I had gone around the other. The sky was empty, the roar had dwindled.

Why, I thought, should a simple, ordinary sound of a plane flying unseen in the sky cause such terror?

The airplane flew back a minute later and on the wings it said: COUNTY FAIR! ATTEND! RACING! FUN!

That's nothing to be afraid of, I thought.

I passed their room at nine-thirty and the door was open. On the walls I saw three calendars lined up with the date August 18, 2035, prominently circled.

"Good evening," I said pleasantly. "Say, you have a lot of nice calendars there. Come in mighty handy."

"Yes," they said.

I went on to my room and stood in the dark before turning on the light and wondered why they should need three calendars, all with the year 2035. It was crazy, but *they* were not. Everything about them was crazy except themselves, they were clean, rational people with beautiful faces, but it began to move in my mind, the calendars, the clocks, the wristwatches they wore, worth a thousand dollars each if I ever saw a wristwatch, and they, themselves, constantly looking at the time. I thought of the handkerchief that wouldn't burn and the seamless clothing, and the sentence "I've always hated Westercott."

I've always hated Westercott.

Lionel Westercott. There wouldn't be two people in the world with an unusual name like that. Lionel Westercott. I said it softly to myself in the summer night. It was a warm evening, with moths dancing softly, in velvet touches, on my screen. I slept fitfully, thinking of my comfortable job, this good little town, everything peaceful, everyone happy, and these two people in the next room, the only people in the town, in the world, it seemed, who were not happy. Their tired mouths haunted me. And sometimes the tired eyes, too tired for ones so young.

I must have slept a bit, for at two o'clock, as usual, I was wakened by her crying, but this time I heard her call out, "Where are we, where are we, how did we get here, where are we?" And his voice, "Hush, hush, now, please," and he soothed her.

"Are we safe, are we safe, are we safe?"

"Yes, yes, dear, yes."

And then the sobbing.

Perhaps I could have thought a lot of things. Most minds would turn to murder, fugitives from justice. My mind did not turn that way. Instead I lay in the dark, listening to her cry, and it broke my heart, it moved in my veins end my head and I was so unbearably touched by her sadness and loneliness that I got up and dressed and left the house. I walked down the street and before I knew it I was on the hill over the lake and there was the library, dark and immense, and I had my janitor's key in my hand. Without thinking why, I entered the big silent place at two in the morning and walked through the empty rooms and down the aisles, turning on a few lights. And then I got a couple of big books out and began tracing some paragraphs and lines down and down, page after page, for about an hour in the early, early dark morning. I drew up a chair and sat down. I fetched some more books. I sent my eye searching. I grew tired. But then at last my hand paused on a name, "William Westercott, politician, New York City. Married to Aimee Ralph on January 1998. One child, Lionel, born February 2000."

I shut the book and locked myself out of the library and walked home, cold, through the summer morning with the stars bright in the black sky.

I stood for a moment in front of the sleeping house with the empty porch and the curtains in every room fluttering with the warm August wind, and I held my cigar in my hand but did not light it. I listened, and there above me, like the cry of some night bird, was the sound of the lonely woman, crying. She had had another nightmare, and, I thought, nightmares are memory, they are based on things remembered, things remembered vividly and horridly and with too much detail, and she had had another of her nightmares and she was afraid.

I looked at the town all around me, the little houses, the houses with people in them, and the country beyond the houses, ten thousand miles of meadow and farm and river and lake, highways and hills and mountains and cities all sizes sleeping in the time before dawn, so quietly, and the streetlights going out now when there was no use for them at this nocturnal hour. And I thought of all the people in the whole land and the years to come, and all of us with good jobs and happy in this year.

Then I went upstairs past their door and went to bed and listened and there, behind the wall, the woman was saying over and over again, "I'm afraid, I'm afraid," faintly, crying.

And lying there I was as cold as an ancient piece of ice placed between the blankets, and I was trembling, though I knew nothing, I knew everything, for now I knew where these travelers were from and what her nightmares were and what she was afraid of, and what they were running away from.

I figured it just before I went to sleep, with her crying faintly in my ears. Lionel Westercott, I thought, will be old enough to be president of the United States in the year 2035.

Somehow, I did not want the sun to rise in the morning.

TO THE FUTURE

THE FIREWORKS SIZZLED ACROSS THE COOL-TILED
square, banged against adobe café walls, then rushed on hot
wires to bash the high church tower, while a fiery bull ran
about the plaza chasing boys and laughing men. It was a spring
night in Mexico in the year 1938.

Mr. and Mrs. William Travis stood on the edge of the yelling crowd, smiling. The bull charged. Ducking, the man and
wife ran, fire pelting them, past the brass band that pulsed out
vast rhythms of La Paloma. The bull passed, a framework of
bamboo and gunpowder, carried lightly on the shoulders of a
charging Mexican.

"I've never enjoyed myself so much in my life," gasped Susan Travis, stopping.

"It's terrific," said William.

"It will go on, won't it? I mean our trip?"

He patted his breast pocket. "I've enough traveler's checks
for a lifetime. Enjoy yourself. Forget it. They'll never find us."

"Never?"

Now someone hurled giant firecrackers from the bell tower.

The bull was dead. The Mexican lifted its framework from

his shoulders. Children clustered to touch the magnificent papier-maché animal.

"Let's examine the bull," said William.

As they walked past the café entrance, Susan saw the strange man looking out at them, a white man in a white suit, with a thin, sunburned face. His eyes coldly watched them as they walked.

She would never have noticed him if it had not been for the bottles at his immaculate elbow; a fat bottle of crème de menthe, a clear bottle of vermouth, a flagon of cognac, and seven other bottles of assorted liqueurs, and, at his fingertips, ten small half-filled glasses from which, without taking his eyes off the street, he sipped, occasionally squinting, pressing his thin mouth shut upon the savor. In his free hand a thin Havana cigar smoked, and on a chair stood twenty cartons of Turkish cigarettes, six boxes of cigars and some packaged colognes.

"Bill—" whispered Susan.

"Take it easy," William said. "That man's nobody."

"I saw him in the plaza this morning."

"Don't look back, keep walking, examine the papier-maché bull—here, that's it, ask questions."

"Do you think he's from the Searchers?"

"They couldn't follow us!"

"They might!"

"What a nice bull," said William to the man who owned it.

"He couldn't have followed us back through two hundred years, could he?"

"Watch yourself!" said William.

She swayed. He crushed her elbow tightly, steering her away.

"Don't faint." He smiled, to make it look good. "You'll be

all right. Let's go right in that café, drink in front of him, so if
he is what we think he is, he won't suspect."

"No, I couldn't."

"We've got to—come on now. And so I said to David, that's
ridiculous!" He spoke this last in a loud voice as they went up
the café steps.

We are here, thought Susan. Who are we? Where are we
going? What do we fear? Start at the beginning, she told herself, holding to her sanity, as she felt the adobe floor underfoot.

My name is Ann Kristen, my husband's name is Roger,
we were born in the year 2155 A.D. And we lived in a world
that was evil. A world that was like a great ship pulling away
from the shore of sanity and civilization, roaring its black horn
in the night, taking two billion people with it, whether they
wanted to go or not, to death, to fall over the edge of the earth
and the sea into radioactive flame and madness.

They walked into the café. The man was staring at them.
A phone rang.

The phone startled Susan. She remembered a phone ring-
ing two hundred years in the future, on that blue April morning in 2155, and herself answering it:

"Ann, this is René! Have you heard? I mean about Travel
In Time, Incorporated? Trips to Rome in 21 A.D., trips to
Napoleon's Waterloo, any time, anyplace!"

"René, you're joking."

"No. Clinton Smith left this morning for Philadelphia in
1776. Travel In Time, Inc., arranges everything. Costs money.
But think, to actually see the burning of Rome, to see Kublai
Khan, Moses and the Red Sea! You've probably got an ad in
your tube-mail now."

She had opened the suction mail tube and there was the metal foil advertisement:

ROME AND THE BORGIÁS!
THE WRIGHT BROTHERS AT KITTY HAWK!
Travel In Time, Inc., can costume you, put you in a crowd during the assassination of Lincoln or Caesar! We guarantee to teach you any language you need to move freely in any civilization, in any year, without friction. Latin, Greek, ancient American colloquial. Take your vacation in Time as well as Place!

René's voice was buzzing on the phone. "Tom and I leave for 1492 tomorrow. They're arranging for Tom to sail with Columbus—isn't it amazing?"

"Yes," murmured Ann, stunned. "What does the government say about this Time Machine Company?"

"Oh, the police have an eye on it. Afraid people might evade the draft, run off and hide in the Past. Everyone has to leave a security bond behind, his house and belongings, to guarantee return. After all, the war's on."

"Yes, the war," murmured Ann. "The war."

Standing there, holding the phone, she had thought: Here is the chance my husband and I have talked and prayed over for so many years. We don't like the world of 2155. We want to run away from his work at the bomb factory—from any position with disease-culture units. Perhaps there is some chance for us, to escape, to run for centuries into a wild country of years where they will never find us and bring us back to burn our books, censor our thoughts, scald our minds with fear, march us, scream at us with radios. . .

The phone rang.

They were in Mexico in the year 1938.

She looked at the stained café wall.

Good workers for the Future State were allowed vacations into the Past to escape fatigue. And so she and her husband had moved back into 1938. They took a room in New York City, and enjoyed the theaters and the Statue of Liberty which still stood green in the harbor. And on the third day, they had changed their clothes and their names, and flown off to hide in Mexico.

"It must be him," whispered Susan, looking at the stranger seated at the table. "Those cigarettes, the cigars, the liquor. They give him away. Remember our first night in the Past?"

A month ago, on their first night in New York, before their flight, they had tasted all the strange drinks, bought odd foods, perfumes, cigarettes of ten dozen rare brands, for they were scarce in the Future, where war was everything. So they had made fools of themselves, rushing in and out of stores, salons, tobacconists, going up to their room to get wonderfully ill.

And now here was this stranger, doing likewise, doing a thing that only a man from the Future would do, who had been starved for liquors and cigarettes too many years.

Susan and William sat and ordered a drink.

The stranger was examining their clothes, their hair, their jewelry, the way they walked and sat. "Sit easily," said William under his breath. "Look as if you've worn this clothing style all your life."

"We should never have tried to escape."

"My God," said William. "He's coming over. Let me do the talking."

The stranger bowed before them. There was the faintest tap of heels knocking together. Susan stiffened. That military sound—unmistakable as that certain ugly rap on your door at midnight.

"Mr. Kristen," said the stranger, "you did not pull up your pant legs when you sat down."

William froze. He looked at his hands lying on either leg, innocently. Susan's heart was beating swiftly.

"You've got the wrong person," said William, quickly. "My name's not Krisler."

"Kristen," corrected the stranger.

"I'm William Travis," said William. "And I don't see what my pant legs have to do with you."

"Sorry." The stranger pulled up a chair. "Let us say I thought I knew you because you did not pull your trousers up. Everyone does. If they don't the trousers bag quickly. I am a long way from home, Mr.—Travis—and in need of company. My name is Simms."

"Mr. Simms, we appreciate your loneliness, but we're tired. We're leaving for Acapulco tomorrow."

"A charming spot. I was just there, looking for some friends of mine. They are somewhere. I shall find them yet. Oh, is the lady a bit sick?"

"Good night, Mr. Simms."

They started out the door, William holding Susan's arm firmly. They did not look back when Mr. Simms called, "Oh, just one other thing." He paused and then slowly spoke the words:

"Twenty-one fifty-five A.D."

Susan shut her eyes and felt the earth falter under her. She kept going, into the fiery plaza, seeing nothing. . .

THEY LOCKED THE DOOR of their hotel room. And then she was crying and they were standing in the dark, and the room tilted under them. Far away, firecrackers exploded, there was laughter in the plaza.

"What a damned, loud nerve," said William. "Him sitting there, looking us up and down like animals, smoking his damn cigarettes, drinking his drinks. I should have killed him then!" His voice was nearly hysterical. "He even had the nerve to use his real name to us. The Chief of the Searchers. And the thing about my pant legs. I should have pulled them up when I sat. It's an automatic gesture of this day and age. When I didn't do it, it set me off from the others. It made him think: Here's a man who never wore pants, a man used to breech-uniforms and future styles. I could kill myself for giving us away!"

"No, no, it was my walk, these high heels, that did it. Our haircuts, so new, so fresh. Everything about us odd and uneasy."

William turned on the light. "He's still testing us. He's not positive of us, not completely. We can't run out on him, then. We can't make him certain. We'll go to Acapulco, leisurely."

"Maybe he is sure of us, but is just playing."

"I wouldn't put it past him. He's got all the time in the world. He can dally here if he wants, and bring us back to the Future sixty seconds after we left it. He might keep us wondering for days, laughing at us."

Susan sat on the bed, wiping the tears from her face, smelling the old smell of charcoal and incense.

"They won't make a scene, will they?"

"They won't dare. They'll have to get us alone to put us in the Time Machine and send us back."

"There's a solution then," she said. "We'll never be alone, we'll always be in crowds."

Footsteps sounded outside their locked door.

They turned out the light and undressed in silence. The footsteps went away.

Susan stood by the window looking down at the plaza in the darkness. "So that building there is a church?"

"Yes."

"I've often wondered what a church looked like. It's been so long since anyone saw one. Can we visit it tomorrow?"

"Of course. Come to bed."

They lay in the dark room.

Half an hour later, their phone rang. She lifted the receiver. "Hello?"

"The rabbits may hide in the forest," said a voice, "but a fox can always find them."

She replaced the receiver and lay back straight and cold in the bed.

Outside, in the year 1938, a man played three tunes upon a guitar, one following another . . .

During the night, she put her hand out and almost touched the year 2155. She felt her fingers slide over cool spaces of time, as over a corrugated surface, and she heard the insistent thump of marching feet, a million bands playing a million military tunes. She saw the fifty thousand rows of disease-culture in their aseptic glass tubes, her hand reaching out to them at her work in that huge factory in the future. She saw the tubes of leprosy, bubonic, typhoid, tuberculosis. She heard the great explosion and saw her hand burned to a wrinkled plum, felt it recoil from a concussion so immense that the world was lifted and let fall, and all the buildings broke and people hemorrhaged and lay silent. Great volcanoes, machines, winds, avalanches slid down to silence and she awoke, sobbing, in the bed, in Mexico, many years away. . . .

In the early morning, drugged with the single hour's sleep they had finally been able to obtain, they awoke to the sound of loud automobiles in the street. Susan peered down from the iron balcony at a small crowd of eight people only now emerging, chattering, yelling, from trucks and cars with red lettering on them. A crowd of Mexicans had followed the trucks.

"Qué pasa?" Susan called to a little boy.

The boy replied.

Susan turned back to her husband.

"An American motion picture company, here on location."

"Sounds interesting." William was in the shower. "Let's watch them. I don't think we'd better leave today. We'll try to lull Simms."

For a moment, in the bright sun, she had forgotten that somewhere in the hotel, waiting, was a man smoking a thousand cigarettes, it seemed. She saw the eight loud, happy Americans below and wanted to call to them: "Save me, hide me, help me! I'm from the year 2155!"

But the words stayed in her throat. The functionaries of Travel In Time, Inc., were not foolish. In your brain, before you left on your trip, they placed a psychological block. You could tell no one your true time or birthplace, nor could you reveal any of the future to those in the past. The past and the future must be protected from each other. Only with this hindrance were people allowed to travel unguarded through the ages. The future must he protected from any change brought about by her people traveling in the past. Even if Susan wanted to with all of her heart, she could not tell any of those happy people below in the plaza who she was, or what her predicament had become.

"What about breakfast?" said William.

BREAKFAST WAS BEING SERVED in the immense dining room. Ham and eggs for everyone. The place was full of tourists. The film people entered, all eight of them, six men and two women, giggling, shoving chairs about. And Susan sat near them feeling the warmth and protection they offered, even when Mr. Simms came down the lobby stairs, smoking his Turkish cigarette with great intensity. He nodded at them from a distance, and Susan nodded back, smiling because he couldn't do anything to them here, in front of eight film people and twenty other tourists.

"Those actors," said William, "Perhaps I could hire two of them, say it was a joke, dress them in our clothes, have them drive off in our car, when Simms is in such a spot where he can't see their faces. If two people pretending to be us could lure him off for a few hours, we might make it to Mexico City. It'd take years to find us there!"

"Hey!"

A fat man, with liquor on his breath, leaned on their table.

"American tourists!" he cried. "I'm so sick of seeing Mexicans, I could kiss you!" He shook their hands. "Come on, eat with us. Misery loves company. I'm Misery, this is Miss Gloom, and Mr. and Mrs. Do-We-Hate-Mexico! We all hate it. But we're here for some preliminary shots for a damn film. The rest of the crew arrives tomorrow. My name's Joe Melton, I'm a director and if this ain't a hell of a country—funerals in the streets, people dying—come on, move over, join the party, cheer us up!"

Susan and William were both laughing.

"Am I funny?" Mr. Melton asked the immediate world.

"Wonderful!" Susan moved over.

Mr. Simms was glaring across the dining room at them. She made a face at him.

Mr. Simms advanced among the tables.

"Mr. and Mrs. Travis!" he called. "I thought we were breakfasting together, alone?"

"Sorry," said William.

"Sit down, pal," said Mr. Melton. "Any friend of theirs is a pal of mine."

Mr. Simms sat. The film people talked loudly and while they talked, Mr. Simms said quietly, "I hope you slept well."

"Did you?"

"I'm not used to spring mattresses," replied Mr. Simms, wryly. "But there are compensations. I stayed up half the night trying new cigarettes and foods. Odd, fascinating. A whole new spectrum of sensation, these ancient vices."

"We don't know what you're talking about," said Susan.

Simms laughed. "Always the play acting. It's no use. Nor is this stratagem of crowds. I'll get you alone soon enough. I'm immensely patient."

"Say," Mr. Melton broke in, "is this guy giving you any trouble?"

"It's all right."

"Say the word and I'll give him the bum's rush."

Melton turned back to yell at his associates. In the laughter, Mr. Simms went on: "Let us come to the point. It took me a month of tracing you through towns and cities to find you, and all of yesterday to be sure of you. If you come with me quietly, I might be able to get you off with no punishment—if you agree to go back to work on the Hydrogen-Plus bomb."

"We don't know what you're talking about."

"Stop it!" cried Simms, irritably. "Use your intelligence! You know we can't let you get away with this escape. Other people in the year 2155 might get the same idea and do the same. We need people."

"To fight your wars," said William.

"Bill!"

"It's all right, Susan. We'll talk on his terms now. We can't escape."

"Excellent," said Simms. "Really, you've both been incredibly romantic, running away from your responsibilities."

"Running away from horror."

"Nonsense. Only a war."

"What are you guys talking about?" asked Mr. Melton.

Susan wanted to tell him. But you could only speak in generalities. The psychological block in your mind allowed that. Generalities, such as Simms and William were now discussing.

"Only the war," said William. "Half the world dead of leprosy bombs!"

"Nevertheless," Simms pointed out, "the inhabitants of the Future resent you two hiding on a tropical isle, as it were, while they drop off the cliff into hell. Death loves death, not life. Dying people love to know that others die with them; it is a comfort to learn you are not alone in the kiln, in the grave. I am the guardian of their collective resentment against you two."

"Look at the guardian of resentments!" said Mr. Melton to his companions.

"The longer you keep me waiting, the harder it will go for you. We need you on the bomb project, Mr. Travis. Return now—no torture. Later, we'll force you to work and after you've finished the bomb, we'll try a number of complicated new devices on you, sir."

"I've got a proposition," said William. "I'll come back with you, if my wife stays here alive, safe, away from that war."

Mr. Simms debated. "All right. Meet me in the plaza in ten minutes. Pick me up in your car. Drive me to a deserted country spot. I'll have the Travel Machine pick us up there."

"Bill!" Susan held his arm tightly.

"Don't argue." He looked over at her. "It's settled." To Simms: "One thing. Last night, you could have got in our room and kidnapped us. Why didn't you?"

"Shall we say that I was enjoying myself?" replied Mr. Simms languidly, sucking his new cigar. "I hate giving up this wonderful atmosphere, this sun, this vacation. I regret leaving behind the wine and the cigarettes. Oh, how I regret it. The plaza then, in ten minutes. Your wife will be protected and may stay here as long as she wishes. Say your good-bys."

Mr. Simms arose and walked out.

"There goes Mr. Big-Talk!" yelled Mr. Melton at the departing gentleman. He turned and looked at Susan. "Hey. Someone's crying. Breakfast's no time for people to cry, now is it?"

At nine fifteen, Susan stood on the balcony of their room, gazing down at the plaza. Mr. Simms was seated there, his neat legs crossed, on a delicate bronze bench. Biting the tip from a cigar, he lighted it tenderly.

Susan heard the throb of a motor, and far up the street, out of a garage and down the cobbled hill, slowly, came William in his car.

The car picked up speed. Thirty, now forty, now fifty miles an hour. Chickens scattered before it.

Mr. Simms took off his white Panama hat and mopped his pink forehead, put his hat back on, and then saw the car.

It was rushing sixty miles an hour, straight on for the plaza.

"William!" screamed Susan.

The car hit the low plaza curb, thundering, jumped up, sped across the tiles toward the green bench where Mr. Simms now dropped his cigar, shrieked, flailed his hands, and was hit by the car. His body flew up and up in the air, and down, crazily, into the street.

On the far side of the plaza, one front wheel broken, the car stopped. People were running.

Susan went in and closed the balcony doors.

THEY CAME DOWN the Official Palace steps together, arm in arm, their faces pale, at twelve noon.

"Adios, señor," said the mayor behind them. "Señora."

They stood in the plaza where the crowd was pointing at the blood.

"Will they want to see you again?" asked Susan.

"No, we went over and over it. It was an accident. I lost control of the car. I wept for them. God knows I had to get my relief out somewhere. I felt like weeping. I hated to kill him. I've never wanted to do anything like that in my life."

"They won't prosecute you?"

"They talked about it, but no. I talked faster. They believe me. It was an accident. It's over."

"Where will we go? Mexico City?"

"The car's in the repair shop. It'll be ready at four this afternoon. Then we'll get the hell out."

"Will we be followed? Was Simms working alone?"

"I don't know. We'll have a little head start on them, I think."

The film people were coming out of the hotel as they approached. Mr. Melton hurried up, scowling. "Hey, I heard what happened. Too bad. Everything okay now? Want to get your minds off it? We're doing some preliminary shots up the street. You want to watch, you're welcome. Come on, do you good."

They went.

They stood on the cobbled street while the film camera was being set up. Susan looked at the road leading down and away, at the highway going to Acapulco and the sea, past pyramids and ruins and little adobe towns with yellow walls, blue walls, purple walls and flaming bougainvillea. She thought: We shall take the roads, travel in clusters and crowds, in markets, in lobbies, bribe police to sleep near, keep double locks, but always the crowds, never alone again, always afraid the next person who passes might be another Simms. Never knowing if we've tricked and lost the Searchers. And always up ahead, in the Future, they'll wait for us to be brought back, waiting with their bombs to burn us and disease to rot us, and their police to tell us to roll over, turn around, jump through the hoop. And so we'll keep running through the forest, and we'll never ever stop or sleep well again in our lives.

A crowd gathered to watch the film being made. And Susan watched the crowd and the streets.

"Seen anyone suspicious?"

"No. What time is it?"

"Three o'clock. The car should be almost ready."

The test film was finished at three forty-five. They all walked down to the hotel, talking. William paused at the garage. "The car'll be ready at six," he said, coming out.

"But no later than that?"

"It'll be ready, don't worry."

In the hotel lobby they looked around for other men traveling alone, men who resembled Mr. Simms, men with new haircuts and too much cigarette smoke and cologne smell about them, but the lobby was empty.

Going up the stairs, Mr. Melton said, "Well, it's been a long, hard day. Who'd like to put a header on it. Martini? Beer?"

"Maybe one."

The whole crowd pushed into Mr. Melton's room and the drinking began.

"Watch the time," said William.

Time, thought Susan, if only they had time. All she wanted was to sit in the plaza all alone, bright day in spring, with not a worry or a thought, with the sun on her face and arms, her eyes closed, smiling at the warmth—and never move, but just sleep in the Mexican sun. . .

Mr. Melton opened the champagne.

"To a very beautiful lady, lovely enough for films," he said, toasting Susan. "I might even give you a test."

She laughed.

"I mean it," said Melton. "You're very nice. I could make you a movie star."

"And take me to Hollywood?"

"Get the hell out of Mexico, sure!"

Susan glanced at William, and he lifted an eyebrow and nodded. It would be a change of scene, clothing, locale, name perhaps, and they would be traveling with eight other people, a good shield against any interference from the future.

"It sounds wonderful," said Susan.

She was feeling the champagne now, the afternoon was slipping by, the party was whirling about her, she felt safe and good and alive and truly happy for the first time in many years.

"What kind of film would my wife be good for?" asked William, refilling his glass.

Melton appraised Susan. The party stopped laughing and listened.

"Well, I'd like to do a story of suspense," said Melton. "A story of a man and wife, like yourselves."

"Go on."

"Sort of a war story, maybe," said the director, examining the color of his drink against the sunlight.

Susan and William waited.

"A story about a man and wife who live in a little house on a little street in the year 2155, maybe," said Melton. "This is ad lib, understand. But this man and wife are faced with a terrible war. Super-Plus Hydrogen bombs, censorship, death, in that year and—here's the gimmick—they escape into the past, followed by a man who they think is evil, but who is only trying to show them what their Duty is."

William dropped his glass to the floor.

Mr. Melton continued. "And this couple take refuge with a group of film people whom they learn to trust. Safety in numbers, they say to themselves."

Susan felt herself slip down into a chair. Everyone was watching the director. He took a little sip of wine. "Ah, that's a fine wine. Well, this man and woman, it seems, don't realize how important they are to the future. The man, especially, is the keystone to a new bomb metal. So the Searchers, let's call them, spare no trouble or expense to find, capture and take home the man and wife, once they get them totally alone, in a hotel room, where no one can see. Strategy. The Searchers work alone, or in groups of eight. One trick or another will do it. Don't you think it would make a wonderful film, Susan? Don't you, Bill?" He finished his drink.

Susan sat with her eyes straight ahead.

"Have a drink?" said Mr. Melton.

William's gun was out and fired, three times, and one of the men fell, and the others ran forward. Susan screamed. A hand was clamped to her mouth. Now the gun was on the floor and William was struggling with the men holding him.

Mr. Melton said, "Please," standing there where he had stood, blood showing on his fingers. "Let's not make matters worse."

Someone pounded on the hall door.

"Let me in!"

"The manager," said Mr. Melton, dryly. He jerked his head. "Everyone, let's move!"

"Let me in. I'll call the police!"

Susan and William looked at each other quickly, and then at the door.

"The manager wishes to come in," said Mr. Melton. "Quick!"

A camera was carried forward. From it shot a blue light which encompassed the room instantly. It widened out and the people of the party vanished, one by one.

"Quickly!"

Outside the window in the instant before she vanished, Susan saw the green land and the purple and yellow and blue and crimson walls and the cobbles flowing like a river, a man upon a burro riding into the warm hills, a boy drinking orange pop. She could feel the sweet liquid in her throat; she could see a man standing under a cool plaza tree with a guitar, could feel her hand upon the strings. And, far away, she could see the sea, the blue and tender sea; she could feel it roll her over and take her in.

And then she was gone. Her husband was gone.

The door burst wide. The manager and his staff rushed in. The room was empty.

"But they were just here! I saw them come in, and now—gone!" cried the manager. "The windows are covered with iron grating; they couldn't get out that way!"

In the late afternoon, the priest was summoned and they opened the room again and aired it out, and had him sprinkle holy water through each corner and give it his cleansing.

"What shall we do with these?" asked the charwoman.

She pointed to the closet, where there were sixty-seven bottles of chartreuse, cognac, crème de cacao, absinthe, vermouth, tequila, 106 cartons of Turkish cigarettes, and 198 yellow boxes of fifty-cent pure Havana-filler cigars . . .

STORY AND ESSAY COLLECTIONS

BRADBURY SPEAKS
Too Soon from the Cave, Too Far from the Stars
ISBN 978-0-06-058569-3 (paperback)
A collection of essays offering commentary on Bradbury's—and America's—greatest influences.

THE ILLUSTRATED MAN
ISBN 978-0-207997-8 (paperback)
Eighteen startling visions of humankind's destiny comprise this phantasmagoric slideshow.

THE GOLDEN APPLES OF THE SUN
And Other Stories
ISBN 978-0-380-73039-1 (paperback)
Thirty-two of Bradbury's most famous tales—prime examples of the poignant poetry of the human soul.

THE OCTOBER COUNTRY
ISBN 978-0-207996-1 (paperback)
A spellbinding journey to the "Undiscovered Country" of the legendary author's imagination.

I SING THE BODY ELECTRIC!
And Other Stories
ISBN 978-0-380-78962-7 (paperback)
Twenty-eight classic Bradbury stories and one luscious poem—a cavalcade of delight and terror.

BRADBURY STORIES
100 of His Most Celebrated Tales
ISBN 978-0-06-054488-1 (paperback)
One hundred treasures from a lifetime of words and ideas—tales that amaze and enthrall.

THE CAT'S PAJAMAS
Stories
ISBN 978-0-06-077733-3 (paperback)
A walk through the six-decade career of this "latter-day O. Henry" (*Booklist*).

WE'LL ALWAYS HAVE PARIS
Stories
ISBN 978-0-06-167014-5 (paperback)
A treasure trove of Bradbury gems—eerie and strange, nostalgic and bittersweet, searching and speculative.

A PLEASURE TO BURN
Fahrenheit 451 Stories
ISBN 978-0-06-207102-6 (paperback)
A collection of sixteen vintage stories and novellas that informed *Fahrenheit 451*.